Susan Lenox
Her Fall and Rise
Volume II

by

David Graham Phillips

Double 9
BOOKS

Susan Lenox
Her Fall and Rise
Volume II
by David Graham Phillips

ISBN: 978-93-67146-92-7

Published by

DOUBLE 9 BOOKS
2/13-B, Ansari Road
Daryaganj, New Delhi – 110002
info@double9books.com
www.double9books.com
Tel. 011-40042856

This book is under public domain

ABOUT THE AUTHOR

David Graham Phillips was an American journalist and novelist known for his incisive social commentary and compelling storytelling. Born in 1867, Phillips began his career as a journalist, writing for publications such as The New York Sun and McClure's Magazine. It was through his investigative journalism that he developed a keen understanding of societal issues, which he later incorporated into his fiction. One of Phillips' most notable works is "The Fortune Hunter," a masterpiece of American literature published in 1909. Set against the backdrop of New York City's high society, the novel explores themes of ambition, greed, and the pursuit of wealth. Through vivid characterizations and intricate plotlines, Phillips paints a vivid portrait of a society consumed by materialism and social climbing. At the heart of "The Fortune Hunter" is the protagonist, Austin Ford, a charismatic and ambitious young man determined to ascend the ranks of society at any cost. As he navigates the complexities of love and ambition, Ford becomes embroiled in a web of deceit and betrayal that ultimately leads to tragic consequences. Phillips' writing is characterized by its sharp social commentary and insightful exploration of human nature. Through "The Fortune Hunter," he offers readers a compelling glimpse into the societal pressures and moral dilemmas faced by individuals striving for success in the Gilded Age.

CONTENTS

CHAPTER I

SUSAN'S impulse was toward the stage. It had become a definite ambition with her, the stronger because Spenser's jealousy and suspicion had forced her to keep it a secret, to pretend to herself that she had no thought but going on indefinitely as his obedient and devoted mistress. The hardiest and best growths are the growths inward—where they have sun and air from without. She had been at the theater several times every week, and had studied the performances at a point of view very different from that of the audience. It was there to be amused; she was there to learn. Spenser and such of his friends as he would let meet her talked plays and acting most of the time. He had forbidden her to have women friends. "Men don't demoralize women; women demoralize each other," was one of his axioms. But such women as she had a bowing acquaintance with were all on the stage—in comic operas or musical farces. She was much alone; that meant many hours every day which could not but be spent by a mind like hers in reading and in thinking. Only those who have observed the difference aloneness makes in mental development, where there is a good mind, can appreciate how rapidly, how broadly, Susan expanded. She read plays more than any other kind of literature. She did not read them casually but was always thinking how they would act. She was soon making in imagination stage scenes out of dramatic chapters in novels as she read. More and more clearly the characters of play and novel took shape and substance before the eyes of her fancy. But the stage was clearly out of the question.

While the idea of a stage career had been dominant, she had thought in other directions, also. Every Sunday, indeed almost every day, she found in the newspapers articles on the subject of work for women.

"Why do you waste time on that stuff?" said Drumley, when he discovered her taste for it.

"Oh, a woman never can tell what may happen," replied she.

"She'll never learn anything from those fool articles," answered he. "You ought to hear the people who get them up laughing about them. I see now why they are printed. It's good for circulation, catches the women— even women like you." However, she persisted in reading. But never did she find an article that contained a really practical suggestion—that is, one applying to the case of a woman who had to live on what she made at the start, who was without experience and without a family to help her. All around her had been women who were making their way; but few indeed of them—even of those regarded as successful—were getting along without outside aid of some kind. So when she read or thought or inquired about work for women, she was sometimes amused and oftener made unhappy by the truth as to the conditions, that when a common worker rises it is almost always by the helping hand of a man, and rarely indeed a generous hand—a painful and shameful truth which a society resolved at any cost to think well of itself fiercely conceals from itself and hypocritically lies about.

She felt now that there was hope in only one direction—hope of occupation that would enable her to live in physical, moral and mental decency. She must find some employment where she could as decently as might be realize upon her physical assets. The stage would be best—but the stage was impossible, at least for the time. Later on she would try for it; there was in her mind not a doubt of that, for unsuspected of any who knew her there lay, beneath her sweet and gentle exterior, beneath her appearance of having been created especially for love and laughter and sympathy, tenacity of purpose and daring of ambition that were—rarely—hinted at the surface in her moments of abstraction. However, just now the stage was impossible. Spenser would find her immediately. She must go into another part of town, must work at something that touched his life at no point.

She had often been told that her figure would be one of her chief assets as a player. And ready-made clothes fitted her with very slight alterations— showing that she had a model figure. The advertisements she had cut out were for cloak models. Within an hour after she left Forty-fourth Street, she found at Jeffries and Jonas, in Broadway a few doors below Houston, a vacancy that had not yet been filled—though as a rule all the help needed was got from the throng of applicants waiting when the store opened.

"Come up to my office," said Jeffries, who happened to be near the door as she entered. "We'll see how you shape up. We want something extra— something dainty and catchy."

He was a short thick man, with flat feet, a flat face and an almost bald head. In his flat nostrils, in the hollows of his great forward bent ears and on the lobes were bunches of coarse, stiff gray hairs. His eyebrows bristled; his small, sly brown eyes twinkled with good nature and with sensuality. His skin had the pallor that suggests kidney trouble. His words issued from his thick mouth as if he were tasting each beforehand—and liked the flavor. He led Susan into his private office, closed the door, took a tape measure from his desk. "Now, my dear," said he, eyeing her form gluttonously, "we'll size you up—eh? You're exactly the build I like."

And under the pretense of taking her measurements, he fumbled and felt, pinched and stroked every part of her person, laughing and chuckling the while. "My, but you are sweet! And so firm! What flesh! Solid—solid! Mighty healthy! You are a good girl—eh?"

"I am a married woman."

"But you've got no ring."

"I've never worn a ring."

"Well—well! I believe that is one of the new wrinkles, but I don't approve. I'm an old-fashioned family man. Let me see again. Now, don't mind a poor old man like me, my dear. I've got a wife—the best woman in the world, and I've never been untrue to her. A look over the fence occasionally—but not an inch out of the pasture. Don't stiffen yourself like that. I can't judge, when you do. Not too much hips—neither sides nor back. Fine! Fine! And the thigh slender—yes—quite lovely, my dear. Thick thighs spoil the hang of garments. Yes—yes—a splendid figure. I'll bet the bosom is a corker—fine skin and nice ladylike size. You can have the place."

"What does it pay?" she asked.

"Ten dollars, to start with. Splendid wages. *I* started on two fifty. But I forgot—you don't know the business?"

"No—nothing about it," was her innocent, honest answer.

"Ah—well, then—nine dollars—eh?"

Susan hesitated.

"You can make quite a neat little bunch on the outside—*you* can. We cater only to the best trade, and the buyers who come to us are big easy spenders. But I'm supposed to know nothing about that. You'll find out from the other girls." He chuckled. "Oh, it's a nice soft life except for a few weeks along at this part of the year—and again in winter. Well—ten dollars, then."

Susan accepted. It was more than she had expected to get; it was less than she could hope to live on in New York in anything approaching the manner a person of any refinement or tastes or customs of comfort regards as merely decent. She must descend again to the tenements, must resume the fight against that physical degradation which sooner or later imposes— upon those *descending* to it—a degradation of mind and heart deeper, more saturating, more putrefying than any that ever originated from within. Not so long as her figure lasted was she the worse off for not knowing a trade. Jeffries was telling the truth; she would be getting splendid wages, not merely for a beginner but for any woman of the working class. Except in rare occasional instances wages and salaries for women were kept down below the standard of decency by woman's peculiar position—by such conditions as that most women took up work as a temporary makeshift or to piece out a family's earnings, and that almost any woman could supplement—and so many did supplement—their earnings at labor with as large or larger earnings in the stealthy shameful way. Where was there a trade that would bring a girl ten dollars a week at the start? Even if she were a semi-professional, a stenographer and typewriter, it would take expertness and long service to lift her up to such wages. Thanks to her figure—to its chancing to please old Jeffries' taste—she was better off than all but a few working women, than all but a few workingmen. She was of the labor aristocracy; and if she had been one of a family of workers she would have been counted an enviable favorite of fortune. Unfortunately, she was alone unfortunately for herself, not at all from the standpoint of the tenement class she was now joining. Among them she would be a person who could afford the luxuries of life as life reveals itself to the tenements.

"Tomorrow morning at seven o'clock," said Jeffries. "You have lost your husband?"

"Yes."

"I saw you'd had great grief. No insurance, I judge? Well—you will find another—maybe a rich one. No—you'll not have to sleep alone long, my dear." And he patted her on the shoulder, gave her a parting fumble of shoulders and arms.

She was able to muster a grateful smile; for she felt a rare kindness of heart under the familiar animalism to which good-looking, well-formed women who go about much unescorted soon grow accustomed. Also, experience had taught her that, as things go with girls of the working class, his treatment was courteous, considerate, chivalrous almost. With men in absolute control of all kinds of work, with women stimulating the sex appetite by openly or covertly using their charms as female to assist them in the cruel struggle for existence—what was to be expected?

Her way to the elevator took her along aisles lined with tables, hidden under masses of cloaks, jackets, dresses and materials for making them. They exuded the odors of the factory—faint yet pungent odors that brought up before her visions of huge, badly ventilated rooms, where women aged or ageing swiftly were toiling hour after hour monotonously—spending half of each day in buying the right to eat and sleep unhealthily. The odors—or, rather, the visions they evoked—made her sick at heart. For the moment she came from under the spell of her peculiar trait—her power to do without whimper or vain gesture of revolt the inevitable thing, whatever it was. She paused to steady herself, half leaning against a lofty up-piling of winter cloaks. A girl, young at first glance, not nearly so young thereafter, suddenly appeared before her—a girl whose hair had the sheen of burnished brass and whose soft smooth skin was of that frog-belly whiteness which suggests an inheritance of some bleaching and blistering disease. She had small regular features, eyes that at once suggested looseness, good-natured yet mercenary too. She was dressed in the sleek tight-fitting trying-on robe of the professional model, and her figure was superb in its firm luxuriousness.

"Sick?" asked the girl with real kindliness.

"No—only dizzy for the moment."

"I suppose you've had a hard day."

"It might have been easier," Susan replied, attempting a smile.

"It's no fun, looking for a job. But you've caught on?"

"Yes. He took me."

"I made a bet with myself that he would when I saw you go in."
The girl laughed agreeably. "He picked you for Gideon."

"What department is that?"

The girl laughed again, with a cynical squinting of the eyes. "Oh, Gideon's our biggest customer. He buys for the largest house in Chicago."

"I'm looking for a place to live," said Susan. "Some place in this part of town."

"How much do you want to spend?"

"I'm to have ten a week. So I can't afford more than twelve or fourteen a month for rent, can I?"

"If you happen to have to live on the ten," was the reply with a sly, merry smile.

"It's all I've got."

Again the girl laughed, the good-humored mercenary eyes twinkling rakishly. "Well—you can't get much for fourteen a month."

"I don't care, so long as it's clean."

"Gee, you're reasonable, ain't you?" cried the girl. "Clean! I pay fourteen a week, and all kinds of things come through the cracks from the other apartments. You must be a stranger to little old New York—bugtown, a lady friend of mine calls it. Alone?"

"Yes."

"Um—" The girl shook her head dubiously. "Rents are mighty steep in New York, and going up all the time. You see, the rich people that own the lands and houses here need a lot of money in their business. You've got either to take a room or part of one in with some tenement family, respectable but noisy and dirty and not at all refined, or else you've got to live in a house where everything goes. You want to live respectable, I judge?"

"Yes."

"That's the way with me. Do what you please, *I* say, but for *God's sake*, don't make yourself *common!* You'll want to be free to have your gentlemen friends come—and at the same time a room you'll not be ashamed for 'em to see on account of dirt and smells and common people around."

"I shan't want to see anyone in my room."

The young woman winced, then went on with hasty enthusiasm.

"I knew you were refined the minute I looked at you. I think you might get a room in the house of a lady friend of mine—Mrs. Tucker, up in Clinton Place near University Place—an elegant neighborhood—that is, the north side of the street. The south side's kind o' low, on account of dagoes having moved in there. They live like vermin—but then all tenement people do."

"They've got to," said Susan.

"Yes, that's a fact. Ain't it awful? I'll write down the name and address of my lady friend. I'm Miss Mary Hinkle."

"My name is Lorna Sackville," said Susan, in response to the expectant look of Miss Hinkle.

"My, what a swell name! You've been sick, haven't you?"

"No, I'm never sick."

"Me too. My mother taught me to stop eating as soon as I felt bad, and not to eat again till I was all right."

"I do that, too," said Susan. "Is it good for the health?"

"It starves the doctors. You've never worked before?"

"Oh, yes—I've worked in a factory."

Miss Hinkle looked disappointed. Then she gave Susan a side glance of incredulity. "I'd never, a' thought it. But I can see you weren't brought up to that. I'll write the address." And she went back through the showroom, presently to reappear with a card which she gave Susan. "You'll find Mrs.

Tucker a perfect lady—too much a lady to get on. I tell her she'll go to ruin— and she will."

Susan thanked Miss Hinkle and departed. A few minutes' walk brought her to the old, high-stooped, brown-stone where Mrs. Tucker lived. The dents, scratches and old paint scales on the door, the dust-streaked windows, the slovenly hang of the imitation lace window curtains proclaimed the cheap middle-class lodging or boarding house of the humblest grade. Respectable undoubtedly; for the fitfully prosperous offenders against laws and morals insist upon better accommodations. Susan's heart sank. She saw that once more she was clinging at the edge of the precipice. And what hope was there that she would get back to firm ground? Certainly not by "honest labor." Back to the tenement! "Yes, I'm on the way back," she said to herself. However, she pulled the loose bell-knob and was admitted to a dingy, dusty hallway by a maid so redolent of stale perspiration that it was noticeable even in the hall's strong saturation of smells of cheap cookery. The parlor furniture was rapidly going to pieces; the chromos and prints hung crazily awry; dust lay thick upon the center table, upon the chimney-piece, upon the picture frames, upon the carving in the rickety old chairs. Only by standing did Susan avoid service as a dust rag. It was typical of the profound discouragement that blights or blasts all but a small area of our modern civilization—a discouragement due in part to ignorance—but not at all to the cause usually assigned—to "natural shiftlessness." It is chiefly due to an unconscious instinctive feeling of the hopelessness of the average lot.

While Susan explained to Mrs. Tucker how she had come and what she could afford, she examined her with results far from disagreeable. One glance into that homely wrinkled face was enough to convince anyone of her goodness of heart—and to Susan in those days of aloneness, of uncertainty, of the feeling of hopelessness, goodness of heart seemed the supreme charm. Such a woman as a landlady, and a landlady in New York, was pathetically absurd. Even to still rather simple-minded Susan she seemed an invitation to the swindler, to the sponger with the hard-luck story, to the sinking who clutch about desperately and drag down with them everyone who permits them to get a hold.

"I've only got one room," said Mrs. Tucker. "That's not any too nice. I did rather calculate to get five a week for it, but you are the kind I like to have in the house. So if you want it I'll let it to you for fourteen a month. And I do hope you'll pay as steady as you can. There's so many in such hard lines that I have a tough time with my rent. I've got to pay my rent, you know."

"I'll go as soon as I can't pay," replied Susan. The landlady's apologetic tone made her sick at heart, as a sensitive human being must ever feel in the presence of a fellow-being doomed to disaster.

"Thank you," said Mrs. Tucker gratefully. "I do wish——" She checked herself. "No, I don't mean that. They do the best they can—and I'll botch along somehow. I look at the bright side of things."

The incurable optimism of the smile accompanying these words moved Susan, abnormally bruised and tender of heart that morning, almost to tears. A woman with her own way to make, and always looking at the bright side!

"How long have you had this house?"

"Only five months. My husband died a year ago. I had to give up our little business six months after his death. Such a nice little stationery store, but I couldn't seem to refuse credit or to collect bills. Then I came here. This looks like losing, too. But I'm sure I'll come out all right. The Lord will provide, as the Good Book says. I don't have no trouble keeping the house full. Only they don't seem to pay. You want to see your room?"

She and Susan ascended three flights to the top story—to a closet of a room at the back. The walls were newly and brightly papered. The sloping roof of the house made one wall a ceiling also, and in this two small windows were set. The furniture was a tiny bed, white and clean as to its linen, a table, two chairs, a small washstand with a little bowl and a less pitcher, a soap dish and a mug. Along one wall ran a row of hooks. On the floor was an old and incredibly dirty carpet, mitigated by a strip of clean matting which ran from the door, between washstand and bed, to one of the windows.

Susan glanced round—a glance was enough to enable her to see all—all that was there, all that the things there implied. Back to the tenement life! She shuddered.

"It ain't much," said Mrs. Tucker. "But usually rooms like these rents for five a week."

The sun had heated the roof scorching hot; the air of this room, immediately underneath, was like that of a cellar where a furnace is in full blast. But Susan knew she was indeed in luck. "It's clean and nice here," said she to Mrs. Tucker, "and I'm much obliged to you for being so reasonable with me." And to clinch the bargain she then and there paid half a month's rent. "I'll give you the rest when my week at the store's up."

"No hurry," said Mrs. Tucker who was handling the money and looking at it with glistening grateful eyes. "Us poor folks oughtn't to be hard on each other—though, Lord knows, if we was, I reckon we'd not be quite so poor. It's them that has the streak of hard in 'em what gets on. But the Bible teaches us that's what to expect in a world of sin. I suppose you want to go now and have your trunk sent?"

"This is all I've got," said Susan, indicating her bag on the table.

Into Mrs. Tucker's face came a look of terror that made Susan realize in an instant how hard-pressed she must be. It was the kind of look that comes into the eyes of the deer brought down by the dogs when it sees the hunter coming up.

"But I've a good place," Susan hastened to say. "I get ten a week.
And as I told you before, when I can't pay I'll go right away."

"I've lost so much in bad debts," explained the landlady humbly. "I don't seem to see which way to turn." Then she brightened. "It'll all come out for the best. I work hard and I try to do right by everybody."

"I'm sure it will," said Susan believingly.

Often her confidence in the moral ideals trained into her from childhood had been sorely tried. But never had she permitted herself more than a hasty, ashamed doubt that the only way to get on was to work and to practice the Golden Rule. Everyone who was prosperous attributed his prosperity to the steadfast following of that way; as for those who were not prosperous, they were either lazy or bad-hearted, or would have been even worse off had they been less faithful to the creed that was best policy as well as best for peace of mind and heart.

In trying to be as inexpensive to Spenser as she could contrive, and also because of her passion for improving herself, Susan had explored far into the almost unknown art of living, on its shamefully neglected material side. She had cultivated the habit of spending much time about her purchases of every kind—had spent time intelligently in saving money intelligently. She had gone from shop to shop, comparing values and prices. She had studied quality in food and in clothing, and thus she had discovered what enormous sums are wasted through ignorance—wasted by poor even more lavishly than by rich or well-to-do, because the shops where the poor dealt had absolutely no check on their rapacity through the occasional canny customer. She had learned the fundamental truth of the material art of living; only when a good thing happens to be cheap is a cheap thing good. Spenser, cross-examining her as to how she passed the days, found out about this education she was acquiring. It amused him. "A waste of time!"

he used to say. "Pay what they ask, and don't bother your head with such petty matters." He might have suspected and accused her of being stingy had not her generosity been about the most obvious and incessant trait of her character.

She was now reduced to an income below what life can be decently maintained upon—the life of a city-dweller with normal tastes for cleanliness and healthfulness. She proceeded without delay to put her invaluable education into use. She must fill her mind with the present and with the future. She must not glance back. She must ignore her wounds—their aches, their clamorous throbs. She took off her clothes, as soon as Mrs. Tucker left her alone, brushed them and hung them up, put on the thin wrapper she had brought in her bag. The fierce heat of the little packing-case of a room became less unendurable; also, she was saving the clothes from useless wear. She sat down at the table and with pencil and paper planned her budget.

Of the ten dollars a week, three dollars and thirty cents must be subtracted for rent—for shelter. This left six dollars and seventy cents for the other two necessaries, food and clothing—there must be no incidental expenses since there was no money to meet them. She could not afford to provide for carfare on stormy days; a rain coat, overshoes and umbrella, more expensive at the outset, were incomparably cheaper in the long run. Her washing and ironing she would of course do for herself in the evenings and on Sundays. Of the two items which the six dollars and seventy cents must cover, food came first in importance. How little could she live on?

That stifling hot room! She was as wet as if she had come undried from a bath. She had thought she could never feel anything but love for the sun of her City of the Sun. But this undreamed-of heat—like the cruel caresses of a too impetuous lover—

How little could she live on?

Dividing her total of six dollars and seventy cents by seven, she found that she had ninety-five cents a day. She would soon have to buy clothes, however scrupulous care she might take of those she possessed. It was modest indeed to estimate fifteen dollars for clothes before October. That meant she must save fifteen dollars in the remaining three weeks of June, in July, August and September—in one hundred and ten days. She must save about fifteen cents a day. And out of that she must buy soap and tooth powder, outer and under clothes, perhaps a hat and a pair of shoes. Thus she could spend for food not more than eighty cents a day, as much less as was consistent with buying the best quality—for she had learned by bitter experience the ravages poor quality food makes in health and looks, had learned why girls of the working class go to pieces swiftly after eighteen. She must fight to keep health—sick she did not dare be. She must fight to keep looks—her figure was her income.

Eighty cents a day. The outlook was not so gloomy. A cup of cocoa in the morning—made at home of the best cocoa, the kind that did not overheat the blood and disorder the skin—it would cost her less than ten cents. She would carry lunch with her to the store. In the evening she would cook a chop or something of that kind on the gas stove she would buy. Some days she would be able to save twenty or even twenty-five cents toward clothing and the like. Whatever else happened, she was resolved never again to sink to dirt and rags. Never again!—never! She had passed through that experience once without loss of self-respect only because it was by way of education. To go through it again would be yielding ground in the fight— the fight for a destiny worth while which some latent but mighty instinct within her never permitted her to forget.

She sat at the table, with the shutters closed against the fiery light of the summer afternoon sun. That hideous unacceptable heat! With eyelids drooped—deep and dark were the circles round them—she listened to the roar of the city, a savage sound like the clamor of a multitude of famished wild beasts. A city like the City of Destruction in "Pilgrim's Progress"—a city where of all the millions, but a few thousands were moving toward or keeping in the sunlight of civilization. The rest, the swarms of the cheap boarding houses, cheap lodging houses, tenements—these myriads were squirming in darkness and squalor, ignorant and never to be less ignorant, ill fed and never to be better fed, clothed in pitiful absurd rags or shoddy vulgar attempts at finery, and never to be better clothed. She would not be of those! She would struggle on, would sink only to mount. She would work; she would try to do as nearly right as she could. And in the end she must triumph. She would get at least a good part of what her soul craved, of what her mind craved, of what her heart craved.

The heat of this tenement room! The heat to which poverty was exposed naked and bound! Would not anyone be justified in doing anything—yes, *anything*—to escape from this fiend?

CHAPTER II

ELLEN, the maid, slept across the hall from Susan, in a closet so dirty that no one could have risked in it any article of clothing with the least pretension to cleanness. It was no better, no worse than the lodgings of more than two hundred thousand New Yorkers. Its one narrow opening, beside the door, gave upon a shaft whose odors were so foul that she kept the window closed, preferring heat like the inside of a steaming pan to the only available "outside air." This in a civilized city where hundreds of dogs with jeweled collars slept in luxurious rooms on downiest beds and had servants to wait upon them! The morning after Susan's coming, Ellen woke her, as they had arranged, at a quarter before five. The night before, Susan had brought up from the basement a large bucket of water; for she had made up her mind, to take a bath every day, at least until the cold weather set in and rendered such a luxury impossible. With this water and what she had in her little pitcher, Susan contrived to freshen herself up. She had bought a gas stove and some indispensable utensils for three dollars and seventeen cents in a Fourteenth Street store, a pound of cocoa for seventy cents and ten cents' worth of rolls—three rolls, well baked, of first quality flour and with about as good butter and other things put into the dough as one can expect in bread not made at home. These purchases had reduced her cash to forty-three cents—and she ought to buy without delay a clock with an alarm attachment. And pay day—Saturday—was two days away.

She made a cup of cocoa, drank it slowly, eating one of the rolls—all in the same methodical way like a machine that continues to revolve after the power has been shut off. It was then, even more than during her first evening alone, even more than when she from time to time startled out of troubled sleep—it was then, as she forced down her lonely breakfast, that she most missed Rod. When she had finished, she completed her toilet. The final glance at herself in the little mirror was depressing. She looked fresh for her new surroundings and for her new class. But in comparison with what she usually looked, already there was a distinct, an ominous falling off. "I'm glad Rod never saw me looking like this," she said aloud drearily. Taking a roll for lunch, she issued forth at half-past six. The hour and three-quarters she had allowed for dressing and breakfasting had been none too much. In the coolness and comparative quiet she went down University

Place and across Washington Square under the old trees, all alive with song and breeze and flashes of early morning light. She was soon in Broadway's deep canyon, was drifting absently along in the stream of cross, mussy-looking workers pushing southward. Her heart ached, her brain throbbed. It was horrible, this loneliness; and every one of the wounds where she had severed the ties with Spenser was bleeding. She was astonished to find herself before the building whose upper floors were occupied by Jeffries and Jonas. How had she got there? Where had she crossed Broadway?

"Good morning, Miss Sackville." It was Miss Hinkle, just arriving. Her eyes were heavy, and there were the criss-cross lines under them that tell a story to the expert in the different effects of different kinds of dissipation. Miss Hinkle was showing her age—and she was "no spring chicken."

Susan returned her greeting, gazing at her with the dazed eyes and puzzled smile of an awakening sleeper.

"I'll show you the ropes," said Miss Hinkle, as they climbed the two flights of stairs. "You'll find the job dead easy. They're mighty nice people to work for, Mr. Jeffries especially. Not easy fruit, of course, but nice for people that have got on. You didn't sleep well?"

"Yes—I think so."

"I didn't have a chance to drop round last night. I was out with one of the buyers. How do you like Mrs. Tucker?"

"She's very good, isn't she?"

"She'll never get along. She works hard, too—but not for herself. In this world you have to look out for Number One. I had a swell dinner last night. Lobster—I love lobster—and elegant champagne—up to Murray's—such a refined place—all fountains and mirrors—really quite artistic. And my gentleman friend was so nice and respectful. You know, we have to go out with the buyers when they ask us. It helps the house sell goods. And we have to be careful not to offend them."

Miss Hinkle's tone in the last remark was so significant that
Susan looked at her—and, looking, understood.

"Sometimes," pursued Miss Hinkle, eyes carefully averted, "sometimes a new girl goes out with an important customer and he gets fresh and she kicks and complains to Mr. Jeffries—or Mr. Jonas—or Mr. Ratney, the head man. They always sympathize with her—but—well, I've noticed that somehow she soon loses her job."

"What do you do when—when a customer annoys you?"

"I!" Miss Hinkle laughed with some embarrassment. "Oh, I do the best I can." A swift glance of the cynical, laughing, "fast" eyes at Susan and away. "The best I can—for the house—and for myself. . . . I talk to you because I know you're a lady and because I don't want to see you thrown down. A woman that's living quietly at home—like a lady—she can be squeamish. But out in the world a woman can't afford to be—no, nor a man, neither. You don't find this set down in the books, and they don't preach it in the churches—leastways they didn't when I used to go to church. But it's true, all the same."

They were a few minutes early; so Miss Hinkle continued the conversation while they waited for the opening of the room where Susan would be outfitted for her work. "I called you Miss Sackville," said she, "but you've been married—haven't you?"

"Yes."

"I can always tell—or at least I can see whether a woman's had experience or not. Well, I've never been regularly married, and I don't expect to, unless something pretty good offers. Think I'd marry one of these rotten little clerks?" Miss Hinkle answered her own question with a scornful sniff. "They can hardly make a living for themselves. And a man who amounts to anything, he wants a refined lady to help him on up, not a working girl. Of course, there're exceptions. But as a rule a girl in our position either has to stay single or marry beneath her—marry some mechanic or such like. Well, I ain't so lazy, or so crazy about being supported, that I'd sink to be cook and slop-carrier—and worse—for a carpenter or a bricklayer. Going out with the buyers—the gentlemanly ones—has spoiled my taste. I can't stand a coarse man—coarse dress and hands and manners. Can you?"

Susan turned hastily away, so that her face was hidden from
Miss Hinkle.

"I'll bet you wasn't married to a coarse man."

"I'd rather not talk about myself," said Susan with an effort.
"It's not pleasant."

Her manner of checking Miss Hinkle's friendly curiosity did not give offense; it excited the experienced working woman's sympathy. She went on:

"Well, I feel sorry for any woman that has to work. Of course most women do—and at worse than anything in the stores and factories. As between being a drudge to some dirty common laborer like most women are, and working in a factory even, give me the factory. Yes, give me a job as a pot slinger even, low as that is. Oh, I *hate* working people! I love refinement. Up to Murray's last night I sat there, eating my lobster and drinking my wine, and I pretended I was a lady—and, my, how happy I was!"

The stockroom now opened. Susan, with the help of Miss Hinkle and the stock keeper, dressed in one of the tight-fitting satin slips that revealed every curve and line of her form, made every motion however slight, every breath she drew, a gesture of sensuousness. As she looked at herself in a long glass in one of the show-parlors, her face did not reflect the admiration frankly displayed upon the faces of the two other women. That satin slip seemed to have a moral quality, an immoral character. It made her feel naked—no, as if she were naked and being peeped at through a crack or keyhole.

"You'll soon get used to it," Miss Hinkle assured her. "And you'll learn to show off the dresses and cloaks to the best advantage." She laughed her insinuating little laugh again, amused, cynical, reckless. "You know, the buyers are men. Gee, what awful jay things we work off on them, sometimes! They can't see the dress for the figure. And you've got such a refined figure, Miss Sackville—the kind I'd be crazy about if I was a man. But I must say——" here she eyed herself in the glass complacently—"most men prefer a figure like mine. Don't they, Miss Simmons?"

The stock keeper shook her fat shoulders in a gesture of indifferent disdain. "They take whatever's handiest—that's *my* experience."

About half-past nine the first customer appeared—Mr. Gideon, it happened to be. He was making the rounds of the big wholesale houses in search of stock for the huge Chicago department store that paid him fifteen thousand a year and expenses. He had been contemptuous of the offerings of Jeffries and Jonas for the winter season, had praised with enthusiasm the models of their principal rival, Icklemeier, Schwartz and Company. They were undecided whether he was really thinking of deserting them or was feeling for lower prices. Mr. Jeffries bustled into the room where Susan stood waiting; his flat face quivered with excitement. "Gid's come!" he said in a hoarse whisper. "Everybody get busy. We'll try Miss Sackville on him."

And he himself assisted while they tricked out Susan in an afternoon costume of pale gray, putting on her head a big pale gray hat with harmonizing feathers. The model was offered in all colors and also in a modified form that permitted its use for either afternoon or evening. Susan had received her instructions, so when she was dressed, she was ready to sweep into Gideon's presence with languid majesty. Jeffries' eyes glistened as he noted her walk. "She looks as if she really was a lady!" exclaimed he. "I wish I could make my daughters move around on their trotters like that."

Gideon was enthroned in an easy chair, smoking a cigar. He was a spare man of perhaps forty-five, with no intention of abandoning the pretensions to youth for many a year. In dress he was as spick and span as a tailor at the trade's annual convention. But he had evidently been "going some" for several days; the sour, worn, haggard face rising above his elegantly fitting collar suggested a moth-eaten jaguar that has been for weeks on short rations or none.

"What's the matter?" he snapped, as the door began to open.

"I don't like to be kept waiting."

In swept Susan; and Jeffries, rubbing his thick hands, said fawningly, "But I think, Mr. Gideon, you'll say it was worth waiting for."

Gideon's angry, arrogant eyes softened at first glimpse of Susan. "Um!" he grunted, some such sound as the jaguar aforesaid would make when the first chunk of food hurtled through the bars and landed on his paws. He sat with cigar poised between his long white fingers while Susan walked up and down before him, displaying the dress at all angles, Jeffries expatiating upon it the while.

"Don't talk so damn much, Jeff!" he commanded with the insolence of a customer containing possibilities of large profit. "I judge for myself. I'm not a damn fool."

"I should say not," cried Jeffries, laughing the merchant's laugh for a customer's pleasantry. "But I can't help talking about it, Gid, it's so lovely!"

Jeffries' shrewd eyes leaped for joy when Gideon got up from his chair and, under pretense of examining the garment, investigated Susan's figure. As his gentle, insinuating hands traveled over her, his eyes sought hers. "Excuse me," said Jeffries. "I'll see that they get the other things ready." And out he went, winking at Mary Hinkle to follow him—an unnecessary gesture as she was already on her way to the door.

Gideon understood as well as did they why they left. "I don't think I've seen you before, my dear," said he to Susan.

"I came only this morning," replied she.

"I like to know everybody I deal with. We must get better acquainted. You've got the best figure in the business—the very best."

"Thank you," said Susan with a grave, distant smile.

"Got a date for dinner tonight?" inquired he; and, assuming that everything would yield precedence to him, he did not wait for a reply, but went on, "Tell me your address. I'll send a cab for you at seven o'clock."

"Thank you," said Susan, "but I can't go."

Gideon smiled. "Oh, don't be shy. Of course you'll go. Ask Jeffries. He'll tell you it's all right."

"There are reasons why I'd rather not be seen in the restaurants."

"That's even better. I'll come in the cab myself and we'll go to a quiet place."

His eyes smiled insinuatingly at her. Now that she looked at him more carefully he was unusually attractive for a man of his type—had strength and intelligence in his features, had a suggestion of mastery, of one used to obedience, in his voice. His teeth were even and sound, his lips firm yet not too thin.

"Come," said he persuasively. "I'll not eat you up—" with a gay and gracious smile—"at least I'll try not to."

Susan remembered what Miss Hinkle had told her. She saw that she must either accept the invitation or give up her position. She said:

"Very well," and gave him her address.

Back came Jeffries and Miss Hinkle carrying the first of the wraps. Gideon waved them away. "You've shown 'em to me before," said he. "I don't want to see 'em again. Give me the evening gowns."

Susan withdrew, soon to appear in a dress that left her arms and neck bare. Gideon could not get enough of this. Jeffries kept her walking up and down until she was ready to drop with weariness of the monotony, of the distasteful play of Gideon's fiery glance upon her arms and shoulders and throat. Gideon tried to draw her into conversation, but she would—indeed could—go no further than direct answers to his direct questions. "Never mind," said he to her in an undertone. "I'll cheer you up this evening. I think I know how to order a dinner."

Her instant conquest of the difficult and valuable Gideon so elated Jeffries that he piled the work on her. He used her with every important buyer who came that day. The temperature was up in the high nineties, the hot moist air stood stagnant as a barnyard pool; the winter models were cruelly hot and heavy. All day long, with a pause of half an hour to eat her roll and drink a glass of water, Susan walked up and down the show parlors weighted with dresses and cloaks, furs for arctic weather. The other girls, even those doing almost nothing, were all but prostrated. It was little short of intolerable, this struggle to gain the "honest, self-respecting living by honest work" that there was so much talk about. Toward five o'clock her nerves abruptly and completely gave way, and she fainted—for the first time in her life. At once the whole establishment was in an uproar. Jeffries cursed himself loudly for his shortsightedness, for his overestimating her young strength. "She'll look like hell this evening," he wailed, wringing his hands like a distracted peasant woman. "Maybe she won't be able to go out at all."

She soon came round. They brought her whiskey, and afterward tea and sandwiches. And with the power of quick recuperation that is the most fascinating miracle of healthy youth, she not only showed no sign of her breakdown but looked much better. And she felt better. We shall some day understand why it is that if a severe physical blow follows upon a mental blow, recovery from the physical blow is always accompanied by a relief of the mental strain. Susan came out of her fit of faintness and exhaustion with a different point of view—as if time had been long at work softening her, grief. Spenser seemed part of the present no longer, but of the past—a past far more remote than yesterday.

Mary Hinkle sat with her as she drank the tea. "Did you make a date with Gid?" inquired she. Her tone let Susan know that the question had been prompted by Jeffries.

"He asked me to dine with him, and I said I would."

"Have you got a nice dress—dinner dress, I mean?"

"The linen one I'm wearing is all. My other dress is for cooler weather."

"Then I'll give you one out of stock—I mean I'll borrow one for you. This dinner's a house affair, you know—to get Gid's order. It'll be worth thousands to them."

"There wouldn't be anything to fit me on such short notice," said Susan, casting about for an excuse for not wearing borrowed finery.

"Why, you've got a model figure. I'll pick you out a white dress—and a black and white hat. I know 'em all, and I know one that'll make you look simply lovely."

Susan did not protest. She was profoundly indifferent to what happened to her. Life seemed a show in which she had no part, and at which she sat a listless spectator. A few minutes, and in puffed Jeffries, solicitous as a fussy old bird with a new family.

"You're a lot better, ain't you?" cried he, before he had looked at her. "Oh, yes, you'll be all right. And you'll have a lovely time with Mr. Gideon. He's a perfect gentleman—knows how to treat a lady. . . . The minute I laid eyes on you I said to myself, said I, 'Jeffries, she's a mascot.' And you are, my dear. You'll get us the order. But you mustn't talk business with him, you understand?"

"Yes," said Susan, wearily.

"He's a gentleman, you know, and it don't do to mix business and social pleasures. You string him along quiet and ladylike and elegant, as if there wasn't any such things as cloaks or dresses in the world. He'll understand all right. . . . If you land the order, my dear, I'll see that you get a nice present. A nice dress—the one we're going to lend you—if he gives us a slice. The dress and twenty-five in cash, if he gives us all. How's that?"

"Thank you," said Susan. "I'll do my best."

"You'll land it. You'll land it. I feel as if we had it with his O. K. on it."

Susan shivered. "Don't—don't count on me too much," she said hesitatingly. "I'm not in very good spirits, I'm sorry to say."

"A little pressed for money?" Jeffries hesitated, made an effort, blurted out what was for him, the business man, a giddy generosity. "On your way out, stop at the cashier's. He'll give you this week's pay in advance." Jeffries hesitated, decided against dangerous liberality. "Not ten, you understand, but say six. You see, you won't have been with us a full week." And he hurried away, frightened by his prodigality, by these hysterical impulses that were rushing him far from the course of sound business sense. "As Jones says, I'm a generous old fool," he muttered. "My soft heart'll ruin me yet."

Jeffries sent Mary Hinkle home with Susan to carry the dress and hat, to help her make a toilet and to "start her off right." In the hour before they left the store there was offered a typical illustration of why and how "business" is able to suspend the normal moral sense and to substitute for it a highly ingenious counterfeit of supreme moral obligation to it. The hysterical Jeffries had infected the entire personnel with his excitement, with the sense that a great battle was impending and that the cause of the house, which was the cause of everyone who drew pay from it, had been intrusted to the young recruit with the fascinating figure and the sweet, sad face. And

Susan's sensitive nature was soon vibrating in response to this feeling. It terrified her that she, the inexperienced, had such grave responsibility. It made her heart heavy to think of probable failure, when the house had been so good to her, had taken her in, had given her unusual wages, had made it possible for her to get a start in life, had intrusted to her its cause, its chance to retrieve a bad season and to protect its employees instead of discharging a lot of them.

"Have you got long white gloves?" asked Mary Hinkle, as they walked up Broadway, she carrying the dress and Susan the hat box.

"Only a few pairs of short ones."

"You must have long white gloves—and a pair of white stockings."

"I can't afford them."

"Oh, Jeffries told me to ask you—and to go to work and buy them if you hadn't."

They stopped at Wanamaker's. Susan was about to pay, when Mary stopped her. "If you pay," said she, "maybe you'll get your money back from the house, and maybe you won't. If I pay, they'll not make a kick on giving it back to me."

The dress Mary had selected was a simple white batiste, cut out at the neck prettily, and with the elbow sleeves that were then the fashion. "Your arms and throat are lovely," said Mary. "And your hands are mighty nice, too—that's why I'm sure you've never been a real working girl—leastways, not for a long time. When you get to the restaurant and draw off your gloves in a slow, careless, ladylike kind of way, and put your elbows on the table— my, how he will take on!" Mary looked at her with an intense but not at all malignant envy. "If you don't land high, it'll be because you're a fool. And you ain't that."

"I'm afraid I am," replied Susan. "Yes, I guess I'm what's called a fool— what probably is a fool."

"You want to look out then," warned Miss Hinkle. "You want to go to work and get over that. Beauty don't count, unless a girl's got shrewdness. The streets are full of beauties sellin' out for a bare living. They thought they couldn't help winning, and they got left, and the plain girls who had to hustle and manage have passed them. Go to Del's or Rector's or the Waldorf or the Madrid or any of those high-toned places, and see the women with the swell clothes and jewelry! The married ones, and the other kind, both. Are they raving tearing beauties? Not often. . . . The trouble with me is I've been too good-hearted and too soft about being flattered. I was too good looking, and a small easy living came too easy. You—I'd say you were—that you had brains but were shy about using them. What's the good of having them? Might as well be a boob. Then, too, you've got to go to work and look out about being too refined. The refined, nice ones goes the lowest—if they get pushed—and this is a pushing world. You'll get pushed just as far as you'll let 'em. Take it from me. I've been down the line."

Susan's low spirits sank lower. These disagreeable truths—for observation and experience made her fear they were truths—filled her with despondency. What was the matter with life? As between the morality she had been taught and the practical morality of this world upon which she had been cast, which was the right? How "take hold"? How avert the impending disaster? What of the "good" should—*must*—she throw away? What should—*must*—she cling to?

Mary Hinkle was shocked by the poor little room. "This is no place for a lady!" cried she. "But it won't last long—not after tonight, if you play your cards halfway right."

"I'm very well satisfied," said Susan. "If I can only keep this!"

She felt no interest in the toilet until the dress and hat were unpacked and laid out upon the bed. At sight of them her eyes became a keen and lively gray—never violet for that kind of emotion—and there surged up the love of finery that dwells in every normal woman—and in every normal man—that is put there by a heredity dating back through the ages to the very beginning of conscious life—and does not leave them until life gives up the battle and prepares to vacate before death. Ellen, the maid, passing the door, saw and entered to add her ecstatic exclamations to the excitement. Down she ran to bring Mrs. Tucker, who no sooner beheld the glory displayed upon the humble bed than she too was in a turmoil. Susan dressed with the aid of three maids as interested and eager as ever robed a queen for coronation. Ellen brought hot water and a larger bowl. Mrs. Tucker wished to lend a highly scented toilet soap she used when she put on gala attire; but Susan insisted upon her own plain soap. They all helped her bathe; they helped her select the best underclothes from her small store. Susan would put on her own stockings; but Ellen got one foot into one of the slippers and Mrs. Tucker looked after the other foot. "Ain't they lovely?" said Ellen to Mrs. Tucker, as they knelt together at their task. "I never see such feet. Not a lump on 'em, but like feet in a picture."

"It takes a mighty good leg to look good in a white stocking," observed Mary. "But yours is so nice and long and slim that they'd stand most anything."

Mrs. Tucker and Ellen stood by with no interference save suggestion and comment, while Mary, who at one time worked for a hairdresser, did Susan's thick dark hair. Susan would permit no elaborations, much to Miss Hinkle's regret. But the three agreed that she was right when the simple sweep of the vital blue-black hair was finished in a loose and graceful knot at the back, and Susan's small, healthily pallid face looked its loveliest, with the violet-gray eyes soft and sweet and serious. Mrs. Tucker brought the hat from the bed, and Susan put it on—a large black straw of a most becoming shape with two pure white plumes curling round the crown and a third, not so long, rising gracefully from the big buckle where the three plumes met. And now came the putting on of the dress. With as much care as if they were handling a rare and fragile vase, Mary and Mrs. Tucker held the dress for Susan to step into it. Ellen kept her petticoat in place while the other two escorted the dress up Susan's form.

Then the three worked together at hooking and smoothing. Susan washed her hands again, refused to let Mrs. Tucker run and bring powder, produced from a drawer some prepared chalk and with it safeguarded her nose against shine; she tucked the powder rag into her stocking. Last of all the gloves went on and a small handkerchief was thrust into the palm of the left glove.

"How do I look?" asked Susan. "Lovely"—"Fine"—"Just grand," exclaimed the three maids.

"I feel awfully dressed up," said she. "And it's so hot!"

"You must go right downstairs where it's cool and you won't get wilted," cried Mrs. Tucker. "Hold your skirts close on the way. The steps and walls ain't none too clean."

In the bathroom downstairs there was a long mirror built into the wall, a relic of the old house's long departed youth of grandeur. As the tenant— Mr. Jessop—was out, Mrs. Tucker led the way into it. There Susan had the first satisfactory look at herself. She knew she was a pretty woman; she would have been weak-minded had she not known it. But she was amazed at herself. A touch here and there, a sinuous shifting of the body within the garments, and the suggestion of "dressed up" vanished before the reflected eyes of her agitated assistants, who did not know what had happened but only saw the results. She hardly knew the tall beautiful woman of fashion gazing at her from the mirror. Could it be that this was her hair?—these eyes hers—and the mouth and nose and the skin? Was this long slender figure her very own? What an astounding difference clothes did make! Never before had Susan worn anything nearly so fine. "This is the way I ought to look all the time," thought she. "And this is the way I *will* look!" Only better—much better. Already her true eye was seeing the defects, the chances for improvement—how the hat could be re-bent and re-trimmed to adapt it to her features, how the dress could be altered to make it more tasteful, more effective in subtly attracting attention to her figure.

"How much do you suppose the dress cost, Miss Hinkle?" asked Ellen—the question Mrs. Tucker had been dying to put but had refrained from putting lest it should sound unrefined.

"It costs ninety wholesale," said Miss Hinkle. "That'd mean a hundred and twenty-five—a hundred and fifty, maybe if you was to try to buy it in a department store. And the hat—well, Lichtenstein'd ask fifty or sixty for it and never turn a hair."

"Gosh—ee?" exclaimed Ellen. "Did you ever hear the like?"

"I'm not surprised," said Mrs. Tucker, who in fact was flabbergasted. "Well—it's worth the money to them that can afford to buy it. The good Lord put everything on earth to be used, I reckon. And Miss Sackville is the build for things like that. Now it'd be foolish on me, with a stomach and sitter that won't let no skirt hang fit to look at."

The bell rang. The excitement died from Susan's face, leaving it pale and cold. A wave of nausea swept through her. Ellen peeped out, Mrs. Tucker and Miss Hinkle listening with anxious faces. "It's him!" whispered Ellen, "and there's a taxi, too."

It was decided that Ellen should go to the door, that as she opened it Susan should come carelessly from the back room and advance along the hall. And this program was carried out with the result that as Gideon said, "Is Miss Sackville here?" Miss Sackville appeared before his widening, wondering, admiring eyes. He was dressed in the extreme of fashion and costliness in good taste; while it would have been impossible for him to look distinguished, he did look what he was—a prosperous business man with prospects. He came perfumed and rustling. But he felt completely outclassed—until he reminded himself that for all her brave show of fashionable lady she was only a model while he was a fifteen-thousand-a-year man on the way to a partnership.

"Don't you think we might dine on the veranda at Sherry's?" suggested he. "It'd be cool there."

At sight of him she had nerved herself, had keyed herself up toward recklessness. She was in for it. She would put it through. No futile cowardly shrinking and whimpering! Why not try to get whatever pleasure there was a chance for? But—Sherry's—was it safe? Yes, almost any of the Fifth Avenue places—except the Waldorf, possibly—was safe enough. The circuit of Spenser and his friends lay in the more Bohemian Broadway district. He had taken her to Sherry's only once, to see as part of a New York education the Sunday night crowd of fashionable people. "If you like," said she.

Gideon beamed. He would be able to show off his prize! As they drove away Susan glanced at the front parlor windows, saw the curtains agitated, felt the three friendly, excited faces palpitating. She leaned from the cab window, waved her hand, smiled. The three faces instantly appeared and immediately hid again lest Gideon should see.

But Gideon was too busy planning conversation. He knew Miss Sackville was "as common as the rest of 'em—and an old hand at the business, no doubt." But he simply could not abruptly break through the barrier; he must squirm through gradually. "That's a swell outfit you've got on," he began.

"Yes," replied Susan with her usual candor. "Miss Hinkle borrowed it out of the stock for me to wear."

Gideon was confused. He knew how she had got the hat and dress, but he expected her to make a pretense. He couldn't understand her not doing it. Such candor—any kind of candor—wasn't in the game of men and women as women had played it in his experience. The women—all sorts of women—lied and faked at their business just as men did in the business of buying and selling goods. And her voice—and her way of speaking—they made him feel more than ever out of his class. He must get something to drink as soon as it could be served; that would put him at his ease. Yes—a drink—that would set him up again. And a drink for her—that would bring her down from this queer new kind of high horse. "I guess she must be a top notcher—the real thing, come down in the world—and not out of the near silks. But she'll be all right after a drink. One drink of liquor makes the whole world kin." That last thought reminded him of his own cleverness and he attacked the situation afresh. But the conversation as they drove up the avenue was on the whole constrained and intermittent—chiefly about the weather. Susan was observing—and feeling—and enjoying. Up bubbled her young spirits perpetually renewed by her healthy, vital youth of body. She was seeing her beloved City of the Sun again. As they turned out of the avenue for Sherry's main entrance Susan realized that she was in Forty-fourth Street. The street where she and Spenser had lived!—had lived only yesterday. No—not yesterday—impossible! Her eyes closed and she leaned back in the cab.

Gideon was waiting to help her alight. He saw that something was wrong; it stood out obviously in her ghastly face. He feared the carriage men round the entrance would "catch on" to the fact that he was escorting a girl so unused to swell surroundings that she was ready to faint with fright. "Don't be foolish," he said sharply. Susan revived herself, descended, and with head bent low and trembling body entered the restaurant. In the agitation of getting a table and settling at it Gideon forgot for the moment her sickly pallor.

He began to order at once, not consulting her—for he prided himself on his knowledge of cookery and assumed that she knew nothing about it. "Have a cocktail?" asked he. "Yes, of course you will. You need it bad and you need it quick."

She said she preferred sherry. She had intended to drink nothing, but she must have aid in conquering her faintness and overwhelming depression. Gideon took a dry martini; ordered a second for himself when the first came, and had them both down before she finished her sherry. "I've ordered champagne," said he. "I suppose you like sweet champagne. Most ladies do, but I can't stand seeing it served even."

"No—I like it very dry," said Susan.

Gideon glinted his eyes gayly at her, showed his white jaguar teeth. "So you're acquainted with fizz, are you?" He was feeling his absurd notion of inequality in her favor dissipate as the fumes of the cocktails rose straight and strong from his empty stomach to his brain. "Do you know, I've a sort of feeling that we're going to like each other a lot. I think we make a handsome couple—eh—what's your first name?"

"Lorna."

"Lorna, then. My name's Ed, but everybody calls me Gid."

As soon as the melon was served, he ordered the champagne opened. "To our better acquaintance," said he, lifting his glass toward her.

"Thank you," said she, in a suffocated voice, touching her glass to her lips.

He was too polite to speak, even in banter, of what he thought was the real cause of her politeness and silence. But he must end this state of overwhelmedness at grand surroundings. Said he:

"You're kind o' shy, aren't you, Lorna? Or is that your game?"

"I don't know. You've had a very interesting life, haven't you? Won't you tell me about it?"

"Oh—just ordinary," replied he, with a proper show of modesty. And straightway, as Susan had hoped, he launched into a minute account of himself—the familiar story of the energetic, aggressive man twisting and kicking his way up from two or three dollars a week. Susan seemed interested, but her mind refused to occupy itself with a narrative so commonplace. After Rod and his friends this boastful business man was dull and tedious. Whenever he laughed at an account of his superior craft—how he had bluffed this man, how he had euchered that one—she smiled. And so in one more case the common masculine delusion that women listen to them on the subject of themselves, with interest and admiration as profound as their own, was not impaired.

"But," he wound up, "I've stayed plain Ed Gideon. I never have let prosperity swell *my* head. And anyone that knows me'll tell you I'm a regular fool for generosity with those that come at me right. . . . I've always been a favorite with the ladies."

As he was pausing for comment from her, she said, "I can believe it." The word "generosity" kept echoing in her mind. Generosity—generosity. How much talk there was about it! Everyone was forever praising himself for his generosity, was reciting acts of the most obvious selfishness in proof. Was there any such thing in the whole world as real generosity?

"They like a generous man," pursued Gid. "I'm tight in business—I can see a dollar as far as the next man and chase it as hard and grab it as tight. But when it comes to the ladies, why, I'm open-handed. If they treat me right, I treat them right." Then, fearing that he had tactlessly raised a doubt of his invincibility, he hastily added, "But they always do treat me right."

While he had been talking on and on, Susan had been appealing to the champagne to help her quiet her aching heart. She resolutely set her thoughts to wandering among the couples at the other tables in that subdued softening light—the beautifully dressed women listening to their male companions with close attention—were they too being bored by such trash by way of talk? Were they too simply listening because it is the man who pays, because it is the man who must be conciliated and put in a good humor with himself, if dinners and dresses and jewels are to be bought? That tenement attic—that hot moist workroom—poverty—privation—"honest work's" dread rewards— —

"Now, what kind of a man would you say I was?" Gideon was inquiring.

"How do you mean?" replied Susan, with the dexterity at vagueness that habitually self-veiling people acquire as an instinct.

"Why, as a man. How do I compare with the other men you've known?" And he "shot" his cuffs with a gesture of careless elegance that his cuff links might assist in the picture of the "swell dresser" he felt he was posing.

"Oh—you—you're—very different."

"I *am* different," swelled Gideon. "You see, it's this way——" And he was off again into another eulogy of himself; it carried them through the dinner and two quarts of champagne. He was much annoyed that she did not take advantage of the pointed opportunity he gave her to note the total of the bill; he was even uncertain whether she had noted that he gave the waiter a dollar. He rustled and snapped it before laying it upon the tray, but her eyes looked vague.

"Well," said he, after a comfortable pull at an expensive-looking cigar, "sixteen seventy-five is quite a lively little peel-off for a dinner for only two. But it was worth it, don't you think?"

"It was a splendid dinner," said Susan truthfully. Gideon beamed in intoxicated good humor. "I knew you'd like it. Nothing pleases me better than to take a nice girl who isn't as well off as I am out and blow her off to a crackerjack dinner. Now, you may have thought a dollar was too much to tip the waiter?"

"A dollar is—a dollar, isn't it?" said Susan.

Gideon laughed. "I used to think so. And most men wouldn't give that much to a waiter. But I feel sorry for poor devils who don't happen to be as lucky or as brainy as I am. What do you say to a turn in the Park? We'll take a hansom, and kind of jog along. And we'll stop at the Casino and at Gabe's for a drink."

"I have to get up so early," began Susan.

"Oh, that's all right." He slowly winked at her. "You'll not have to bump the bumps for being late tomorrow—if you treat *me* right."

He carried his liquor easily. Only in his eyes and in his ever more slippery smile that would slide about his face did he show that he had been drinking. He helped her into a hansom with a flourish and, overruling her protests, bade the driver go to the Casino. Once under way she was glad; her hot skin and her weary heart were grateful for the air blowing down the avenue from the Park's expanse of green. When Gideon attempted to put his arm around her, she moved close into the corner and went on talking so calmly about calm subjects that he did not insist. But when he had tossed down a drink of whiskey at the Casino and they resumed the drive along the moonlit, shady roads, he tried again.

"Please," said she, "don't spoil a delightful evening."

"Now look here, my dear—haven't I treated you right?"

"Indeed you have, Mr. Gideon."

"Oh, don't be so damned formal. Forget the difference between our positions. Tomorrow I'm going to place a big order with your house, if you treat me right. I'm dead stuck on you—and that's a God's fact. You've taken me clean off my feet. I'm thinking of doing a lot for you."

Susan was silent.

"What do you say to throwing up your job and coming to Chicago with me? How much do you get?"

"Ten."

"Why, *you* can't live on that."

"I've lived on less—much less."

"Do you like it?"

"Naturally not."

"You want to get on—don't you?"

"I must."

"You're down in the heart about something. Love?"

Susan was silent.

"Cut love out. Cut it out, my dear. That ain't the way to get on. Love's a good consolation prize, if you ain't going to get anywhere, and know you ain't. And it's a good first prize after you've arrived and can afford the luxuries of life. But for a man—or a woman—that's pushing up, it's sheer ruination! Cut it out!"

"I am cutting it out," said Susan. "But that takes time."

"Not if you've got sense. The way to cut anything out is—cut it out!—a quick slash—just cut. If you make a dozen little slashes, each of them hurts as much as the one big slash—and the dozen hurt twelve times as much—bleed twelve times as much—put off the cure a lot more than twelve times as long."

He had Susan's attention for the first time.

"Do you know why women don't get on?"

"Tell me," said she. "That's what I want to hear."

"Because they don't play the game under the rules. Now, what does a man do? Why, he stakes everything he's got—does whatever's necessary, don't stop at *nothing* to help him get there. How is it with women? Some try to be virtuous—when their bodies are their best assets. God! I wish I'd 'a' had your looks and your advantages as a woman to help me. I'd be a millionaire this minute, with a house facing this Park and a yacht and all the rest of it. A woman that's squeamish about her virtue can't hope to win— unless she's in a position to make a good marriage. As for the loose ones, they are as big fools as the virtuous ones. The virtuous ones lock away their best asset; the loose ones throw it away. Neither one *use* it. Do you follow me?"

"I think so." Susan was listening with a mind made abnormally acute by the champagne she had freely drunk. The coarse bluntness and directness of the man did not offend her. It made what he said the more effective, producing a rude arresting effect upon her nerves. It made the man himself seem more of a person. Susan was beginning to have a kind of respect for him, to change her first opinion that he was merely a vulgar, pushing commonplace.

"Never thought of that before?"

"Yes—I've thought of it. But— —" She paused.

"But—what?"

"Oh, nothing."

"Never mind. Some womanish heart nonsense, I suppose. Do you see the application of what I've said to you and me?"

"Go on." She was leaning forward, her elbows on the closed doors of the hansom, her eyes gazing dreamily into the moonlit dimness of the cool woods through which they were driving.

"You don't want to stick at ten per?"

"No."

"It'll be less in a little while. Models don't last. The work's too hard."

"I can see that."

"And anyhow it means tenement house."

"Yes. Tenement house."

"Well—what then? What's your plan?"

"I haven't any."

"Haven't a plan—yet want to get on! Is that good sense? Did ever anybody get anywhere without a plan?"

"I'm willing to work. I'm going to work. I *am* working."

"Work, of course. Nobody can keep alive without working. You might as well say you're going to breathe and eat—Work don't amount to anything, for getting on. It's the kind of work—working in a certain direction—working with a plan."

"I've got a plan. But I can't begin at it just yet."

"Will it take money?"

"Some."

"Have you got it?"

"No," replied Susan. "I'll have to get it."

"As an honest working girl?" said he with good-humored irony.

Susan laughed. "It does sound ridiculous, doesn't it?" said she.

"Here's another thing that maybe you haven't counted in. Looking as you do, do you suppose men that run things'll let you get past without paying toll? Not on your life, my dear. If you was ugly, you might after several years get twenty or twenty-five by working hard—unless you lost your figure first. But the men won't let a good looker rise that way. Do you follow me?"

"Yes."

"I'm not talking theory. I'm talking life. Take you and me for example. I can help you—help you a lot. In fact I can put you on your feet. And I'm willing. If you was a man and I liked you and wanted to help you, I'd make you help me, too. I'd make you do a lot of things for me—maybe some of 'em not so very nice—maybe some of 'em downright dirty. And you'd do 'em, as all young fellows, struggling up, have to. But you're a woman. So I'm willing to make easier terms. But I can't help you with you not showing any appreciation. That wouldn't be good business—would it?—to get no return but, 'Oh, thank you so much, Mr. Gideon. So sweet of you. I'll remember you in my prayers.' Would that be sensible?"

"No," said Susan.

"Well, then! If I do you a good turn, you've got to do me a good turn—not one that I don't want done, but one I do want done. Ain't I right? Do you follow me?"

"I follow you."

Some vague accent in Susan's voice made him feel dissatisfied with her response. "I hope you do," he said sharply. "What I'm saying is dresses on your back and dollars in your pocket—and getting on in the world—if you work it right."

"Getting on in the world," said Susan, pensively.

"I suppose that's a sneer."

"Oh, no. I was only thinking."

"About love being all a woman needs to make her happy, I suppose?"

"No. Love is—Well, it isn't happiness."

"Because you let it run you, instead of you running it. Eh?"

"Perhaps."

"Sure! Now, let me tell you, Lorna dear. Comfort and luxury, money in bank, property, a good solid position—*that's* the foundation. Build on *that* and you'll build solid. Build on love and sentiment and you're building upside down. You're putting the gingerbread where the rock ought to be. Follow me?"

"I see what you mean."

He tried to find her hand. "What do you say?"

"I'll think of it."

"Well, think quick, my dear. Opportunity doesn't wait round in anybody's outside office . . . Maybe you don't trust me—don't think I'll deliver the goods?"

"No. I think you're honest."

"You're right I am. I do what I say I'll do. That's why I've got on. That's why I'll keep on getting on. Let's drive to a hotel."

She turned her head and looked at him for the first time since he began his discourse on making one's way in the world. Her look was calm, inquiring—would have been chilling to a man of sensibility—that is, of sensibility toward an unconquered woman.

"I want to give your people that order, and I want to help you."

"I want them to get the order. I don't care about the rest," she replied dully.

"Put it any way you like."

Again he tried to embrace her. She resisted firmly. "Wait," said she. "Let me think."

They drove the rest of the way to the upper end of the Park in silence.

He ordered the driver to turn. He said to her; "Well, do you get the sack or does the house get the order?"

She was silent.

"Shall I drive you home or shall we stop at Gabe's for a drink?"

"Could I have champagne?" said she.

"Anything you like if you choose right."

"I haven't any choice," said she.

He laughed, put his arm around her, kissed her unresponsive but unresisting lips. "You're right, you haven't," said he. "It's a fine sign that you have the sense to see it. Oh, you'll get on. You don't let trifles stand in your way."

CHAPTER III

AT the lunch hour the next day Mary Hinkle knocked at the garret in Clinton Place. Getting no answer, she opened the door. At the table close to the window was Susan in a nightgown, her hair in disorder as if she had begun to arrange it and had stopped halfway. Her eyes turned listlessly in Mary's direction—dull eyes, gray, heavily circled.

"You didn't answer, Miss Sackville. So I thought I'd come in and leave a note," explained Mary. Her glance was avoiding Susan's.

"Come for the dress and hat?" said Susan. "There they are." And she indicated the undisturbed bed whereon hat and dress were carelessly flung.

"My, but it's hot in this room!" exclaimed Mary. "You must move up to my place. There's a room and bath vacant—only seven per."

Susan seemed not to hear. She was looking dully at her hands upon the table before her.

"Mr. Jeffries sent me to ask you how you were. He was worried because you didn't come." With a change of voice, "Mr. Gideon telephoned down the order a while ago. Mr. Jeffries says you are to keep the dress and hat."

"No," said Susan. "Take them away with you."

"Aren't you coming down this afternoon?"

"No," replied Susan. "I've quit."

"Quit?" cried Miss Hinkle. Her expression gradually shifted from astonishment to pleased understanding. "Oh, I see! You've got something better."

"No. But I'll find something."

Mary studied the situation, using Susan's expressionless face as a guide. After a time she seemed to get from it a clew. With the air of friendly experience bent on aiding helpless inexperience she pushed aside the dress and made room for herself on the bed. "Don't be a fool, Miss Sackville," said she. "If you don't like that sort of thing—you know what I mean— why, you can live six months—maybe a year—on the reputation of what you've done and their hope that you'll weaken down and do it again. That'll give you time to look round and find something else. For pity's sake, don't turn yourself loose without a job. You got your place so easy that you think you can get one any old time. There's where you're wrong. Believe me, you played in luck—and luck don't come round often. I know what I'm talking about. So I say, don't be a fool!"

"I am a fool," said Susan.

"Well—get over it. And don't waste any time about it, either."

"I can't go back," said Susan stolidly. "I can't face them."

"Face who?" cried Mary. "Business is business. Everybody understands that. All the people down there are crazy about you now. You got the house a hundred-thousand-dollar order. You don't *suppose* anybody in business bothers about how an order's got—do you?"

"It's the way *I* feel—not the way *they* feel."

"As for the women down there—of course, there's some that pretend they won't do that sort of thing. Look at 'em—at their faces and figures—and you'll see why they don't. Of course a girl keeps straight when there's nothing in not being straight—leastways, unless she's a fool. She knows that if the best she can do is marry a fellow of her own class, why she'd only get left if she played any tricks with them cheap skates that have to get married or go without because they're too poor to pay for anything—and by marrying can get that and a cook and a washwoman and mender besides—and maybe, too, somebody who can go out and work if they're laid up sick. But if a girl sees a chance to get on——don't be a fool, Miss Sackville."

Susan listened with a smile that barely disturbed the stolid calm of her features. "I'm not going back," she said.

Mary Hinkle was silenced by the quiet finality of her voice. Studying that delicate face, she felt, behind its pallid impassiveness, behind the refusal to return, a reason she could not comprehend. She dimly realized that she would respect it if she could understand it; for she suspected it had its origin somewhere in Susan's "refined ladylike nature." She knew that once in a while among the women she was acquainted with there did happen one who preferred death in any form of misery to leading a lax life—and indisputable facts had convinced her that not always were these women "just stupid ignorant fools." She herself possessed no such refinement of nerves or of whatever it was. She had been brought up in a loose family and in a loose neighborhood. She was in the habit of making all sorts of pretenses, because that was the custom, while being candid about such matters was regarded as bad form. She was not fooled by these pretenses in other girls, though they often did fool each other. In Susan, she instinctively felt, it was not pretense. It was something or other else—it was a dangerous reality. She liked Susan; in her intelligence and physical charm were the possibilities of getting far up in the world; it seemed a pity that she was thus handicapped. Still, perhaps Susan would stumble upon some worth while man who, attempting to possess her without marriage and failing, would pay the heavy price. There was always that chance—a small chance, smaller even than finding by loose living a worth while man who would marry you because you happened exactly to suit him—to give him enough only to make him feel that he wanted more. Still, Susan was unusually attractive, and luck sometimes did come a poor person's way—sometimes.

"I'm overdue back," said Mary. "You want me to tell 'em that?"

"Yes."

"You'll have hard work finding a job at anything like as much as ten per. I've got two trades, and I couldn't at either one."

"I don't expect to find it."

"Then what are you going to do?"

"Take what I can get—until I've been made hard enough—or strong enough—or whatever it is—to stop being a fool."

This indication of latent good sense relieved Miss Hinkle. "I'll tell 'em you may be down tomorrow. Think it over for another day."

Susan shook her head. "They'll have to get somebody else." And, as Miss Hinkle reached the threshold, "Wait till I do the dress up. You'll take it for me?"

"Why send the things back?" urged Mary. "They belong
to you.
God knows you earned 'em."

Susan, standing now, looked down at the finery. "So I did.
I'll keep them," said she. "They'd pawn for something."

"With your looks they'd wear for a heap more. But keep 'em, anyhow. And I'll not tell Jeffries you've quit. It'll do no harm to hold your job open a day or so."

"As you like," said Susan, to end the discussion. "But I have quit."

"No matter. After you've had something to eat, you'll feel different."

And Miss Hinkle nodded brightly and departed. Susan resumed her seat at the bare wobbly little table, resumed her listless attitude. She did not move until Ellen came in, holding out a note and saying, "A boy from your store brung this—here."

"Thank you," said Susan, taking the note. In it she found a twenty-dollar bill and a five. On the sheet of paper round it was scrawled:

Take the day off. Here's your commission. We'll raise your pay in a few weeks, L. L. J.

So Mary Hinkle had told them either that she was quitting or that she was thinking of quitting, and they wished her to stay, had used the means they believed she could not resist. In a dreary way this amused her. As if she cared whether or not life was kept in this worthless body of hers, in her tired heart, in her disgusted mind! Then she dropped back into listlessness. When she was aroused again it was by Gideon, completely filling the small doorway. "Hello, my dear!" cried he cheerfully. "Mind my smoking?"

Susan slowly turned her head toward him, surveyed him with an expression but one removed from the blank look she would have had if there had been no one before her.

"I'm feeling fine today," pursued Gideon, advancing a step and so bringing himself about halfway to the table. "Had a couple of pick-me-ups and a fat breakfast. How are you?"

"I'm always well."

"Thought you seemed a little seedy." His shrewd sensual eyes were exploring the openings in her nightdress. "You'll be mighty glad to get out of this hole. Gosh! It's hot. Don't see how you stand it. I'm a law abiding citizen but I must say I'd turn criminal before I'd put up with this."

In the underworld from which Gideon had sprung—the underworld where welters the overwhelming mass of the human race—there are three main types. There are the hopeless and spiritless—the mass—who welter passively on, breeding and dying. There are the spirited who also possess both shrewdness and calculation; they push upward by hook and by crook, always mindful of the futility of the struggle of the petty criminal of the slums against the police and the law; they arrive and found the aristocracies of the future. The third is the criminal class. It is also made up of the spirited—but the spirited who, having little shrewdness and no calculation—that is, no ability to foresee and measure consequences—wage clumsy war upon society and pay the penalty of their fatuity in lives of wretchedness even more wretched than the common lot. Gideon belonged to the second class—the class that pushes upward without getting into jail; he was a fair representative of this type, neither its best nor its worst, but about midway of its range between arrogant, all-dominating plutocrat and shystering merchant or lawyer or politician who barely escapes the criminal class.

"You don't ask me to sit down, dearie," he went on facetiously.

"But I'm not so mad that I won't do it."

He took the seat Miss Hinkle had cleared on the bed. His glance wandered disgustedly from object to object in the crowded yet bare attic. He caught a whiff of the odor from across the hall—from the fresh-air shaft—and hastily gave several puffs at his cigar to saturate his surroundings with its perfume. Susan acted as if she were alone in the room. She had not even drawn together her nightgown.

"I phoned your store about you," resumed Gideon. "They said you hadn't showed up—wouldn't till tomorrow. So I came round here and your landlady sent me up. I want to take you for a drive this afternoon. We can dine up to Claremont or farther, if you like."

"No, thanks," said Susan. "I can't go."

"Upty-tupty!" cried Gideon. "What's the lady so sour about?"

"I'm not sour."

"Then why won't you go?"

"I can't."

"But we'll have a chance to talk over what I'm going to do for you."

"You've kept your word," said Susan.

"That was only part. Besides, I'd have given your house the order, anyhow."

Susan's eyes suddenly lighted up. "You would?" she cried.

"Well—a part of it. Not so much, of course. But I never let pleasure interfere with business. Nobody that does ever gets very far."

Her expression made him hasten to explain—without being conscious why. "I said—*part* of the order, my dear. They owe to you about half of what they'll make off me. . . . What's that money on the table? Your commission?"

"Yes."

"Twenty-five? Um!" Gideon laughed. "Well, I suppose it's as generous as I'd be, in the same circumstances. Encourage your employees, but don't swell-head 'em—that's the good rule. I've seen many a promising young chap ruined by a raise of pay. . . . Now, about you and me." Gideon took a roll of bills from his trousers pocket, counted off five twenties, tossed them on the table. "There!"

One of the bills in falling touched Susan's hand. She jerked the hand away as if the bill had been afire. She took all five of them, folded them, held them out to him. "The house has paid me," said she.

"That's honest," said he, nodding approvingly. "I like it. But in your case it don't apply."

These two, thus facing a practical situation, revealed an important, overlooked truth about human morals. Humanity divides broadly into three classes: the arrived; those who will never arrive and will never try; those in a state of flux, attempting and either failing or succeeding. The arrived and the inert together preach and to a certain extent practice an idealistic system of morality that interferes with them in no way. It does not interfere with the arrived because they have no need to infringe it, except for amusement; it does not interfere with the inert, but rather helps them to bear their lot by giving them a cheering notion that their insignificance is due to their goodness. This idealistic system receives the homage of lip service from the third and struggling section of mankind, but no more, for in practice it would hamper them at every turn in their efforts to fight their way up. Susan was, at that stage of her career, a candidate for membership in the struggling class. Her heart was set firmly against the unwritten, unspoken, even unwhispered code of practical morality which dominates the struggling class. But life had at least taught her the folly of intolerance. So when Gideon talked in terms of that practical morality, she listened without offense; and she talked to him in terms of it because to talk the idealistic morality in which she had been bred and before which she bowed the knee in sincere belief would have been simply to excite his laughter at her innocence and his contempt for her folly.

"I feel that I've been paid," said she. "I did it for the house—because I owed it to them."

"Only for the house?" said he with insinuating tenderness. He took and pressed the fingers extended with the money in them.

"Only for the house," she repeated, a hard note in her voice. And her fingers slipped away, leaving the money in his hand. "At least, I suppose it must have been for the house," she added, reflectively, talking to herself aloud. "Why did I do it? I don't know. I don't know. They say one always has a reason for what one does. But I often can't find any reason for things I do—that, for instance. I simply did it because it seemed to me not to matter much what *I* did with myself, and they wanted the order so badly." Then she happened to become conscious of his presence and to see a look of uneasiness, self-complacence, as if he were thinking that he quite understood this puzzle. She disconcerted him with what vain men call a cruel snub. "But whatever the reason, it certainly couldn't have been you," said she.

"Now, look here, Lorna," protested Gideon, the beginnings of anger in his tone. "That's not the way to talk if you want to get on."

She eyed him with an expression which would have raised a suspicion that he was repulsive in a man less self-confident, less indifferent to what the human beings he used for pleasure or profit thought of him.

"To say nothing of what I can do for you, there's the matter of future orders. I order twice a year—in big lots always."

"I've quit down there."

"Oh! Somebody else has given you something good—eh? *That's* why you're cocky."

"No."

"Then why've you quit?"

"I wish you could tell me. I don't understand. But—I've done it."

Gideon puzzled with this a moment, decided that it was beyond him and unimportant, anyhow. He blew out a cloud of smoke, stretched his legs and took up the main subject. "I was about to say, I've got a place for you. I'd like to take you to Chicago, but there's a Mrs. G.—as dear, sweet, good a soul as ever lived—just what a man wants at home with the children and to make things respectable. I wouldn't grieve her for worlds. But I can't live without a little fun—and Mrs. G. is a bit slow for me. . . . Still, it's no use talking about having you out there. She ought to be able to understand that an active man needs two women. One for the quiet side of his nature, the other for the lively side. Sometimes I think she—like a lot of wives— wouldn't object if it wasn't that she was afraid the other lady would get me away altogether and she'd be left stranded."

"Naturally," said Susan.

"Not at all!" cried he. "Don't you get any such notion in that lovely little head of yours, my dear. You women don't understand honor—a man's sense of honor."

"Naturally," repeated Susan.

He gave a glance of short disapproval. Her voice was not to his liking. "Let's drop Mrs. G. out of this," said he. "As I was saying, I've arranged for you to take a place here—easy work—something to occupy you—and I'll foot the bills over and above— —"

He stopped short or, rather, was stopped by the peculiar smile Susan had turned upon him. Before it he slowly reddened, and his eyes reluctantly shifted. He had roused her from listlessness, from indifference. The poisons in her blood were burned up by the fresh, swiftly flowing currents set in motion by his words, by the helpfulness of his expression, of his presence. She became again the intensely healthy, therefore intensely alive, therefore energetic and undaunted Susan Lenox, who, when still a child, had not hesitated to fly from home, from everyone she knew, into an unknown world.

"What are you smiling at me that way for?" demanded he in a tone of extreme irritation.

"So you look on me as your mistress?" And never in all her life had her eyes been so gray—the gray of cruelest irony.

"Now what's the use discussing those things? You know the world. You're a sensible woman."

Susan made closer and more secure the large loose coil of her hair, rose and leaned against the table. "You don't understand. You couldn't. I'm not one of those respectable women, like your Mrs. G., who belong to men. And I'm not one of the other kind who also throw in their souls with their bodies for good measure. Do *you* think you had *me?*" She laughed with maddening gentle mockery, went on: "I don't hate you. I don't despise you even. You mean well. But the sight of you makes me sick. It makes me feel as I do when I think of a dirty tenement I used to have to live in, and of the things that I used to have to let crawl over me. So I want to forget you as soon as I can—and that will be soon after you get out of my sight."

Her blazing eyes startled him. Her voice, not lifted above its usual quiet tones, enraged him. "You—you!" he cried. "You must be crazy, to talk to *me* like that!"

She nodded. "Yes—crazy," said she with the same quiet intensity. "For I know what kind of a beast you are—a clean, good-natured beast, but still a beast. And how could you understand?"

He had got upon his feet. He looked as if he were going to strike her.

She made a slight gesture toward the door. He felt at a hopeless disadvantage with her—with this woman who did not raise her voice, did not need to raise it to express the uttermost of any passion. His jagged teeth gleamed through his mustache; his shrewd little eyes snapped like an angry rat's. He fumbled about through the steam of his insane rage for adequate insults—in vain. He rushed from the room and bolted downstairs.

Within an hour Susan was out, looking for work. There could be no turning back now. Until she went with Gideon it had been as if her dead were still unburied and in the house. Now— —

Never again could she even indulge in dreams of going to Rod. That part of her life was finished with all the finality of the closed grave. Grief—yes. But the same sort of grief as when a loved one, after a long and painful illness, finds relief in death. Her love for Rod had been stricken of a mortal illness the night of their arrival in New York. After lingering for a year between life and death, after a long death agony, it had expired. The end came—these matters of the exact moment of inevitable events are unimportant but have a certain melancholy interest—the end came when she made choice where there was no choice, in the cab with Gideon.

For better or for worse she was free. She was ready to begin her career.

CHAPTER IV

AFTER a few days, when she was viewing her situation in a calmer, more normal mood with the practical feminine eye, she regretted that she had refused Gideon's money. She was proud of that within herself which had impelled and compelled her to refuse it; but she wished she had it. Taking it, she felt, would have added nothing to her humiliation in her own sight; and for what he thought of her, one way or the other, she cared not a pin. It is one of the familiar curiosities of human inconsistency which is at bottom so completely consistent, that she did not regret having refused his far more valuable offer to aid her.

She did not regret even during those few next days of disheartening search for work. We often read how purpose can be so powerful that it compels. No doubt if Susan's purpose had been to get temporary relief — or, perhaps, had it been to get permanent relief by weaving a sex spell — she would in that desperate mood have been able to compel. Unfortunately she was not seeking to be a pauper or a parasite; she was trying to find steady employment at living wages — that is, at wages above the market value for female and for most male — labor. And that sort of purpose cannot compel.

Our civilization overflows with charity — which is simply willingness to hand back to labor as generous gracious alms a small part of the loot from the just wages of labor. But of real help — just wages for honest labor — there is little, for real help would disarrange the system, would abolish the upper classes.

She had some faint hopes in the direction of millinery and dressmaking, the things for which she felt she had distinct talent. She was soon disabused. There was nothing for her, and could be nothing until after several years of doubtful apprenticeship in the trades to which any female person seeking employment to piece out an income instinctively turned first and offered herself at the employer's own price. Day after day, from the first moment of the industrial day until its end, she hunted — wearily, yet unweariedly — with resolve living on after the death of hope. She answered advertisements; despite the obviously sensible warnings of the working girls she talked with she even consulted and took lists from the religious and charitable organizations, patronized by those whose enthusiasm about honest work had never been cooled by doing or trying to do any of it, and managed by those who, beginning as workers, had made all haste to escape from it into positions where they could live by talking about it and lying about it— saying the things comfortable people subscribe to philanthropies to hear.

There was work, plenty of it. But not at decent wages, and not leading to wages that could be earned without viciously wronging those under her in an executive position. But even in those cases the prospect of promotion was vague and remote, with illness and failing strength and poor food, worse clothing and lodgings, as certainties straightway. At some places she was refused with the first glance at her. No good-looking girls wanted; even though they behaved themselves and attracted customers, the customers lost sight of matters of merchandise in the all-absorbing matter of sex. In offices a good-looking girl upset discipline, caused the place to degenerate into a deer-haunt in the mating season. No place did she find offering more than four dollars a week, except where the dress requirements made the nominally higher wages even less. Everywhere women's wages were based upon the assumption that women either lived at home or made the principal part of their incomes by prostitution, disguised or frank. In fact, all wages even the wages of men except in a few trades—were too small for an independent support. There had to be a family—and the whole family had to work—and even then the joint income was not enough for decency. She had no family or friends to help her—at least, no friends except those as poor as herself, and she could not commit the crime of adding to their miseries.

She had less than ten dollars left. She must get to work at once—and what she earned must supply her with all. A note came from Jeffries—a curt request that she call—curt to disguise the eagerness to have her back. She tore it up. She did not even debate the matter. It was one of her significant qualities that she never had the inclination, apparently lacked the power, to turn back once she had turned away. Mary Hinkle came, urged her. Susan listened in silence, merely shook her head for answer, changed the subject.

In the entrance to the lofts of a tall Broadway building she saw a placard: "Experienced hands at fancy ready-to-wear hat trimming wanted." She climbed three steep flights and was in a large, low-ceilinged room where perhaps seventy-five girls were at work. She paused in the doorway long enough to observe the kind of work—a purely mechanical process of stitching a few trimmings in exactly the same way upon a cheap hat frame. Then she went to an open window in a glass partition and asked employment of a young Jew with an incredibly long nose thrusting from the midst of a pimply face which seemed merely its too small base.

"Experienced?" asked the young man.

"I can do what those girls are doing."

With intelligent eyes he glanced at her face, then let his glance rove contemptuously over the room full of workers. "I should hope so," said he. "Forty cents a dozen. Want to try it?"

"When may I go to work?"

"Right away. Write your name here."

Susan signed her name to what she saw at a glance was some sort of contract. She knew it contained nothing to her advantage, much to her disadvantage. But she did not care. She had to have work—something, anything that would stop the waste of her slender capital. And within fifteen minutes she was seated in the midst of the sweating, almost nauseatingly odorous women of all ages, was toiling away at the simple task of making an ugly hat frame still more ugly by the addition of a bit of tawdry cotton ribbon, a buckle, and a bunch of absurdly artificial flowers. She was soon able to calculate roughly what she could make in six days. She thought she could do two dozen of the hats a day; and twelve dozen hats at forty cents the dozen would mean four dollars and eighty cents a week!

Four dollars and eighty cents! Less than she had planned to set aside for food alone, out of her ten dollars as a model.

Next her on the right sat a middle-aged woman, grossly fat, repulsively shapeless, piteously homely—one of those luckless human beings who are foredoomed from the outset never to know any of the great joys of life the joys that come through our power to attract our fellow-beings. As this woman stitched away, squinting through the steel-framed spectacles set upon her snub nose, Susan saw that she had not even good health to mitigate her lot, for her color was pasty and on her dirty skin lay blotches of dull red. Except a very young girl here and there all the women had poor or bad skins. And Susan was not made disdainful by the odor which is far worse than that of any lower animal, however dirty, because the human animal must wear clothing. She had lived in wretchedness in a tenement; she knew that this odor was an inevitable part of tenement life when one has neither the time nor the means to be clean. Poor food, foul air, broken sleep—bad health, disease, unsightly faces, repulsive bodies!

No wonder the common people looked almost like another race in contrast with their brothers and sisters of the comfortable classes. Another race! The race into which she would soon be reborn under the black magic of poverty! As she glanced and reflected on what she saw, viewed it in the light of her experience, her fingers slackened, and she could speed them up only in spurts.

"If I stay here," thought she, "in a few weeks I shall be like these others. No matter how hard I may fight, I'll be dragged down." As impossible to escape the common lot as for a swimmer alone in mid-ocean to keep up indefinitely whether long or brief, the struggle could have but, the one end—to be sunk in, merged in, the ocean.

It took no great amount of vanity for her to realize that she was in every way the superior of all those around her—in every way except one. What did she lack? Why was it that with her superior intelligence, her superior skill both of mind and of body, she could be thus dragged down and held far below her natural level? Why could she not lift herself up among the sort of people with whom she belonged—or even make a beginning toward lifting herself up? Why could she not take hold? What did she lack? What must she acquire—or what get rid of?

At lunch time she walked with the ugly woman up and down the first side street above the building in which the factory was located. She ate a roll she bought from a pushcart man, the woman munched an apple with her few remnants of teeth. "Most of the girls is always kicking," said the woman. "But I'm mighty satisfied. I get enough to eat and to wear, and I've got a bed to sleep in—and what else is there in life for anybody, rich or poor?"

"There's something to be said for that," replied Susan, marveling to find in this piteous creature the only case of thorough content she had ever seen.

"I make my four to five per," continued the woman. "And I've got only myself. Thank God, I was never fool enough to marry. It's marrying that drags us poor people down and makes us miserable. Some says to me, 'Ain't you lonesome?' And I says to them, says I, 'Why, I'm used to being alone. I don't want anything else.' If they was all like me, they'd not be fightin' and drinkin' and makin' bad worse. The bosses always likes to give me work. They say I'm a model worker, and I'm proud to say they're right. I'm mighty grateful to the bosses that provide for the like of us. What'd we do without 'em? That's what I'd like to know."

She had pitied this woman because she could never hope to experience any of the great joys of life. What a waste of pity, she now thought. She had overlooked the joy of joys—delusions. This woman was secure for life against unhappiness.

A few days, and Susan was herself regarded as a model worker. She turned out hats so rapidly that the forewoman, urged on by Mr. Himberg, the proprietor, began to nag at the other girls. And presently a notice of general reduction to thirty-five cents a dozen was posted. There had been a union; it had won a strike two years before—and then had been broken up by shrewd employing of detectives who had got themselves elected officers. With the union out of the way, there was no check upon the bosses in their natural and lawful effort to get that profit which is the most high god of our civilization. A few of the youngest and most spirited girls—those from families containing several workers—indignantly quit. A few others murmured, but stayed on. The mass dumbly accepted the extra twist in the screw of the mighty press that was slowly squeezing them to death. Neither to them nor to Susan herself did it happen to occur that she was the cause of the general increase of hardship and misery. However, to have blamed her would have been as foolish and as unjust as to blame any other individual. The system ordained it all. Oppression and oppressed were both equally its helpless instruments. No wonder all the vast beneficent discoveries of science that ought to have made the whole human race healthy, long-lived and prosperous, are barely able to save the race from swift decay and destruction under the ravages of this modern system of labor worse than slavery—for under slavery the slave, being property whose loss could not be made good without expense, was protected in life and in health.

Susan soon discovered that she had miscalculated her earning power. She had been deceived by her swiftness in the first days, before the monotony of her task had begun to wear her down. Her first week's earnings were only four dollars and thirty cents. This in her freshness, and in the busiest season when wages were at the highest point.

In the room next hers—the same, perhaps a little dingier—lived a man. Like herself he had no trade—that is, none protected by a powerful union and by the still more powerful—in fact, the only powerful shield—requirements of health and strength and a certain grade of intelligence that together act rigidly to exclude most men and so to keep wages from dropping to the neighborhood of the line of pauperism. He was the most industrious and, in his small way, the most resourceful of men. He was insurance agent, toilet soap agent, piano tuner, giver of piano lessons, seller of pianos and of music on commission. He worked fourteen and sixteen hours a day. He made nominally about twelve to fifteen a week. Actually—because of the poverty of his customers and his too sympathetic nature he made five to six a week—the most any working person could hope for unless in one of the few favored trades. Barely enough to keep body and soul together. And why should capital that needs so much for fine houses and wines and servants and automobiles and culture and charity and the other luxuries—why should capital pay more when so many were competing for the privilege of being allowed to work?

She gave up her room at Mrs. Tucker's—after she had spent several evenings walking the streets and observing and thinking about the miseries of the fast women of the only class she could hope to enter. "A woman," she decided, "can't even earn a decent living that way unless she has the money to make the right sort of a start. 'To him that hath shall be given; from him that hath not shall be taken away even that which he hath.' Gideon was my chance and I threw it away."

Still, she did not regret. Of all the horrors the most repellent seemed to her to be dependence upon some one man who could take it away at his whim.

She disregarded the advice of the other girls and made the rounds of the religious and charitable homes for working girls. She believed she could endure perhaps better than could girls with more false pride, with more awe of snobbish conventionalities—at least she could try to endure—the superciliousness, the patronizing airs, the petty restraints and oppressions, the nauseating smugness, the constant prying and peeping, the hypocritical lectures, the heavy doses of smug morality. She felt that she could bear with almost any annoyances and humiliations to be in clean surroundings and to get food that was at least not so rotten that the eye could see it and the nose smell it. But she found all the homes full, with long waiting lists, filled for the most part, so the working girls said, with professional objects of charity. Thus she had no opportunity to judge for herself whether there was any truth in the prejudice of the girls against these few and feeble attempts to mitigate the miseries of a vast and ever vaster multitude of girls. Adding together all the accommodations offered by all the homes of every description, there was a total that might possibly have provided for the homeless girls of a dozen factories or sweatshops—and the number of homeless girls was more than a quarter of a million, was increasing at the rate of more than a hundred a day.

Charity is so trifling a force that it can, and should be, disregarded. It serves no *good* useful service. It enables comfortable people to delude themselves that all that can be done is being done to mitigate the misfortunes which the poor bring upon themselves. It obscures the truth that modern civilization has been perverted into a huge manufacturing of decrepitude and disease, of poverty and prostitution. The reason we talk so much and listen so eagerly when our magnificent benevolences are the subject is that we do not wish to be disturbed—and that we dearly love the tickling sensation in our vanity of generosity.

Susan was compelled to the common lot—the lot that will be the common lot as long as there are people to be made, by taking advantage of human necessities, to force men and women and children to degrade themselves into machines as wage-slaves. At two dollars a week, double what her income justified—she rented a room in a tenement flat in Bleecker street. It was a closet of a room whose thin, dirt-adorned walls were no protection against sound or vermin, not giving even privacy from prying eyes. She might have done a little better had she been willing to share room and bed with one or more girls, but not enough better to compensate for what that would have meant.

The young Jew with the nose so impossible that it elevated his countenance from commonplace ugliness to weird distinction had taken a friendly fancy to her. He was Julius Bam, nephew of the proprietor. In her third week he offered her the forewoman's place. "You've got a few brains in your head," said he. "Miss Tuohy's a boob. Take the job and you'll push up. We'll start you at five per."

Susan thanked him but declined. "What's the use of my taking a job I couldn't keep more than a day or two?" explained she. "I haven't it in me to boss people."

"Then you've got to get it, or you're done for," said he. "Nobody ever gets anywhere until he's making others work for him."

It was the advice she had got from Matson, the paper box manufacturer in Cincinnati. It was the lesson she found in all prosperity on every hand. Make others work for you—and the harder you made them work the more prosperous you were—provided, of course, you kept all or nearly all the profits of their harder toil. Obvious common sense. But how could she goad these unfortunates, force their clumsy fingers to move faster, make their long and weary day longer and wearier—with nothing for them as the result but duller brain, clumsier fingers, more wretched bodies? She realized why those above lost all patience with them, treated them with contempt. Only as one of them could any intelligent, energetic human being have any sympathy for them, stupid and incompetent from birth, made ever more and more stupid and incapable by the degrading lives they led. She could scarcely conceal her repulsion for their dirty bodies, their stained and rotting clothing saturated with stale sweat, their coarse flesh reeking coarse food smells. She could not listen to their conversation, so vulgar, so inane. Yet she felt herself—for the time—one of them, and her heart bled for them. And while she knew that only their dullness of wit and ignorance kept them from climbing up and stamping and trampling full as savagely and cruelly as did those on top, still the fact remained that they were not stamping and trampling.

As she was turning in some work, Miss Tuohy said abruptly:

"You don't belong here. You ought to go back."

Susan started, and her heart beat wildly. She was going to lose her job!

The forelady saw, and instantly understood. "I don't mean that," she said. "You can stay as long as you like—as long as your health lasts. But isn't there somebody somewhere—*anybody*—you can go to and ask them to help you out of this?"

"No—there's no one," said she.

"That can't be true," insisted the forelady. "Everybody has somebody—or can get somebody—that is, anyone who looks like you. I wouldn't suggest such a thing to a fool. But *you* could keep your head. There isn't any other way, and you might as well make up your mind to it."

To confide is one of the all but universal longings—perhaps needs—of human nature. Susan's honest, sympathetic eyes, her look and her habit of reticence, were always attracting confidences from such unexpected sources as hard, forbidding Miss Tuohy. Susan was not much surprised when Miss Tuohy went on to say:

"I was spoiled when I was still a kid—by getting to know well a man who was above my class. I had tastes that way, and he appealed to them. After him I couldn't marry the sort of man that wanted me. Then my looks went—like a flash—it often happens that way with us Irish girls. But I can get on. I know how to deal with these people—and *you* never could learn. You'd treat em like ladies and they'd treat you as easy fruit. Yes, I get along all right, and I'm happy—away from here."

Susan's sympathetic glance of inquiry gave the necessary encouragement. "It's a baby," Miss Tuohy explained—and Susan knew it was for the baby's sake that this good heart had hardened itself to the dirty work of forelady. Her eyes shifted as she said, "A child of my sister's—dead in Ireland. How I do love that baby——"

They were interrupted and it so happened that the confidence was never resumed and finished. But Miss Tuohy had made her point with Susan—had set her to thinking less indefinitely. "I *must* take hold!" Susan kept saying to herself. The phrase was always echoing in her brain. But how?—*how?* And to that question she could find no answer.

Every morning she bought a one-cent paper whose big circulation was in large part due to its want ads—its daily section of closely printed columns of advertisements of help wanted and situations wanted. Susan read the columns diligently. At first they acted upon her like an intoxicant, filling her not merely with hope but with confident belief that soon she would be in a situation where the pay was good and the work agreeable, or at least not disagreeable. But after a few weeks she ceased from reading.

Why? Because she answered the advertisements, scores of them, more than a hundred, before she saw through the trick and gave up. She found that throughout New York all the attractive or even tolerable places were filled by girls helped by their families or in other ways, girls working at less than living wages because they did not have to rely upon their wages for their support. And those help wanted advertisements were simply appeals for more girls of that sort—for cheaper girls; or they were inserted by employment agencies, masquerading in the newspaper as employers and lying in wait to swindle working girls by getting a fee in exchange for a false promise of good work at high wages; or they were the nets flung out by crafty employers who speeded and starved their slaves, and wished to recruit fresh relays to replace those that had quit in exhaustion or in despair.

"Why do you always read the want ads?" she said to Lany Ricardo, who spent all her spare time at those advertisements in two papers she bought and one she borrowed every day. "Did you ever get anything good, or hear of anybody that did?"

"Oh, my, no," replied Lany with a laugh. "I read for the same reason that all the rest do. It's a kind of dope. You read and then you dream about the places—how grand they are and how well off you'll be. But nobody'd be fool enough to answer one of 'em unless she was out of a job and had to get another and didn't care how rotten it was. No, it's just dope—like buyin' policy numbers or lottery tickets. You know you won't git a prize, but you have a lot of fun dreaming about it."

As Susan walked up and down at the lunch hour, she talked with workers, both men and women, in all sorts of employment. Some were doing a little better than she; others—the most—were worse off chiefly because her education, her developed intelligence, enabled her to ward off savage blows—such as illness from rotten food—against which their ignorance made them defenseless. Whenever she heard a story of someone's getting on, how grotesquely different it was from the stories she used to get out of the Sunday school library and dream over! These almost actualities of getting on had nothing in them about honesty and virtue. According to them it was always some sort of meanness or trickery; and the particular meanness or tricks were, in these practical schools of success in session at each lunch hour, related in detail as lessons in how to get on. If the success under discussion was a woman's, it was always how her boss or employer had "got stuck on her" and had given her an easier job with good pay so that she could wear clothes more agreeable to his eyes and to his touch. Now and then it was a wonderful dazzling success—some girl had got her rich employer so "dead crazy" about her that he had taken her away from work altogether and had set her up in a flat with a servant and a "swell trap"; there was even talk of marriage.

Was it true? Were the Sunday school books through and through lies—ridiculous, misleading lies, wicked lies—wicked because they hid the shameful truth that ought to be proclaimed from the housetops? Susan was not sure. Perhaps envy twisted somewhat these tales of rare occasional successes told by the workers to each other. But certain it was that, wherever she had the opportunity to see for herself, success came only by hardness of heart, by tricks and cheats. Certain it was also that the general belief among the workers was that success could be got in those ways only—and this belief made the falsehood, if it was a falsehood, or the partial truth, if it was a twisted truth, full as poisonous as if it had been true throughout. Also, if the thing were not true, how came it that everyone in practical life believed it to be so—how came it that everyone who talked in praise of honesty and virtue looked, as he talked, as if he were canting and half expected to be laughed at?

All about her as badly off as she, or worse off. Yet none so unhappy as she—not even the worse off. In fact, the worse off as the better off were not so deeply wretched. Because they had never in all their lives known the decencies of life clean lodgings, clean clothing, food fit to eat, leisure and the means of enjoying leisure. And Susan had known all these things. When she realized why her companions in misery, so feeble in self-restraint, were able to endure patiently and for the most part even cheerfully, how careful she was never to say or to suggest anything that might put ideas of what life might be, of what it was for the comfortable few, into the minds of these girls who never had known and could only be made wretched by knowing! How fortunate for them, she thought, that they had gone to schools where they met only their own kind! How fortunate that the devouring monster of industry had snatched them away from school before their minds had been awakened to the realities of life! How fortunate that their imaginations were too dull and too heavy to be touched by the sights of luxury they saw in the streets or by what they read in the newspapers and in the cheap novels! To them, as she soon realized, their world seemed the only world, and the world that lived in comfort seemed a vague unreality, as must seem whatever does not come into our own experience.

One lunch hour an apostle of discontent preaching some kind of politics or other held forth on the corner above the shop. Susan paused to listen. She had heard only a few words when she was incensed to the depths of her heart against him. He ought to be stopped by the police, this scoundrel trying to make these people unhappy by awakening them to the misery and degradation of their lot! He looked like an honest, earnest man. No doubt he fancied that he was in some way doing good. These people who were always trying to do the poor good—they ought all to be suppressed! If someone could tell them how to cease to be poor, that would indeed be good. But such a thing would be impossible. In Sutherland, where the best off hadn't so painfully much more than the worst off, and where everybody but the idle and the drunken, and even they most of the time, had enough to eat, and a decent place to sleep, and some kind of Sunday clothes—in Sutherland the poverty was less than in Cincinnati, infinitely less than in this vast and incredibly rich New York where in certain districts wealth, enormous wealth, was piled up and up. So evidently the presence of riches did not help poverty but seemed to increase it. No, the disease was miserable, thought Susan. For most of the human race, disease and bad food and vile beds in dingy holes and days of fierce, poorly paid toil—that was the law of this hell of a world. And to escape from that hideous tyranny, you must be hard, you must trample, you must rob, you must cease to be human.

The apostle of discontent insisted that the law could be changed, that the tyranny could be abolished. She listened, but he did not convince her. He sounded vague and dreamy—as fantastically false in his new way as she had found the Sunday school books to be. She passed on.

She continued to pay out a cent each day for the newspaper. She no longer bothered with the want ads. Pipe dreaming did not attract her; she was too fiercely bent upon escape, actual escape, to waste time in dreaming of ways of escape that she never could realize. She read the paper because, if she could not live in the world but was battered down in its dark and foul and crowded cellar, she at least wished to know what was going on up in the light and air. She found every day news of great doings, of wonderful rises, of rich rewards for industry and thrift, of abounding prosperity and of opportunity fairly forcing itself into acceptance. But all this applied only to the few so strangely and so luckily chosen, while the mass was rejected. For that mass, from earliest childhood until death, there was only toil in squalor—squalid food, squalid clothing, squalid shelter. And when she read one day—in an obscure paragraph in her newspaper—that the income of the average American family was less than twelve dollars a week—less than two dollars and a half a week for each individual—she realized that what she was seeing and living was not New York and Cincinnati, but was the common lot, country wide, no doubt world wide.

"*Must* take hold!" her mind cried incessantly to her shrinking heart. "Somehow—anyhow—take hold!—must—must—*must!*"

Those tenement houses! Those tenement streets! Everywhere wandering through the crowds the lonely old women—holding up to the girls the mirror of time and saying: "Look at my misery! Look at my disease-blasted body. Look at my toil-bent form and toil-wrecked hands. Look at my masses of wrinkles, at my rags, at my leaky and rotten shoes. Think of my aloneness—not a friend—feared and cast off by my relatives because they are afraid they will have to give me food and lodgings. Look at me—think of my life—and know that I am *you* as you will be a few years from now whether you work as a slave to the machine or as a slave to the passions of one or of many men. I am *you*. Not one in a hundred thousand escape my fate except by death."

"Somehow—anyhow—I must take hold," cried Susan to her swooning heart.

When her capital had dwindled to three dollars Mrs. Tucker appeared. Her face was so beaming bright that Susan, despite her being clad in garments on which a pawnshop would advance nothing, fancied she had come with good news.

"Now that I'm rid of that there house," said she, "I'll begin to perk up. I ain't got nothing left to worry me. I'm ready for whatever blessings the dear Master'll provide. My pastor tells me I'm the finest example of Christian fortitude he ever Saw. But"—and Mrs. Tucker spoke with genuine modesty—"I tell him I don't deserve no credit for leaning on the Lord. If I can trust Him in death, why not in life?"

"You've got a place? The church has——"

"Bless you, no," cried Mrs. Tucker. "Would I burden 'em with myself, when there's so many that has to be looked after? No, I go direct to the Lord."

"What are you going to do? What place have you got?"

"None as yet. But He'll provide something—something better'n
I deserve."

Susan had to turn away, to hide her pity—and her disappointment. Not only was she not to be helped, but also she must help another. "You might get a job at the hat factory," said she.

Mrs. Tucker was delighted. "I knew it!" she cried. "Don't you see how He looks after me?"

Susan persuaded Miss Tuohy to take Mrs. Tucker on. She could truthfully recommend the old woman as a hard worker. They moved into a room in a tenement in South Fifth Avenue. Susan read in the paper about a model tenement and went to try for what was described as real luxury in comfort and cleanliness. She found that sort of tenements filled with middle-class families on their way down in the world and making their last stand against rising rents and rising prices. The model tenement rents were far, far beyond her ability to pay. She might as well think of moving to the Waldorf. She and Mrs. Tucker had to be content with a dark room on the fifth floor, opening on a damp air shaft whose odor was so foul that in comparison the Clinton Place shaft was as the pure breath of the open sky. For this shelter—more than one-half the free and proud citizens of prosperous America dwelling in cities occupy its like, or worse they paid three dollars a week—a dollar and a half apiece. They washed their underclothing at night, slept while it was drying. And Susan, who could not bring herself to imitate the other girls and wear a blouse of dark color that was not to be washed, rose at four to do the necessary ironing. They did their own cooking. It was no longer possible for Susan to buy quality and content herself with small quantity. However small the quantity of food she could get along on, it must be of poor quality—for good quality was beyond her means.

It maddened her to see the better class of working girls. Their fairly good clothing, their evidences of some comfort at home, seemed to mock at her as a poor fool who was being beaten down because she had not wit enough to get on. She knew these girls were either supporting themselves in part by prostitution or were held up by their families, by the pooling of the earnings of several persons. Left to themselves, to their own earnings at work, they would be no better off than she, or at best so little better off that the difference was unimportant. If to live decently in New York took an income of fifteen dollars a week, what did it matter whether one got five or ten or twelve? Any wages below fifteen meant a steady downward drag—meant exposure to the dirt and poison of poverty tenements—meant the steady decline of the power of resistance, the steady oozing away of self-respect, of the courage and hope that give the power to rise. To have less than the fifteen dollars absolutely necessary for decent surroundings, decent clothing, decent food—that meant one was drowning. What matter whether the death of the soul was quick, or slow, whether the waters of destruction were twenty feet deep or twenty thousand?

Mrs. Reardon, the servant woman on the top floor, was evicted and Susan and Mrs. Tucker took her in. She protested that she could sleep on the floor, that she had done so a large part of her life—that she preferred it to most beds. But Susan made her up a kind of bed in the corner. They would not let her pay anything. She had rheumatism horribly, some kind of lung trouble, and the almost universal and repulsive catarrh that preys upon working people. Her hair had dwindled to a meager wisp. This she wound into a hard little knot and fastened with an imitation tortoise-shell comb, huge, high, and broken, set with large pieces of glass cut like diamonds. Her teeth were all gone and her cheeks almost met in her mouth.

One day, when Mrs. Tucker and Mrs. Reardon were exchanging eulogies upon the goodness of God to them, Susan shocked them by harshly ordering them to be silent. "If God hears you," she said, "He'll think you're mocking Him. Anyhow, I can't stand any more of it. Hereafter do your talking of that kind when I'm not here."

Another day Mrs. Reardon told about her sister. The sister had worked in a factory where some sort of poison that had a rotting effect on the human body was used in the manufacture. Like a series of others the sister caught the disease. But instead of rotting out a spot, a few fingers, or part of the face, it had eaten away the whole of her lower jaw so that she had to prepare her food for swallowing by first pressing it with her fingers against her upper teeth. Used as Susan was to hearing horrors in this region where disease and accident preyed upon every family, she fled from the room and walked shuddering about the streets—the streets with their incessant march past of blighted and blasted, of maimed and crippled and worm-eaten. Until that day Susan had been about as unobservant of the obvious things as is the rest of the race. On that day she for the first time noticed the crowd in the street, with mind alert to signs of the ravages of accident and disease. Hardly a sound body, hardly one that was not piteously and hideously marked.

When she returned—and she did not stay out long—Mrs. Tucker was alone. Said she:

"Mrs. Reardon says the rotten jaw was sent on her sister as a punishment for marrying a Protestant, she being a Catholic. How ignorant some people is! Of course, the good Lord sent the judgment on her for being a Catholic at all."

"Mrs. Tucker," said Susan, "did you ever hear of Nero?"

"He burned up Rome—and he burned up the Christian martyrs," said Mrs. Tucker. "I had a good schooling. Besides, sermons is highly educating."

"Well," said Susan, "if I had a choice of living under Nero or of living under that God you and Mrs. Reardon talk about, I'd take Nero and be thankful and happy."

Mrs. Tucker would have fled if she could have afforded it. As it was all she ventured was a sigh and lips moving in prayer.

On a Friday in late October, at the lunch hour, Susan was walking up and down the sunny side of Broadway. It was the first distinctly cool day of the autumn; there had been a heavy downpour of rain all morning, but the New York sun that is ever struggling to shine and is successful on all but an occasional day was tearing up and scattering the clouds with the aid of a sharp north wind blowing down the deep canyon. She was wearing her summer dress still—old and dingy but clean. That look of neatness about the feet—that charm of a well-shaped foot and a well-turned ankle properly set off—had disappeared—with her the surest sign of the extreme of desperate poverty. Her shoes were much scuffed, were even slightly down at the heel; her sailor hat would have looked only the worse had it had a fresh ribbon on its crown. This first hint of winter had stung her fast numbing faculties into unusual activity. She was remembering the misery of the cold in Cincinnati—the misery that had driven her into prostitution as a drunken driver's lash makes the frenzied horse rush he cares not where in his desire to escape. This wind of Broadway—this first warning of winter— it was hissing in her ears: "Take hold! Winter is coming! Take hold!"

Summer and winter—fiery heat and brutal cold. Like the devils in the poem, the poor—the masses, all but a few of the human race—were hurried from fire to ice, to vary their torment and to make it always exquisite.

To shelter herself for a moment she paused at a spot that happened to be protected to the south by a projecting sidewalk sign. She was facing, with only a tantalizing sheet of glass between, a display of winter underclothes on wax figures. To show them off more effectively the sides and the back of the window were mirrors. Susan's gaze traveled past the figures to a person she saw standing at full length before her. "Who is that pale, stooped girl?" she thought. "How dreary and sad she looks! How hard she is fighting to make her clothes look decent, when they aren't! She must be something like me—only much worse off." And then she realized that she was gazing at her own image, was pitying her own self. The room she and Mrs. Tucker and the old scrubwoman occupied was so dark, even with its one little gas jet lighted, that she was able to get only a faint look at herself in the little cracked and water-marked mirror over its filthy washstand—filthy because the dirt was so ground in that only floods of water and bars of soap could have cleaned down to its original surface. She was having a clear look at herself for the first time in three months.

She shrank in horror, yet gazed on fascinated. Why, her physical charm had gone gone, leaving hardly a trace! Those dull, hollow eyes—that thin and almost ghastly face—the emaciated form—the once attractive hair now looking poor and stringy because it could not be washed properly—above all, the sad, bitter expression about the mouth. Those pale lips! Her lips had been from childhood one of her conspicuous and most tempting beauties; and as the sex side of her nature had developed they had bloomed into wonderful freshness and vividness of form and color. Now— —

Those pale, pale lips! They seemed to form a sort of climax of tragedy to the melancholy of her face. She gazed on and on. She noted every detail. How she had fallen! Indeed, a fallen woman! These others had been born to the conditions that were destroying her; they were no worse off, in many cases better off. But she, born to comfort and custom of intelligent educated associations and associates— —

A fallen woman!

Honest work! Even if it were true that this honest work was a sort of probation through which one rose to better things—even if this were true, could it be denied that only a few at best could rise, that the most—including all the sensitive, and most of the children—must wallow on, must perish? Oh, the lies, the lies about honest work!

Rosa Mohr, a girl of her own age who worked in the same room, joined her. "Admiring yourself?" she said laughing. "Well, I don't blame you. You *are* pretty."

Susan at first thought Rosa was mocking her. But the tone and expression were sincere.

"It won't last long," Rosa went on. "I wasn't so bad myself when I quit the high school and took a job because father lost his business and his health. He got in the way of one of those trusts. So of course they handed it to him good and hard. But he wasn't a squealer. He always said they'd done only what he'd been doing himself if he'd had the chance. I always think of what papa used to say when I hear people carrying on about how wicked this or that somebody else is."

"Are you going to stay on—at this life?" asked Susan, still looking at her own image.

"I guess so. What else is there? . . . I've got a steady. We'll get married as soon as he has a raise to twelve per. But I'll not be any better off. My beau's too stupid ever to make much. If you see me ten years from now I'll probably be a fat, sloppy old thing, warming a window sill or slouching about in dirty rags."

"Isn't there any way to—to escape?"

"It does look as though there ought to be—doesn't it? But I've thought and thought, and *I* can't see it—and I'm pretty near straight Jew. They say things are better than they used to be, and I guess they are. But not enough better to help me any. Perhaps my children—*if* I'm fool enough to have any—perhaps they'll get a chance. . . . But I wouldn't gamble on it."

Susan was still looking at her rags—at her pale lips—was avoiding meeting her own eyes. "Why not try the streets?"

"Nothing in it," said Rosa, practically. "I did try it for a while and quit. Lots of the girls do, and only the fools stay at it. Once in a while there's a girl who's lucky and gets a lover that's kind to her or a husband that can make good. But that's luck. For one that wins out, a thousand lose."

"Luck?" said Susan.

Rosa laughed. "You're right. It's something else besides luck. The trouble is a girl loses her head—falls in love—supports a man—takes to drink—don't look out for her health—wastes her money. Still—where's the girl with head enough to get on where there's so many temptations?"

"But there's no chance at all, keeping straight, you say."

"The other thing's worse. The street girls—of our class, I mean—don't average as much as we do. And it's an awful business in winter. And they spend so much time in station houses and over on the Island. And, gosh! how the men do treat them! You haven't any idea. You wouldn't believe the horrible things the girls have to do to earn their money—a quarter or half a dollar—and maybe the men don't pay them even that. A girl tries to get her money in advance, but often she doesn't. And as they have to dress better than we do, and live where they can clean up a little, they 'most starve. Oh, that life's hell."

Susan had turned away from her image, was looking at Rosa.

"As for the fast houses——" Rosa shuddered—"I was in one for a week. I ran away—it was the only way I could escape. I'd never tell any human being what I went through in that house. . . . Never!" She watched Susan's fine sympathetic face, and in a burst of confidence said: "One night the landlady sent me up with seventeen men. And she kept the seventeen dollars I made, and took away from me half a dollar one drunken longshoreman gave me as a present. She said I owed it for board and clothes. In those houses, high and low, the girls always owes the madam. They haven't a stitch of their own to their backs."

The two girls stood facing each other, each looking past the other into the wind-swept canyon of Broadway—the majestic vista of lofty buildings, symbols of wealth and luxury so abundant that it flaunted itself, overflowed in gaudy extravagance. Finally Susan said:

"Do you ever think of killing yourself?"

"I thought I would," replied the other girl. "But I guess I wouldn't have. Everybody knows there's no hope, yet they keep on hopin'. And I've got pretty good health yet, and once in a while I have some fun. You ought to go to dances—and drink. You wouldn't be blue *all* the time, then."

"If it wasn't for the sun," said Susan.

"The sun?" inquired Rosa.

"Where I came from," explained Susan, "it rained a great deal, and the sky was covered so much of the time. But here in New York there is so much sun. I love the sun. I get desperate—then out comes the sun, and I say to myself, 'Well, I guess I can go on a while longer, with the sun to help me.'"

"I hadn't thought of it," said Rosa, "but the sun is a help."

That indefatigable New York sun! It was like Susan's own courage. It fought the clouds whenever clouds dared to appear and contest its right to shine upon the City of the Sun, and hardly a day was so stormy that for a moment at least the sun did not burst through for a look at its beloved.

For weeks Susan had eaten almost nothing. During her previous sojourn in the slums—the slums of Cincinnati, though they were not classed as slums—the food had seemed revolting. But she was less discriminating then. The only food she could afford now—the food that is the best obtainable for a majority of the inhabitants of any city—was simply impossible for her. She ate only when she could endure no longer. This starvation no doubt saved her from illness; but at the same time it drained her strength. Her vitality had been going down, a little each day—lower and lower. The poverty which had infuriated her at first was now acting upon her like a soothing poison. The reason she had not risen to revolt was this slow and subtle poison that explains the inertia of the tenement poor from babyhood. To be spirited one must have health or a nervous system diseased in some of the ways that cause constant irritation. The disease called poverty is not an irritant, but an anesthetic. If Susan had been born to that life, her naturally vivacious temperament would have made her gay in unconscious wretchedness; as it was, she knew her own misery and suffered from it keenly—at times hideously—yet was rapidly losing the power to revolt.

Perhaps it was the wind—yes, it must have been the wind with its threat of winter—that roused her sluggish blood, that whipped thought into action. Anything—anything would be right, if it promised escape. Right—wrong! Hypocritical words for comfortable people!

That Friday night, after her supper of half-cooked corn meal and tea, she went instantly to work at washing out clothes. Mrs. Tucker spent the evening gossiping with the janitress, came in about midnight. As usual she was full to the brim with news of misery—of jobs lost, abandoned wives, of abused children, of poisoning from rotten "fresh" food or from "embalmed" stuff in cans, of sickness and yet more sickness, of maiming accidents, of death—news that is the commonplace of tenement life. She loved to tell these tales with all the harrowing particulars and to find in each some evidence of the goodness of God to herself. Often Susan could let her run on and on without listening. But not that night. She resisted the impulse to bid her be silent, left the room and stood at the hall window. When she returned Mrs. Tucker was in bed, was snoring in a tranquillity that was the reverse of contagious. With her habitual cheerfulness she had adapted herself to her changed condition without fretting. She had become as ragged and as dirty as her neighbors; she so wrought upon Susan's sensibilities, blunted though they were, that the girl would have been unable to sleep in the same bed if she had not always been tired to exhaustion when she lay down. But for that matter only exhaustion could have kept her asleep in that vermin-infested hole. Even the fiercest swarms of the insects that flew or ran or crawled and bit, even the filthy mice squeaking as they played upon the covers or ran over the faces of the sleepers, did not often rouse her.

While Mrs. Tucker snored, Susan worked on, getting every piece of at all fit clothing in her meager wardrobe into the best possible condition. She did not once glance at the face of the noisy sleeper—a face homely enough in Mrs. Tucker's waking hours, hideous now with the mouth open and a few scattered rotten teeth exposed, and the dark yellow-blue of the unhealthy gums and tongue.

At dawn Mrs. Tucker awoke with a snort and a start. She rubbed her eyes with her dirty and twisted and wrinkled fingers—the nails were worn and broken, turned up as if warped at the edges, blackened with dirt and bruisings. "Why, are you up already?" she said to Susan.

"I've not been to bed," replied the girl.

The woman stretched herself, sat up, thrust her thick, stockinged legs over the side of the bed. She slept in all her clothing but her skirt, waist, and shoes. She kneeled down upon the bare, sprung, and slanting floor, said a prayer, arose with a beaming face. "It's nice and warm in the room. How I do dread the winter, the cold weather—though no doubt we'll make out all right! Everything always does turn out well for me. The Lord takes care of me. I must make me a cup of tea."

"I've made it," said Susan.

The tea was frightful stuff—not tea at all, but cheap adulterants colored poisonously. Everything they got was of the same quality; yet the prices they paid for the tiny quantities they were able to buy at any one time were at a rate that would have bought the finest quality at the most expensive grocery in New York.

"Wonder why Mrs. Reardon don't come?" said Mrs. Tucker. Mrs. Reardon had as her only work a one night job at scrubbing. "She ought to have come an hour ago."

"Her rheumatism was bad when she started," said Susan. "I guess she worked slow."

When Mrs. Tucker had finished her second cup she put on her shoes, overskirt and waist, made a few passes at her hair. She was ready to go to work.

Susan looked at her, murmured: "An honest, God-fearing working woman!"

"Huh?" said Mrs. Tucker.

"Nothing," replied Susan who would not have permitted her to hear. It would be cruel to put such ideas before one doomed beyond hope.

Susan was utterly tired, but even the strong craving for a stimulant could not draw that tea past her lips. She ate a piece of dry bread, washed her face, neck, and hands. It was time to start for the factory.

That day—Saturday—was a half-holiday. Susan drew her week's earnings—four dollars and ten cents—and came home. Mrs. Tucker, who had drawn—"thanks to the Lord"—three dollars and a quarter, was with her. The janitress halted them as they passed and told them that Mrs. Reardon was dead. She looked like another scrubwoman, living down the street, who was known always to carry a sum of money in her dress pocket, the banks being untrustworthy. Mrs. Reardon, passing along in the dusk of the early morning, had been hit on the head with a blackjack. The one blow had killed her.

Violence, tragedy of all kinds, were too commonplace in that neighborhood to cause more than a slight ripple. An old scrubwoman would have had to die in some peculiarly awful way to receive the flattery of agitating an agitated street. Mrs. Reardon had died what was really almost a natural death. So the faint disturbance of the terrors of life had long since disappeared. The body was at the Morgue, of course.

"We'll go up, right away," said Mrs. Tucker.

"I've something to do that can't be put, off," replied Susan.

"I don't like for anyone as young as you to be so hard," reproached Mrs. Tucker.

"Is it hard," said Susan, "to see that death isn't nearly so terrible as life? She's safe and at peace. I've got to *live*."

Mrs. Tucker, eager for an emotional and religious opportunity, hastened away. Susan went at her wardrobe ironing, darning, fixing buttonholes, hooks and eyes. She drew a bucket of water from the tap in the hall and proceeded to wash her hair with soap; she rinsed it, dried it as well as she could with their one small, thin towel, left it hanging free for the air to finish the job.

It had rained all the night before—the second heavy rain in two months. But at dawn the rain had ceased, and the clouds had fled before the sun that rules almost undisputed nine months of the year and wars valiantly to rule the other three months—not altogether in vain. A few golden strays found their way into that cavelike room and had been helping her wonderfully. She bathed herself and scrubbed herself from head to foot. She manicured her nails, got her hands and feet into fairly good condition. She put on her best underclothes, her one remaining pair of undarned stockings, the pair of ties she had been saving against an emergency. And once more she had the charm upon which she most prided herself—the charm of an attractive look about the feet and ankles. She then took up the dark-blue hat frame—one of a lot of "seconds"—she had bought for thirty-five cents at a bargain sale, trimmed it with a broad dark-blue ribbon for which she had paid sixty cents. She was well pleased—and justly so—with the result. The trimmed hat might well have cost ten or fifteen dollars—for the largest part of the price of a woman's hat is usually the taste of the arrangement of the trimming.

By this time her hair was dry. She did it up with a care she had not had time to give it in many a week. She put on the dark-blue serge skirt of the between seasons dress she had brought with her from Forty-fourth Street; she had not worn it at all. With the feeble aid of the mirror that distorted her image into grotesqueness, she put on her hat with the care that important detail of a woman's toilet always deserves.

She completed her toilet with her one good and unworn blouse—plain white, the yoke gracefully pointed—and with a blue neck piece she had been saving. She made a bundle of all her clothing that was fit for anything—including the unworn batiste dress Jeffries and Jonas had given her. And into it she put the pistol she had brought away from Forty-fourth Street. She made a separate bundle of the Jeffries and Jonas hat with its valuable plumes. With the two bundles she descended and went to a pawnshop in Houston Street, to which she had made several visits.

A dirty-looking man with a short beard fluffy and thick like a yellow hen's tail lurked behind the counter in the dark little shop. She put her bundles on the counter, opened them. "How much can I get for these things?" she asked.

The man examined every piece minutely. "There's really nothing here but the summer dress and the hat," said he. "And they're out of style. I can't give you more than four dollars for the lot—and one for the pistol which is good but old style now. Five dollars. How'll you have it?"

Susan folded the things and tied up the bundles. "Sorry to have troubled you," she said, taking one in either hand.

"How much did you expect to get, lady?" asked the pawnbroker.

"Twenty-five dollars."

He laughed, turned toward the back of the shop. As she reached the door he called from his desk at which he seemed about to seat himself, "I might squeeze you out ten dollars."

"The plumes on the hat will sell for thirty dollars," said Susan. "You know as well as I do that ostrich feathers have gone up."

The man slowly advanced. "I hate to see a customer go away unsatisfied," said he. "I'll give you twenty dollars."

"Not a cent less than twenty-five. At the next place I'll ask thirty—and get it."

"I never can stand out against a lady. Give me the stuff."

Susan put it on the counter again. Said she:

"I don't blame you for trying to do me. You're right to try to buy your way out of hell."

The pawnbroker reflected, could not understand this subtlety, went behind his counter. He produced a key from his pocket, unlocked a drawer underneath and took out a large tin box. With another key from another pocket he unlocked this, threw back the lid revealing a disorder of papers. From the depths he fished a paper bag. This contained a roll of bills. He gave Susan a twenty and a five, both covered with dirt so thickly that she could scarcely make out the denominations.

"You'll have to give me cleaner money than this," said she.

"You are a fine lady," grumbled he. But he found cleaner bills.

She turned to her room. At sight of her Mrs. Tucker burst out laughing with delight. "My, but you do look like old times!" cried she. "How neat and tasty you are! I suppose it's no need to ask if you're going to church?"

"No," said Susan. "I've got nothing to give, and I don't beg."

"Well, I ain't going there myself, lately—somehow. They got so they weren't very cordial—or maybe it was me thinking that way because I wasn't dressed up like. Still I do wish you was more religious. But you'll come to it, for you're naturally a good girl. And when you do, the Lord'll give you a more contented heart. Not that you complain. I never knew anybody, especially a young person, that took things so quiet. . . . It can't be you're going to a dance?"

"No," said Susan. "I'm going to leave—go back uptown."

Mrs. Tucker plumped down upon the bed. "Leave for good?" she gasped.

"I've got Nelly Lemayer to take my place here, if you want her," said Susan. "Here is my share of the rent for next week and half a dollar for the extra gas I've burned last night and today."

"And Mrs. Reardon gone, too!" sobbed Mrs. Tucker, suddenly remembering the old scrubwoman whom both had forgotten. "And up to that there Morgue they wouldn't let me see her except where the light was so poor that I couldn't rightly swear it was her. How brutal everybody is to the poor! If they didn't have the Lord, what would become of them! And you leaving me all alone!"

The sobs rose into hysteria. Susan stood impassive. She had seen again and again how faint the breeze that would throw those shallow waters into commotion and how soon they were tranquil again. It was by observing Mrs. Tucker that she first learned an important unrecognized truth about human nature that amiable, easily sympathetic and habitually good-humored people are invariably hard of heart. In this parting she had no sense of loss, none of the melancholy that often oppresses us when we separate from someone to whom we are indifferent yet feel bound by the tie of misfortunes borne together. Mrs. Tucker, fallen into the habits of their surroundings, was for her simply part of them. And she was glad she was leaving them—forever, she hoped. *Christian*, fleeing the City of Destruction, had no sterner mandate to flight than her instinct was suddenly urging upon her.

When Mrs. Tucker saw that her tears were not appreciated, she decided that they were unnecessary. She dried her eyes and said:

"Anyhow, I reckon Mrs. Reardon's taking-off was a mercy."

"She's better dead," said Susan. She had abhorred the old woman, even as she pitied and sheltered her. She had a way of fawning and cringing and flattering—no doubt in well meaning attempt to show gratitude—but it was unendurable to Susan. And now that she was dead and gone, there was no call for further pretenses.

"You ain't going right away?" said Mrs. Tucker.

"Yes," said Susan.

"You ought to stay to supper."

Supper! That revolting food! "No, I must go right away," replied Susan.

"Well, you'll come to see me. And maybe you'll be back with us. You might go farther and do worse. On my way from the morgue I dropped in to see a lady friend on the East Side. I guess the good Lord has abandoned the East Side, there being nothing there but Catholics and Jews, and no true religion. It's dreadful the way things is over there—the girls are taking to the streets in droves. My lady friend was telling me that some of the mothers is sending their little girls out streetwalking, and some's even taking out them that's too young to be trusted to go alone. And no money in it, at that. And food and clothing prices going up and up. Meat and vegetables two and three times what they was a few years ago. And rents!" Mrs. Tucker threw up her hands.

"I must be going," said Susan. "Good-by."

She put out her hand, but Mrs. Tucker insisted on kissing her. She crossed Washington Square, beautiful in the soft evening light, and went up Fifth Avenue. She felt that she was breathing the air of a different world as she walked along the broad clean sidewalk with the handsome old houses on either side, with carriages and automobiles speeding past, with clean, happy-faced, well dressed human beings in sight everywhere. It was like coming out of the dank darkness of Dismal Swamp into smiling fields with a pure, star-spangled sky above. She was free—free! It might be for but a moment; still it was freedom, infinitely sweet because of past slavery and because of the fear of slavery closing in again. She had abandoned the old toilet articles. She had only the clothes she was wearing, the thirty-one dollars divided between her stockings, and the two-dollar bill stuffed into the palm of her left glove.

She had walked but a few hundred feet. She had advanced into a region no more prosperous to the eye than that she had been working in every day. Yet she had changed her world—because she had changed her point of view. The strata that form society lie in roughly parallel lines one above the other. The flow of all forms of the currents of life is horizontally along these strata, never vertically from one stratum to another. These strata, lying apparently in contact, one upon another, are in fact abysmally separated. There is not—and in the nature of things never can be any genuine human sympathy between any two strata. We *sympathize* in our own stratum, or class; toward other strata—other classes—our attitude is necessarily a looking up or a looking down. Susan, a bit of flotsam, ascending, descending, ascending across the social layers—belonging nowhere having attachments, not sympathies, a real settled lot nowhere—Susan was once more upward bound.

At the corner of Fourteenth Street there was a shop with large mirrors in the show windows. She paused to examine herself. She found she had no reason to be disturbed about her appearance. Her dress and hat looked well; her hair was satisfactory; the sharp air had brought some life to the pallor of her cheeks, and the release from the slums had restored some of the light to her eyes. "Why did I stay there so long?" she demanded of herself. Then, "How have I suddenly got the courage to leave?" She had no answer to either question. Nor did she care for an answer. She was not even especially interested in what was about to happen to her.

The moment she found herself above Twenty-third Street and in the old familiar surroundings, she felt an irresistible longing to hear about Rod Spenser. She was like one who has been on a far journey, leaving behind him everything that has been life to him; he dismisses it all because he must, until he finds himself again in his own country, in his old surroundings. She went into the Hoffman House and at the public telephone got the *Herald* office. "Is Mr. Drumley there?"

"No," was the reply. "He's gone to Europe."

"Did Mr. Spenser go with him?"

"Mr. Spenser isn't here—hasn't been for a long time. He's abroad too. Who is this?"

"Thank you," said Susan, hanging up the receiver.

She drew a deep breath of relief.

She left the hotel by the women's entrance in Broadway. It was six o'clock. The sky was clear—a typical New York sky with air that intoxicated blowing from it—air of the sea—air of the depths of heaven. A crescent moon glittered above the Diana on the Garden tower. It was Saturday night and Broadway was thronged—with men eager to spend in pleasure part of the week's wages or salary they had just drawn; with women sparkling-eyed and odorous of perfumes and eager to help the men. The air was sharp—was the ocean air of New York at its delicious best. And the slim, slightly stooped girl with the earnest violet-gray eyes and the sad bitter mouth from whose lips the once brilliant color had now fled was ready for whatever might come. She paused at the corner, and gazed up brilliantly lighted Broadway.

"Now!" she said half aloud and, like an expert swimmer adventuring the rapids, she advanced into the swift-moving crowd of the highway of New York's gayety.

CHAPTER V

AT the corner of Twenty-sixth Street a man put himself squarely across her path. She was attracted by the twinkle in his good-natured eyes. He was a youngish man, had the stoutness of indulgence in a fondness for eating and drinking—but the stoutness was still well within the bounds of decency. His clothing bore out the suggestion of his self-assured way of stopping her—the suggestion of a confidence-giving prosperity.

"You look as if you needed a drink, too," said he. "How about it, lady with the lovely feet?"

For the first time in her life she was feeling on an equality with man. She gave him the same candidly measuring glance that man gives man. She saw good-nature, audacity without impudence—at least not the common sort of impudence. She smiled merrily, glad of the chance to show her delight that she was once more back in civilization after the long sojourn in the prison workshops where it is manufactured. She said:

"A drink? Thank you—yes."

"That's a superior quality of smile you've got there," said he. "That, and those nice slim feet of yours ought to win for you anywhere. Let's go to the Martin."

"Down University Place?"

The stout young man pointed his slender cane across the street.

"You must have been away."

"Yes," said the girl. "I've been—dead."

"I'd like to try that myself—if I could be sure of coming to life in little old New York." And he looked round with laughing eyes as if the lights, the crowds, the champagne-like air intoxicated him.

At the first break in the thunderous torrent of traffic they crossed Broadway and went in at the Twenty-sixth Street entrance. The restaurant, to the left, was empty. Its little tables were ready, however, for the throng of diners soon to come. Susan had difficulty in restraining herself. She was almost delirious with delight. She was agitated almost to tears by the freshness, the sparkle in the glow of the red-shaded candles, in the colors and odors of the flowers decorating every table. While she had been down there all this had been up here—waiting for her! Why had she stayed down there? But then, why had she gone? What folly, what madness! To suffer such horrors for no reason—beyond some vague, clinging remnant of a superstition—or had it been just plain insanity? "Yes, I've been crazy—out of my head. The break with—Rod—upset my mind."

Her companion took her into the café to the right. He seated her on one of the leather benches not far from the door, seated himself in a chair opposite; there was a narrow marble-topped table between them. On Susan's right sat a too conspicuously dressed but somehow important looking actress; on her left, a shopkeeper's fat wife. Opposite each woman sat the sort of man one would expect to find with her. The face of the actress's man interested her. It was a long pale face, the mouth weary, in the eyes a strange hot fire of intense enthusiasm. He was young—and old—and neither. Evidently he had lived every minute of every year of his perhaps forty years. He was wearing a quiet suit of blue and his necktie was of a darker shade of the same color. His clothes were draped upon his good figure with a certain fascinating distinction. He was smoking an unusually long and thick cigarette. The slender strong white hand he raised and lowered was the hand of an artist. He might be a bad man, a very bad man— his face had an expression of freedom, of experience, that made such an idea as conventionality in connection with him ridiculous. But however bad he might be, Susan felt sure it would be an artistic kind of badness, without vulgarity. He might have reached the stage at which morality ceases to be a conviction, a matter of conscience, and becomes a matter of preference, of tastes—and he surely had good taste in conduct no less than in dress and manner. The woman with him evidently wished to convince him that she loved him, to convince those about her that they were lovers; the man evidently knew exactly what she had in mind—for he was polite, attentive, indifferent, and—Susan suspected—secretly amused.

Susan's escort leaned toward her and said in a low tone, "The two at the next table—the woman's Mary Rigsdall, the actress, and the man's Brent, the fellow who writes plays." Then in a less cautious tone, "What are you drinking?"

"What are *you* drinking?" asked Susan, still covertly watching Brent.

"You are going to dine with me?"

"I've no engagement."

"Then let's have Martinis—and I'll go get a table and order dinner while the waiter's bringing them."

When Susan was alone, she gazed round the crowded café, at the scores of interesting faces—thrillingly interesting to her after her long sojourn among countenances merely expressing crude elemental appetites if anything at all beyond toil, anxiety, privation, and bad health. These were the faces of the triumphant class—of those who had wealth or were getting it, fame or were striving for it, of those born to or acquiring position of some sort among the few thousands who lord it over the millions. These were the people among whom she belonged. Why was she having such a savage struggle to attain it? Then, all in an instant the truth she had been so long groping for in vain flung itself at her. None of these women, none of the women of the prosperous classes would be there but for the assistance and protection of the men. She marveled at her stupidity in not having seen the obvious thing clearly long ago. The successful women won their success by disposing of their persons to advantage—by getting the favor of some man of ability. Therefore, she, a woman, must adopt that same policy if she was to have a chance at the things worth while in life. She must make the best bargain—or series of bargains—she could. And as her necessities were pressing she must lose no time. She understood now the instinct that had forced her to fly from South Fifth Avenue, that had overruled her hesitation and had compelled her to accept the good-natured, prosperous man's invitation. . . . There was no other way open to her. She must not evade that fact; she must accept it. Other ways there might be—for other women. But not for her, the outcast without friends or family, the woman alone, with no one to lean upon or to give her anything except in exchange for what she had to offer that was marketable. She must make the bargain she could, not waste time in the folly of awaiting a bargain to her liking. Since she was living in the world and wished to continue to live there, she must accept the world's terms. To be sad or angry either one because the world did not offer her as attractive terms as it apparently offered many other women— the happy and respected wives and mothers of the prosperous classes, for instance—to rail against that was silly and stupid, was unworthy of her intelligence. She would do as best she could, and move along, keeping her eyes open; and perhaps some day a chance for much better terms might offer—for the best—for such terms as that famous actress there had got. She looked at Mary Rigsdall. An expression in her interesting face—the latent rather than the surface expression—set Susan to wondering whether, if she knew Rigsdall's *whole* story—or any woman's whole story—she might not see that the world was not bargaining so hardly with her, after all. Or any man's whole story. There her eyes shifted to Rigsdall's companion, the famous playwright of whom she had so often heard Rod and his friends talk.

She was startled to find that his gaze was upon her—an all-seeing look that penetrated to the very core of her being. He either did not note or cared nothing about her color of embarrassment. He regarded her steadily until, so she felt, he had seen precisely what she was, had become intimately acquainted with her. Then he looked away. It chagrined her that his eyes did not again turn in her direction; she felt that he had catalogued her as not worth while. She listened to the conversation of the two. The woman did the talking, and her subject was herself—her ability as an actress, her conception of some part she either was about to play or was hoping to play. Susan, too young to have acquired more than the rudiments of the difficult art of character study, even had she had especial talent for it—which she had not—Susan decided that the famous Rigsdall was as shallow and vain as Rod had said all stage people were.

The waiter brought the cocktails and her stout young companion came back, beaming at the thought of the dinner he had painstakingly ordered. As he reached the table he jerked his head in self-approval. "It'll be a good one," said he. "Saturday night dinner—and after—means a lot to me. I work hard all week. Saturday nights I cut loose. Sundays I sleep and get ready to scramble again on Monday for the dollars." He seated himself, leaned toward her with elevated glass. "What name?" inquired he.

"Susan."

"That's a good old-fashioned name. Makes me see the hollyhocks, and the hens scratching for worms. Mine's Howland. Billy Howland. I came from Maryland . . . and I'm mighty glad I did. I wouldn't be from anywhere else for worlds, and I wouldn't be there for worlds. Where do you hail from?"

"The West," said Susan.

"Well, the men in your particular corner out yonder must be a pretty poor lot to have let you leave. I spotted you for mine the minute I saw you— Susan. I hope you're not as quiet as your name. Another cocktail?"

"Thanks."

"Like to drink?"

"I'm going to do more of it hereafter."

"Been laying low for a while—eh?"

"Very low," said Susan. Her eyes were sparkling now; the cocktail had begun to stir her long languid blood.

"Live with your family?"

"I haven't any. I'm free."

"On the stage?"

"I'm thinking of going on."

"And meanwhile?"

"Meanwhile—whatever comes."

Billy Howland's face was radiant. "I had a date tonight and the lady threw me down. One of those drummer's wives that take in washing to add to the family income while hubby's flirting round the country. This hubby came home unexpectedly. I'm glad he did."

He beamed with such whole-souled good-nature that Susan laughed. "Thanks. Same to you," said she.

"Hope you're going to do a lot of that laughing," said he. "It's the best I've heard—such a quiet, gay sound. I sure do have the best luck. Until five years ago there was nothing doing for Billy—hall bedroom—Wheeling stogies—one shirt and two pairs of cuffs a week—not enough to buy a lady an ice-cream soda. All at once—bang! The hoodoo busted, and everything that arrived was for William C. Howland. Better get aboard."

"Here I am."

"Hold on tight. I pay no attention to the speed laws, and round the corners on two wheels. Do you like good things to eat?"

"I haven't eaten for six months."

"You must have been out home. Ah!—There's the man to tell us dinner's ready."

They finished the second cocktail. Susan was pleased to note that Brent was again looking at her; and she thought—though she suspected it might be the cocktail—that there was a question in his look—a question about her which he had been unable to answer to his satisfaction. When she and Howland were at one of the small tables against the wall in the restaurant, she said to him:

"You know Mr. Brent?"

"The play man? Lord, no. I'm a plain business dub. He wouldn't bother with me. You like that sort of man?"

"I want to get on the stage, if I can," was Susan's diplomatic reply.

"Well—let's have dinner first. I've ordered champagne, but if you prefer something else——"

"Champagne is what I want. I hope it's very dry."

Howland's eyes gazed tenderly at her. "I do like a woman who knows the difference between champagne and carbonated sirup. I think you and I've got a lot of tastes in common. I like eating—so do you. I like drinking—so do you. I like a good time—so do you. You're a little bit thin for my taste, but you'll fatten up. I wonder what makes your lips so pale."

"I'd hate to remind myself by telling you," said Susan.

The restaurant was filling. Most of the men and women were in evening dress. Each arriving woman brought with her a new exhibition of extravagance in costume, diffused a new variety of powerful perfume. The orchestra in the balcony was playing waltzes and the liveliest Hungarian music and the most sensuous strains from Italy and France and Spain. And before her was food!—food again!—not horrible stuff unfit for beasts, worse than was fed to beasts, but human food—good things, well cooked and well served. To have seen her, to have seen the expression of her eyes, without knowing her history and without having lived as she had lived, would have been to think her a glutton. Her spirits giddied toward the ecstatic. She began to talk—commenting on the people about her—the one subject she could venture with her companion. As she talked and drank, he ate and drank, stuffing and gorging himself, but with a frankness of gluttony that delighted her. She found she could not eat much, but she liked to see eating; she who had so long been seeing only poverty, bolting wretched food and drinking the vilest kinds of whiskey and beer, of alleged coffee and tea—she reveled in Howland's exhibition. She must learn to live altogether in her senses, never to think except about an appetite. Where could she find a better teacher? . . . They drank two quarts of champagne, and with the coffee she took *crème de menthe* and he brandy. And as the sensuous temperament that springs from intense vitality reasserted itself, the opportunity before her lost all its repellent features, became the bright, vivid countenance of lusty youth, irradiating the joy of living.

"I hear there's a lively ball up at Terrace Garden," said he. "Want to go?"

"That'll be fine!" cried she.

She saw it would have taken nearly all the money she possessed to have paid that bill. About four weeks' wages for one dinner! Thousands of families living for two weeks on what she and he had consumed in two hours! She reached for her half empty champagne glass, emptied it. She must forget all those things! "I've played the fool once. I've learned my lesson. Surely I'll never do it again." As she drank, her eyes chanced upon the clock. Half-past ten. Mrs. Tucker had probably just fallen asleep. And Mrs. Reardon was going out to scrub—going out limping and groaning with rheumatism. No, Mrs. Reardon was lying up at the morgue dead, her one chance to live lost forever. Dead! Yet better off than Mrs. Tucker lying alive. Susan could see her—the seamed and broken and dirty old remnant of a face—could see the vermin—and the mice could hear the snoring—the angry grunt and turning over as the insects——

"I want another drink—right away," she cried.

"Sure!" said Howland. "I need one more, too."

They drove in a taxi to Terrace Garden, he holding her in his arms and kissing her with an intoxicated man's enthusiasm. "You certainly are sweet," said he. "The wine on your breath is like flowers. Gosh, but I'm glad that husband came home! Like me a little?"

"I'm so happy, I feel like standing up and screaming," declared she.

"Good idea," cried he. Whereupon he released a war whoop and they both went off into a fit of hysterical laughter. When it subsided he said, "I sized you up as a live wire the minute I saw you. But you're even better than I thought. What are you in such a good humor about?"

"You couldn't understand if I told you," replied she. "You'd have to go and live where I've been living—live there as long as I have."

"Convent?"

"Worse. Worse than a jail."

The ball proved as lively as they hoped. A select company from the Tenderloin was attending, and the regulars were all of the gayest crowd among the sons and daughters of artisans and small merchants up and down the East Side. Not a few of the women were extremely pretty. All, or almost all, were young, and those who on inspection proved to be older than eighteen or twenty were acting younger than the youngest. Everyone had been drinking freely, and continued to drink. The orchestra played continuously. The air was giddy with laughter and song. Couples hugged and kissed in corners, and finally openly on the dancing floor. For a while Susan and Howland danced together. But soon they made friends with the crowd and danced with whoever was nearest. Toward three in the morning it flashed upon her that she had not even seen him for many a dance. She looked round—searched for him—got a blond-bearded man in evening dress to assist her.

"The last seen of your stout friend," this man finally reported, "he was driving away in a cab with a large lady from Broadway. He was asleep, but I guess she wasn't."

A sober thought winked into her whirling brain—he had warned her to hold on tight, and she had lost her head—and her opportunity. A bad start—a foolishly bad start. But out winked the glimpse of sobriety and Susan laughed. "That's the last I'll ever see of *him*," said she.

This seemed to give Blond-Beard no regrets. Said he: "Let's you and I have a little supper. I'd call it breakfast, only then we couldn't have champagne."

And they had supper—six at the table, all uproarious, Susan with difficulty restrained from a skirt dance on the table up and down among the dishes and bottles. It was nearly five o'clock when she and Blond-Beard helped each other toward a cab.

"What's your address?" said he.

"The same as yours," replied she drowsily.

Late that afternoon she established herself in a room with a bath in West Twenty-ninth Street not far from Broadway. The exterior of the house was dingy and down-at-the-heel. But the interior was new and scrupulously clean. Several other young women lived there alone also, none quite so well installed as Susan, who had the only private bath and was paying twelve dollars a week. The landlady, frizzled and peroxide, explained— without adding anything to what she already knew—that she could have "privileges," but cautioned her against noise. "I can't stand for it," said she. "First offense—out you go. This house is for ladies, and only gentlemen that know how to conduct themselves as a gentleman should with a lady are allowed to come here."

Susan paid a week in advance, reducing to thirty-one dollars her capital which Blond-Beard had increased to forty-three. The young lady who lived at the other end of the hall smiled at her, when both happened to glance from their open doors at the same time. Susan invited her to call and she immediately advanced along the hall in the blue silk kimono she was wearing over her nightgown.

"My name's Ida Driscoll," said she, showing a double row of charming white teeth—her chief positive claim to beauty.

She was short, was plump about the shoulders but slender in the hips. Her reddish brown hair was neatly done over a big rat, and was so spread that its thinness was hidden well enough to deceive masculine eyes. Nor would a man have observed that one of her white round shoulders was full two inches higher than the other. Her skin was good, her features small and irregular, her eyes shrewd but kindly.

"My name's"—Susan hesitated—"Lorna Sackville."

"I guess Lorna and Ida'll be enough for us to bother to remember," laughed Miss Driscoll. "The rest's liable to change. You've just come, haven't you?"

"About an hour ago. I've got only a toothbrush, a comb, a washrag and a cake of soap. I bought them on my way here."

"Baggage lost—eh?" said Ida, amused.

"No," admitted Susan. "I'm beginning an entire new deal."

"I'll lend you a nightgown. I'm too short for my other things to fit you."

"Oh, I can get along. What's good for a headache? I'm nearly crazy with it."

"Wine?"

"Yes."

"Wait a minute." Ida, with bedroom slippers clattering, hurried back to her room, returned with a bottle of bromo seltzer and in the bathroom fixed Susan a dose. "You'll feel all right in half an hour or so. Gee, but you're swell—with your own bathroom."

Susan shrugged her shoulders and laughed.

Ida shook her head gravely. "You ought to save your money. I do."

"Later—perhaps. Just now—I *must* have a fling."

Ida seemed to understand. She went on to say: "I was in millinery. But in this town there's nothing in anything unless you have capital or a backer. I got tired of working for five per, with ten or fifteen as the top notch. So I quit, kissed my folks up in Harlem good-by and came down to look about. As soon as I've saved enough I'm going to start a business. That'll be about a couple of years—maybe sooner, if I find an angel."

"I'm thinking of the stage."

"Cut it out!" cried Ida. "It's on the bum. There's more money and less worry in straight sporting—if you keep respectable. Of course, there's nothing in out and out sporting."

"Oh, I haven't decided on anything. My head is better."

"Sure! If the dose I gave you don't knock it you can get one at the drug store two blocks up Sixth Avenue that'll do the trick. Got a dinner date?"

"No. I haven't anything on hand."

"I think you and I might work together," said Ida. "You're thin and tallish. I'm short and fattish. We'd catch 'em coming and going."

"That sounds good," said Susan.

"You're new to—to the business?"

"In a way—yes."

"I thought so. We all soon get a kind of a professional look. You haven't got it. Still, so many dead respectable women imitate nowadays, and paint and use loud perfumes, that sporting women aren't nearly so noticeable. Seems to me the men's tastes even for what they want at home are getting louder and louder all the time. They hate anything that looks slow. And in our business it's harder and harder to please them—except the yaps from the little towns and the college boys. A woman has to be up to snuff if she gets on. If she looks what she is, men won't have her—nor if she is what she looks."

Susan had not lived where every form of viciousness is openly discussed and practiced, without having learned the things necessary to a full understanding of Ida's technical phrases and references. The liveliness that had come with the departure of the headache vanished. To change the subject she invited Ida to dine with her.

"What's the use of your spending money in a restaurant?" objected Ida. "You eat with me in my room. I always cook myself something when I ain't asked out by some one of my gentleman friends. I can cook you a chop and warm up a can of French peas and some dandy tea biscuits I bought yesterday."

Susan accepted the invitation, promising that when she was established she would reciprocate. As it was about six, they arranged to have the dinner at seven, Susan to dress in the meantime. The headache had now gone, even to that last heaviness which seems to be an ominous threat of a return. When she was alone, she threw off her clothes, filled the big bathtub with water as hot as she could stand it. Into this she gently lowered herself until she was able to relax and recline without discomfort. Then she stood up and with the soap and washrag gave herself the most thorough scrubbing of her life. Time after time she soaped and rubbed and scrubbed, and dipped herself in the hot water. When she felt that she had restored her body to some where near her ideal of cleanness, she let the water run out and refilled the tub with even hotter water. In this she lay luxuriously, reveling in the magnificent sensations of warmth and utter cleanliness. Her eyes closed; a delicious languor stole over her and through her, soothing every nerve. She slept.

She was awakened by Ida, who had entered after knocking and calling at the outer door in vain. Susan slowly opened her eyes, gazed at Ida with a soft dreamy smile. "You don't know what this means. It seems to me I was never quite so comfortable or so happy in my life."

"It's a shame to disturb you," said Ida. "But dinner's ready.

Don't stop to dress first. I'll bring you a kimono."

Susan turned on the cold water, and the bath rapidly changed from warm to icy. When she had indulged in the sense of cold as delightful in its way as the sense of warmth, she rubbed her glowing skin with a rough towel until she was rose-red from head to foot. Then she put on stockings, shoes and the pink kimono Ida had brought, and ran along the hall to dinner. As she entered Ida's room, Ida exclaimed, "How sweet and pretty you do look! You sure ought to make a hit!"

"I feel like a human being for the first time in—it seems years—ages—to me."

"You've got a swell color—except your lips. Have they always been pale like that?"

"No."

"I thought not. It don't seem to fit in with your style. You ought to touch 'em up. You look too serious and innocent, anyhow. They make a rouge now that'll stick through everything—eating, drinking—anything."

Susan regarded herself critically in the glass. "I'll see," she said.

The odor of the cooking chops thrilled Susan like music. She drew a chair up to the table, sat in happy-go-lucky fashion, and attacked the chop, the hot biscuit, and the peas, with an enthusiasm that inspired Ida to imitation. "You know how to cook a chop," she said to Ida. "And anybody who can cook a chop right can cook. Cooking's like playing the piano. If you can do the simple things perfectly, you're ready to do anything."

"Wait till I have a flat of my own," said Ida. "I'll show you what eating means. And I'll have it, too, before very long. Maybe we'll live together. I was to a fortune teller's yesterday. That's the only way I waste money. I go to fortune tellers nearly every day. But then all the girls do. You get your money's worth in excitement and hope, whether there's anything in it or not. Well, the fortune teller she said I was to meet a dark, slender person who was to change the whole course of my life—that all my troubles would roll away—and that if any more came, they'd roll away, too. My, but she did give me a swell fortune, and only fifty cents! I'll take you to her."

Ida made black coffee and the two girls, profoundly contented, drank it and talked with that buoyant cheerfulness which bubbles up in youth on the slightest pretext. In this case the pretext was anything but slight, for both girls had health as well as youth, had that freedom from harassing responsibility which is the chief charm of every form of unconventional life. And Susan was still in the first flush of the joy of escape from the noisome prison whose poisons had been corroding her, soul and body. No, poison is not a just comparison; what poison in civilization parallels, or even approaches, in squalor, in vileness of food and air, in wretchedness of shelter and clothing, the tenement life that is really the typical life of the city? From time to time Susan, suffused with the happiness that is too deep for laughter, too deep for tears even, gazed round like a dreamer at those cheerful comfortable surroundings and drew a long breath—stealthily, as if she feared she would awaken and be again in South Fifth Avenue, of rags and filth, of hideous toil without hope.

"You'd better save your money to put in the millinery business with me," Ida advised. "I can show you how to make a lot. Sometimes I clear as high as a hundred a week, and I don't often fall below seventy-five. So many girls go about this business in a no account way, instead of being regular and business-like."

Susan strove to hide the feelings aroused by this practical statement of what lay before her. Those feelings filled her with misgiving. Was the lesson still unlearned? Obviously Ida was right; there must be plan, calculation, a definite line laid out and held to, or there could not but be failure and disaster. And yet—Susan's flesh quivered and shrank away. She struggled against it, but she could not conquer it. Experience had apparently been in vain; her character had remained unchanged. . . . She must compel herself. She must do what she had to do; she must not ruin everything by imitating the people of the tenements with their fatal habit of living from day to day only, and taking no thought for the morrow except fatuously to hope and dream that all would be well.

While she was fighting with herself, Ida had been talking on—the same subject. When Susan heard again, Ida was saying:

"Now, take me, for instance. I don't smoke or drink. There's nothing in either one—especially drink. Of course sometimes a girl's got to drink. A man watches her too close for her to dodge out. But usually you can make him think you're as full as he is, when you really are cold sober."

"Do the men always drink when they—come with—with—us?" asked Susan.

"Most always. They come because they want to turn themselves loose. That's why a girl's got to be careful not to make a man feel nervous or shy. A respectable woman's game is to be modest and innocent. With us, the opposite. They're both games; one's just as good as the other."

"I don't think I could get along at all—at this," confessed Susan with an effort, "unless I drank too much—so that I was reckless and didn't care what happened."

Ida looked directly into her eyes; Susan's glance fell and a flush mounted. After a pause Ida went on:

"A girl does feel that way at first. A girl that marries as most of them do—because the old ones are pushing her out of the nest and she's got no place else to go—she feels the same way till she hardens to it. Of course, you've got to get broke into any business."

"Go on," said Susan eagerly. "You are so sensible. You must teach me."

"Common sense is a thing you don't often hear—especially about getting on in the world. But, as I was saying—one of my gentlemen friends is a lawyer—such a nice fellow—so liberal. Gives me a present of twenty or twenty-five extra, you understand—every time he makes a killing downtown. He asked me once how I felt when I started in; and when I told him, he said, 'That's exactly the way I felt the first time I won a case for a client I knew was a dirty rascal and in the wrong. But now—I take that sort of thing as easy as you do.' He says the thing is to get on, no matter how, and that one way's as good as another. And he's mighty right. You soon learn that in little old New York, where you've got to have the money or you get the laugh and the foot—the swift, hard kick. Clean up after you've arrived, he says—and don't try to keep clean while you're working—and don't stop for baths and things while you're at the job."

Susan was listening with every faculty she possessed.

"He says he talks the other sort of thing—the dope—the fake stuff—just as the rest of the hustlers do. He says it's necessary in order to keep the people fooled—that if they got wise to the real way to succeed, then there'd be nobody to rob and get rich off of. Oh, he's got it right. He's a smart one."

The sad, bitter expression was strong in Susan's face.

After a pause, Ida went on: "If a girl's an ignorant fool or squeamish, she don't get up in this business any more than in any other. But if she keeps a cool head, and don't take lovers unless they pay their way, and don't drink, why she can keep her self-respect and not have to take to the streets."

Susan lifted her head eagerly. "Don't have to take to the streets?" she echoed.

"Certainly not," declared Ida. "I very seldom let a man pick me up after dark—unless he looks mighty good. I go out in the daytime. I pretend I'm an actress out of a job for the time being, or a forelady in a big shop who's taking a day or so off, or a respectable girl living with her parents. I put a lot of money into clothes—quiet, ladylike clothes. Mighty good investment. If you ain't got clothes in New York you can't do any kind of business. I go where a nice class of men hangs out, and I never act bold, but just flirt timidly, as so many respectable girls or semi-respectables do. But when a girl plays that game, she has to be careful not to make a man think he ain't expected to pay. The town's choked full of men on the lookout for what they call love—which means, for something cheap or, better still, free. Men are just crazy about themselves. Nothing easier than to fool 'em—and nothing's harder than to make 'em think you ain't stuck on 'em. I tell you, a girl in our life has a chance to learn men. They turn themselves inside out to us."

Susan, silent, her thoughts flowing like a mill race, helped Ida with the dishes. Then they dressed and went together for a walk. It being Sunday evening, the streets were quiet. They sauntered up Fifth Avenue as far as Fifty-ninth Street and back. Ida's calm and sensible demeanor gave Susan much needed courage every time a man spoke to them. None of these men happened to be up to Ida's standard, which was high.

"No use wasting time on snide people," explained she. "We don't want drinks and a gush of loose talk, and I saw at a glance that was all those chappies were good for."

They returned home at half-past nine without adventure. Toward midnight one of Ida's regulars called and Susan was free to go to bed. She slept hardly at all. Ever before her mind hovered a nameless, shapeless horror. And when she slept she dreamed of her wedding night, woke herself screaming, "Please, Mr. Ferguson—please!"

Ida had three chief sources of revenue.

The best was five men—her "regular gentleman friends"—who called by appointment from time to time. These paid her ten dollars apiece, and occasionally gave her presents of money or jewelry—nothing that amounted to much. From them she averaged about thirty-five dollars a week. Her second source was a Mrs. Thurston who kept in West Fifty-sixth Street near Ninth Avenue a furnished-room house of the sort that is on the official— and also the "revenue"—lists of the police and the anti-vice societies. This lady had a list of girls and married women upon whom she could call. Gentlemen using her house for rendezvous were sometimes disappointed by the ladies with whom they were intriguing. Again a gentleman grew a little weary of his perhaps too respectable or too sincerely loving ladylove and appealed to Mrs. Thurston. She kept her list of availables most select and passed them off as women of good position willing to supplement a small income, or to punish stingy husbands or fathers and at the same time get the money they needed for dress and bridge, for matinées and lunches. Mrs. Thurston insisted—and Ida was inclined to believe—that there were genuine cases of this kind on the list.

"It's mighty hard for women with expensive tastes and small means to keep straight in New York," said she to Susan. "It costs so much to live, and there are so many ways to spend money. And they always have rich lady friends who set an extravagant pace. They've got to dress—and to kind of keep up their end. So—" Ida laughed, went on: "Besides the city women are getting so they like a little sporty novelty as much as their brothers and husbands and fathers do. Oh, I'm not ashamed of my business any more. We're as good as the others, and we're not hypocrites. As my lawyer friend says, everybody's got to make a *good* living, and good livings can't be made on the ways that used to be called on the level—they're called damfool ways now."

Ida's third source of income was to her the most attractive because it had such a large gambling element in it. This was her flirtations as a respectable woman in search of lively amusement and having to take care not to be caught. There are women of all kinds who delight in deceiving men because it gives them a sweet stealthy sense of superiority to the condescending sex. In women of the Ida class this pleasure becomes as much a passion as it is in the respectable woman whom her husband tries to enslave. With Susan, another woman and one in need of education, Ida was simple and scrupulously truthful. But it would have been impossible for a man to get truth as to anything from her. She amused herself inventing plausible romantic stories about herself that she might enjoy the gullibility of the boastfully superior and patronizing male. She was devoid of sentiment, even of passion. Yet at times she affected both in the most extreme fashion. And afterward, with peals of laughter, she would describe to Susan how the man had acted, what an ass she had made of him.

"Men despise us," she said. "But it's nothing to the way I despise them. The best of them are rotten beasts when they show themselves as they are. And they haven't any mercy on us. It's too ridiculous. Men despise a man who is virtuous and a woman who isn't. What rot!"

She deceived the "regulars" without taking the trouble to remember her deceptions. They caught her lying so often that she knew they thought her untruthful through and through. But this only gave her an opportunity for additional pleasure—the pleasure of inventing lies that they would believe in spite of their distrust of her. "Anyhow," said she, "haven't you noticed the liars everybody's on to are always believed and truthful people are doubted?"

Upon the men with whom she flirted, she practiced the highly colored romances it would have been useless to try upon the regulars. Her greatest triumph at this game was a hard luck story she had told so effectively that the man had given her two hundred dollars. Most of her romances turned about her own ruin. As a matter of fact, she had told Susan the exact truth when she said she had taken up her mode of life deliberately; she had grown weary and impatient of the increasing poverty of a family which, like so many of the artisan and small merchant and professional classes in this day of concentrating wealth and spreading tastes for comfort and luxury, was on its way down from comfort toward or through the tenements. She was a type of the recruits that are swelling the prostitute class in ever larger numbers and are driving the prostitutes of the tenement class toward starvation—where they once dominated the profession even to its highest ranks, even to the fashionable *cocotes* who prey upon the second generation of the rich. But Ida never told her lovers her plain and commonplace tale of yielding to the irresistible pressure of economic forces. She had made men weep at her recital of her wrongs. It had even brought her offers of marriage—none, however, worth accepting.

"I'd be a boob to marry a man with less than fifteen or twenty thousand a year, wouldn't I?" said she. "Why, two of the married men who come to see me regularly give me more than they give their wives for pin money. And in a few years I'll be having my own respectable business, with ten thousand income—maybe more—and as well thought of as the next woman."

Ida's dream was a house in the country, a fine flat in town, a husband in some "refined" profession and children at high-class schools. "And I'll get there, don't you doubt it!" exclaimed she. "Others have—of course, you don't know about them—they've looked out for that. Yes, lots of others have—but—well, just you watch your sister Ida."

And Susan felt that she would indeed arrive. Already she had seen that there was no difficulty such as she had once imagined about recrossing the line to respectability. The only real problem in that matter was how to get together enough to make the crossing worth while—for what was there in respectability without money, in a day when respectability had ceased to mean anything but money?

Ida wished to take her to Mrs. Thurston and get her a favored place on the list. Susan thanked her, but said, "Not yet—not quite yet." Ida suggested that they go out together as two young married women whose husbands had gone on the road. Susan put her off from day to day. Ida finally offered to introduce her to one of the regulars: "He's a nice fellow—knows how to treat a lady in a gentlemanly way. Not a bit coarse or familiar." Susan would not permit this generosity. And all this time her funds were sinking. She had paid a second week's rent, had bought cooking apparatus, some food supplies, some necessary clothing. She was down to a five-dollar bill and a little change.

"Look here, Lorna," said Ida, between remonstrance and exasperation, "when *are* you going to start in?"

Susan looked fixedly at her, said with a slow smile, "When I can't hold out another minute."

Ida tossed her head angrily. "You've got brains—more than I have," she cried. "You've got every advantage for catching rich men—even a rich husband. You're educated. You speak and act and look refined. Why you could pretend to be a howling fashionable swell. You've got all the points. But what have you got 'em for? Not to use that's certain."

"You can't be as disgusted with me as I am."

"If you're going to do a thing, why, *do* it!"

"That's what I tell myself. But—I can't make a move."

Ida gave a gesture of despair. "I don't see what's to become of you. And you could do *so* well! . . . Let me phone Mr. Sterling. I told him about you. He's anxious to meet you. He's fond of books—like you. You'd like him. He'd give up a lot to you, because you're classier than I am."

Susan threw her arms round Ida and kissed her. "Don't bother about me," she said. "I've got to act in my own foolish, stupid way. I'm like a child going to school. I've got to learn a certain amount before I'm ready to do whatever it is I'm going to do. And until I learn it, I can't do much of anything. I thought I had learned in the last few months. I see I haven't."

"Do listen to sense, Lorna," pleaded Ida. "If you wait till the last minute, you'll get left. The time to get the money's when you have money. And I've a feeling that you're not particularly flush."

"I'll do the best I can. And I can't move till I'm ready."

Meanwhile she continued to search for work—work that would enable her to live *decently*, wages less degrading than the wages of shame. In a newspaper she read an advertisement of a theatrical agency. Advertisements of all kinds read well; those of theatrical agencies read—like the fairy tales that they were. However, she found in this particular offering of dazzling careers and salaries a peculiar phrasing that decided her to break the rule she had made after having investigated scores of this sort of offers.

Rod was abroad; anyhow, enough time had elapsed. One of the most impressive features of the effect of New York—meaning by "New York" only that small but significant portion of the four millions that thinks—at least, after a fashion, and acts, instead of being mere passive tools of whatever happens to turn up—the most familiar notable effect of this New York is the speedy distinction in the newcomer of those illusions and delusions about life and about human nature, about good and evil, that are for so many people the most precious and the only endurable and beautiful thing in the world. New York, destroyer of delusions and cherished hypocrisies and pretenses, therefore makes the broadly intelligent of its citizens hardy, makes the others hard—and between the hardy and hard, between sense and cynicism, yawns a gulf like that between Absalom and Dives. Susan, a New Yorker now, had got the habit—in thought, at least—of seeing things with somewhat less distortion from the actual. She no longer exaggerated the importance of the Rod-Susan episode. She saw that in New York, where life is crowded with events, everything in one's life, except death, becomes incident, becomes episode, where in regions offering less to think about each rare happening took on an aspect of vast importance. The Rod-Susan love adventure, she now saw, was not what it would have seemed—therefore, would have been—in Sutherland, but was mere episode of a New York life, giving its light and shade to a certain small part of the long, variedly patterned fabric of her life, and of his, not determining the whole. She saw that it was simply like a bend in the river, giving a new turn to current and course but not changing the river itself, and soon left far behind and succeeded by other bends giving each its equal or greater turn to the stream.

Rod had passed from her life, and she from his life. Thus she was free to begin her real career—the stage—if she could. She went to the suite of offices tenanted by Mr. Josiah Ransome. She was ushered in to Ransome himself, instead of halting with underlings. She owed this favor to advantages which her lack of vanity and of self-consciousness prevented her from surmising. Ransome—smooth, curly, comfortable looking—received her with a delicate blending of the paternal and the gallant. After he had inspected her exterior with flattering attentiveness and had investigated her qualifications with a thoroughness that was convincing of sincerity he said:

"Most satisfactory! I can make you an exceptional assurance. If you register with me, I can guarantee you not less than twenty-five a week."

Susan hesitated long and asked many questions before she finally—with reluctance paid the five dollars. She felt ashamed of her distrust, but might perhaps have persisted in it had not Mr. Ransome said:

"I don't blame you for hesitating, my dear young lady. And if I could I'd put you on my list without payment. But you can see how unbusiness-like that would be. I am a substantial, old-established concern. You—no doubt you are perfectly reliable. But I have been fooled so many times. I must not let myself forget that after all I know nothing about you."

As soon as Susan had paid he gave her a list of vaudeville and musical comedy houses where girls were wanted. "You can't fail to suit one of them," said he. "If not, come back here and get your money."

After two weary days of canvassing she went back to Ransome. He was just leaving. But he smiled genially, opened his desk and seated himself. "At your service," said he. "What luck?"

"None," replied Susan. "I couldn't live on the wages they offered at the musical comedy places, even if I could get placed."

"And the vaudeville people?"

"When I said I could only sing and not dance, they looked discouraged. When I said I had no costumes they turned me down."

"Excellent!" cried Ransome. "You mustn't be so easily beaten. You must take dancing lessons—perhaps a few singing lessons, too. And you must get some costumes."

"But that means several hundred dollars."

"Three or four hundred," said Ransome airily. "A matter of a few weeks."

"But I haven't anything like that," said Susan. "I haven't so much as— —"

"I comprehend perfectly," interrupted Ransome. She interested him, this unusual looking girl, with her attractive mingling of youth and experience. Her charm that tempted people to give her at once the frankest confidences, moved him to go out of his way to help her. "You haven't the money," he went on.

"You must have it. So—I promised to place you, and I will. I don't usually go so far in assisting my clients. It's not often necessary—and where it's necessary it's usually imprudent. However—I'll give you the address of a flat where there is a lady—a trustworthy, square sort, despite her— her profession. She will put you in the way of getting on a sound financial basis."

Ransome spoke in a matter-of-fact tone, like a man stating a simple business proposition. Susan understood. She rose. Her expression was neither shock nor indignation; but it was none the less a negative.

"It's the regular thing, my dear," urged Ransome. "To make a start, to get in right, you can't afford to be squeamish. The way I suggest is the simplest and most direct of several that all involve the same thing. And the surest. You look steady-headed—self-reliant. You look sensible— —"

Susan smiled rather forlornly. "But I'm not," said she. "Not yet."

Ransome regarded her with a sympathy which she felt was genuine. "I'm sorry, my dear. I've done the best I can for you. You may think it a very poor best—and it is. But"—he shrugged his shoulders—"I didn't make this world and its conditions for living. I may say also that I'm not the responsible party—the party in charge. However— —"

To her amazement he held out a five-dollar bill. "Here's your fee back." He laughed at her expression. "Oh, I'm not a robber," said he. "I only wish I could serve you. I didn't think you were so—" his eyes twinkled—"so unreasonable, let us say. Among those who don't know anything about life there's an impression that my sort of people are in the business of dragging women down. Perhaps one of us occasionally does as bad—about a millionth part as bad—as the average employer of labor who skims his profits from the lifeblood of his employees. But as a rule we folks merely take those that are falling and help them to light easy—or even to get up again."

Susan felt ashamed to take her money. But he pressed it on her. "You'll need it," said he. "I know how it is with a girl alone and trying to get a start. Perhaps later on you'll be more in the mood where I can help you."

"Perhaps," said Susan.

"But I hope not. It'll take uncommon luck to pull you through—and I hope you'll have it."

"Thank you," said Susan. He took her hand, pressed it friendlily—and she felt that he was a man with real good in him, more good than many who would have shrunk from him in horror.

She was waiting for a thrust from fate. But fate, disappointing as usual, would not thrust. It seemed bent on the malicious pleasure of compelling her to degrade herself deliberately and with calculation, like a woman marrying for support a man who refuses to permit her to decorate with any artificial floral concealments of faked-up sentiment the sordid truth as to what she is about. She searched within herself in vain for the scruple or sentiment or timidity or whatever it was that held her back from the course that was plainly inevitable. She had got down to the naked fundamentals of decency and indecency that are deep hidden by, and for most of us under, hypocrisies of conventionality. She had found out that a decent woman was one who respected her body and her soul, that an indecent woman was one who did not, and that marriage rites or the absence of them, the absence of financial or equivalent consideration, or its presence, or its extent or its form, were all irrelevant non-essentials. Yet—she hesitated, knowing the while that she was risking a greater degradation, and a stupid and fatal folly to boot, by shrinking from the best course open to her—unless it were better to take a dose of poison and end it all. She probably would have done that had she not been so utterly healthy, therefore overflowing with passionate love of life. Except in fiction suicide and health do not go together, however superhumanly sensitive the sore beset hero or heroine. Susan was sensitive enough; whenever she did things incompatible with our false and hypocritical and unscientific notions of sensitiveness, allowances should be made for her because of her superb and dauntless health. If her physical condition had been morbid, her conduct might have been, would have been, very different.

She was still hesitating when Saturday night came round again—swiftly despite long disheartening days, and wakeful awful nights. In the morning her rent would be due. She had a dollar and forty-five cents.

After dinner alone a pretense at dinner—she wandered the streets of the old Tenderloin until midnight. An icy rain was falling. Rains such as this—any rains except showers—were rare in the City of the Sun. That rain by itself was enough to make her downhearted. She walked with head down and umbrella close to her shoulders. No one spoke to her. She returned dripping; she had all but ruined her one dress. She went to bed, but not to sleep. About nine—early for that house she rose, drank a cup of coffee and ate part of a roll. Her little stove and such other things as could not be taken along she rolled into a bundle, marked it, "For Ida." On a scrap of paper she wrote this note:

Don't think I'm ungrateful, please. I'm going without saying good-by because I'm afraid if I saw you, you'd be generous enough to put up for me, and I'd be weak enough to accept. And if I did that, I'd never be able to get strong or even to hold my head up. So—good-by. I'll learn sooner or later—learn how to live. I hope it won't be too long—and that the teacher won't be too hard on me.

Yes, I'll learn, and I'll buy fine hats at your grand millinery store yet. Don't forget me altogether.

She tucked this note into the bundle and laid it against the door behind which Ida and one of her regulars were sleeping peacefully. The odor of Ida's powerful perfume came through the cracks in the door; Susan drew it eagerly into her nostrils, sobbed softly, turned away, It was one of the perfumes classed as immoral; to Susan it was the aroma of a friendship as noble, as disinterested, as generous, as human sympathy had ever breathed upon human woe. With her few personal possessions in a package she descended the stairs unnoticed, went out into the rain. At the corner of Sixth Avenue she paused, looked up and down the street. It was almost deserted. Now and then a streetwalker, roused early by a lover with perhaps a family waiting for him, hurried by, looking piteous in the daylight which showed up false and dyed hair, the layers of paint, the sad tawdriness of battered finery from the cheapest bargain troughs.

Susan went slowly up Sixth Avenue. Two blocks, and she saw a girl enter the side door of a saloon across the way. She crossed the street, pushed in at the same door, went on to a small sitting-room with blinds drawn, with round tables, on every table a match stand. It was one of those places where streetwalkers rest their weary legs between strolls, and sit for company on rainy or snowy nights, and take shy men for sociability-breeding drinks and for the preliminary bargaining. The air of the room was strong with stale liquor and tobacco, the lingering aroma of the night's vanished revels. In the far corner sat the girl she had followed; a glass of raw whiskey and another of water stood on the table before her. Susan seated herself near the door and when the swollen-faced, surly bartender came, ordered whiskey. She poured herself a drink—filled the glass to the brim. She drank it in two gulps, set the empty glass down. She shivered like an animal as it is hit in the head with a poleax. The mechanism of life staggered, hesitated, went on with a sudden leaping acceleration of pace. Susan tapped her glass against the matchstand. The bartender came.

"Another," said she.

The man stared at her. "The—hell!" he ejaculated. "You must be afraid o' catchin' cold. Or maybe you're looking for the menagerie?"

Susan laughed and so did the girl in the corner. "Won't you have a drink with me?" asked Susan.

"That's very kind of you," replied the girl, in the manner of one eager to show that she, too, is a perfect lady in every respect, used to the ways of the best society. She moved to a chair at Susan's table.

She and Susan inventoried each other. Susan saw a mere child—hardly eighteen—possibly not seventeen—but much worn by drink and irregular living—evidently one of those who rush into the fast woman's life with the idea that it is a career of gayety—and do not find out their error until looks and health are gone. Susan drank her second drink in three gulps, several minutes apart. The girl was explaining in a thin, common voice, childish yet cracked, that she had come there seeking a certain lady friend because she had an extra man and needed a side partner.

"Suppose you come with me," she suggested. "It's good money,
I think. Want to get next?"

"When I've had another drink," said Susan. Her eyes were gorgeously brilliant. She had felt almost as reckless several times before; but never had she felt this devil-may-care eagerness to see what the turn of the next card would bring. "You'll take one?"

"Sure. I feel like the devil. Been bumming round all night. My lady friend that I had with me—a regular lady friend—she was suddenly took ill. Appendicitis complicated with d.t.'s the ambulance guy said. The boys are waiting for me to come back, so's we can go on. They've got some swell rooms in a hotel up in Forty-second Street. Let's get a move on."

The bartender served the third drink and Susan paid for them, the other girl insisting on paying for the one she was having when Susan came. Susan's head was whirling. Her spirits were spiraling up and up. Her pale lips were wreathed in a reckless smile. She felt courageous for adventure—any adventure. Her capital had now sunk to three quarters and a five-cent piece. They issued forth, talking without saying anything, laughing without knowing or caring why. Life was a joke—a coarse, broad joke—but amusing if one drank enough to blunt any refinement of sensibility. And what was sensibility but a kind of snobbishness? And what more absurd than snobbishness in an outcast?

"That's good whiskey they had, back there," said Susan.

"Good? Yes—if you don't care what you say."

"If you don't want to care what you say or do," explained Susan.

"Oh, all booze is good for that," said the girl.

CHAPTER VI

THEY went through to Broadway and there stood waiting for a car, each under her own umbrella. "Holy Gee!" cried Susan's new acquaintance. "Ain't this rain a soaker?"

It was coming in sheets, bent and torn and driven horizontally by the wind. The umbrella, sheltering the head somewhat, gave a wholly false impression of protection. Both girls were soon sopping wet. But they were more than cheerful about it; the whiskey made them indifferent to external ills as they warmed themselves by its bright fire. At that time a famous and much envied, admired and respected "captain of industry," having looted the street-car systems, was preparing to loot them over again by the familiar trickery of the receivership and the reorganization. The masses of the people were too ignorant to know what was going on; the classes were too busy, each man of each of them, about his own personal schemes for graft of one kind and another. Thus, the street-car service was a joke and a disgrace. However, after four or five minutes a north-bound car appeared.

"But it won't stop," cried Susan. "It's jammed."

"That's why it will stop," replied her new acquaintance. "You don't suppose a New York conductor'd miss a chance to put his passengers more on the bum than ever?"

She was right, at least as to the main point; and the conductor with much free handling of their waists and shoulders added them to the dripping, straining press of passengers, enduring the discomforts the captain of industry put upon them with more patience than cattle would have exhibited in like circumstances. All the way up Broadway the new acquaintance enlivened herself and Susan and the men they were squeezed in among by her loud gay sallies which her young prettiness made seem witty. And certainly she did have an amazing and amusing acquaintance with the slang at the moment current. The worn look had vanished, her rounded girlhood freshness had returned. As for Susan, you would hardly have recognized her as the same person who had issued from the house in Twenty-ninth Street less than an hour before. Indeed, it was not the same person. Drink nervifies every character; here it transformed, suppressing the characteristics that seemed, perhaps were, essential in her normal state, and causing to bloom in sudden audacity of color and form the passions and gayeties at other times subdued by her intelligence and her sensitiveness. Her brilliant glance moved about the car full as boldly as her companion's. But there was this difference: Her companion gazed straight into the eyes of the men; Susan's glance shot past above or just below their eyes.

As they left the car at Forty-second Street the other girl gave her short skirt a dexterous upward flirt that exhibited her legs almost to the hips. Susan saw that they were well shaped legs, surprisingly plump from the calves upward, considering the slightness of her figure above the waist.

"I always do that when I leave a car," said the girl. "Sometimes it starts something on the trail. You forgot your package—back in the saloon!"

"Then I didn't forget much," laughed Susan. It appealed to her, the idea of entering the new life empty-handed.

The hotel was one that must have been of the first class in its day—not a distant day, for the expansion of New York in craving for showy luxury has been as sudden as the miraculous upward thrust of a steel skyscraper. It had now sunk to relying upon the trade of those who came in off Broadway for a few minutes. It was dingy and dirty; the walls and plastering were peeling; the servants were slovenly and fresh. The girl nodded to the evil-looking man behind the desk, who said:

"Hello, Miss Maud. Just in time. The boys were sending out for some others."

"They've got a nerve!" laughed Maud. And she led Susan down a rather long corridor to a door with the letter B upon it. Maud explained: "This is the swellest suite in the house parlor, bedroom, bath." She flung open the door, disclosing a sitting-room in disorder with two young men partly dressed, seated at a small table on which were bottles, siphons, matches, remains of sandwiches, boxes of cigarettes—a chaotic jumble of implements to dissipation giving forth a powerful, stale odor. Maud burst into a stream of picturesque profanity which set the two men to laughing. Susan had paused on the threshold. The shock of this scene had for the moment arrested the triumphant march of the alcohol through blood and nerve and brain.

"Oh, bite it off!" cried the darker of the two men to Maud, "and have a drink. Ain't you ashamed to speak so free before your innocent young lady friend?" He grinned at Susan. "What Sunday school do you hail from?" inquired he.

The other young man was also looking at Susan; and it was an arresting and somewhat compelling gaze. She saw that he was tall and well set up. As he was dressed only in trousers and a pale blue silk undershirt, the strength of his shoulders, back and arms was in full evidence. His figure was like that of the wonderful young prize-fighters she had admired at moving picture shows to which Drumley had taken her. He had a singularly handsome face, blond yet remotely suggesting Italian. He smiled at Susan and she thought she had never seen teeth more beautiful—pearl-white, regular, even. His eyes were large and sensuous; smiling though they were, Susan was ill at ease—for in them there shone the same untamed, uncontrolled ferocity that one sees in the eyes of a wild beast. His youth, his good looks, his charm made the sinister savagery hinted in the smile the more disconcerting. He poured whiskey from a bottle into each of the two tall glasses, filled them up with seltzer, extended one toward Susan.

"Shut the door, Queenie," he said to her in a pleasant tone that subtly mingled mockery and admiration. "And let's drink to love."

"Didn't I do well for you, Freddie?" cried Maud.

"She's my long-sought affinity," declared Freddie with the same attractive mingling of jest and flattery.

Susan closed the door, accepted the glass, laughed into his eyes. The whiskey was once more asserting its power. She took about half the drink before she set the glass down.

The young man said, "Your name's Queenie, mine's Freddie." He came to her, holding her gaze fast by the piercing look from his handsome eyes. He put his arms round her and kissed her full upon the pale, laughing lips. His eyes were still smiling in pleasant mockery; yet his kiss burned and stung, and the grip of his arm round her shoulders made her vaguely afraid. Her smile died away. The grave, searching, wondering expression reappeared in the violet-gray eyes for a moment.

"You're all right," said he. "Except those pale lips. You're going to be my girl. That means, if you ever try to get away from me unless I let you go—I'll kill you—or worse." And he laughed as if he had made the best joke in the world. But she saw in his eyes a sparkle that seemed to her to have something of the malignance of the angry serpent's.

She hastily finished her drink.

Maud was jerking off her clothes, crying, "I want to get out of these nasty wet rags." The steam heat was full on; the sitting-room, the whole suite, was intensely warm. Maud hung her skirt over the back of a chair close to the radiator, took off her shoes and stockings and put them to dry also. In her chemise she curled herself on a chair, lit a cigarette and poured a drink. Her feet were not bad, but neither were they notably good; she tucked them out of sight. She looked at Susan. "Get off those wet things," urged she, "or you'll take your death."

"In a minute," said Susan, but not convincingly.

Freddie forced another drink and a cigarette upon her. As a girl at home in Sutherland, she had several times—she and Ruth—smoked cigarettes in secrecy, to try the new London and New York fashion, announced in the newspapers and the novels. So the cigarette did not make her uncomfortable. "Look at the way she's holding it?" cried Maud, and she and the men burst out laughing. Susan laughed also and, Freddie helping, practiced a less inexpert manner. Jim, the dark young man with the sullen heavy countenance, rang for more sandwiches and another bottle of whiskey. Susan continued to drink but ate nothing.

"Have a sandwich," said Freddie.

"I'm not hungry."

"Well, they say that to eat and drink means to die of paresis, while to only drink means dying of delirium tremens. I guess you're right. I'd prefer the d.t.'s. It's quicker and livelier."

Jim sang a ribald song with some amusing comedy business. Maud told several stories whose only claim to point lay in their frankness about things not usually spoken. "Don't you tell any more, Maudie," advised Freddie. "Why is it that a woman never takes up a story until every man on earth has heard it at least twice?" The sandwiches disappeared, the second bottle of whiskey ran low. Maud told story after story of how she had played this man and that for a sucker—was as full of such tales and as joyous and self-pleased over them as an honest salesman telling his delighted, respectable, pew-holding employer how he has "stuck" this customer and that for a "fancy" price. Presently Maud again noticed that Susan was in her wet clothes and cried out about it. Susan pretended to start to undress. Freddie and Jim suddenly seized her. She struggled, half laughing; the whiskey was sending into her brain dizzying clouds. She struggled more fiercely. But it was in vain.

"Gee, you *have* got a prize, Freddie!" exclaimed Jim at last, angry. "A regular tartar!"

"A damn handsome one," retorted Freddie. "She's even got feet."

Susan, amid the laughter of the others, darted for the bedroom. Cowering in a corner, trying to cover herself, she ordered Freddie to leave her. He laughed, seized her in his iron grip. She struck at him, bit him in the shoulder. He gave a cry of pain and drove a savage blow into her cheek.

Then he buried his fingers in her throat and the gleam of his eyes made her soul quail.

"Don't kill me!" she cried, in the clutch of cowardice for the first time. It was not death that she feared but the phantom of things worse than death that can be conjured to the imagination by the fury of a personality which is utterly reckless and utterly cruel. "Don't kill me!" she shrieked. "What the hell are you doing?" shouted Jim from the other room.

"Shut that door," replied Freddie. "I'm going to attend to my lady friend."

As the door slammed, he dragged Susan by the throat and one arm to the bed, flung her down. "I saw you were a high stepper the minute I looked at you," said he, in a pleasant, cooing voice that sent the chills up and down her spine. "I knew you'd have to be broke. Well, the sooner it's done, the sooner we'll get along nicely." His blue eyes were laughing into hers. With the utmost deliberation he gripped her throat with one hand and with the other began to slap her, each blow at his full strength. Her attempts to scream were only gasps. Quickly the agony of his brutality drove her into unconsciousness. Long after she had ceased to feel pain, she continued to feel the impact of those blows, and dully heard her own deep groans.

When she came to her senses, she was lying sprawled upon the far side of the bed. Her head was aching wildly; her body was stiff and sore; her face felt as if it were swollen to many times its normal size. In misery she dragged herself up and stood on the floor. She went to the bureau and stared at herself in the glass. Her face was indeed swollen, but not to actual disfigurement. Under her left eye there was a small cut from which the blood had oozed to smear and dry upon her left cheek. Upon her throat were faint bluish finger marks. The damage was not nearly so great as her throbbing nerves reported—the damage to her body. But—her soul—it was a crushed, trampled, degraded thing, lying prone and bleeding to death. "Shall I kill myself?" she thought. And the answer came in a fierce protest and refusal from every nerve of her intensely vital youth. She looked straight into her own eyes—without horror, without shame, without fear. "You are as low as the lowest," she said to her image—not to herself but to her image; for herself seemed spectator merely of that body and soul aching and bleeding and degraded.

It was the beginning of self-consciousness with her—a curious kind of self-consciousness—her real self, aloof and far removed, observing calmly, critically, impersonally the adventures of her body and the rest of her surface self.

She turned round to look again at the man who had outraged them. His eyes were open and he was gazing dreamily at her, as smiling and innocent as a child. When their eyes met, his smile broadened until he was showing his beautiful teeth. "You *are* a beauty!" said he. "Go into the other room and get me a cigarette."

She continued to look fixedly at him.

Without change of expression he said gently, "Do you want another lesson in manners?"

She went to the door, opened it, entered the sitting-room. The other two had pulled open a folding bed and were lying in it, Jim's head on Maud's bosom, her arms round his neck. Both were asleep. His black beard had grown out enough to give his face a dirty and devilish expression. Maud looked far more youthful and much prettier than when she was awake. Susan put a cigarette between her lips, lit it, carried a box of cigarettes and a stand of matches in to Freddie.

"Light one for me," said he.

She obeyed, held it to his lips.

"Kiss me, first."

Her pale lips compressed.

"Kiss me," he repeated, far down in his eyes the vicious gleam of that boundlessly ferocious cruelty which is mothered not by rage but by pleasure.

She kissed him on the cheek.

"On the lips," he commanded.

Their lips met, and it was to her as if a hot flame, terrible yet thrilling, swept round and embraced her whole body.

"Do you love me?" he asked tenderly.

She was silent.

"You love me?" he asked commandingly.

"You can call it that if you like."

"I knew you would. I understand women. The way to make a woman love is to make her afraid."

She gazed at him. "I am not afraid," she said.

He laughed. "Oh, yes. That's why you do what I say—and always will."

"No," replied she. "I don't do it because I am afraid, but because I want to live."

"I should think! . . . You'll be all right in a day or so," said he, after inspecting her bruises. "Now, I'll explain to you what good friends we're going to be."

He propped himself in an attitude of lazy grace, puffed at his cigarette in silence for a moment, as if arranging what he had to say. At last he began:

"I haven't any regular business. I wasn't born to work. Only damn fools work—and the clever man waits till they've got something, then he takes it away from 'em. You don't want to work, either."

"I haven't been able to make a living at it," said the girl.

She was sitting cross-legged, a cover draped around her.

"You're too pretty and too clever. Besides, as you say, you couldn't make a living at it—not what's a living for a woman brought up as you've been. No, you can't work. So we're going to be partners."

"No," said Susan. "I'm going to dress now and go away."

Freddie laughed. "Don't be a fool. Didn't I say we were to be partners? . . . You want to keep on at the sporting business, don't you?"

Hers was the silence of assent.

"Well—a woman—especially a young one like you—is no good unless she has someone—some man—behind her. Married or single, respectable or lively, working or sporting—N. G. without a man. A woman alone doesn't amount to any more than a rich man's son."

There had been nothing in Susan's experience to enable her to dispute this.

"Now, I'm going to stand behind you. I'll see that you don't get pinched, and get you out if you do. I'll see that you get the best the city's got if you're sick—and so on. I've got a pull with the organization. I'm one of Finnegan's lieutenants. Some day—when I'm older and have served my apprenticeship—I'll pull off something good. Meanwhile—I manage to live. I always have managed it—and I never did a stroke of real work since I was a kid—and never shall. God was mighty good to me when he put a few brains in this nut of mine."

He settled his head comfortably in the pillow and smiled at his own thoughts. In spite of herself Susan had been not only interested but attracted. It is impossible for any human being to contemplate mystery in any form without being fascinated. And here was the profoundest mystery she had ever seen. He talked well, and his mode of talking was that of education, of refinement even. An extraordinary man, certainly—and in what a strange way!

"Yes," said he presently, looking at her with his gentle, friendly smile. "We'll be partners. I'll protect you and we'll divide what you make."

What a strange creature! Had he—this kindly handsome youth—done that frightful thing? No—no. It was another instance of the unreality of the outward life. *He* had not done it, any more than she—her real self—had suffered it. Her reply to his restatement of the partnership was:

"No, thank you. I want nothing to do with it."

"You're dead slow," said he, with mild and patient persuasion. "How would you get along at your business in this town if you didn't have a backer? Why, you'd be taking turns at the Island and the gutter within six months. You'd be giving all your money to some rotten cop or fly cop who couldn't protect you, at that. Or you'd work the street for some cheap cadet who'd beat you up oftener than he'd beat up the men who welched on you."

"I'll look out for myself," persisted she.

"Bless the baby!" exclaimed he, immensely amused. "How lucky that you found me! I'm going to take care of you in spite of yourself. Not for nothing, of course. You wouldn't value me if you got me for nothing. I'm going to help you, and you're going to help me. You need me, and I need you. Why do you suppose I took the trouble to tame you? What *you* want doesn't go. It's what *I* want."

He let her reflect on this a while. Then he went on:

"You don't understand about fellows like Jim and me—though Jim's a small potato beside me, as you'll soon find out. Suppose you didn't obey orders—just as I do what Finnegan tells me—just as Finnegan does what the big shout down below says? Suppose you didn't obey—what then?"

"I don't know," confessed Susan.

"Well, it's time you learned. We'll say, you act stubborn. You dress and say good-by to me and start out. Do you think I'm wicked enough to let you make a fool of yourself? Well, I'm not. You won't get outside the door before your good angel here will get busy. I'll be telephoning to a fly cop of this district. And what'll he do? Why, about the time you are halfway down the block, he'll pinch you. He'll take you to the station house. And in Police Court tomorrow the Judge'll give you a week on the Island for being a streetwalker."

Susan shivered. She instinctively glanced toward the window. The rain was still falling, changing the City of the Sun into a city of desolation. It looked as though it would never see the sun again—and her life looked that way, also.

Freddie was smiling pleasantly. He went on:

"You do your little stretch on the Island. When your time's up I send you word where to report to me. We'll say you don't come. The minute you set foot on the streets again alone, back to the Island you go. . . . Now, do you understand, Queenie?" And he laughed and pulled her over and kissed her and smoothed her hair. "You're a very superior article—you are," he murmured. "I'm stuck on you."

Susan did not resist. She did not care what happened to her. The more intelligent a trapped animal is, the less resistance it offers, once it realizes. Helpless—absolutely helpless. No money—no friends. No escape but death. The sun was shining. Outside lay the vast world; across the street on a flagpole fluttered the banner of freedom. Freedom! Was there any such thing anywhere? Perhaps if one had plenty of money—or powerful friends. But not for her, any more than for the masses whose fate of squalid and stupid slavery she was trying to escape. Not for her; so long as she was helpless she would simply move from one land of slavery to another. Helpless! To struggle would not be courageous, but merely absurd.

"If you don't believe me, ask Maud," said Freddie. "I don't want you to get into trouble. As I told you, I'm stuck on you." With his cigarette gracefully loose between those almost too beautifully formed lips of his and with one of his strong smooth white arms about his head, he looked at her, an expression of content with himself, of admiration for her in his handsome eyes. "You don't realize your good luck. But you will when you find how many girls are crazy to get on the good side of me. This is a great old town, and nobody amounts to anything in it unless he's got a pull or is next to somebody else that has."

Susan's slow reflective nod showed that this statement explained, or seemed to explain, certain mysteries of life that had been puzzling her.

"You've got a lot in you," continued he. "That's my opinion, and I'm a fair judge of yearlings. You're liable to land somewhere some day when you've struck your gait. . . . If I had the mon I'd be tempted to set you up in a flat and keep you all to myself. But I can't afford it. It takes a lot of cash to keep me going. . . . You'll do well. You won't have to bother with any but classy gents. I'll see that the cops put you wise when there's anyone round throwing his money away. And I can help you, myself. I've got quite a line of friends among the rich chappies from Fifth Avenue. And I always let my girls get the benefit of it."

My girls! Susan's mind, recovering now from its daze, seized upon this phrase. And soon she had fathomed how these two young men came to be so luxuriously dressed, so well supplied with money. She had heard of this system under which the girls in the streets were exploited as thoroughly as the girls in the houses. In all the earth was there anyone who was suffered to do for himself or herself without there being a powerful idle someone else to take away all the proceeds but a bare living? Helpless! Helpless!

"How many girls have you?" she asked.

"Jealous already!" And he laughed and blew a cloud of smoke into her face.

She took the quarters he directed—a plain clean room two flights up at seven dollars a week, in a furnished room house on West Forty-third Street near Eighth Avenue. She was but a few blocks from where she and Rod had lived. New York—to a degree unrivaled among the cities of the world—illustrates in the isolated lives of its never isolated inhabitants how little relationship there is between space and actualities of distance. Wherever on earth there are as many as two human beings, one may see an instance of the truth. That an infinity of spiritual solitude can stretch uncrossable even between two locked in each other's loving arms! But New York's solitudes, its separations, extend to the surface things. Susan had no sense of the apparent nearness of her former abode. Her life again lay in the same streets; but there again came the sense of strangeness which only one who has lived in New York could appreciate. The streets were the same; but to her they seemed as the streets of another city, because she was now seeing in them none of the things she used to see, was seeing instead kinds of people, aspects of human beings, modes of feeling and acting and existing of which she used to have not the faintest knowledge. There were as many worlds as kinds of people. Thus, though we all talk to each other as if about the same world, each of us is thinking of his own kind of world, the only one he sees. And that is why there can never be sympathy and understanding among the children of men until there is some approach to resemblance in their various lots; for the lot determines the man.

The house was filled with women of her own kind. They were allowed all privileges. There was neither bath nor stationary washstand, but the landlady supplied tin tubs on request. "Oh, Mr. Palmer's recommendation," said she; "I'll give you two days to pay. My terms are in advance. But Mr. Palmer's a dear friend of mine."

She was a short woman with a monstrous bust and almost no hips. Her thin hair was dyed and frizzled, and her voice sounded as if it found its way out of her fat lips after a long struggle to pass through the fat of her throat and chest. Her second chin lay upon her bosom in a soft swollen bag that seemed to be suspended from her ears. Her eyes were hard and evil, of a brownish gray. She affected suavity and elaborate politeness; but if the least thing disturbed her, she became red and coarse of voice and vile of language. The vile language and the nature of her business and her private life aside, she would have compared favorably with anyone in the class of those who deal—as merchants, as landlords, as boarding-house keepers—with the desperately different classes of uncertain income. She was reputed rich. They said she stayed on in business to avoid lonesomeness and to keep in touch with all that was going on in the life that had been hers from girlhood.

"And she's a mixer," said Maud to Susan. In response to Susan's look of inquiry, she went on to explain, "A mixer's a white woman that keeps a colored man." Maud laughed at Susan's expression of horror. "You are a greenie," she mocked. "Why, it's all the rage. Nearly all the girls do—from the headliners that are kept by the young Fifth Avenue millionaires down to nine out of ten of the girls of our set that you see in Broadway. No, I'm not lying. It's the truth. I don't do it—at least, not yet. I may get round to it."

After the talk with Maud about the realities of life as it is lived by several hundred thousand of the inhabitants of Manhattan Island Susan had not the least disposition to test by defiance the truth of Freddie Palmer's plain statement as to his powers and her duties. He had told her to go to work that very Sunday evening, and Jim had ordered Maud to call for her and to initiate her. And at half-past seven Maud came. At once she inspected Susan's swollen face.

"Might be a bit worse," she said. "With a veil on, no one'd notice it."

"But I haven't a veil," said Susan.

"I've got mine with me—pinned to my garter. I haven't been home since this afternoon." And Maud produced it.

"But I can't wear a veil at night," objected Susan.

"Why not?" said Maud. "Lots of the girls do. A veil's a dandy hider. Besides, even where a girl's got nothing to hide and has a face that's all to the good, still it's not a bad idea to wear a veil. Men like what they can't see. One of the ugliest girls I know makes a lot of money—all with her veil. She fixes up her figure something grand. Then she puts on that veil—one of the kind you think you can see a face through but you really can't. And she never lifts it till the 'come on' has given up his cash. Then——" Maud laughed. "Gee, but she has had some hot run-ins after she hoists her curtain!"

"Why don't you wear a veil all the time?" asked Susan.

Maud tossed her head. "What do you take me for? I've got too good an opinion of my looks for that."

Susan put on the veil. It was not of the kind that is a disguise. Still, diaphanous though it seemed, it concealed astonishingly the swelling in Susan's face. Obviously, then, it must at least haze the features, would do something toward blurring the marks that go to make identity.

"I shall always wear a veil," said Susan.

"Oh, I don't know," deprecated Maud. "I think you're quite pretty—though a little too proper and serious looking to suit some tastes."

Susan had removed veil and hat, was letting down her hair.

"What are you doing that for?" cried Maud impatiently. "We're late now and——"

"I don't like the way my hair's done," cried Susan.

"Why, it was all right—real swell—good as a hairdresser could have done."

But Susan went on at her task. Ever since she came East she had worn it in a braid looped at the back of her head. She proceeded to change this radically. With Maud forgetting to be impatient in admiration of her swift fingers she made a coiffure much more elaborate—wide waves out from her temples and a big round loose knot behind. She was well content with the result—especially when she got the veil on again and it was assisting in the change.

"What do you think?" she said to Maud when she was ready.

"My, but you look different!" exclaimed Maud. "A lot dressier—and sportier. More—more Broadway."

"That's it—Broadway," said Susan. She had always avoided looking like Broadway. Now, she would take the opposite tack. Not loud toilets—for they would defeat her purpose. Not loud but—just common.

"But," added Maud, "you do look swell about the feet. Where *do* you get your shoes? No, I guess it's the feet."

As they sallied forth Maud said, "First, I'll show you our hotel." And they went to a Raines Law hotel in Forty-second Street near Eighth Avenue. "The proprietor's a heeler of Finnegan's. I guess Freddie comes in for some rake-off. He gives us twenty-five cents of every dollar the man spends," explained she. "And if the man opens wine we get two dollars on every bottle. The best way is to stay behind when the man goes and collect right away. That avoids rows—though they'd hardly dare cheat you, being as you're on Freddie's staff. Freddie's got a big pull. He's way up at the top. I wish to God I had him instead of Jim. Freddie's giving up fast. They say he's got some things a lot better'n this now, and that he's likely to quit this and turn respectable. You ought to treat me mighty white, seeing what I done for you. I've put you in right—and that's everything in this here life."

Susan looked all round—looked along the streets stretching away with their morning suggestion of freedom to fly, freedom to escape—helpless! "Can't I get a drink?" asked she. There was a strained look in her eyes, a significant nervousness of the lips and hands. "I must have a drink."

"Of course. Max has been on a vacation, but I hear he's back. When I introduce you, he'll probably set 'em up. But I wouldn't drink if I were you till I went off duty."

"I must have a drink," replied Susan.

"It'll get you down. It got me down. I used to have a fine sucker—gave me a hundred a week and paid my flat rent. But I had nothing else to do, so I took to drinking, and I got so reckless that I let him catch me with my lover that time. But I had to have somebody to spend the money on. Anyhow, it's no fun having a John."

"A John?" said Susan. "What's that?"

"You are an innocent——!" laughed Maud. "A John's a sucker—a fellow that keeps a girl. Well, it'd be no fun to have a John unless you fooled him—would it?"

They now entered the side door of the hotel and ascended the stairs. A dyspeptic looking man with a red nose that stood out the more strongly for the sallowness of his skin and the smallness of his sunken brown eyes had his hands spread upon the office desk and was leaning on his stiff arms. "Hello, Max," said Maud in a fresh, condescending way. "How's business?"

"Slow. Always slack on Sundays. How goes it with you, Maudie?"

"So—so. I manage to pick up a living in spite of the damn chippies. I don't see why the hell they don't go into the business regular and make something out of it, instead of loving free. I'm down on a girl that's neither the one thing nor the other. This is my lady friend, Miss Queenie." She turned laughingly to Susan. "I never asked your last name."

"Brown."

"My, what a strange name!" cried Maud. Then, as the proprietor laughed with the heartiness of tradesman at good customer's jest, she said, "Going to set 'em up, Max?"

He pressed a button and rang a bell loudly. The responding waiter departed with orders for a whiskey and two lithias. Maud explained to Susan:

"Max used to be a prize-fighter. He was middleweight champion."

"I've been a lot of things in my days," said Max with pride.

"So I've heard," joked Maud. "They say they've got your picture at headquarters."

"That's neither here nor there," said Max surlily. "Don't get too flip." Susan drank her whiskey as soon as it came, and the glow rushed to her ghastly face. Said Max with great politeness:

"You're having a little neuralgia, ain't you? I see your face is swhole some."

"Yes," said Susan. "Neuralgia." Maud laughed hilariously. Susan herself had ceased to brood over the incident. In conventional lives, visited but rarely by perilous storms, by disaster, such an event would be what is called concise. But in life as it is lived by the masses of the people—life in which awful disease, death, maiming, eviction, fire, violent event of any and every kind, is part of the daily routine in that life of the masses there is no time for lingering upon the weathered storm or for bothering about and repairing its ravages. Those who live the comparatively languid, the sheltered life should not use their own standards of what is delicate and refined, what is conspicuous and strong, when they judge their fellow beings as differently situated. Nevertheless, they do—with the result that we find the puny mud lark criticizing the eagle battling with the hurricane.

When Susan and Maud were in the street again, Susan declared that she must have another drink. "I can't offer to pay for one for you," said she to Maud. "I've almost no money. And I must spend what I've got for whiskey before I—can—can—start in."

Maud began to laugh, looked at Susan, and was almost crying instead. "I can lend you a fiver," she said. "Life's hell—ain't it? My father used to have a good business—tobacco. The trust took it away from him—and then he drank—and mother, she drank, too. And one day he beat her so she died—and he ran away. Oh, it's all awful! But I've stopped caring. I'm stuck on Jim—and another little fellow he don't know about. For God's sake don't tell him or he'd have me pinched for doing business free. I get full every night and raise old Nick. Sometimes I hate Jim. I've tried to kill him twice when I was loaded. But a girl's got to have a backer with a pull. And Jim lets me keep a bigger share of what I make than some fellows. Freddie's pretty good too, they say—except when he's losing on the races or gets stuck on some actress that's too classy to be shanghaied—like you was—and that makes him cough up."

Maud went on to disclose that Jim usually let her have all she made above thirty dollars a week, and in hard weeks had sometimes let her beg off with fifteen. Said she:

"I can generally count on about fifteen or twenty for myself. Us girls that has backers make a lot more money than the girls that hasn't. They're always getting pinched too—though they're careful never to speak first to a man. We can go right up and brace men with the cops looking on. A cop that'd touch us would get broke—unless we got too gay or robbed somebody with a pull. But none of our class of girls do any robbing. There's nothing in it. You get caught sooner or later, and then you're down and out."

While Susan was having two more drinks Maud talked about Freddie. She seemed to know little about him, though he was evidently one of the conspicuous figures. He had started in the lower East Side—had been leader of one of those gangs that infest tenement districts—the young men who refuse to submit to the common lot of stupid and badly paid toil and try to fight their way out by the quick methods of violence instead of the slower but surer methods of robbing the poor through a store of some kind. These gangs were thieves, blackmailers, kidnapers of young girls for houses of prostitution, repeaters. Most of them graduated into habitual jailbirds, a few—the cleverest—became saloon-keepers and politicians and high-class professional gamblers and race track men.

Freddie, Maud explained, was not much over twenty-five, yet was already well up toward the place where successful gang leaders crossed over into the respectable class—that is, grafted in "big figures." He was a great reader, said Maud, and had taken courses at some college. "They say he and his gang used to kill somebody nearly every night. Then he got a lot of money out of one of his jobs—some say it was a bank robbery and some say they killed a miner who was drunk with a big roll on him. Anyhow, Freddie got next to Finnegan—he's worth several millions that he made out of policy shops and poolrooms, and contracts and such political things. So he's in right—and he's got the brains. He's a good one for working out schemes for making people work hard and bring him their money. And everybody's afraid of him because he won't stop at nothing and is too slick to get caught."

Maud broke off abruptly and rose, warned by the glazed look in Susan's eyes. Susan was so far gone that she had difficulty in not staggering and did not dare speak lest her uncertain tongue should betray her. Maud walked her up and down the block several times to give the fresh air a chance, then led her up to a man who had looked at them in passing and had paused to look back. "Want to go have a good time, sweetheart?" said Maud to the man. He was well dressed, middle-aged, with a full beard and spectacles, looked as if he might be a banker, or perhaps a professor in some college.

"How much?" asked he.

"Five for a little while. Come along, sporty. Take me or my lady friend."

"How much for both of you?"

"Ten. We don't cut rates. Take us both, dearie. I know a hotel where it'd be all right."

"No. I guess I'll take your lady friend." He had been peering at Susan through his glasses. "And if she treats me well, I'll take her again. You're sure you're all right? I'm a married man."

"We've both been home visiting for a month, and walking the chalk. My, but ma's strict! We got back tonight," said Maud glibly. "Go ahead, Queenie. I'll be chasing up and down here, waiting." In a lower tone: "Get through with him quick. Strike him for five more after you get the first five. He's a blob."

When Susan came slinking through the office of the hotel in the wake of the man two hours later, Maud sprang from the little parlor. "How much did you get?" she asked in an undertone.

Susan looked nervously at the back of the man who was descending the stairway to the street. "He said he'd pay me next time," she said. "I didn't know what to do. He was polite and——"

Maud seized her by the arm. "Come along!" she cried. As she passed the desk she said to the clerk, "A dirty bilker! Tryin' to kiss his way out!"

"Give him hell," said the clerk.

Maud, still gripping Susan, overtook the man at the sidewalk.

"What do you mean by not paying my lady friend?" she shouted.

"Get out!" said the man in a low tone, with an uneasy glance round. "If you annoy me I'll call the police."

"If you don't cough up mighty damn quick," cried Maud so loudly that several passers-by stopped, "I'll do the calling myself, you bum, and have you pinched for insulting two respectable working girls." And she planted herself squarely before him. Susan drew back into the shadow of the wall.

Up stepped Max, who happened to be standing outside his place.

"What's the row about?" he demanded.

"These women are trying to blackmail me," said the man, sidling away.

Maud seized him by the arm. "Will you cough up or shall I scream?" she cried.

"Stand out of the way, girls," said Max savagely, "and let me take a crack at the— —."

The man dived into his pocket, produced a bill, thrust it toward Susan. Maud saw that it was a five. "That's only five," she cried. "Where's the other five?"

"Five was the bargain," whined the man.

"Do you want me to push in your blinkers, you damned old bilk, you?" cried Max, seizing him violently by the arm. The man visited his pocket again, found another five, extended the two. Maud seized them. "Now, clear out!" said Max. "I hate to let you go without a swift kick in the pants."

Maud pressed the money on Susan and thanked Max. Said Max,

"Don't forget to tell Freddie what I done for his girl."

"She'll tell him, all right," Maud assured him.

As the girls went east through Forty-second Street, Susan said,

"I'm afraid that man'll lay for us."

"Lay for us," laughed Maud. "He'll run like a cat afire if he ever sights us again."

"I feel queer and faint," said Susan. "I must have a drink."

"Well—I'll go with you. But I've got to get busy. I want a couple of days off this week for my little fellow, so I must hustle. You let that dirty dog keep you too long. Half an hour's plenty enough. Always make 'em cough up in advance, then hustle 'em through. And don't listen to their guff about wanting to see you again if you treat 'em right. There's nothing in it."

They went into a restaurant bar near Broadway. Susan took two drinks of whiskey raw in rapid succession; Maud took one drink—a green mint with ice. "While you was fooling away time with that thief," said she, "I had two men—got five from one, three from the other. The five-dollar man took a three-dollar room—that was seventy-five for me. The three-dollar man wouldn't stand for more than a dollar room—so I got only a quarter there. But he set 'em up to two rounds of drinks—a quarter more for me. So I cleared nine twenty-five. And you'd 'a' got only your twenty-five cents commission on the room if it hadn't been for me. You forgot to collect your commission. Well, you can get it next time. Only I wouldn't *ask* for it, Max was so nice in helping out. He'll give you the quarter."

When Susan had taken her second stiff drink, her eyes were sparkling and she was laughing recklessly. "I want a cigarette," she said.

"You feel bully, don't you?"

"I'm ready for anything," declared she giddily. "I don't give a damn. I'm over the line. I—*don't*—give—a—damn!"

"I used to hate the men I went up with," said Maud, "but now I hardly look at their faces. You'll soon be that way. Then you'll only drink for fun. Drink—and dope—they are about the only fun we have—them and caring about some fellow."

"How many girls has Freddie got?"

"Search me. Not many that he'd speak to himself. Jim's his wardman—does his collecting for him. Freddie's above most of the men in this business. The others are about like Jim—tough straight through, but Freddie's a kind of a pullman. The other men-even Jim—hate him for being such a snare and being able to hide it that he's in such a low business. They'd have done him up long ago, if they could. But he's to wise for them. That's why they have to do what he says. I tell you, you're in right, for sure. You'll have Freddie eating out of your hand, if you play a cool hand."

Susan ordered another drink and a package of Egyptian cigarettes. "They don't allow ladies to smoke in here," said Maud. "We'll go to the washroom."

And in the washroom they took a few hasty puffs before sallying forth again. Usually Sunday night was dull, all the men having spent their spare money the night before, and it being a bad night for married men to make excuses for getting away from home. Maud explained that, except "out-of-towners," the married men were the chief support of their profession—"and most of the cornhuskers are married men, too." But Susan had the novice's luck. When she and Maud met Maud's "little gentleman friend" Harry Tucker at midnight and went to Considine's for supper, Susan had taken in "presents" and commissions twenty-nine dollars and a half. Maud had not done so badly, herself; her net receipts were twenty-two fifty.

She would not let Susan pay any part of the supper bill, but gave Harry the necessary money. "Here's a five," said she, pressing the bill into his hand, "and keep the change."

And she looked at him with loving eyes of longing. He was a pretty, common-looking fellow, a mere boy, who clerked in a haberdashery in the neighborhood. As he got only six dollars a week and had to give five to his mother who sewed, he could not afford to spend money on Maud, and she neither expected nor wished it. When she picked him up, he like most of his fellow-clerks had no decent clothing but the suit he had to have to "make a front" at the store. Maud had outfitted him from the skin with the cheap but showy stuff exhibited for just such purposes in the Broadway windows. She explained confidentially to Susan:

"It makes me sort of feel that I own him. Then, too, in love there oughtn't to be any money. If he paid, I'd be as cold to him as I am to the rest. The only reason I like Jim at all is I like a good beating once in a while. It's exciting. Jim—he treats me like the dirt under his feet. And that's what we are—dirt under the men's feet. Every woman knows it, when it comes to a showdown between her and a man. As my pop used to say, the world was made for men, not for women. Still, our graft ain't so bum, at that—if we work it right."

Freddie called on Susan about noon the next day. She was still in bed. He was dressed in the extreme of fashion, was wearing a chinchilla-lined coat. He looked the idle, sportively inclined son of some rich man in the Fifth Avenue district. He was having an affair with a much admired young actress—was engaged in it rather as a matter of vanity and for the fashionable half-world associations into which it introduced him rather than from any present interest in the lady. He stood watching Susan with a peculiar expression—one he might perhaps have found it hard to define himself. He bent over her and carelessly brushed her ear with his lips. "How did your royal highness make out?" inquired he.

"The money's in the top bureau drawer," replied she, the covers up to her eyes and her eyes closed.

He went to the bureau, opened the drawer, with his gloved hands counted the money. As he counted his eyes had a look in them that was strangely like jealous rage. He kept his back toward her for some time after he had crossed to look at the money. When he spoke it was to say:

"Not bad. And when you get dressed up a bit and lose your stage fright, you'll do a smashing business. I'll not take my share of this. I had a good run with the cards last night. Anyhow, you've got to pay your rent and buy some clothes. I've got to invest something in my new property. It's badly run down. You'll get busy again tonight, of course. Never lay off, lady, unless the weather's bad. You'll find you won't average more than twenty good business days a month in summer and fall, and only about ten in winter and spring, when it's cold and often lots of bad weather in the afternoons and evenings. That means hustle."

No sign from Susan. He sat on the bed and pulled the covers away from her face. "What are you so grouchy about, pet?" he inquired, chucking her under the chin.

"Nothing."

"Too much booze, I'll bet. Well, sleep your grouch off. I've got a date with Finnegan. The election's coming on, and I have to work—lining up the vote and getting the repeaters ready. It all means good money for me. Look out about the booze, lady. It'll float you into trouble—trouble with me, I mean." And he patted her bare shoulders, laughed gently, went to the door. He paused there, struggled with an impulse to turn—departed.

CHAPTER VII

BUT she did not "look out about the booze." Each morning she awoke in a state of depression so horrible that she wondered why she could not bring herself to plan suicide. Why was it? Her marriage? Yes—and she paid it its customary tribute of a shudder. Yes, her marriage had made all things thereafter possible. But what else? Lack of courage? Lack of self-respect? Was it not always assumed that a woman in her position, if she had a grain of decent instinct, would rush eagerly upon death? Was she so much worse than others? Or was what everybody said about these things—everybody who had experience—was it false, like nearly everything else she had been taught? She did not understand; she only knew that hope was as strong within her as health itself—and that she did not want to die—and that at present she was helpless.

One evening the man she was with—a good-looking and unusually interesting young chap—suddenly said:

"What a heart action you have got! Let me listen to that again."

"Is it all wrong?" asked Susan, as he pressed his ear against her chest.

"You ask that as if you rather hoped it was."

"I do—and I don't."

"Well," said he, after listening for a third time, "you'll never die of heart trouble. I never heard a heart with such a grand action—like a big, powerful pump, built to last forever. You're never ill, are you?"

"Not thus far."

"And you'll have a hard time making yourself ill. Health? Why, your health must be perfect. Let me see." And he proceeded to thump and press upon her chest with an expertness that proclaimed the student of medicine. He was all interest and enthusiasm, took a pencil and, spreading a sheet upon her chest over her heart, drew its outlines. "There!" he cried.

"What is it?" asked Susan. "I don't understand."

The young man drew a second and much smaller heart within the outline of hers. "This," he explained, "is about the size of an ordinary heart. You can see for yourself that yours is fully one-fourth bigger than the normal."

"What of it?" said Susan.

"Why, health and strength—and vitality—courage—hope—all one-fourth above the ordinary allowance. Yes, more than a fourth. I envy you. You ought to live long, stay young until you're very old—and get pretty much anything you please. You don't belong to this life. Some accident, I guess. Every once in a while I run across a case something like yours. You'll go back where you belong. This is a dip, not a drop."

"You sound like a fortune-teller." She was smiling mockingly. But in truth she had never in all her life heard words that thrilled her so, that heartened her so.

"I am. A scientific fortune-teller. And what that kind says comes true, barring accidents. As you're not ignorant and careless this life of yours isn't physiologically bad. On the contrary, you're out in the open air much of the time and get the splendid exercise of walking—a much more healthful life, in the essential ways, than respectable women lead. They're always stuffing, and rumping it. They never move if they can help. No, nothing can stop you but death—unless you're far less intelligent than you look. Oh, yes—death and one other thing."

"Drink." And he looked shrewdly at her.

But drink she must. And each day, as soon as she dressed and was out in the street, she began to drink, and kept it up until she had driven off the depression and had got herself into the mood of recklessness in which she found a certain sardonic pleasure in outraging her own sensibilities. There is a stage in a drinking career when the man or the woman becomes depraved and ugly as soon as the liquor takes effect. But she was far from this advanced stage. Her disposition was, if anything, more sweet and generous when she was under the influence of liquor. The whiskey—she almost always drank whiskey—seemed to act directly and only upon the nerves that ached and throbbed when she was sober, the nerves that made the life she was leading seem loathsome beyond the power of habit to accustom. With these nerves stupefied, her natural gayety asserted itself, and a fondness for quiet and subtle mockery—her indulgence in it did not make her popular with vain men sufficiently acute to catch her meaning.

By observation and practice she was soon able to measure the exact amount of liquor that was necessary to produce the proper state of intoxication at the hour for going "on duty." That gayety of hers was of the surface only. Behind it her real self remained indifferent or somber or sardonic, according to her mood of the day. And she had the sense of being in the grasp of a hideous, fascinating nightmare, of being dragged through some dreadful probation from which she would presently emerge to ascend to the position she would have earned by her desperate fortitude. The past—unreal. The present—a waking dream. But the future—ah, the future!

He has not candidly explored far beneath the surface of things who does not know the strange allure, charm even, that many loathsome things possess. And drink is peculiarly fitted to bring out this perverse quality— drink that blurs all the conventionalities, even those built up into moral ideas by centuries and ages of unbroken custom. The human animal, for all its pretenses of inflexibility, is almost infinitely adaptable—that is why it has risen in several million years of evolution from about the humblest rank in the mammalian family to overlordship of the universe. Still, it is doubtful if, without drink to help her, a girl of Susan's intelligence and temperament would have been apt to endure. She would probably have chosen the alternative—death. Hundreds, perhaps thousands, of girls, at least her equals in sensibility, are caught in the same calamity every year, tens of thousands, ever more and more as our civilization transforms under the pressure of industrialism, are caught in the similar calamities of soul-destroying toil. And only the few survive who have perfect health and abounding vitality. Susan's iron strength enabled her to live; but it was drink that enabled her to endure. Beyond question one of the greatest blessings that could now be conferred upon the race would be to cure it of the drink evil. But at the same time, if drink were taken away before the causes of drink were removed, there would be an appalling increase in suicide—in insanity, in the general total of human misery. For while drink retards the growth of intelligent effort to end the stupidities in the social system, does it not also help men and women to bear the consequences of those stupidities? Our crude and undeveloped new civilization, strapping men and women and children to the machines and squeezing all the energy out of them, all the capacity for vital life, casts them aside as soon as they are useless but long before they are dead. How unutterably wretched they would be without drink to give them illusions!

Susan grew fond of cigarettes, fond of whiskey; to the rest she after a few weeks became numb—no new or strange phenomenon in a world where people with a cancer or other hideous running sore or some gross and frightful deformity of fat or excrescence are seen laughing, joining freely and comfortably in the company of the unafflicted. In her affliction Susan at least saw only those affected like herself—and that helped not a little, helped the whiskey to confuse and distort her outlook upon life.

The old Cartesian formula—"I think, therefore I am"—would come nearer to expressing a truth, were it reversed—"I am, therefore I think." Our characters are compressed, and our thoughts bent by our environment. And most of us are unconscious of our slavery because our environment remains unchanged from birth until death, and so seems the whole universe to us.

In spite of her life, in spite of all she did to disguise herself, there persisted in her face—even when she was dazed or giddied or stupefied with drink—the expression of the woman on the right side of the line. Whether it was something in her character, whether it was not rather due to superiority of breeding and intelligence, would be difficult to say. However, there was the *different* look that irritated many of the other girls, interfered with her business and made her feel a hypocrite. She heard so much about the paleness of her lips that she decided to end that comment by using paint— the durable kind Ida had recommended. When her lips flamed carmine, a strange and striking effect resulted. The sad sweet pensiveness of her eyes— the pallor of her clear skin—then, that splash of bright red, artificial, bold, defiant—the contrast of the combination seemed somehow to tell the story of her life her past no less than her present. And when her beauty began to come back—for, hard though her life was, it was a life of good food, of plenty of sleep, of much open air; so it put no such strain upon her as had the life of the factory and the tenement—when her beauty came back, the effect of that contrast of scarlet splash against the sad purity of pallid cheeks and violet-gray eyes became a mark of individuality, of distinction. It was not long before Susan would have as soon thought of issuing forth with her body uncovered as with her lips unrouged.

She turned away from men who sought her a second time. She was difficult to find, she went on "duty" only enough days each week to earn a low average of what was expected from the girls by their protectors. Yet she got many unexpected presents—and so had money to lend to the other girls, who soon learned how "easy" she was.

Maud, sometimes at her own prompting, sometimes prompted by Jim, who was prompted by Freddie—warned her every few days that she was skating on the thinnest of ice. But she went her way. Not until she accompanied a girl to an opium joint to discover whether dope had the merits claimed for it as a deadener of pain and a producer of happiness— not until then did Freddie come in person.

"I hear," said he and she wondered whether he had heard from Max or from loose-tongued Maud—"that you come into the hotel so drunk that men sometimes leave you right away again—go without paying you."

"I must drink," said Susan.

"You must *stop* drink," retorted he, amiable in his terrible way. "If you don't, I'll have you pinched and sent up. That'll bring you to your senses."

"I must drink," said Susan.

"Then I must have you pinched," said he with his mocking laugh. "Don't be a fool," he went on. "You can make money enough to soon buy the right sort of clothes so that I can afford to be seen with you. I'd like to take you out once in a while and give you a swell time. But what'd we look like together—with you in those cheap things out of bargain troughs? Not that you don't look well—for you do. But the rest of you isn't up to your feet and to the look in your face. The whole thing's got to be right before a lady can sit opposite *me* in Murray's or Rector's."

"All I ask is to be let alone," said Susan.

"That isn't playing square—and you've got to play square. What I want is to set you up in a nice parlor trade—chaps from the college and the swell clubs and hotels. But I can't do anything for you as long as you drink this way. You'll have to stay on the streets."

"That's where I want to stay."

"Well, there's something to be said for the streets," Freddie admitted. "If a woman don't intend to make sporting her life business, she don't want to get up among the swells of the profession, where she'd become known and find it hard to sidestep. Still, even in the street you ought to make a hundred, easy—and not go with any man that doesn't suit you."

"Any man that doesn't suit me," said Susan. And, after a pause, she said it again: "Any man that doesn't suit me."

The young man, with his shrewdness of the street-graduate and his sensitiveness of the Italian, gave her an understanding glance. "You look as if you couldn't decide whether to laugh or cry. I'd try to laugh if I was you."

She had laughed as he spoke.

Freddie nodded approval. "That sounded good to me. You're getting broken in. Don't take yourself so seriously. After all, what are you doing? Why, learning to live like a man."

She found this new point of view interesting—and true, too. Like a man—like all men, except possibly a few—not enough exceptions to change the rule. Like a man; getting herself hardened up to the point where she could take part in the cruel struggle on equal terms with the men. It wasn't their difference of body any more than it was their difference of dress that handicapped women; it was the idea behind skirt and sex—and she was getting rid of that. . . .

The theory was admirable; but it helped her not at all in practice. She continued to keep to the darkness, to wait in the deep doorways, so far as she could in her "business hours," and to repulse advances in the day time or in public places—and to drink. She did not go again to the opium joint, and she resisted the nightly offers of girls and their "gentlemen friends" to try cocaine in its various forms. "Dope," she saw, was the medicine of despair. And she was far from despair. Had she not youth? Had she not health and intelligence and good looks? Some day she would have finished her apprenticeship. Then—the career!

Freddie let her alone for nearly a month, though she was earning less than fifty dollars a week—which meant only thirty for him. He had never "collected" from her directly, but always through Jim; and she had now learned enough of the methods of the system of which she was one of the thousands of slaves to appreciate that she was treated by Jim with unique consideration. Not only by the surly and brutal Jim, but also by the police who oppressed in petty ways wherever they dared because they hated Freddie's system which took away from them a part of the graft they regarded as rightfully theirs.

Yes, rightfully theirs. And anyone disposed to be critical of police morality—or of Freddie Palmer morality—in this matter of graft would do well to pause and consider the source of his own income before he waxes too eloquent and too virtuous. Graft is one of those general words that mean everything and nothing. What is graft and what is honest income? Just where shall we draw the line between rightful exploitation of our fellow-beings through their necessities and their ignorance of their helplessness, and wrongful exploitation? Do attempts to draw that line resolve down to making virtuous whatever I may appropriate and vicious whatever is appropriated in ways other than mine? And if so are not the police and the Palmers entitled to their day in the moral court no less than the tariff-baron and market-cornerer, the herder and driver of wage slaves, the retail artists in cold storage filth, short weight and shoddy goods? However, "we must draw the line somewhere" or there will be no such thing as morality under our social system. So why not draw it at anything the other fellow does to make money. In adopting this simple rule, we not only preserve the moralities from destruction but also establish our own virtue and the other fellow's villainy. Truly, never is the human race so delightfully, so unconsciously, amusing as when it discusses right and wrong.

When she saw Freddie again, he was far from sober. He showed it by his way of beginning. Said he:

"I've got to hand you a line of rough talk, Queenie. I took on this jag for your especial benefit," said he. "I'm a fool about you and you take advantage of it. That's bad for both of us. . . . You're drinking as much as ever?"

"More," replied she. "It takes more and more."

"How can you expect to get on?" cried he, exasperated.

"As I told you, I couldn't make a cent if I didn't drink."

Freddie stared moodily at her, then at the floor—they were in her room. Finally he said:

"You get the best class of men. I put my swell friends on to where you go slipping by, up and down in the shadow—and it's all they can do to find you. The best class of men—men all the swell respectable girls in town are crazy to hook up with—those of 'em that ain't married already. If you're good enough for those chaps they ought to be good enough for you. Yet some of 'em complain to me that they get thrown down—and others kick because you were too full—and, damn it, you act so queer that you scare 'em away. What am I to do about it?"

She was silent.

"I want you to promise me you'll take a brace."

No answer.

"You won't promise?"

"No—because I don't intend to. I'm doing the best I can."

"You think I'm a good thing. You think I'll take anything off you, because I'm stuck on you—and appreciate that you ain't on the same level with the rest of these heifers. Well—I'll not let any woman con me. I never have. I never will. And I'll make you realize that you're not square with me. I'll let you get a taste of life as it is when a girl hasn't got a friend with a pull."

"As you please," said Susan indifferently. "I don't in the least care what happens to me."

"We'll see about that," cried he, enraged. "I'll give you a week to brace up in."

The look he shot at her by way of finish to his sentence was menacing enough. But she was not disturbed; these signs of anger tended to confirm her in her sense of security from him. For it was wholly unlike the Freddie Palmer the rest of the world knew, to act in this irresolute and stormy way. She knew that Palmer, in his fashion, cared for her—better still, liked her—

liked to talk with her, liked to show—and to develop—the aspiring side of his interesting, unusual nature for her benefit.

A week passed, during which she did not see him. But she heard that he was losing on both the cards and the horses and was drinking wildly. A week—ten days—then— —

One night, as she came out of a saloon a block or so down Seventh
Avenue from Forty-second, a fly cop seized her by the arm.

"Come along," said he roughly. "You're drinking and soliciting. I've got to clear the streets of some of these tarts. It's got so decent people can't move without falling over 'em."

Susan had not lived in the tenement districts where the ignorance and the helplessness and the lack of a voice that can make itself heard among the ruling classes make the sway of the police absolute and therefore tyrannical—she had not lived there without getting something of that dread and horror of the police which to people of the upper classes seems childish or evidence of secret criminal hankerings. And this nervousness had latterly been increased to terror by what she had learned from her fellow-outcasts—the hideous tales of oppression, of robbery, of bodily and moral degradation. But all this terror had been purely fanciful, as any emotion not of experience proves to be when experience evokes the reality. At that touch, at the sound of those rough words—at that *reality* of the terror she had imagined from the days when she went to work at Matson's and to live with the Brashears, she straightway lost consciousness. When her senses returned she was in a cell, lying on a wooden bench.

There must have been some sort of wild struggle; for her clothes were muddy, her hat was crushed into shapelessness, her veil was so torn that she had difficulty in arranging it to act as any sort of concealment. Though she had no mirror at which to discover the consolation, she need have had no fear of being recognized, so distorted were all her features by the frightful paroxysms of grief that swept and ravaged her body that night. She fainted again when they led her out to put her in the wagon.

She fainted a third time when she heard her name—"Queenie Brown"—bellowed out by the court officer. They shook her into consciousness, led her to the court-room. She was conscious of a stifling heat, of a curious crowd staring at her with eyes which seemed to bore red hot holes into her flesh. As she stood before the judge, with head limp upon her bosom, she heard in her ear a rough voice bawling, "You're discharged. The judge says don't come here again." And she was pushed through an iron gate. She walked unsteadily up the aisle, between two masses of those burning-eyed human monsters. She felt the cold outside air like a vast drench of icy water flung upon her. If it had been raining, she might have gone toward the river. But than that day New York had never been more radiantly the City of the Sun. How she got home she never knew, but late in the afternoon she realized that she was in her own room.

Hour after hour she lay upon the bed, body and mind
inert.
Helpless—no escape—no courage to live—yet no wish to
die.
How much longer would it last? Surely the waking from
this
dream must come soon.

About noon the next day Freddie came. "I let you off easy," said he, sitting on the bed upon which she was lying dressed as when she came in the day before. "Have you been drinking again?"

"No," she muttered.

"Well—don't. Next time, a week on the Island. . . . Did you hear?"

"Yes."

"Don't turn me against you. I'd hate to have to make an awful example of you."

"I must drink," she repeated in the same stolid way.

He abruptly but without shock lifted her to a sitting position. His arm held her body up; her head was thrown back and her face was looking calmly at him. She realized that he had been drinking—drinking hard. Her eyes met his terrible eyes without flinching. He kissed her full upon the lips. With her open palm she struck him across the cheek, bringing the red fierily to its smooth fair surface. The devil leaped into his eyes, the devil of cruelty and lust. He smiled softly and wickedly. "I see you've forgotten the lesson I gave you three months ago. You've got to be taught to be afraid all over again."

"I *am* not afraid," said she. "I *was* not afraid. You can't make me afraid."

"We'll see," murmured he. And his fingers began to caress her round smooth throat.

"If you ever strike me again," she said quietly, "I'll kill you."

His eyes flinched for an instant—long enough to let her know his innermost secret. "I want you—I want *you*—damn you," he said, between his clinched teeth. "You're the first one I couldn't get. There's something in you I can't get!"

"That's *me*," she replied.

"You hate me, don't you?"

"No."

"Then you love me?"

"No. I care nothing about you."

He let her drop back to the bed, went to the window, stood looking out moodily. After a while he said without turning:

"My mother kept a book shop—on the lower East Side. She brought me up at home. At home!" And he laughed sardonically. "She hated me because I looked like my father."

Silence, then he spoke again:

"You've never been to my flat. I've got a swell place. I want
to cut out this part of the game. I can get along without it. You're going to move in with me, and stop this street business.
I make good money. You can have everything you want."

"I prefer to keep on as I am."

"What's the difference? Aren't you mine whenever I want you?"

"I prefer to be free."

"*Free!* Why, you're not free. Can't I send you to the Island any time I feel like it—just as I can the other girls?"

"Yes—you can do that. But I'm free, all the same."

"No more than the other girls."

"Yes."

"What do you mean?"

"Unless you understand, I couldn't make you see it," she said. She was sitting on the edge of the bed, doing up her hair, which had partly fallen down. "I think you do understand."

"What in the hell do you want, anyhow?" he demanded.

"If I knew—do you suppose I'd be here?"

He watched her with baffled, longing eyes. "What is it," he muttered, "that's so damn peculiar about you?"

It was the question every shrewd observant person who saw her put to himself in one way or another; and there was excellent reason why this should have been.

Life has a certain set of molds—lawyer, financier, gambler, preacher, fashionable woman, prostitute, domestic woman, laborer, clerk, and so on through a not extensive list of familiar types with which we all soon become acquainted. And to one or another of these patterns life fits each of us as we grow up. Not one in ten thousand glances into human faces is arrested because it has lit upon a personality that cannot be immediately located, measured, accounted for. The reason for this sterility of variety which soon makes the world rather monotonous to the seeing eye is that few of us are born with any considerable amount of personality, and what little we have is speedily suppressed by a system of training which is throughout based upon an abhorrence of originality. We obey the law of nature—and nature so abhors variety that, whenever a variation from a type happens, she tries to kill it, and, that failing, reproduces it a myriad times to make it a type. When an original man or woman appears and all the strenuous effort to suppress him or her fails, straightway spring up a thousand imitators and copiers, and the individuality is lost in the school, the fashion, the craze. We have not the courage to be ourselves, even where there is anything in us that might be developed into something distinctive enough to win us the rank of real identity. Individuality—distinction—where it does exist, almost never shows until experience brings it out—just as up to a certain stage the embryo of any animal is like that of every other animal, though there is latent in it the most positive assertion of race and sex, of family, type, and so on.

Susan had from childhood possessed certain qualities of physical beauty, of spiritedness, of facility in mind and body—the not uncommon characteristic of the child that is the flower of passionate love. But now there was beginning to show in her a radical difference from the rest of the crowd pouring through the streets of the city. It made the quicker observers in the passing throng turn the head for a second and wondering glance. Most of them assumed they had been stirred by her superiority of face and figure. But striking faces and figures of the various comely types are frequent in the streets of New York and of several other American cities. The truth was that they were interested by her expression—an elusive expression telling of a soul that was being moved to its depths by experience which usually finds and molds mere passive material. This expression was as evident in her mouth as in her eyes, in her profile as in her full face. And as she sat there on the edge of the bed twisting up her thick dark hair, it was this expression that disconcerted Freddie Palmer, for the first time in all his contemptuous dealings with the female sex. In his eyes was a ferocious desire to seize her and again try to conquer and to possess.

She had become almost unconscious of his presence. He startled her by suddenly crying, "Oh, you go to hell!" and flinging from the room, crashing the door shut behind him.

Maud had grown tired of the haberdasher's clerk and his presumptions upon her frank fondness which he wholly misunderstood. She had dropped him for a rough looking waiter-singer in a basement drinking place. He was beating her and taking all the money she had for herself, and was spending it on another woman, much older than Maud and homely—and Maud knew, and complained of him bitterly to everyone but himself. She was no longer hanging round Susan persistently, having been discouraged by the failure of her attempts at intimacy with a girl who spent nearly all her spare time at reading or at plays and concerts. Maud was now chumming with a woman who preyed upon the patrons of a big Broadway hotel—she picked them up near the entrance, robbed them, and when they asked the hotel detectives to help them get back their stolen money, the detectives, who divided with her, frightened them off by saying she was a mulatto and would compel them to make a public appearance against her in open court. This woman, older and harder than most of the girls, though of quiet and refined appearance and manner, was rapidly dragging Maud down. Also, Maud's looks were going because she ate irregularly all kinds of trash, and late every night ate herself full to bursting and drank herself drunk to stupefaction.

Susan's first horror of the men she met—men of all classes—was rapidly modified into an inconsistent, therefore characteristically human, mingling of horror and tolerance. Nobody, nothing, was either good or bad, but all veered like weathercocks in the shifting wind. She decided that people were steadily good only where their lot happened to be cast in a place in which the good wind held steadily, and that those who were usually bad simply had the misfortune to have to live where the prevailing winds were bad.

For instance, there was the handsome, well educated, well mannered young prize-fighter, Ned Ballou, who was Estelle's "friend." Ballou, big and gentle and as incapable of bad humor as of constancy or of honesty about money matters, fought under the name of Joe Geary and was known as Upper Cut Joe because usually, in the third round, never later than the fifth, he gave the knockout to his opponent by a cruelly swift and savage uppercut. He had educated himself marvelously well. But he had been brought up among thieves and had by some curious freak never learned to know what a moral sense was, which is one—and a not unattractive—step deeper down than those who know what a moral sense is but never use it. At supper in Gaffney's he related to Susan and Estelle how he had won his greatest victory—the victory of Terry the Cyclone, that had lifted him up into the class of secure money-makers. He told how he always tried to "rattle" his opponent by talking to him, by pouring out in an undertone a stream of gibes, jeers, insults. The afternoon of the fight Terry's first-born had died, but the money for the funeral expenses and to save the wife from the horrors and dangers of the free wards had to be earned. Joe Geary knew that he must win this fight or drop into the working or the criminal class. Terry was a "hard one"; so circumstances compelled, those desperate measures which great men, from financiers and generals down to prize-fighters, do not shrink from else they would not be great, but small.

As soon as he was facing Terry in the ring—Joe so he related with pride in his cleverness—began to "guy"—"Well, you Irish fake—so the kid's dead—eh? Who was its pa, say?—the dirty little bastard—or does the wife know which one it was——" and so on. And Terry, insane with grief and fury, fought wild—and Joe became a champion.

As she listened Susan grew cold with horror and with hate. Estelle said:

"Tell the rest of it, Joe."

"Oh, that was nothing," replied he.

When he strolled away to talk with some friends Estelle told "the rest" that was "nothing." The championship secure, Joe had paid all Terry's bills, had supported Terry and his wife for a year, had relapsed into old habits and "pulled off a job" of safe-cracking because, the prize-fighting happening to pay poorly, he would have had a default on the payments for a month or so. He was caught, did a year on the Island before his "pull" could get him out. And all the time he was in the "pen" he so arranged it with his friends that the invalid Terry and his invalid wife did not suffer. And all this he had done not because he had a sense of owing Terry, but because he was of the "set" in which it is the custom to help anybody who happens to need it, and aid begun becomes an obligation to "see it through."

It was an extreme case of the moral chaos about her—the chaos she had begun to discover when she caught her aunt and Ruth conspiring to take Sam away from her.

What a world! If only these shifting, usually evil winds of circumstance could be made to blow good!

A few evenings after the arrest Maud came for Susan, persuaded her to go out. They dined at about the only good restaurant where unescorted women were served after nightfall. Afterward they went "on duty." It was fine overhead and the air was cold and bracing—one of those marvelous New York winter nights which have the tonic of both sea and mountains and an exhilaration, in addition, from the intense bright-burning life of the mighty city. For more than a week there had been a steady downpour of snow, sleet and finally rain. Thus, the women of the streets had been doing almost no business. There was not much money in sitting in drinking halls and the back rooms of saloons and picking up occasional men; the best trade was the men who would not venture to show themselves in such frankly disreputable places, but picked out women in the crowded streets and followed them to quiet dark places to make the arrangements—men stimulated by good dinners, or, later on, in the evening, those who left parties of elegant respectability after theater or opera. On this first night of business weather in nearly two weeks the streets were crowded with women and girls. They were desperately hard up and they made open dashes for every man they could get at. All classes were made equally bold—the shop and factory and office and theater girls with wages too small for what they regarded as a decent living; the women with young children to support and educate; the protected professional regulars; the miserable creatures who had to get along as best they could without protection, and were prey to every blackmailing officer of an anti-vice society and to every policeman and fly-cop not above levying upon women who were "too low to be allowed to live, anyhow." Out from all kinds of shelters swarmed the women who were demonstrating how prostitution flourishes and tends to spread to every class of society whenever education develops tastes beyond the earning power of their possessors. And with clothes and food to buy, rent to pay, dependents to support, these women, so many days hampered in the one way that was open to them to get money, made the most piteous appeals to the men. Not tearful appeals, not appeals to sympathy or even to charity, but to passion. They sought in every way to excite. They exhibited their carefully gotten-up legs; they made indecent gestures; they said the vilest things; they offered the vilest inducements; they lowered their prices down and down. And such men as did not order them off with disdain, listened with laughter, made jokes at which the wretched creatures laughed as gayly as if they were not mad with anxiety and were not hating these men who were holding on to that which they must have to live.

"Too many out tonight," said Maud as they walked their beat—Forty-second between Broadway and Eighth Avenue. "I knew it would be this way. Let's go in here and get warm."

They went into the back room of a saloon where perhaps half a dozen women were already seated, some of them gray with the cold against which their thin showy garments were no protection. Susan and Maud sat at a table in a corner; Maud broke her rule and drank whiskey with Susan. After they had taken perhaps half a dozen drinks, Maud grew really confidential. She always, even in her soberest moments, seemed to be telling everything she knew; but Susan had learned that there were in her many deep secrets, some of which not even liquor could unlock.

"I'm going to tell you something," she now said to Susan. "You must promise not to give me away."

"Don't tell me," replied Susan. She was used to being flattered—or victimized, according to the point of view—with confidences. She assumed Maud was about to confess some secret about her own self, as she had the almost universal habit of never thinking of anyone else. "Don't tell me," said she. "I'm tired of being used to air awful secrets. It makes me feel like a tenement wash line."

"This is about you," said Maud. "If it's ever found out that I put you wise, Jim'll have me killed. Yes—killed."

Susan, reckless by this time, laughed. "Oh, trash!" she said.

"No trash at all," insisted Maud. "When you know this town through and through you'll know that murder's something that can be arranged as easy as buying a drink. What risk is there in making one of *us* disappear'? None in the world. I always feel that Jim'll have me killed some day—unless I go crazy sometime and kill him. He's stuck on me—or, at least, he's jealous of me—and if he ever found out I had a lover—somebody—anybody that didn't pay—why, it'd be all up with me. Little Maud would go on the grill."

She ordered and slowly drank another whiskey before she recalled what she had set out to confide. By way of a fresh start she said, "What do you think of Freddie?"

"I don't know," replied Susan. And it was the truth. Her instinctive belief in a modified kind of fatalism made her judgments of people—even of those who caused her to suffer—singularly free from personal bitterness. Freddie, a mere instrument of destiny, had his good side, his human side, she knew. At his worst he was no worse than the others, And aside from his queer magnetism, there was a certain force in him that compelled her admiration; at least he was not one of the petty instruments of destiny. He had in him the same quality she felt gestating within herself. "I don't know what to think," she repeated.

Maud had been reflecting while Susan was casting about, as she had many a time before, for her real opinion of her master who was in turn the slave of Finnegan, who was in his turn the slave of somebody higher up, she didn't exactly know who—or why—or the why of any of it—or the why of the grotesque savage purposeless doings of destiny in general. Maud now burst out:

"I don't care. I'm going to put you wise if I die for it."

"Don't," said Susan. "I don't want to know."

"But I've *got* to tell you. Do you know what Freddie's going to do?"

Susan smiled disdainfully. "I don't care. You mustn't tell me—when you've been drinking this way——"

"Finnegan's police judge is a man named Bennett. As soon as Bennett comes back to Jefferson Market Police Court, Freddie's going to have you sent up for three months."

Susan's glass was on the way to her lips. She set it down again. The drunken old wreck of an entertainer at the piano in the corner was bellowing out his favorite song—"I Am the King of the Vikings." Susan began to hum the air.

"It's gospel," cried Maud, thinking Susan did not believe her. "He's a queer one, is Freddie. They're all afraid of him. You'd think he was a coward, the way he bullies women and that. But somehow he ain't—not a bit. He'll be a big man in the organization some day, they all say. He never lets up till he gets square. And he thinks you're not square—after all he's done for you."

"Perhaps not—as he looks at it," said Susan.

"And Jim says he's crazy in love with you, and that he wants to put you where other men can't see you and where maybe he can get over caring about you. That's the real reason. He's a queer devil. But then all men are though none quite like Freddie."

"So I'm to go to the Island for three months," said Susan reflectively.

"You don't seem to care. It's plain you never was there. . . . And you've got to go. There's no way out of it—unless you skip to another city. And if you did you never could come back here. Freddie'd see that you got yours as soon as you landed."

Susan sat looking at her glass. Maud watched her in astonishment. "You're as queer as Freddie," said she at length. "I never feel as if I was acquainted with you—not really. I never had a lady friend like that before.

You don't seem to be a bit excited about what Freddie's going to do. Are you in love with him?"

Susan lifted strange, smiling eyes to Maud's curious gaze. "I—in *love*—with a *man*," she said slowly. And then she laughed.

"Don't laugh that way," cried Maud. "It gives me the creeps.
What are you going to do?"

"What can I do?"

"Nothing."

"Then if there's nothing to do, I'll no nothing."

"Go to the Island for three months?"

Susan shrugged her shoulders. "I haven't gone yet." She rose.
"It's too stuffy and smelly in here," said she. "Let's move out."

"No. I'll wait. I promised to meet a gentleman friend here. You'll not tell that I tipped you off?"

"You'd not have told me if you hadn't known I wouldn't."

"That's so. But—why don't you make it up with Freddie?"

"I couldn't do that."

"He's dead in love. I'm sure you could."

Again Susan's eyes became strange. "I'm sure I couldn't. Good night." She got as far as the door, came back. "Thank you for telling me."

"Oh, that's all right," murmured the girl. She was embarrassed by Susan's manner. She was frightened by Susan's eyes. "You ain't going to——" There she halted.

"What?"

"To jump off? Kill yourself?"

"Hardly," said Susan. "I've got a lot to do before I die."

She went directly home. Palmer was lying on the bed, a cigarette between his lips, a newspaper under his feet to prevent his boots from spoiling the spread—one of the many small indications of the prudence, thrift and calculation that underlay the almost insane recklessness of his surface character, and that would save him from living as the fool lives and dying as the fool dies.

"I thought you wouldn't slop round in these streets long," said he, as she paused upon the threshold. "So I waited."

She went to the bureau, unlocked the top drawer, took the ten-dollar bill she had under some undershirts there, put it in her right stocking where there were already a five and a two. She locked the drawer, tossed the key into an open box of hairpins. She moved toward the door.

"Where are you going?" asked he, still staring at the ceiling.

"Out. I've made almost nothing this week."

"Sit down. I want to talk to you."

She hesitated, seated herself on a chair near the bed.

He frowned at her. "You've been drinking?"

"Yes."

"I've been drinking myself, but I've got a nose like a hunting dog. What do you do it for?"

"What's the use of explaining? You'd not understand."

"Perhaps I would. I'm one-fourth Italian—and they understand everything. . . . You're fond of reading, aren't you?"

"It passes the time."

"While I was waiting for you I glanced at your new books—Emerson—Dickens—Zola." He was looking toward the row of paper backs that filled almost the whole length of the mantel. "I must read them. I always like your books. You spend nearly as much time reading as I do—and you don't need it, for you've got a good education. What do you read for? To amuse yourself?"

"No."

"To get away from yourself?"

"No."

"Then why?" persisted he.

"To find out about myself."

He thought a moment, turned his face toward her. "You *are* clever!" he said admiringly. "What's your game?"

"My game?"

"What are you aiming for? You've got too much sense not to be aiming for something."

She looked at him; the expression that marked her as a person peculiar and apart was glowing in her eyes like a bed of red-hot coals covered with ashes.

"What?" he repeated.

"To get strong," replied she. "Women are born weak and bred weaker. I've got to get over being a woman. For there isn't any place in this world for a woman except under the shelter of some man. And I don't want that." The underlying strength of her features abruptly came into view. "And I won't have it," she added.

He laughed. "But the men'll never let *you* be anything but a woman."

"We'll see," said she, smiling. The strong look had vanished into the soft contour of her beautiful youth.

"Personally, I like you better when you've been drinking," he went on. "You're sad when you're sober. As you drink you liven up."

"When I get over being sad if I'm sober, when I learn to take things as they come, just like a man—a strong man, then I'll be——" She stopped.

"Be what?"

"Ready."

"Ready for what?"

"How do I know?"

He swung himself to a sitting position. "Meanwhile, you're coming to live with me. I've been fighting against it, but I give up. I need you. You're the one I've been looking for. Pack your traps. I'll call a cab and we'll go over to my flat. Then we'll go to Rector's and celebrate."

She shook her head. "I'm sorry, but I can't."

"Why not?"

"I told you. There's something in me that won't let me."

He rose, walked to her very deliberately. He took one of her hands from her lap, drew her to her feet, put his hands strongly on her shoulders. "You belong to me," he said, his lips smiling charmingly, but the devil in the gleam of his eyes and in the glistening of his beautiful, cruel teeth. "Pack up."

"You know that I won't."

He slowly crushed her in his arms, slowly pressed his lips upon hers. A low scream issued from her lips and she seized him by the throat with both hands, one hand over the other, and thrust him backward. He reeled, fell upon his back on the bed; she fell with him, clung to him—like a bull dog—not as if she would not, but as if she could not, let go. He clutched at her fingers; failing to dislodge them, he tried to thrust his thumbs into her eyes. But she seized his right thumb between her teeth and bit into it until they almost met. And at the same time her knees ground into his abdomen. He choked, gurgled, grew dark red, then gray, then a faint blackish blue, lay limp under her. But she did not relax until the blue of his face had deepened to black and his eyes began to bulge from their sockets. At those signs that he was beyond doubt unconscious, she cautiously relaxed her fingers. She unclenched her teeth; his arm, which had been held up by the thumb she was biting, dropped heavily. She stood over him, her eyes blazing insanely at him. She snatched out her hatpin, flung his coat and waistcoat from over his chest, felt for his heart. With the murderous eight inches of that slender steel poniard poised for the drive, she began to sob, flung the weapon away, took his face between her hands and kissed him.

"You fiend! You fiend!" she sobbed.

She changed to her plainest dress. Leaving the blood-stained blouse on the bed beside him where she had flung it down after tearing it off, she turned out the light, darted down stairs and into the street. At Times Square she took the Subway for the Bowery. To change one's world, one need not travel far in New York; the ocean is not so wide as is the gap between the Tenderloin and the lower East Side.

CHAPTER VIII

SHE had thought of escape daily, hourly almost, for nearly five months. She had advanced not an inch toward it; but she never for an instant lost hope. She believed in her destiny, felt with all the strength of her health and vitality that she had not yet found her place in the world, that she would find it, and that it would be high. Now—she was compelled to escape, and this with only seventeen dollars and in the little time that would elapse before Palmer returned to consciousness and started in pursuit, bent upon cruel and complete revenge. She changed to an express train at the Grand Central Subway station, left the express on impulse at Fourteenth Street, took a local to Astor Place, there ascended to the street.

She was far indeed from the Tenderloin, in a region not visited by the people she knew. As for Freddie, he never went below Fourteenth Street, hated the lower East Side, avoided anyone from that region of his early days, now shrouded in a mystery that would not be dispelled with his consent. Freddie would not think of searching for her there; and soon he would believe she was dead—drowned, and at the bottom of river or bay. As she stepped from the exit of the underground, she saw in the square before her, under the Sunset Cox statue, a Salvation Army corps holding a meeting. She heard a cry from the center of the crowd:

"The wages of sin is death!"

She drifted into the fringe of the crowd and glanced at the little group of exhorters and musicians. The woman who was preaching had taken the life of the streets as her text. Well fed and well clad and certain of a clean room to sleep in—certain of a good living, she was painting the moral horrors of the street life.

"The wages of sin is death!" she shouted.

She caught Susan's eye, saw the cynical-bitter smile round her lips. For Susan had the feeling that, unsuspected by the upper classes, animates the masses as to clergy and charity workers of all kinds—much the same feeling one would have toward the robber's messenger who came bringing from his master as a loving gift some worthless trifle from the stolen goods. Not from clergy, not from charity worker, not from the life of the poor as they take what is given them with hypocritical cringe and tear of thanks, will the upper classes get the truth as to what is thought of them by the masses in this day of awakening intelligence and slow heaving of crusts so long firm that they have come to be regarded as bed-rock of social foundation.

Cried the woman, in response to Susan's satirical look:

"You mock at that, my lovely young sister. Your lips are painted, and they sneer. But you know I'm right—yes, you show in your eyes that you know it in your aching heart! The wages of sin is *death!* Isn't that so, sister?"

Susan shook her head.

"Speak the truth, sister! God is watching you. The wages of sin is *death!*"

"The wages of weakness is death," retorted Susan. "But—the wages of sin—well, it's sometimes a house in Fifth Avenue."

And then she shrank away before the approving laughter of the little crowd and hurried across into Eighth Street. In the deep shadow of the front of Cooper Union she paused, as the meaning of her own impulsive words came to her. The wages of sin! And what was sin, the supreme sin, but weakness? It was exactly as Burlingham had explained. He had said that, whether for good or for evil, really to live one must be strong. Strong!

What a good teacher he had been—one of the rare kind that not only said things interestingly but also said them so that you never forgot. How badly she had learned!

She strolled on through Eighth Street, across Third Avenue and into Second Avenue. It was ten o'clock. The effects of the liquor she had drunk had worn away. In so much wandering she had acquired the habit of closing up an episode of life as a traveler puts behind him the railway journey at its end. She was less than half an hour from her life in the Tenderloin; it was as completely in her past as it would ever be. The cards had once more been shuffled; a new deal was on.

A new deal. What? To fly to another city—that meant another Palmer, or the miseries of the unprotected woman of the streets, or slavery to the madman of what the French with cruel irony call a *maison de joie.* To return to work— —

What was open to her, educated as the comfortable classes educate their women? Work meant the tenements. She loathed the fast life, but not as she loathed vermin-infected tenements. To toil all day at a monotonous task, the same task every day and all day long! To sleep at night with Tucker and the vermin! To her notion the sights and sounds and smells and personal contacts of the tenements were no less vicious; were—for her at least—far more degrading than anything in the Tenderloin and its like. And there she got money to buy whiskey that whirled her almost endurably, sometimes even gayly, over the worst things—money to buy hours, whole days of respite that could be spent in books, in dreams and plannings, in the freedom of a clean and comfortable room, or at the theater or concert. There were degrees in horror; she was paying a hateful price, but not so hateful as she had paid when she worked. The wages of shame were not so hard earned as the wages of toil, were larger, brought her many of the things she craved. The wages of toil brought her nothing but the right to bare existence in filth and depravity and darkness. Also, she felt that if she were tied down to some dull and exhausting employment, she would be settled and done for. In a few years she would be an old woman, with less wages or flung out diseased or maimed—to live on and on like hundreds of wretched old creatures adrift everywhere in the tenement streets. No, work had nothing to offer her except "respectability." And what a mocking was "respectability," in rags and filth! Besides, what had *she*, the outcast born, to do with this respectability?

No—not work—never again. So long as she was roving about, there was hope and chance somehow to break through into the triumphant class that ruled the world, that did the things worth while—wore the good clothes, lived in the good houses, ate the good food, basked in the sunshine of art.

Either she would soar above respectability, or she would remain beneath it. Respectability might be an excellent thing; surely there must be some merit in a thing about which there was so much talk, after which there was so much hankering, and to which there was such desperate clinging. But as a sole possession, as a sole ambition, it seemed thin and poor and even pitiful. She had emancipated herself from its tyranny; she would not resume the yoke. Among so many lacks of the good things of life its good would not be missed. Perhaps, when she had got a few other of the good things she might try to add it to them—or might find herself able to get comfortably along without it, as had George Eliot and Aspasia, George Sand and Duse and Bernhardt and so many of the world's company of self-elected women members of the triumphant class.

A new deal! And a new deal meant at least even chance for good luck.

As she drifted down the west side of Second Avenue, her thoughts so absorbed her that she was oblivious of the slushy sidewalk, even of the crossings where one had to pick one's way as through a shallow creek with stepping stones here and there. There were many women alone, as in every other avenue and every frequented cross street throughout the city—women made eager to desperation by the long stretch of impossible weather. Every passing man was hailed, sometimes boldly, sometimes softly. Again and again that grotesque phrase "Let's go have a good time" fell upon the ears. After several blocks, when her absent-mindedness had got her legs wet to the knees in the shallow shiny slush, she was roused by the sound of music—an orchestra playing and playing well a lively Hungarian dance. She was standing before the winter garden from which the sounds came. As she opened the door she was greeted by a rush of warm air pleasantly scented with fresh tobacco smoke, the odors of spiced drinks and of food, pastry predominating. Some of the tables were covered ready for those who would wish to eat; but many of them were for the drinkers. The large, low-ceilinged room was comfortably filled. There were but a few women and they seemed to be wives or sweethearts. Susan was about to retreat when a waiter—one of those Austrians whose heads end abruptly an inch or so above the eyebrows and whose chins soon shade off into neck—advanced smilingly with a polite, "We serve ladies without escorts."

She chose a table that had several other vacant tables round it. On the recommendation of the waiter she ordered a "burning devil"; he assured her she would find it delicious and the very thing for a cold slushy night. At the far end of the room on a low platform sat the orchestra. A man in an evening suit many sizes too large for him sang in a strong, not disagreeable tenor a German song that drew loud applause at the end of each stanza. The "burning devil" came—an almost black mixture in a large heavy glass. The waiter touched a match to it, and it was at once wreathed in pale flickering flames that hovered like butterflies, now rising as if to float away, now lightly descending to flit over the surface of the liquid or to dance along the edge of the glass.

"What shall I do with it?" said Susan.

"Wait till it goes out," said the waiter. "Then drink, as you would anything else." And he was off to attend to the wants of a group of card players a few feet away.

Susan touched her finger to the glass, when the flame suddenly vanished. She found it was not too hot to drink, touched her lips to it. The taste, sweetish, suggestive of coffee and of brandy and of burnt sugar, was agreeable. She slowly sipped it, delighting in the sensation of warmth, of comfort, of well being that speedily diffused through her. The waiter came to receive her thanks for his advice. She said to him:

"Do you have women sing, too?"

"Oh, yes—when we can find a good-looker with a voice. Our customers know music."

"I wonder if I could get a trial?"

The waiter was interested at once. "Perhaps. You sing?"

"I have sung on the stage."

"I'll ask the boss."

He went to the counter near the door where stood a short thick-set Jew of the East European snub-nosed type in earnest conversation with a seated blonde woman. She showed that skill at clinging to youth which among the lower middle and lower classes pretty clearly indicates at least some experience at the fast life. For only in the upper and upper middle class does a respectable woman venture thus to advertise so suspicious a guest within as a desire to be agreeable in the sight of men. Susan watched the waiter as he spoke to the proprietor, saw the proprietor's impatient shake of the head, sent out a wave of gratitude from her heart when her waiter friend persisted, compelled the proprietor to look toward her. She affected an air of unconsciousness; in fact, she was posing as if before a camera. Her heart leaped when out of the corner of her eye she saw the proprietor coming with the waiter. The two paused at her table, and the proprietor said in a sharp, impatient voice:

"Well, lady—what is it?"

"I want a trial as a singer."

The proprietor was scanning her features and her figure which was well displayed by the tight-fitting jacket. The result seemed satisfactory, for in a voice oily with the softening influence of feminine charm upon male, he said:

"You've had experience?"

"Yes—a lot of it. But I haven't sung in about two years."

"Sing German?"

"Only ballads in English. But I can learn anything."

"English'll do—if you can sing. What costume do you wear?"

And the proprietor seated himself and motioned the waiter away.

"I have no costume. As I told you, I've not been singing lately."

"We've got one that might fit—a short blue silk skirt—low neck and blue stockings. Slippers too, but they might be tight—I forget the number."

"I did wear threes. But I've done a great deal of walking. I wear a five now." Susan thrust out a foot and ankle, for she knew that despite the overshoe they were good to look at.

The proprietor nodded approvingly and there was the note of personal interest in his voice as he said: "They can try your voice tomorrow morning. Come at ten o'clock."

"If you decide to try me, what pay will I get?"

The proprietor smiled slyly. "Oh, we don't pay anything to the singers. That man who sang—he gets his board here. He works in a factory as a bookkeeper in the daytime. Lots of theatrical and musical people come here. If a man or a girl can do any stunt worth while, there's a chance."

"I'd have to have something more than board," said Susan.

The proprietor frowned down at his stubby fingers whose black and cracked nails were drumming on the table. "Well—I might give you a bed. There's a place I could put one in my daughter's room. She sings and dances over at Louis Blanc's garden in Third Avenue. Yes, I could put you there. But—no privileges, you understand."

"Certainly. . . . I'll decide tomorrow. Maybe you'll not want me."

"Oh, yes—if you can sing at all. Your looks'd please my customers." Seeing the dubious expression in Susan's face, he went on, "When I say 'no privilege' I mean only about the room. Of course, it's none of my business what you do outside. Lots of well fixed gents comes here. My girls have all had good luck. I've been open two years, and in that time one of my singers got an elegant delicatessen owner to keep her."

"Really," said Susan, in the tone that was plainly expected of her.

"Yes—an *elegant* gentleman. I'd not be surprised if he married her. And another married an electrician that cops out forty a week. You'll find it a splendid chance to make nice friends—good spenders. And I'm a practical man."

"I suppose there isn't any work I could do in the daytime?"

"Not here."

"Perhaps——"

"Not nowhere, so far as I know. That is, work you'd care to do. The factories and stores is hard on a woman, and she don't get much. And besides they ain't very classy to my notion. Of course, if a woman ain't got looks or sense or any tone to her, if she's satisfied to live in a bum tenement and marry some dub that can't make nothing, why, that's different. But you look like a woman that had been used to something and wanted to get somewhere. I wouldn't have let *my* daughter go into no such low, foolish life."

She had intended to ask about a place to stop for the night. She now decided that the suggestion that she was homeless might possibly impair her chances. After some further conversation—the proprietor repeating what he had already said, and repeating it in about the same language— she paid the waiter fifteen cents for the drink and a tip of five cents out of the change she had in her purse, and departed. It had clouded over, and a misty, dismal rain was trickling through the saturated air to add to the messiness of the churn of cold slush. Susan went on down Second Avenue. On a corner near its lower end she saw a Raines Law hotel with awnings, indicating that it was not merely a blind to give a saloon a hotel license but was actually open for business. She went into the "family" entrance of the saloon, was alone in a small clean sitting-room with a sliding window between it and the bar. A tough but not unpleasant young face appeared at the window. It was the bartender.

"Evening, cutie," said he. "What'll you have?"

"Some rye whiskey," replied Susan. "May I smoke a cigarette here?"

"Sure, go as far as you like. Ten-cent whiskey—or fifteen?"

"Fifteen—unless it's out of the same bottle as the ten."

"Call it ten—seeing as you are a lady. I've got a soft heart for you ladies. I've got a wife in the business, myself."

When he came in at the door with the drink, a young man followed him—a good-looking, darkish youth, well dressed in a ready made suit of the best sort. At second glance Susan saw that he was at least partly of Jewish blood, enough to elevate his face above the rather dull type which predominates among clerks and merchants of the Christian races. He had small, shifty eyes, an attractive smile, a manner of assurance bordering on insolence. He dropped into a chair at Susan's table with a, "You don't mind having a drink on me."

As Susan had no money to spare, she acquiesced. She said to the bartender, "I want to get a room here—a plain room. How much?"

"Maybe this gent'll help you out," said the bartender with a grin and a wink. "He's got money to burn—and burns it."

The bartender withdrew. The young man struck a match and held it for her to light the cigarette she took from her purse. Then he lit one himself. "Next time try one of mine," said he. "I get 'em of a fellow that makes for the swellest uptown houses. But I get 'em ten cents a package instead of forty. I haven't seen you down here before. What a good skin you've got! It's been a long time since I've seen a skin as fine as that, except on a baby now and then. And that shape of yours is all right, too. I suppose it's the real goods?"

With that he leaned across the table and put his hand upon her bosom. She drew back indifferently.

"You don't give anything for nothing—eh?" laughed he. "Been in the business long?"

"It seems long."

"It ain't what it used to be. The competition's getting to be something fierce. Looks as if all the respectable girls and most of the married women were coming out to look for a little extra money. Well—why not?"

Susan shrugged her shoulders. "Why not?" echoed she carelessly.

She did not look forward with pleasure to being alone. The man was clean and well dressed, and had an unusual amount of personal charm that softened his impertinence of manner. Evidently he has the habit of success with women. She much preferred him sitting with her to her own depressing society. So she accepted his invitation. She took one of his cigarettes, and it was as good as he had said. He rattled on, mingling frank coarse compliments with talk about "the business" from a standpoint so practical that she began to suspect he was somehow in it himself. He clearly belonged to those more intelligent children of the upper class tenement people, the children who are too bright and too well educated to become working men and working women like their parents; they refuse to do any kind of manual labor, as it could never in the most favorable circumstances pay well enough to give them the higher comforts they crave, the expensive comforts which every merchant is insistently and temptingly thrusting at a public for the most part too poor to buy; so these cleverer children of the working class develop into shyster lawyers, politicians, sports, prostitutes, unless chance throws into their way some respectable means of getting money. Vaguely she wondered—without caring to question or guess what particular form of activity this young man had taken in avoiding monotonous work at small pay.

After her second drink came she found that she did not want it. She felt tired and sleepy and wished to get her wet stockings off and to dry her skirt which, for all her careful holding up, had not escaped the fate of whatever was exposed to that abominable night. "I'm going along with you," said the young man as she rose. "Here's to our better acquaintance."

"Thanks, but I want to be alone," replied she affably. And, not to seem unappreciative of his courtesy, she took a small drink from her glass. It tasted very queer. She glanced suspiciously at the young man. Her legs grew suddenly and strangely heavy. Her heart began to beat violently, and a black fog seemed to be closing in upon her eyes. Through it she saw the youth grinning sardonically. And instantly she knew. "What a fool I am!" she thought.

She had been trapped by another form of the slave system. This man was a recruiting sergeant for houses of prostitution—was one of the "cadets." They search the tenement districts for good-looking girls and young women. They hang about the street corners, flirting. They attend the balls where go the young people of the lower middle class and upper lower class. They learn to make love seductively; they understand how to tempt a girl's longing for finery, for an easier life, her dream of a husband above her class in looks and in earning power. And for each recruit "broken in" and hardened to the point of willingness to go into a sporting house, they get from the proprietor ten to twenty-five dollars according to her youth and beauty. Susan knew all about the system, had heard stories of it from the lips of girls who had been embarked through it—embarked a little sooner than they would have embarked under the lash of want, or of that other and almost equally compelling brute, desire for the comforts and luxuries that mean decent living. Susan knew; yet here she was, because of an unguarded moment, and because of a sense of security through experience—here she was, succumbing to knockout drops as easily as the most innocent child lured away from its mother's door to get a saucer of ice cream! She tried to rise, to scream, though she knew any such effort was futile.

With a gasp and a sigh her head fell forward and she was unconscious.

She awakened in a small, rather dingy room. She was lying on her back with only stockings on. Beyond the foot of the bed was a little bureau at which a man, back full to her, stood in trousers and shirt sleeves tying his necktie. She saw that he was a rough looking man, coarsely dressed—an artisan or small shop-keeper. Used as she was to the profound indifference of men of all classes and degrees of education and intelligence to what the woman thought—used as she was to this sensual selfishness which men at least in part conceal from their respectable wives, Susan felt a horror of this man who had not minded her unconsciousness. Her head was aching so fiercely that she had not the courage to move. Presently the man turned toward her a kindly, bearded face. But she was used to the man of general good character who with little shame and no hesitation became beast before her, the free woman.

"Hello, pretty!" cried he, genially. "Slept off your jag, have you?"

He was putting on his coat and waistcoat. He took from the waistcoat pocket a dollar bill. "You're a peach," said he. "I'll come again, next time my old lady goes off guard." He made the bill into a pellet, dropped it on her breast. "A little present for you. Put it in your stocking and don't let the madam grab it."

With a groan Susan lifted herself to a sitting position, drew the spread about her—a gesture of instinct rather than of conscious modesty. "They drugged me and brought me here," said she. "I want you to help me get out."

"Good Lord!" cried the man, instantly all a-quiver with nervousness. "I'm a married man. I don't want to get mixed up in this." And out of the room he bolted, closing the door behind him.

Susan smiled at herself satirically. After all her experience, to make this silly appeal—she who knew men! "I must be getting feeble-minded," thought she. Then — —

Her clothes! With a glance she swept the little room. No closet! Her own clothes gone! On the chair beside the bed a fast-house parlor dress of pink cotton silk, and a kind of abbreviated chemise. The stockings on her legs were not her own, but were of pink cotton, silk finished. A pair of pink satin slippers stood on the floor beside the two galvanized iron wash basins.

The door opened and a burly man, dressed in cheap ready-made clothes but with an air of authority and prosperity, was smiling at her. "The madam told me to walk right in and make myself at home," said he. "Yes, you're up to her account of you. Only she said you were dead drunk and would probably be asleep. Now, honey, you treat me right and I'll treat you right."

"Get out of here!" cried Susan. "I'm going to leave this house. They drugged me and brought me here."

"Oh, come now. I've got nothing to do with your quarrels with the landlady. Cut those fairy tales out. You treat me right and — —"

A few minutes later in came the madam. Susan, exhausted, sick, lay inert in the middle of the bed. She fixed her gaze upon the eyes looking through the hideous mask of paint and powder partially concealing the madam's face.

"Well, are you going to be a good girl now?" said the madam.

"I want to sleep," said Susan.

"All right, my dear." She saw and snatched the five-dollar bill from the pillow. "It'll go toward paying your board and for the parlor dress. God, but you was drunk when they brought you up from the bar!"

"When was that?" asked Susan.

"About midnight. It's nearly four now. We've shut the house for the night. You're in a first-rate house, my dear, and if you behave yourself, you'll make money—a lot more than you ever could at a dive like Zeist's.

If you don't behave well, we'll teach you how. This building belongs to one of the big men in politics, and he looks after my interests—and he ought to, considering the rent I pay—five hundred a month—for the three upper floors. The bar's let separate. Would you like a nice drink?"

"No," said Susan. Trapped! Hopelessly trapped! And she would never escape until, diseased, her looks gone, ruined in body and soul, she was cast out into the hospital and the gutter.

"As I was saying," ventured the madam, "you might as well settle down quietly."

"I'm very well satisfied," said Susan. "I suppose you'll give me a square deal on what I make." She laughed quietly as if secretly amused at something. "In fact, I know you will," she added in a tone of amused confidence.

"As soon as you've paid up your twenty-five a week for room and board and the fifty for the parlor dress——"

Susan interrupted her with a laugh. "Oh, come off," said she.

"I'll not stand for that. I'll go back to Jim Finnegan."

The old woman's eyes pounced for her face instantly. "Do you know Finnegan?"

"I'm his girl," said Susan carelessly. She stretched herself and yawned. "I got mad at him and started out for some fun. He's a regular damn fool about me. But I'm sick of him. Anything but a jealous man! And spied on everywhere I go. How much can I make here?"

"Ain't you from Zeist's?" demanded the madam. Her voice was quivering with fright. She did not dare believe the girl; she did not dare disbelieve her.

"Zeist's? What's that?" said Susan indifferently.

"The joint two blocks down. Hasn't Joe Bishop had you in there for a couple of months?"

Susan yawned. "Lord, how my head does ache! Who's Joe Bishop? I'm dead to the world. I must have had an awful jag!" She turned on her side, drew the spread over her. "I want to sleep. So long!"

"Didn't you run away from home with Joe Bishop?" demanded the madam shrilly. "And didn't he put you to work for Zeist?"

"Who's Joe Bishop? Where's Zeist's?" Susan said, cross and yawning. "I've been with Jim about a year. He took me off the street. I was broke in five years ago."

The madam gave a kind of howl. "And that Joe Bishop got twenty-five off me!" she screamed. "And you're Finnegan's girl, and he'll make trouble for me."

"He's got a nasty streak in him," said Susan, drowsily. "He put me on the Island once for a little side trip I made." She laughed, yawned. "But he sent and got me out in two days—and gave me a present of a hundred. It's funny how a man'll make a fool of himself about a woman. Put out the light."

"No, I won't put out the light," shrieked the madam. "You can't work here. I'm going to telephone Jim Finnegan to come and get you."

Susan started up angrily, as if she were half-crazed by drink. "If you do, you old hag," she cried, "I'll tell him you doped me and set these men on me. I'll tell him about Joe Bishop. And Jim'll send the whole bunch of you to the pen. I'll not go back to him till I get good and ready. And that means, I won't go back at all, no matter what he offers me." She began to cry in a maudlin way. "I hate him. I'm tired of living as if I was back in the convent."

The madam stood, heaving to and fro and blowing like a chained elephant. "I don't know what to do," she whined. "I wish Joe Bishop was in hell."

"I'm going to get out of here," shrieked Susan, raving and blazing again and waving her arms. "You don't know a good thing when you get it. What kind of a bum joint is this, anyway? Where's my clothes? They must be dry by this time."

"Yes—yes—they're dry, my dear," whined the madam. "I'll bring 'em to you."

And out she waddled, returning in a moment with her arms full of the clothing. She found Susan in the bed and nestling comfortably into the pillows. "Here are your clothes," she cried.

"No—I want to sleep," was Susan's answer in a cross, drowsy tone. "I think I'll stay. You won't telephone Jim. But when he finds me, I'll tell him to go to the devil."

"For God's sake!" wailed the madam. "I can't let you work here. You don't want to ruin me, do you?"

Susan sat up, rubbed her eyes, yawned, brushed her hair back, put a sly, smiling look into her face. "How much'll you give me to go?" she asked. "Where's the fifteen that was in my stocking?"

"I've got it for you," said the madam.

"How much did I make tonight?"

"There was three at five apiece."

Three!—not only the two, but a third while she lay in a dead stupor. Susan shivered.

"Your share's four dollars," continued the madam.

"Is that all!" cried Susan, jeering. "A bum joint! Oh, there's my five the man gave me as a present."

"Yes—yes," quavered the madam.

"And another man gave me a dollar." She looked round. "Where the devil is it?" She found it in a fold of the spread. "Then you owe me twenty altogether, counting the money I had on me." She yawned. "I don't want to go!" she protested, pausing halfway in taking off the second pink stocking. Then she laughed. "Lord, what hell Jim will raise if he finds I spent the night working in this house. Why is it that, as soon as men begin to care for a woman, they get prim about her?"

"Do get dressed, dear," wheedled the madam.

"I don't see why I should go at this time of night," objected Susan pettishly. "What'll you give me if I go?"

The madam uttered a groan.

"You say you paid Joe Bishop twenty-five——"

"I'll kill him!" shrieked the madam. "He's ruined me—ruined me!"

"Oh, he's all right," said Susan cheerfully. "I like him. He's a pretty little fellow. I'll not give him away to Jim."

"Joe was dead stuck on you," cried the madam eagerly. "I might 'a' knowed he hadn't seen you before. I had to pay him the twenty-five right away, to get him out of the house and let me put you to work. He wanted to stay on."

Susan shivered, laughed to hide it. "Well, I'll go for twenty-five."

"Twenty-five!" shrieked the madam.

"You'll get it back from Joe."

"Maybe I won't. He's a dog—a dirty dog."

"I think I told Joe about Jim," said Susan reflectively. "I was awful gabby downstairs. Yes—I told him."

And her lowered eyes gleamed with satisfaction when the madam cried out: "You did! And after that he brought you here! He's got it in for me. But I'll ruin him! I'll tear him up!"

Susan dressed with the utmost deliberation, the madam urging her to make haste. After some argument, Susan yielded to the madam's pleadings and contented herself with the twenty dollars. The madam herself escorted Susan down to the outside door and slathered her with sweetness and politeness. The rain had stopped again. Susan went up Second Avenue slowly. Two blocks from the dive from which she had escaped, she sank down on a stoop and fainted.

CHAPTER IX

THE dash of cold rain drops upon her face and the chill of moisture soaking through her clothing revived her. Throughout the whole range of life, whenever we resist we suffer. As Susan dragged her aching, cold wet body up from that stoop, it seemed to her that each time she resisted the penalty grew heavier. Could she have been more wretched had she remained in that dive? From her first rebellion that drove her out of her uncle's house had she ever bettered herself by resisting? She had gone from bad to worse, from worse to worst.

Worst? "This *must* be the worst!" she thought. "Surely there can be no lower depth than where I am now." And then she shuddered and her soul reeled. Had she not thought this at each shelf of the precipice down which she had been falling? "Has it a bottom? Is there no bottom?"

Wet through, tired through, she put up her umbrella and forced herself feebly along. "Where am I going? Why do I not kill myself? What is it that drives me on and on?"

There came no direct answer to that last question. But up from those deep vast reservoirs of vitality that seemed sufficient whatever the drain upon them—up from those reservoirs welled strength and that unfaltering will to live which breathes upon the corpse of hope and quickens it. And she had a sense of an invisible being, a power that had her in charge, a destiny, walking beside her, holding up her drooping strength, compelling her toward some goal hidden in the fog and the storm.

At Eighth Street she turned west; at Third Avenue she paused, waiting for chance to direct her. Was it not like the maliciousness of fate that in the city whose rarely interrupted reign of joyous sunshine made her call it the city of the Sun her critical turn of chance should have fallen in foul weather? Evidently fate was resolved on a thorough test of her endurance. In the open square, near the Peter Cooper statue, stood a huge all-night lunch wagon. She moved toward it, for she suddenly felt hungry. It was drawn to the curb; a short flight of ladder steps led to an interior attractive to sight and smell. She halted at the foot of the steps and looked in. The only occupant was the man in charge. In a white coat he was leaning upon the counter, reading a newspaper which lay flat upon it. His bent head was extensively and roughly thatched with black hair so thick that to draw a comb through it would have been all but impossible. As Susan let down her umbrella and began to ascend, he lifted his head and gave her a full view of a humorous young face, bushy of eyebrows and mustache and darkly stained by his beard, close shaven though it was. He looked like a Spaniard or an Italian, but he was a black Irishman, one of the West coasters who recall in their eyes and coloring the wrecking of the Armada.

"Good morning, lady," said he. "Breakfast or supper?"

"Both," replied Susan. "I'm starved."

The air was gratefully warm in the little restaurant on wheels. The dominant odor was of hot coffee; but that aroma was carried to a still higher delight by a suggestion of pastry. "The best thing I've got," said the restaurant man, "is hot corn beef hash. It's so good I hate to let any of it go. You can have griddle cakes, too—and coffee, of course."

"Very well," said Susan.

She was ascending upon a wave of reaction from the events of the night. Her headache had gone. The rain beating upon the roof seemed musical to her now, in this warm shelter with its certainty of the food she craved.

The young man was busy at the shiny, compact stove; the odors of the good things she was presently to have grew stronger and stronger, stimulating her hunger, bringing joy to her heart and a smile to her eyes. She wondered at herself. After what she had passed through, how could she feel thus happy—yes, positively happy? It seemed to her this was an indication of a lack in her somewhere—of seriousness, of sensibility, of she knew not what. She ought to be ashamed of that lack. But she was not ashamed. She was shedding her troubles like a child—or like a philosopher.

"Do you like hash?" inquired the restaurant man over his shoulder.

"Just as you're making it," said she. "Dry but not too dry. Brown but not too brown."

"You don't think you'd like a poached egg on top of it?"

"Exactly what I want!"

"It isn't everybody that can poach an egg," said the restaurant man. "And it isn't every egg that can be poached. Now, my eggs are the real thing. And I can poach 'em so you'd think they was done with one of them poaching machines. I don't have 'em with the yellow on a slab of white. I do it so that the white's all round the yellow, like in the shell. And I keep 'em tender, too. Did you say one egg or a pair?"

"Two," said Susan.

The dishes were thick, but clean and whole. The hash—"dry but not too dry, brown but not too brown"—was artistically arranged on its platter, and the two eggs that adorned its top were precisely as he had promised. The coffee, boiled with the milk, was real coffee, too. When the restaurant man had set these things before her, as she sat expectant on a stool, he viewed his handiwork with admiring eyes.

"Delmonico couldn't beat it," said he. "No, nor Oscar, neither. That'll take the tired look out of your face, lady, and bring the beauty back."

Susan ate slowly, listening to the music of the beating rain. It was like an oasis, a restful halt between two stretches of desert journey; she wished to make it as long as possible. Only those who live exposed to life's buffetings ever learn to enjoy to the full the great little pleasures of life—the halcyon pauses in the storms—the few bright rays through the break in the clouds, the joy of food after hunger, of a bath after days of privation, of a jest or a smiling face or a kind word or deed after darkness and bitterness and contempt. She saw the restaurant man's eyes on her, a curious expression in them.

"What's the matter?" she inquired.

"I was thinking," said he, "how miserable you must have been to be so happy now."

"Oh, I guess none of us has any too easy a time," said she.

"But it's mighty hard on women. I used to think different, before I had bad luck and got down to tending this lunch wagon. But now I understand about a lot of things. It's all very well for comfortable people to talk about what a man or a woman ought to do and oughtn't to do. But let 'em be slammed up against it. They'd sing a different song—wouldn't they?"

"Quite different," said Susan.

The man waved a griddle spoon. "I tell you, we do what we've got to do. Yes—the thieves and—and—all of us. Some's used for foundations and some for roofing and some for inside fancy work and some for outside wall. And some's used for the rubbish heap. But all's used. They do what they've got to do. I was a great hand at worrying what I was going to be used for. But I don't bother about it any more." He began to pour the griddle cake dough. "I think I'll get there, though," said he doggedly, as if he expected to be derided for vanity.

"You will," said Susan.

"I'm twenty-nine. But I've been being got ready for something. They don't chip away at a stone as they have at me without intending to make some use of it."

"No, indeed," said the girl, hope and faith welling up in her own heart.

"And what's more, I've stood the chipping. I ain't become rubbish; I'm still a good stone. That's promising, ain't it?"

"It's a sure sign," declared Susan. Sure for herself, no less than for him.

The restaurant man took from under the counter several well-worn schoolbooks. He held them up, looked at Susan and winked. "Good business—eh?"

She laughed and nodded. He put the books back under the counter, finished the cakes and served them. As he gave her more butter he said:

"It ain't the best butter—not by a long shot. But it's good—as good as you get on the average farm—or better. Did you ever eat the best butter?"

"I don't know. I've had some that was very good."

"Eighty cents a pound?"

"Mercy, no," exclaimed Susan.

"Awful price, isn't it? But worth the money—yes, sir! Some time when you've got a little change to spare, go get half a pound at one of the swell groceries or dairies. And the best milk, too. Twelve cents a quart. Wait till I get money. I'll show 'em how to live. I was born in a tenement. Never had nothing. Rags to wear, and food one notch above a garbage barrel."

"I know," said Susan.

"But even as a boy I wanted the high-class things. It's wanting the best that makes a man push his way up."

Another customer came—a keeper of a butcher shop, on his way to market. Susan finished the cakes, paid the forty cents and prepared to depart. "I'm looking for a hotel," said she to the restaurant man, "one where they'll take me in at this time, but one that's safe not a dive."

"Right across the square there's a Salvation Army shelter—very good—clean. I Don't know of any other place for a lady."

"There's a hotel on the next corner," put in the butcher, suspending the violent smacking and sipping which attended his taking rolls and coffee. "It ain't neither the one thing nor the other. It's clean and cheap, and they'll let you behave if you want to."

"That's all I ask," said the girl. "Thank you." And she departed, after an exchange of friendly glances with the restaurant man. "I feel lots better," said she.

"It was a good breakfast," replied he.

"That was only part. Good luck!"

"Same to you, lady. Call again. Try my chops."

At the corner the butcher had indicated Susan found the usual Raines Law hotel, adjunct to a saloon and open to all comers, however "transient." But she took the butcher's word for it, engaged a dollar-and-a-half room from the half-asleep clerk, was shown to it by a colored bellboy who did not bother to wake up. It was a nice little room with barely space enough for a bed, a bureau, a stationary washstand, a chair and a small radiator. As she undressed by the light of a sad gray dawn, she examined her dress to see how far it needed repair and how far it might be repaired. She had worn away from Forty-third Street her cheapest dress because it happened to be of an inconspicuous blue. It was one of those suits that look fairly well at a glance on the wax figure in the department store window, that lose their bloom as quickly as a country bride, and at the fourth or fifth wearing begin to make frank and sweeping confession of the cheapness of every bit of the material and labor that went into them. These suits are typical of all that poverty compels upon the poor, all that they in their ignorance and inexperience of values accept without complaint, fancying they are getting money's worth and never dreaming they are more extravagant than the most prodigal of the rich. However, as their poverty gives them no choice, their ignorance saves them from futilities of angry discontent. Susan had bought this dress because she had to have another dress and could not afford to spend more than twelve dollars, and it had been marked down from twenty-five. She had worn it in fair weather and had contrived to keep it looking pretty well. But this rain had finished it quite. Thereafter, until she could get another dress, she must expect to be classed as poor and seedy—therefore, on the way toward deeper poverty—therefore, an object of pity and of prey. If she went into a shop, she would be treated insultingly by the shopgirls, despising her as a poor creature like themselves. If a man approached her, he would calculate upon getting her very cheap because a girl in such a costume could not have been in the habit of receiving any great sum. And if she went with him, he would treat her with far less consideration than if she had been about the same business in smarter attire. She spread the dress on bureau and chair, smoothing it, wiping the mud stains from it. She washed out her stockings at the stationary stand, got them as dry as her remarkably strong hands could wring them, hung them on a rung of the chair near the hot little radiator. She cleaned her boots and overshoes with an old newspaper she found in a drawer, and wet at the washstand. She took her hat to pieces and made it over into something that looked almost fresh enough to be new. Then, ready for bed, she got the office of the hotel on the telephone and left a call for half-past nine o'clock—three hours and a half away. When she was throwing up the window, she glanced into the street.

The rain had once more ceased. Through the gray dimness the men and women, boys and girls, on the way to the factories and shops for the day's work, were streaming past in funereal procession. Some of the young ones were lively. But the mass was sullen and dreary. Bodies wrecked or rapidly wrecking by ignorance of hygiene, by the foul air and foul food of the tenements, by the monotonous toil of factory and shop—mindless toil—toil that took away mind and put in its place a distaste for all improvement— toil of the factories that distorted the body and enveloped the soul in sodden stupidity—toil of the shops that meant breathing bad air all day long, meant stooped shoulders and varicose veins in the legs and the arches of the insteps broken down, meant dull eyes, bad skin, female complaints, meant the breeding of desires for the luxury the shops display, the breeding of envy and servility toward those able to buy these luxuries.

Susan lingered, fascinated by this exhibit of the price to the many of civilization for the few. Work? Never! Not any more than she would. "Work" in a dive! Work—either branch of it, factory and shop or dive meant the sale of all the body and all the soul; her profession—at least as she practiced it—meant that perhaps she could buy with part of body and part of soul the privilege of keeping the rest of both for her own self. If she had stayed on at work from the beginning in Cincinnati, where would she be now? Living in some stinking tenement hole, with hope dead. And how would she be looking? As dull of eye as the rest, as pasty and mottled of skin, as ready for any chance disease. Work? Never! Never! "Not at anything that'd degrade me more than this life. Yes—more." And she lifted her head defiantly. To her hunger Life was thus far offering only a plate of rotten apples; it was difficult to choose among them—but there was choice.

She was awakened by the telephone bell; and it kept on ringing until she got up and spoke to the office through the sender. Never had she so craved sleep; and her mental and physical contentment of three hours and a half before had been succeeded by headache, a general soreness, a horrible attack of the blues. She grew somewhat better, however, as she washed first in hot water, then in cold at the stationary stand which was quite as efficient if not so luxurious as a bathtub. She dressed in a rush, but not so hurriedly that she failed to make the best toilet the circumstances permitted. Her hair went up unusually well; the dress did not look so badly as she had feared it would. "As it's a nasty day," she reflected, "it won't do me so much damage. My hat and my boots will make them give me the benefit of the doubt and think I'm saving my good clothes."

She passed through the office at five minutes to ten. When she reached Lange's winter garden, its clock said ten minutes past ten, but she knew it must be fast. Only one of the four musicians had arrived—the man who played the drums, cymbals, triangle and xylophone—a fat, discouraged old man who knew how easily he could be replaced. Neither Lange nor his wife had come; her original friend, the Austrian waiter, was wiping off tables and cleaning match stands. He welcomed her with a smile of delight that showed how few teeth remained in the front of his mouth and how deeply yellow they were. But Susan saw only his eyes—and the kind heart that looked through them.

"Maybe you haven't had breakfast already?" he suggested.

"I'm not hungry, thank you."

"Perhaps some coffee—yes?"

Susan thought the coffee would make her feel better. So he brought it—Vienna fashion—an open china pot full of strong, deliciously aromatic black coffee, a jug of milk with whipped white of egg on top, a basket of small sweet rolls powdered with sugar and caraway seed. She ate one of the rolls, drank the coffee. Before she had finished, the waiter stood beaming before her and said:

"A cigarette—yes?"

"Oh, no," replied Susan, a little sadly.

"But yes," urged he. "It isn't against the rules. The boss's wife smokes. Many ladies who come here do—real ladies. It is the custom in Europe. Why not?" And he produced a box of cigarettes and put it on the table. Susan lit one of them and once more with supreme physical content came a cheerfulness that put color and sprightliness into the flowers of hope. And the sun had won its battle with the storm; the storm was in retreat. Sunshine was streaming in at the windows, into her heart. The waiter paused in his work now and then to enjoy himself in contemplating the charming picture she made. She was thinking of what the wagon restaurant man had said. Yes, Life had been chipping away at her; but she had remained good stone, had not become rubbish.

About half-past ten Lange came down from his flat which was overhead. He inspected her by daylight and finding that his electric light impressions were not delusion was highly pleased with her. He refused to allow her to pay for the coffee. "Johann!" he called, and the leader of the orchestra approached and made a respectful bow to his employer. He had a solemn pompous air and the usual pompadour. He and Susan plunged into the music question, found that the only song they both knew was Tosti's "Good Bye."

"That'll do to try," said Lange. "Begin!"

And after a little tuning and voice testing, Susan sang the "Good Bye" with full orchestra accompaniment. It was not good; it was not even pretty good; but it was not bad. "You'll do all right," said Lange. "You can stay. Now, you and Johann fix up some songs and get ready for tonight." And he turned away to buy supplies for restaurant and bar.

Johann, deeply sentimental by nature, was much pleased with Susan's contralto. "You do not know how to sing," said he. "You sing in your throat and you've got all the faults of parlor singers. But the voice is there—and much expressiveness—much temperament. Also, you have intelligence— and that will make a very little voice go a great way."

Before proceeding any further with the rehearsal, he took Susan up to a shop where sheet music was sold and they selected three simple songs: "Gipsy Queen," "Star of My Life" and "Love in Dreams." They were to try "Gipsy Queen" that night, with "Good Bye" and, if the applause should compel, "Suwanee River."

When they were back at the restaurant Susan seated herself in a quiet corner and proceeded to learn the words of the song and to get some notion of the tune.

She had lunch with Mr. and Mrs. Lange and Katy, whose hair was very golden indeed and whose voice and manner proclaimed the Bowery and its vaudeville stage. She began by being grand with Susan, but had far too good a heart and far too sensible a nature to keep up long. It takes more vanity, more solemn stupidity and more leisure than plain people have time for, to maintain the force of fake dignity. Before lunch was over it was Katy and Lorna; and Katy was distressed that her duties at the theater made it impossible for her to stay and help Lorna with the song.

At the afternoon rehearsal Susan distinguished herself. To permit business in the restaurant and the rehearsal at the same time, there was a curtain to divide the big room into two unequal parts. When Susan sang her song through for the first time complete, the men smoking and drinking on the other side of the curtain burst into applause. Johann shook hands with Susan, shook hands again, kissed her hand, patted her shoulder. But in the evening things did not go so well.

Susan, badly frightened, got away from the orchestra, lagged when it speeded to catch up with her. She made a pretty and engaging figure in the costume, low in the neck and ending at the knees. Her face and shoulders, her arms and legs, the lines of her slender, rounded body made a success. But they barely saved her from being laughed at. When she finished, there was no applause so no necessity for an encore. She ran upstairs, and, with nerves all a-quiver, hid herself in the little room she and Katy were to share. Until she failed she did not realize how much she had staked upon this venture. But now she knew; and it seemed to her that her only future was the streets. Again her chance had come; again she had thrown it away. If there were anything in her—anything but mere vain hopes—that could not have occurred. In her plight anyone with a spark of the divinity that achieves success would have scored. "I belong in the streets," said she. Before dinner she had gone out and had bought a ninety-five cent night-dress and some toilet articles. These she now bundled together again. She changed to her street dress; she stole down the stairs.

She was out at the side door, she was flying through the side street toward the Bowery. "Hi!" shouted someone behind her. "Where you going?" And overtaking her came her staunch friend Albert, the waiter. Feeling that she must need sympathy and encouragement, he had slipped away from his duties to go up to her. He had reached the hall in time to see what she was about and had darted bareheaded after her.

"Where you going?" he repeated, excitedly.

A crowd began to gather. "Oh, good-by," she cried. "I'm getting out before I'm told to go—that's all. I made a failure. Thank you, Albert." She put out her hand; she was still moving and looking in the direction of the Bowery.

"Now you mustn't be foolish,", said he, holding on tightly to her hand. "The boss says it's all right. Tomorrow you do better."

"I'd never dare try again."

"Tomorrow makes everything all right. You mustn't act like a baby. The first time Katy tried, they yelled her off the stage. Now she gets eleven a week. Come back right away with me. The boss'd be mad if you won't. You ain't acting right, Miss Lorna. I didn't think you was such a fool."

He had her attention now. Unmindful of the little crowd they had gathered, they stood there discussing until to save Albert from pneumonia she returned with him. He saw her started up the stairs, then ventured to take his eye off her long enough to put his head into the winter garden and send a waiter for Lange. He stood guard until Lange came and was on his way to her.

The next evening, a Saturday, before a crowded house she sang well, as well as she had ever sung in her life—sang well enough to give her beauty of face and figure, her sweetness, her charm the opportunity to win a success. She had to come back and sing "Suwanee River." She had to come for a second encore; and, flushed with her victory over her timidity, she sang Tosti's sad cry of everlasting farewell with all the tenderness there was in her. That song exactly fitted her passionate, melancholy voice; its words harmonized with the deep sadness that was her real self, that is the real self of every sensitive soul this world has ever tried with its exquisite torments for flesh and spirit. The tears that cannot be shed were in her voice, in her face, as she stood there, with her violet-gray eyes straining into vacancy. But the men and the women shed tears; and when she moved, breaking the spell of silence, they not only applauded, they cheered.

The news quickly spread that at Lange's there was a girl singer worth hearing and still more worth looking at. And Lange had his opportunity to arrive.

But several things stood in his way, things a man of far more intelligence would have found it hard to overcome.

Like nearly all saloon-keepers, he was serf to a brewery; and the particular brewery whose beer his mortgage compelled him to push did not make a beer that could be pushed. People complained that it had a disagreeably bitter aftertaste. In the second place, Mrs. Lange was a born sitter. She had married to rest—and she was resting. She was always piled upon a chair. Thus, she was not an aid but a hindrance, an encourager of the help in laziness and slovenliness. Again, the cooking was distinctly bad; the only really good thing the house served was coffee, and that was good only in the mornings. Finally, Lange was a saver by nature and not a spreader. He could hold tightly to any money he closed his stubby fingers upon; he did not know how to plant money and make it grow, but only how to hoard.

Thus it came to pass that, after the first spurt, the business fell back to about where it had been before Susan came. Albert, the Austrian waiter, explained to Susan why it was that her popularity did the house apparently so little good—explained with truth where she suspected kind-hearted plotting, that she had arrested its latterly swift-downward slide. She was glad to hear what he had to say, as it was most pleasant to her vanity; but she could not get over the depression of the central fact—she was not making the sort of business to justify asking Lange for more than board and lodging; she was not in the way of making the money that was each day more necessary, as her little store dwindled.

The question of getting money to live on is usually dismissed in a princely way by writers about human life. It is in reality, except with the few rich, the ever-present question—as ever-present as the necessity of breathing—and it is not, like breathing, a matter settled automatically. It dominates thought; it determines action. To leave it out of account ever, in writing a human history, is to misrepresent and distort as utterly as would a portrait painter who neglected to give his subject eyes, or a head, even. With the overwhelming mass of us, money is at all times all our lives long the paramount question—for to be without it is destruction worse than death, and we are almost all perilously near to being without it. Thus, airily to pass judgment upon men and women as to their doings in getting money for necessaries, for what the compulsion of custom and habit has made necessaries to them—airily to judge them for their doings in such dire straits is like sitting calmly on shore and criticizing the conduct of passengers and sailors in a storm-beset sinking ship. It is one of the favorite pastimes of the comfortable classes; it makes an excellent impression as to one's virtue upon one's audience; it gives us a pleasing sense of superior delicacy and humor. But it is none the less mean and ridiculous. Instead of condemnation, the world needs to bestir itself to remove the stupid and cruel creatures that make evil conduct necessary; for can anyone, not a prig, say that the small part of the human race that does well does so because it is naturally better than the large part that does ill?

Spring was slow in opening. Susan's one dress was in a deplorable state. The lining hung in rags. The never good material was stretched out of shape, was frayed and worn gray in spots, was beyond being made up as presentable by the most careful pressing and cleaning. She had been forced to buy a hat, shoes, underclothes. She had only three dollars and a few cents left, and she simply did not dare lay it all out in dress materials. Yet, less than all would not be enough; all would not be enough.

Lange had from time to time more than hinted at the opportunities she was having as a public singer in his hall. But Susan, for all her experience, had remained one of those upon whom such opportunities must be thrust if they are to be accepted.

So long as she had food and shelter, she could not make advances; she could not even go so far as passive acquiescence. She knew she was again violating the fundamental canon of success; whatever one's business, do it thoroughly if at all. But she could not overcome her temperament which had at this feeble and false opportunity at once resented itself. She knew perfectly that therein was the whole cause of her failure to make the success she ought to have made when she came up from the tenements, and again when she fell into the clutches of Freddie Palmer. But it is one thing to know; it is another thing to do. Susan ignored the attempts of the men; she pretended not to understand Lange when they set him on to intercede with her for them. She saw that she was once more drifting to disaster—and that she had not long to drift. She was exasperated against herself; she was disgusted with herself. But she drifted on.

Growing seedier looking every day, she waited, defying the plain teachings of experience. She even thought seriously of going to work. But the situation in that direction remained unchanged. She was seeing things, the reasons for things, more clearly now, as experience developed her mind. She felt that to get on in respectability she ought to have been either more or less educated. If she had been used from birth to conditions but a step removed from savagery, she might have been content with what offered, might even have felt that she was rising. Or if she had been bred to a good trade, and educated only to the point where her small earnings could have satisfied her desires, then she might have got along in respectability. But she had been bred a "lady"; a Chinese woman whose feet have been bound from babyhood until her fifteenth or sixteenth year—how long it would be, after her feet were freed, before she could learn to walk at all!—and would she ever be able to learn to walk well?

What is luxury for one is squalor for another; what is elevation for one degrades another. In respectability she could not earn what was barest necessity for her—what she was now getting at Lange's—decent shelter, passable food. Ejected from her own class that shelters its women and brings them up in unfitness for the unsheltered life, she was dropping as all such women must and do drop—was going down, down, down—striking on this ledge and that, and rebounding to resume her ever downward course.

She saw her own plight only too vividly. Those whose outward and inward lives are wide apart get a strong sense of dual personality. It was thus with Susan. There were times when she could not believe in the reality of her external life.

She often glanced through the columns on columns, pages on pages of "want ads" in the papers—not with the idea of answering them, for she had served her apprenticeship at that, but simply to force herself to realize vividly just how matters stood with her. Those columns and pages of closely printed offerings of work! Dreary tasks, all of them—tasks devoid of interest, of personal sense of usefulness, tasks simply to keep degrading soul in degenerating body, tasks performed in filthy factories, in foul-smelling workrooms and shops, in unhealthful surroundings. And this, throughout civilization, was the "honest work" so praised—by all who don't do it, but live pleasantly by making others do it. Wasn't there something in the ideas of Etta's father, old Tom Brashear? Couldn't sensible, really loving people devise some way of making most tasks less repulsive, of lessening the burdens of those tasks that couldn't be anything but repulsive? Was this stupid system, so cruel, so crushing, and producing at the top such absurd results as flashy, insolent autos and silly palaces and overfed, overdressed women, and dogs in jeweled collars, and babies of wealth brought up by low menials—was this system really the best?

"If they'd stop canting about 'honest work' they might begin to get somewhere."

In the effort to prevent her downward drop from beginning again she searched all the occupations open to her. She could not find one that would not have meant only the most visionary prospect of some slight remote advancement, and the certain and speedy destruction of what she now realized was her chief asset and hope—her personal appearance. And she resolved that she would not even endanger it ever again. The largest part of the little capital she took away from Forty-third Street had gone to a dentist who put in several fillings of her back teeth. She had learned to value every charm—hair, teeth, eyes, skin, figure, hands. She watched over them all, because she felt that when her day finally came—and come it would, she never allowed long to doubt—she must be ready to enter fully into her own. Her day! The day when fate should change the life her outward self would be compelled to live, would bring it into harmony with the life of inward self—the self she could control.

Katy had struck up a friendship at once profitable and sentimental with her stage manager. She often stayed out all night. On one of these nights Susan, alone in the tiny room and asleep, was roused by feeling hands upon her. She started up half awake and screamed.

"Sh!" came in Lange's voice. "It's me."

Susan had latterly observed sly attempts on his part to make advances without his wife and daughter's suspecting; but she had thought her way of quietly ignoring was effective. "You must go," she whispered. "Mrs. Lange must have heard."

"I had to come," said he hoarsely, a mere voice in the darkness. "I can't hold out no longer without you, Lorna."

"Go—go," urged Susan.

But it was too late. In the doorway, candle in hand, appeared Mrs. Lange. Despite her efforts at "dressiness" she was in her best hour homely and nearly shapeless. In night dress and released from corsets she was hideous and monstrous. "I thought so!" she shrieked. "I thought so!"

"I heard a burglar, mother," whined Lange, an abject and guilty figure.

"Shut your mouth, you loafer!" shrieked Mrs. Lange. And she turned to Susan. "You gutter hussy, get on your clothes and clear out!"

"But—Mrs. Lange——" began Susan.

"Clear out!" she shouted, opening the outer hall. "Dress mighty damn quick and clear out!"

"Mother, you'll wake the people upstairs," pleaded Lange—and Susan had never before realized how afraid of his wife the little man was. "For God's sake, listen to sense."

"After I've thrown you—into the streets," cried his wife, beside herself with jealous fury. "Get dressed, I tell you!" she shouted at Susan.

And the girl hurried into her clothes, making no further attempt to speak. She knew that to plead and to explain would be useless; even if Mrs. Lange believed, still she would drive from the house the temptation to her husband. Lange, in a quaking, cowardly whine, begged his wife to be sensible and believe his burglar story. But with each half-dozen words he uttered, she interrupted to hurl obscene epithets at him or at Susan. The tenants of the upstairs flats came down. She told her wrongs to a dozen half-clad men, women and children; they took her side at once, and with the women leading showered vile insults upon Susan. The uproar was rising, rising. Lange cowered in a corner, crying bitterly like a whipped child. Susan, only partly dressed, caught up her hat and rushed into the hall. Several women struck at her as she passed. She stumbled on the stairs, almost fell headlong. With the most frightful words in tenement house vocabulary pursuing her she fled into the street, and did not pause until she was within a few yards of the Bowery. There she sat down on a doorstep and, half-crazed by the horror of her sudden downfall, laced her shoes and buttoned her blouse and put on her hat with fumbling, shaking fingers. It had all happened so quickly that she would have thought she was dreaming but for the cold night air and the dingy waste of the Bowery with the streetwalkers and drunken bums strolling along under the elevated tracks. She had trifled with the opportunity too long. It had flown in disgust, dislodging her as it took flight. If she would be over nice and critical, would hesitate to take the only upward path fate saw fit to offer, then—let her seek the bottom! Susan peered down, and shuddered.

She went into the saloon at the corner, into the little back room. She poured down drink after drink of the frightful poison sold as whiskey with the permission of a government owned by every interest that can make big money out of a race of free men and so can afford to pay big bribes. It is characteristic of this poison of the saloon of the tenement quarter that it produces in anyone who drinks it a species of quick insanity, of immediate degeneration—a desire to commit crime, to do degraded acts. Within an hour of Susan's being thrown into the streets, no one would have recognized her. She had been drinking, had been treating the two faded but young and decently dressed streetwalkers who sat at another table. The three, fired and maddened by the poison, were amusing themselves and two young men as recklessly intoxicated as they. Susan, in an attitude she had seen often enough but had never dreamed of taking, was laughing wildly at a coarse song, was standing up, skirts caught high and body swaying in drunken rhythm as she led the chorus.

When the barkeeper announced closing time, one of the young men said to her:

"Which way?"

"To hell," laughed she. "I've been thrown out everywhere else.
Want to go along?"

"I'll never desert a perfect lady," replied he.

CHAPTER X

SHE was like one who has fallen bleeding and broken into a cave; who after a time gathers himself together and crawls toward a faint and far distant gleam of light; who suddenly sees the light no more and at the same instant lurches forward and down into a deeper chasm.

Occasionally sheer exhaustion of nerves made it impossible for her to drink herself again into apathy before the effects of the last doses of the poison had worn off. In these intervals of partial awakening—she never permitted them to lengthen out, as such sensation as she had was of one falling—falling—through empty space—with whirling brain and strange sounds in the ears and strange distorted sights or hallucinations before the eyes—falling down—down—whither?—to how great a depth?—or was there no bottom, but simply presently a plunging on down into the black of death's bottomless oblivion?

Drink—always drink. Yet in every other way she took care of her health—a strange mingling of prudence and subtle hope with recklessness and frank despair. All her refinement, baffled in the moral ways, concentrated upon the physical. She would be neat and well dressed; she would not let herself be seized of the diseases on the pariah in those regions—the diseases through dirt and ignorance and indifference.

In the regions she now frequented recklessness was the keynote. There was the hilarity of the doomed; there was the cynical or stolid indifference to heat or cold, to rain or shine, to rags, to filth, to jail, to ejection for nonpayment of rent, to insult of word or blow. The fire engines—the ambulance—the patrol wagon—the city dead wagon—these were all ever passing and repassing through those swarming streets. It was the vastest, the most populous tenement area of the city. Its inhabitants represented the common lot—for it is the common lot of the overwhelming mass of mankind to live near to nakedness, to shelterlessness, to starvation, without ever being quite naked or quite roofless or quite starved. The masses are eager for the necessities; the classes are eager for the comforts and luxuries. The masses are ignorant; the classes are intelligent—or, at least, shrewd. The unconscious and inevitable exploitation of the masses by the classes automatically and of necessity stops just short of the catastrophe point—

for the masses must have enough to give them the strength to work and reproduce. To go down through the social system as had Susan from her original place well up among the classes is like descending from the beautiful dining room of the palace where the meat is served in taste and refinement upon costly dishes by well mannered servants to attractively dressed people—descending along the various stages of the preparation of the meat, at each stage less of refinement and more of coarseness, until one at last arrives at the slaughter pen. The shambles, stinking and reeking blood and filth! The shambles, with hideous groan or shriek, or more hideous silent look of agony! The shambles of society where the beauty and grace and charm of civilization are created out of noisome sweat and savage toil, out of the health and strength of men and women and children, out of their ground up bodies, out of their ground up souls. Susan knew those regions well. She had no theories about them, no resentment against the fortunate classes, no notion that any other or better system might be possible, any other or better life for the masses. She simply accepted life as she found it, lived it as best she could.

Throughout the masses of mankind life is sustained by illusions—illusions of a better lot tomorrow, illusions of a heaven beyond a grave, where the nightmare, life in the body, will end and the reality, life in the spirit, will begin. She could not join the throngs moving toward church and synagogue to indulge in their dream that the present was a dream from which death would be a joyful awakening. She alternately pitied and envied them. She had her own dream that this dream, the present, would end in a joyful awakening to success and freedom and light and beauty. She admitted to herself that the dream was probably an illusion, like that of the pious throngs. But she was as unreasonably tenacious of her dream as they were of theirs. She dreamed it because she was a human being—and to be human means to hope, and to hope means to dream of a brighter future here or hereafter, or both here and hereafter. The earth is peopled with dreamers; she was but one of them. The last thought of despair as the black earth closes is a hope, perhaps the most colossal of hope's delusions, that there will be escape in the grave.

There is the time when we hope and know it and believe in it. There is the time when we hope and know it but have ceased to believe in it. There is the time when we hope, believing that we have altogether ceased to hope. That time had come for Susan. She seemed to think about the present. She moved about like a sleepwalker.

What women did she know—what men? She only dimly remembered from day to day—from hour to hour. Blurred faces passed before her, blurred voices sounded in her ears, blurred personalities touched hers. It was like the jostling of a huge crowd in night streets. A vague sense of buffetings—of rude contacts—of momentary sensations of pain, of shame, of disgust, all blunted and soon forgotten.

In estimating suffering, physical or mental, to fail to take into account a more important factor—the merciful paralysis or partial paralysis of any center of sensibility—that is insistently assaulted.

She no longer had headaches or nausea after drinking deeply. And where formerly it had taken many stiff doses of liquor to get her into the state of recklessness or of indifference, she was now able to put herself into the mood in which life was endurable with two or three drinks, often with only one. The most marked change was that never by any chance did she become gay; the sky over her life was steadily gray—gray or black, to gray again—never lighter.

How far she had fallen! But swift descent or gradual, she had adapted herself—had, in fact, learned by much experience of disaster to mitigate the calamities, to have something to keep a certain deep-lying self of selfs intact—unaffected by what she had been forced to undergo. It seemed to her that if she could get the chance—or could cure herself of the blindness which was always preventing her from seeing and seizing the chance that doubtless offered again and again—she could shed the surface her mode of life had formed over her and would find underneath a new real surface, stronger, sightly, better able to bear—like the skin that forms beneath the healing wound.

In these tenements, as in all tenements of all degrees, she and the others of her class were fiercely resented by the heads of families where there was any hope left to impel a striving upward. She had the best furnished room in the tenement. She was the best dressed woman—a marked and instantly recognizable figure because of her neat and finer clothes. Her profession kept alive and active the instincts for care of the person that either did not exist or were momentary and feeble in the respectable women. The slovenliness, the scurrilousness of even the wives and daughters of the well-to-do and the rich of that region would not have been tolerated in any but the lowest strata of her profession, hardly even in those sought by men of the laboring class. Also, the deep horror of disease, which her intelligence never for an instant permitted to relax its hold, made her particular and careful when in other circumstances drink might have reduced her to squalor. She spent all her leisure time—for she no longer read—in the care of her person.

She was watched with frightened, yet longing and curious, eyes by all the girls who were at work. The mothers hated her; many of them spat upon the ground after she had passed. It was a heart-breaking struggle, that of these mothers to save their daughters, not from prostitution, not from living with men outside marriage, not from moral danger, but from the practical danger, the danger of bringing into the world children with no father to help feed and clothe them. In the opinion of these people—an opinion often frankly expressed, rarely concealed with any but the thinnest hypocrisy—the life of prostitution was not so bad. Did the life of virtue offer any attractive alternative? Whether a woman was "bad" or "good," she must live in travail and die in squalor to be buried in or near the Potter's Field. But if the girl still living at home were not "good," that would mean a baby to be taken care of, would mean the girl herself not a contributor to the family support but a double burden. And if she went into prostitution, would her family get the benefit? No.

The mothers made little effort to save their sons; they concentrated on the daughters. It was pitiful to see how in their ignorance they were unaware of the strongest forces working against them. The talk of all this motley humanity—of "good" no less than "bad" women, of steady workingmen, of political heelers, thieves and bums and runners for dives—was frankly, often hideously, obscene. The jammed together way of living made modesty impossible, or scantest decency—made the pictures of it among the aspiring few, usually for the benefit of religion or charitable visitors, a pitiful, grotesque hypocrisy. Indeed, the prostitute class was the highest in this respect. The streetwalkers, those who prospered, had better masters, learned something about the pleasures and charms of privacy, also had more leisure in which to think, in however crude a way, about the refinements of life, and more money with which to practice those refinements. The boys from the earliest age were on terms of licentious freedom with the girls. The favorite children's games, often played in the open street with the elders looking on and laughing, were sex games. The very babies used foul language—that is, used the language they learned both at home and in the street. It was primitive man; Susan was at the foundation of the world.

To speak of the conditions there as a product of civilization is to show ignorance of the history of our race, is to fancy that we are civilized today, when in fact we are—historically—in a turbulent and painful period of transition from a better yesterday toward a tomorrow in which life will be worth living as it never has been before in all the ages of duration. In this today of movement toward civilization which began with the discovery of iron and will end when we shall have discovered how to use for the benefit of all the main forces of nature—in this today of agitation incident to journeying, we are in some respects better off, in other respects worse off, than the race was ten or fifteen thousand years ago. We have lost much of the freedom that was ours before the rise of governments and ruling classes; we have gained much—not so much as the ignorant and the unthinking and the uneducated imagine, but still much. In the end we which means the masses of us—will gain infinitely. But gain or loss has not been in so-called morality. There is not a virtue that has not existed from time ages before record. Not a vice which is shallowly called "effete" or the "product of over-civilization," but originated before man was man.

To speak of the conditions in which Susan Lenox now lived as savagery is to misuse the word. Every transitional stage is accompanied by a disintegration. Savagery was a settled state in which every man and every woman had his or her fixed position, settled duties and rights. With the downfall of savagery with the beginning of the journey toward that hope of tomorrow, civilization, everything in the relations of men with men and men with women, became unsettled. Such social systems as the world has known since have all been makeshift and temporary—like our social systems of today, like the moral and extinct codes rising and sinking in power over a vast multitude of emigrants moving from a distant abandoned home toward a distant promised land and forced to live as best they can in the interval. In the historic day's journey of perhaps fifteen thousand years our present time is but a brief second. In that second there has come a breaking up of the makeshift organization which long served the working multitudes fairly well. The result is an anarchy in which the strong oppress the weak, in which the masses are being crushed by the burdens imposed upon them by the classes. And in that particular part of the human race en route into which fate had flung Susan Lenox conditions not of savagery but of primitive chaos were prevailing. A large part of the population lived off the unhappy workers by prostitution, by thieving, by petty swindling, by politics, by the various devices in coarse, crude and small imitation of the devices employed by the ruling classes. And these petty parasites imitated the big parasites in their ways of spending their dubiously got gains. To have a "good time" was the ideal here as in idle Fifth Avenue; and the notions of a "good time" in vogue in the two opposite quarters differed in degree rather than in kind.

Nothing to think about but the appetites and their vices. Nothing to hope for but the next carouse. Susan had brought down with her from above one desire unknown to her associates and neighbors—the desire to forget. If she could only forget! If the poison would not wear off at times!

She could not quite forget. And to be unable to forget is to remember— and to remember is to long—and to long is to hope.

Several times she heard of Freddie Palmer. Twice she chanced upon his name in the newspaper—an incidental reference to him in connection with local politics. The other times were when men talking together in the drinking places frequented by both sexes spoke of him as a minor power in the organization. Each time she got a sense of her remoteness, of her security. Once she passed in Grand Street a detective she had often seen with him in Considine's at Broadway and Forty-second. The "bull" looked sharply at her. Her heart stood still. But he went on without recognizing her. The sharp glance had been simply that official expression of see-all and know-all which is mere formality, part of the official livery, otherwise meaningless. However, it is not to that detective's discredit that he failed to recognize her. She had adapted herself to her changed surroundings.

Because she was of a different and higher class, and because she picked and chose her company, even when drink had beclouded her senses and instinct alone remained on drowsy guard, she prospered despite her indifference. For that region had its aristocracy of rich merchants, tenement-owners, politicians whose sons, close imitators of the uptown aristocracies in manners and dress, spent money freely in the amusements that attract nearly all young men everywhere. Susan made almost as much as she could have made in the more renowned quarters of the town. And presently she was able to move into a tenement which, except for two workingmen's families of a better class, was given over entirely to fast women. It was much better kept, much cleaner, much better furnished than the tenements for workers chiefly; they could not afford decencies, much less luxuries. All that sort of thing was, for the neighborhood, concentrated in the saloons, the dance halls, the fast houses and the fast flats.

Her walks in Grand Street and the Bowery, repelling and capricious though she was with her alternating moods of cold moroseness and sardonic and mocking gayety, were bringing her in a good sum of money for that region. Sometimes as much as twenty dollars a week, rarely less than twelve or fifteen. And despite her drinking and her freehandedness with her fellow-professionals less fortunate and with the street beggars and for tenement charities, she had in her stockings a capital of thirty-one dollars.

She avoided the tough places, the hang-outs of the gangs. She rarely went alone into the streets at night—and the afternoons were, luckily, best for business as well as for safety. She made no friends and therefore no enemies. Without meaning to do so and without realizing that she did so, she held herself aloof without haughtiness through sense of loneliness, not at all through sense of superiority. Had it not been for her scarlet lips, a far more marked sign in that region than anywhere uptown, she would have passed in the street for a more or less respectable woman—not thoroughly respectable; she was too well dressed, too intelligently cared for to seem the good working girl.

On one of the few nights when she lingered in the little back room of the saloon a few doors away at the corner, as she entered the dark passageway of the tenement, strong fingers closed upon her throat and she was borne to the floor. She knew at once that she was in the clutch of one of those terrors of tenement fast women, the lobbygows—men who live by lying in wait in the darkness to seize and rob the lonely, friendless fast woman. She struggled—and she was anything but weak. But not a sound could escape from her tight-pressed throat. Soon she became unconscious.

One of the workingmen, returning drunk from the meeting of the union, in the corner saloon, stumbled over her, gave her a kick in his anger. This roused her; she uttered a faint cry. "Thought it was a man," mumbled he, dragging her to a sitting position. He struck a match. "Oh—it's you! Don't make any noise. If my old woman came out, she'd kill us both."

"Never mind me," said Susan. "I was only stunned."

"Oh, I thought it was the booze. They say you hit it something fierce."

"No—a lobbygow." And she felt for her stockings. They were torn away from her garters. Her bosom also was bare, for the lobbygow had searched there, also.

"How much did he get?"

"About thirty-five."

"The hell he did! Want me to call a cop?"

"No," replied Susan, who was on her feet again. "What's the use?"

"Those damn cops!" cursed the workingman. "They'd probably pinch you—or both of us. Ten to one the lobbygows divide with them."

"I didn't mean that," said Susan. The police were most friendly and most kind to her. She was understanding the ways of the world better now, and appreciated that the police themselves were part of the same vast system of tyranny and robbery that was compelling her. The police made her pay because they dared not refuse to be collectors. They bound whom the mysterious invisible power compelled them to bind; they loosed whom that same power bade them loose. She had no quarrel with the police, who protected her from far worse oppressions and oppressors than that to which they subjected her. And if they tolerated lobbygows and divided with them, it was because the overshadowing power ordained it so.

"Needn't be afraid I'll blow to the cop," said the drunken artisan. "You can damn the cops all you please to me. They make New York worse than Russia."

"I guess they do the best they can—like everybody else," said the girl wearily.

"I'll help you upstairs."

"No, thank you," said she. Not that she did not need help; but she wished no disagreeable scene with the workingman's wife who might open the door as they passed his family's flat.

She went upstairs, the man waiting below until she should be safe—and out of the way. She staggered into her room, tottered to the bed, fell upon it. A girl named Clara, who lived across the hall, was sitting in a rocking-chair in a nightgown, reading a Bertha Clay novel and smoking a cigarette. She glanced up, was arrested by the strange look in Susan's eyes.

"Hello—been hitting the pipe, I see," said she. "Down in Gussie's room?"

"No. A lobbygow," said Susan.

"Did he get much?"

"About thirty-five."

"The ——!" cried Clara. "I'll bet it was Gussie's fellow. I've suspected him. Him and her stay in, hitting the pipe all the time. That costs money, and she hasn't been out for I don't know how long. Let's go down there and raise hell."

"What's the use?" said Susan.

"You ought to 'a' put it in the savings bank. That's what I do—when I have anything. Then, when I'm robbed, they only get what I've just made. Last time, they didn't get nothing—but me." And she laughed. Her teeth were good in front, but out on one side and beginning to be discolored on the other. "How long had you been saving?"

"Nearly six months."

"Gee! *Isn't* that hell!" Presently she laughed. "Six months' work and only thirty-five to show for it. Guess you're about as poor at hiving it up as I am. I give it to that loafer I live with. You give it away to anybody that wants a stake. Well—what's the diff? It all goes."

"Give me a cigarette," said Susan, sitting up and inspecting the bruises on her bosom and legs. "And get that bottle of whiskey from under the soiled clothes in the bottom of the washstand."

"It *is* something to celebrate, isn't it?" said Clara. "My fellow's gone to his club tonight, so I didn't go out. I never do any more, unless he's there to hang round and see that I ain't done up. You'll have to get a fellow. You'll have to come to it, as I'm always telling you. They're expensive, but they're company—anybody you can count on for shining up, even if it is for what they can get out of you, is better than not having nobody nowhere. And they keep off bums and lobbygows and scare the bilkers into coughing up."

"Not for me," replied Susan.

The greater the catastrophe, the longer the time before it is fully realized. Susan's loss of the money that represented so much of savage if momentary horror, and so much of unconscious hope this calamity did not overwhelm her for several days. Then she yielded for the first time to the lure of opium. She had listened longingly to the descriptions of the delights as girls and men told; for practically all of them smoked—or took cocaine. But to Clara's or Gussie's invitations to join the happy band of dreamers, she had always replied, "Not yet. I'm saving that." Now, however, she felt that the time had come. Hope in this world she had none. Before the black adventure, why not try the world of blissful unreality to which it gave entrance? Why leave life until she had exhausted all it put within her reach?

She went to Gussie's room at midnight and flung herself down in a wrapper upon a couch opposite a sallow, delicate young man. His great dark eyes were gazing unseeingly at her, were perhaps using her as an outline sketch from which his imagination could picture a beauty of loveliness beyond human. Gussie taught her how to prepare the little ball of opium, how to put it on the pipe and draw in its fumes. Her system was so well prepared for it by the poisons she had drunk that she had satisfactory results from the outset. And she entered upon the happiest period of her life thus far. All the hideousness of her profession disappeared under the gorgeous draperies of the imagination. Opium's magic transformed the vile, the obscene, into the lofty, the romantic, the exalted. The world she had been accustomed to regard as real ceased to be even the blur the poisonous liquors had made of it, became a vague, distant thing seen in a dream. Her opium world became the vivid reality.

The life she had been leading had made her extremely thin, had hardened and dulled her eyes, had given her that sad, shuddering expression of the face upon which have beaten a thousand mercenary and lustful kisses. The opium soon changed all this. Her skin, always tending toward pallor, became of the dead amber-white of old ivory. Her thinness took on an ethereal transparency that gave charm even to her slight stoop. Her face became dreamy, exalted, rapt; and her violet-gray eyes looked from it like the vents of poetical fires burning without ceasing upon an altar to the god of dreams. Never had she been so beautiful; never had she been so happy—not with the coarser happiness of dancing eye and laughing lip, but with the ecstasy of soul that is like the shimmers of a tranquil sea quivering rhythmically under the caresses of moonlight.

In her descent she had now reached that long narrow shelf along which she would walk so long as health and looks should last—unless some accident should topple her off on the one side into suicide or on the other side into the criminal prostitute class. And such accidents were likely to happen. Still there was a fair chance of her keeping her balance until loss of looks and loss of health—the end of the shelf—should drop her abruptly to the very bottom. She could guess what was there. Every day she saw about the streets, most wretched and most forlorn of its wretched and forlorn things, the solitary old women, bent and twisted, wrapped in rotting rags, picking papers and tobacco from the gutters and burrowing in garbage barrels, seeking somehow to get the drink or the dope that changed hell into heaven for them.

Despite liquor and opium and the degradations of the street-woman's life she walked that narrow ledge with curious steadiness. She was unconscious of the cause. Indeed, self-consciousness had never been one of her traits. The cause is interesting.

In our egotism, in our shame of what we ignorantly regard as the lowliness of our origin we are always seeking alleged lofty spiritual explanations of our doings, and overlook the actual, quite simple real reason. One of the strongest factors in Susan's holding herself together in face of overwhelming odds, was the nearly seventeen years of early training her Aunt Fanny Warham had given her in orderly and systematic ways—a place for everything and everything in its place; a time for everything and everything at its time, neatness, scrupulous cleanliness, no neglecting of any of the small, yet large, matters that conserve the body. Susan had not been so apt a pupil of Fanny Warham's as was Ruth, because Susan had not Ruth's nature of the old-maidish, cut-and-dried conventional. But during the whole fundamentally formative period of her life Susan Lenox had been trained to order and system, and they had become part of her being, beyond the power of drink and opium and prostitution to disintegrate them until the general break-up should come. In all her wanderings every man or woman or girl she had met who was not rapidly breaking up, but was offering more or less resistance to the assaults of bad habits, was one who like herself had acquired in childhood strong good habits to oppose the bad habits and to fight them with. An enemy must be met with his own weapons or stronger.

The strongest weapons that can be given a human animal for combating the destructive forces of the struggle for existence are not good sentiments or good principles or even pious or moral practices—for, bad habits can make short work of all these—but are good habits in the practical, material matters of life. They operate automatically, they apply to all the multitude of small, every day; semi-unconscious actions of the daily routine. They preserve the *morale*. And not morality but morals is the warp of character— the part which, once destroyed or even frayed, cannot be restored.

Susan, unconsciously and tenaciously practicing her early training in order and system whenever she could and wherever she could, had an enormous advantage over the mass of the girls, both respectable and fast. And while their evidence was always toward "going to pieces" her tendency was always to repair and to put off the break-up.

One June evening she was looking through the better class of dance halls and drinking resorts for Clara, to get her to go up to Gussie's for a smoke. She opened a door she had never happened to enter before—a dingy door with the glass frosted. Just inside there was a fetid little bar; view of the rest of the room was cut off by a screen from behind which came the sound of a tuneless old piano. She knew Clara would not be in such a den, but out of curiosity she glanced round the screen. She was seeing a low-ceilinged room, the walls almost dripping with the dirt of many and many a hard year. In a corner was the piano, battered, about to fall to pieces, its ancient and horrid voice cracked by the liquor which had been poured into it by facetious drunkards. At the keyboard sat an old hunchback, broken-jawed, dressed in slimy rags, his one eye instantly fixed upon her with a lecherous expression that made her shiver as it compelled her to imagine the embrace he was evidently imagining. His filthy fingers were pounding out a waltz. About the floor were tottering in the measure of the waltz a score of dreadful old women. They were in calico. They had each a little biscuit knot of white hair firmly upon the crown of the head. From their bleached, seamed old faces gleamed the longings or the torments of all the passions they could no longer either inspire or satisfy. They were one time prostitutes, one time young, perhaps pretty women, now descending to death—still prostitutes in heart and mind but compelled to live as scrub women, cleaners of all manner of loathsome messes in dives after the drunkards had passed on. They were now enjoying the reward of their toil, the pleasures of which they dreamed and to which they looked forward as they dragged their stiff old knees along the floors in the wake of the brush and the cloth. They were drinking biting poisons from tin cups—for those hands quivering with palsy could not be trusted with glass-dancing with drunken, disease-swollen or twisted legs—venting from ghastly toothless mouths strange cries of merriment that sounded like shrieks of damned souls at the licking of quenchless flames.

Susan stood rooted to the threshold of that frightful scene—that vision of the future toward which she was hurrying. A few years—a very few years—and, unless she should have passed through the Morgue, here she would be, abandoning her body to abominations beyond belief at the hands of degenerate oriental sailors to get a few pennies for the privileges of this dance hall. And she would laugh, as did these, would enjoy as did these, would revel in the filth her senses had been trained to find sweet. "No! No!" she protested. "I'd kill myself first!" And then she cowered again, as the thought came that she probably would not, any more than these had killed themselves. The descent would be gradual—no matter how swift, still gradual. Only the insane put an end to life. Yes—she would come here some day.

She leaned against the wall, her throat contracting in a fit of nausea. She grew cold all over; her teeth chattered. She tried in vain to tear her gaze from the spectacle; some invisible power seemed to be holding her head in a vise, thrusting her struggling eyelids violently open.

There were several men, dead drunk, asleep in old wooden chairs against the wall. One of these men was so near her that she could have touched him. His clothing was such an assortment of rags slimy and greasy as one sometimes sees upon the top of a filled garbage barrel to add its horrors of odor of long unwashed humanity to the stenches from vegetable decay. His wreck of a hard hat had fallen from his head as it dropped forward in drunken sleep. Something in the shape of the head made her concentrate upon this man. She gave a sharp cry, stretched out her hand, touched the man's shoulder.

"Rod!" she cried. "Rod!"

The head slowly lifted, and the bleary, blowsy wreck of Roderick Spenser's handsome face was turned stupidly toward her. Into his gray eyes slowly came a gleam of recognition. Then she saw the red of shame burst into his hollow cheeks, and the head quickly drooped.

She shook him. "Rod! It's *you!*"

"Get the hell out," he mumbled. "I want to sleep."

"You know me," she said. "I see the color in your face. Oh, Rod—you needn't be ashamed before *me.*"

She felt him quiver under her fingers pressing upon his shoulder. But he pretended to snore.

"Rod," she pleaded, "I want you to come along with me. I can't do you any harm now."

The hunchback had stopped playing. The old women were crowding round Spenser and her, were peering at them, with eyes eager and ears a-cock for romance—for nowhere on this earth do the stars shine so sweetly as down between the precipices of shame to the black floor of the slum's abyss. Spenser, stooped and shaking, rose abruptly, thrust Susan aside with a sweep of the arm that made her reel, bolted into the street. She recovered her balance and amid hoarse croakings of "That's right, honey! Don't give him up!" followed the shambling, swaying figure. He was too utterly drunk to go far; soon down he sank, a heap of rags and filth, against a stoop.

She bent over him, saw he was beyond rousing, straightened and looked about her. Two honest looking young Jews stopped. "Won't you help me get him home?" she said to them. "Sure!" replied they in chorus. And, with no outward sign of the disgust they must have felt at the contact, they lifted up the sot, in such fantastic contrast to Susan's clean and even stylish appearance, and bore him along, trying to make him seem less the helpless whiskey-soaked dead weight. They dragged him up the two flights of stairs and, as she pushed back the door, deposited him on the floor. She assured them they could do nothing more, thanked them, and they departed. Clara appeared in her doorway.

"God Almighty, Lorna!" she cried. "*What* have you got there?
How'd it get in?"

"You've been advising me to take a fellow," said Susan. "Well—here he is."

Clara looked at her as if she thought her crazed by drink or dope. "I'll call the janitor and have him thrown out."

"No, he's my lover," said Susan. "Will you help me clean him up?"

Clara, looking at Spenser's face now, saw those signs which not the hardest of the world's hard uses can cut or tear away. "Oh!" she said, in a tone of sympathy. "He *is* down, isn't he?
But he'll pull round all right."

She went into her room to take off her street clothes and to get herself into garments as suitable as she possessed for one of those noisome tasks that are done a dozen times a day by the bath nurses in the receiving department of a charity hospital. When she returned, Susan too was in her chemise and ready to begin the search for the man, if man there was left deep buried in that muck. While Susan took off the stinking and rotten rags, and flung them into the hall, Clara went to the bathroom they and Mollie shared, and filled the tub with water as hot as her hand could bear. With her foot Susan pushed the rags along the hall floor and into the garbage closet. Then she and Clara lifted the emaciated, dirt-streaked, filth-smeared body, carried it to the bathroom, let it down into the water. There were at hand plenty of those strong, specially prepared soaps and other disinfectants constantly used by the women of their kind who still cling to cleanliness and health. With these they attacked him, not as if he were a human being, but as if he were some inanimate object that must be scoured before it could be used.

Again and again they let out the water, black, full of dead and dying vermin; again and again they rinsed him, attacked him afresh. Their task grew less and less repulsive as the man gradually appeared, a young man with a soft skin, a well-formed body, unusually good hands and feet, a distinguished face despite its savage wounds from dissipation, hardly the less handsome for the now fair and crisp beard which gave it a look of more years than Spenser had lived.

If Spenser recovered consciousness—and it seems hardly possible that he did not—he was careful to conceal the fact. He remained limp, inert, apparently in a stupor. They gave him one final scrubbing, one final rinsing, one final thorough inspection. "Now, he's all right," declared Clara. "What shall we do with him?"

"Put him to bed," said Susan.

They had already dried him off in the empty tub. They now rubbed him down with a rough towel, lifted him, Susan taking the shoulders, Clara the legs, and put him in Susan's bed. Clara ran to her room, brought one of the two nightshirts she kept for her fellow. When they had him in this and with a sheet over him, they cleaned and straightened the bathroom, then lit cigarettes and sat down to rest and to admire the work of their hands.

"Who is he?" asked Clara.

"A man I used to know," said Susan. Like all the girls in that life with a real story to tell, she never told about her past self. Never tell? They never even remember if drink and drugs will do their duty.

"I don't blame you for loving him," said Clara. "Somehow, the lower a man sinks the more a woman loves him. It's the other way with men. But then men don't know what love is. And a woman don't really know till she's been through the mill."

"I don't love him," said Susan.

"Same thing," replied the practical Clara, with a wave of the bare arm at the end of which smoked the cigarette. "What're you going to do with him?"

"I don't know," confessed Susan.

She was not a little uneasy at the thought of his awakening. Would he despise her more than ever now—fly from her back to his filth? Would he let her try to help him? And she looked at the face which had been, in that other life so long, long ago, dearer to her than any face her eyes had ever rested upon; a sob started deep down within her, found its slow and painful way upward, shaking her whole body and coming from between her clenched teeth in a groan. She forgot all she had suffered from Rod—forgot the truth about him which she had slowly puzzled out after she left him and as experience enabled her to understand actions she had not understood at the time. She forgot it all. That past—that far, dear, dead past! Again she was a simple, innocent girl upon the high rock, eating that wonderful dinner. Again the evening light faded, stars and moon came out, and she felt the first sweet stirring of love for him. She could hear his voice, the light, clear, entrancing melody of the Duke's song—

La Donna è mobile
Qua penna al vento—

She burst into tears—tears that drenched her soul as the rain drenches the blasted desert and makes the things that could live in beauty stir deep in its bosom. And Clara, sobbing in sympathy, kissed her and stole away, softly closing the door. "If a man die, shall he live again?" asked the old Arabian philosopher. If a woman die, shall she live again?. . . Shall not that which dies in weakness live again in strength?. . . Looking at him, as he lay there sleeping so quietly, her being surged with the heaving of high longings and hopes. If *they* could only live again! Here they were, together, at the lowest depth, at the rock bottom of life. If they could build on that rock, build upon the very foundation of the world, then would they indeed build in strength! Then, nothing could destroy—nothing!. . . If they could live again! If they could build!

She had something to live for—something to fight for. Into her eyes came a new light; into her soul came peace and strength. Something to live for—someone to redeem.

CHAPTER XI

SHE fell asleep, her head resting upon her hand, her elbow on the arm of the chair. She awoke with a shiver; she opened her eyes to find him gazing at her. The eyes of both shifted instantly. "Wouldn't you like some whiskey?" she asked.

"Thanks," replied he, and his unchanged voice reminded her vividly of his old self, obscured by the beard and by the dissipated look.

She took the bottle from its concealment in the locked washstand drawer, poured him out a large drink. When she came back where he could see the whiskey in the glass, his eyes glistened and he raised himself first on his elbow, then to a sitting position. His shaking hand reached out eagerly and his expectant lips quivered. He gulped the whiskey down.

"Thank you," he said, gazing longingly at the bottle as he held the empty glass toward her.

"More?"

"I *would* like a little more," said he gratefully.

Again she poured him a large drink, and again he gulped it down. "That's strong stuff," said he. "But then they sell strong stuff in this part of town. The other kind tastes weak to me now."

He dropped back against the pillows. She poured herself a drink. Halfway to her lips the glass halted. "I've got to stop that," thought she, "if I'm going to do anything for him or for myself." And she poured the whiskey back and put the bottle away. The whole incident took less than five seconds. It did not occur that she was essaying and achieving the heroic, that she had in that instant revealed her right to her dream of a career high above the common lot.

"Don't *you* drink?" said he.

"I've decided to cut it out," replied she carelessly. "There's nothing in it."

"I couldn't live without it—and wouldn't."

"It *is* a comfort when one's on the way down," said she. "But I'm going to try the other direction—for a change."

She held a box of cigarettes toward him. He took one, then she; she held the lighted match for him, lit her own cigarette, let the flame of the match burn on, she absently watching it.

"Look out! You'll burn yourself!" cried he.

She started, threw the match into the slop jar. "How do you feel?" inquired she.

"Like the devil," he answered. "But then I haven't known what it was to feel any other way for several months except when I couldn't feel at all." A long silence, both smoking, he thinking, she furtively watching him. "You haven't changed so much," he finally said. "At least, not on the outside."

"More on the outside than on the inside," said she. "The inside doesn't change much. There I'm almost as I was that day on the big rock. And I guess you are, too—aren't you?"

"The devil I am! I've grown hard and bitter."

"That's all outside," declared she. "That's the shell—like the scab that stays over the sore spot till it heals."

"Sore spot? I'm nothing but sore spots. I've been treated like a dog."

And he proceeded to talk about the only subject that interested him—himself. He spoke in a defensive way, as if replying to something she had said or thought. "I've not got down in the world without damn good excuse. I wrote several plays, and they were tried out of town. But we never could get into New York. I think Brent was jealous of me, and his influence kept me from a hearing. I know it sounds conceited, but I'm sure I'm right."

"Brent?" said she, in a queer voice. "Oh, I think you must be mistaken. He doesn't look like a man who could do petty mean things. No, I'm sure he's not petty."

"Do you know him?" cried Spenser, in an irritated tone.

"No. But—someone pointed him out to me once—a long time ago—one night in the Martin. And then—you'll remember—there used to be a great deal of talk about him when we lived in Forty-third Street. You admired him tremendously."

"Well, he's responsible," said Spenser, sullenly. "The men on top are always trampling down those who are trying to climb up. He had it in for me. One of my friends who thought he was a decent chap gave him my best play to read. He returned it with some phrases about its showing talent—one of those phrases that don't mean a damn thing. And a few weeks ago—" Spenser raised himself excitedly—"the thieving hound produced a play that was a clean steal from mine. I'd be laughed at if I protested or sued. But I *know*, curse him!"

He fell back shaking so violently that his cigarette dropped to the sheet. Susan picked it up, handed it to him. He eyed her with angry suspicion. "You don't believe me, do you?" he demanded.

"I don't know anything about it," replied she. "Anyhow, what does it matter? The man I met on that show boat—the Mr. Burlingham I've often talked about—he used to say that the dog that stopped to lick his scratches never caught up with the prey."

He flung himself angrily in the bed. "You never did have any heart— any sympathy. But who has? Even Drumley went back on me—let 'em put a roast of my last play in the *Herald*—a telegraphed roast from New Haven— said it was a dead failure. And who wrote it? Why, some newspaper correspondent in the pay of the *Syndicate*—and that means Brent. And of course it was a dead failure. So—I gave up—and here I am. . . . This your room?"

"Yes."

"Where's this nightshirt come from?"

"It belongs to the friend of the girl across the hall." He laughed sneeringly. "The hell it does!" mocked he. "I understand perfectly. I want my clothes."

"No one is coming," said Susan. "There's no one to come."

He was looking round the comfortable little room that was the talk of the whole tenement and was stirring wives and fast women alike to "do a little fixing up." Said he:

"A nice little nest you've made for him. You always were good at that."

"I've made it for myself," said she. "I never bring men here."

"I want my clothes," cried he. "I haven't sunk that low, you——!"

The word he used did not greatly disturb Susan. The shell she had formed over herself could ward off brutal contacts of languages no less than of the other kinds. It did, however, shock her a little to hear Rod Spenser use a word so crude.

"Give me my clothes," he ordered, waving his fists in a fierce, feeble gesture.

"They were torn all to pieces. I threw them away. I'll get you some more in the morning."

He dropped back again, a scowl upon his face. "I've got no money—not a damn cent. I did half a day's work on the docks and made enough to quiet me last night." He raised himself. "I can work again. Give me my clothes!"

"They're gone," said Susan. "They were completely used up."

This brought back apparently anything but dim memory of what his plight had been. "How'd I happen to get so clean?"

"Clara and I washed you off a little. You had fallen down."

He lay silent a few minutes, then said in a hesitating, ashamed tone, "My troubles have made me a boor. I beg your pardon. You've been tremendously kind to me."

"Oh, it wasn't much. Don't you feel sleepy?"

"Not a bit." He dragged himself from the bed. "But *you* do. I must go."

She laughed in the friendliest way. "You can't. You haven't any clothes."

He passed his hand over his face and coughed violently, she holding his head and supporting his emaciated shoulders. After several minutes of coughing and gagging, gasping and groaning and spitting, he was relieved by the spasm and lay down again. When he got his breath, he said—with rest between words—"I'd ask you to send for the ambulance, but if the doctors catch me, they'll lock me away. I've got consumption. Oh, I'll soon be out of it."

Susan sat silent. She did not dare look at him lest he should see the pity and horror in her eyes.

"They'll find a cure for it," pursued he. "But not till the day after I'm gone. That is the way my luck runs. Still, I don't see why I should care to stay—and I don't! Have you any more of that whiskey?"

Susan brought out the bottle again, gave him the last of the whiskey—a large drink. He sat up, sipping it to make it last. He noted the long row of books on the shelf fastened along the wall beside the bed, the books and magazines on the table. Said he:

"As fond of reading as ever, I see?"

"Fonder," said she. "It takes me out of myself."

"I suppose you read the sort of stuff you really like, now—not the things you used to read to make old Drumley think you were cultured and intellectual."

"No—the same sort," replied she, unruffled by his contemptuous, unjust fling. "Trash bores me."

"Come to think of it, I guess you did have pretty good taste in books."

But he was interested in himself, like all invalids; and, like them, he fancied his own intense interest could not but be shared by everyone. He talked on and on of himself, after the manner of failures—told of his wrongs, of how friends had betrayed him, of the jealousies and enmities his talents had provoked. Susan was used to these hard-luck stories, was used to analyzing them. With the aid of what she had worked out as to his character after she left him, she had no difficulty in seeing that he was deceiving himself, was excusing himself. But after all she had lived through, after all she had discovered about human frailty, especially in herself, she was not able to criticize, much less condemn, anybody. Her doubts merely set her to wondering whether he might not also be self-deceived as to his disease.

"Why do you think you've got consumption?" asked she.

"I was examined at the free dispensary up in Second Avenue the other day. I've suspected what was the matter for several months. They told me I was right."

"But the doctors are always making mistakes. I'd not give up if I were you."

"Do you suppose I would if I had anything to live for?"

"I was thinking about that a while ago—while you were asleep."

"Oh, I'm all in. That's a cinch."

"So am I," said she. "And as we've nothing to lose and no hope, why, trying to do something won't make us any worse off. . . . We've both struck the bottom. We can't go any lower." She leaned forward and, with her earnest eyes fixed upon him, said, "Rod—why not try—together?"

He closed his eyes.

"I'm afraid I can't be of much use to you," she went on. "But you can help me. And helping me will make you help yourself. I can't get up alone. I've tried. No doubt it's my fault. I guess I'm one of those women that aren't hard enough or self-confident enough to do what's necessary unless I've got some man to make me do it. Perhaps I'd get the—the strength or whatever it is, when I was much older. But by that time in my case—I guess it'd be too late. Won't you help me, Rod?"

He turned his head away, without opening his eyes.

"You've helped me many times—beginning with the first day we met."

"Don't," he said. "I went back on you. I did sprain my ankle, but I could have come."

"That wasn't anything," replied she. "You had already done a thousand times more than you needed to do."

His hand wandered along the cover in her direction. She touched it. Their hands clasped.

"I lied about where I got the money yesterday. I didn't work. I begged. Three of us—from the saloon they call the Owl's Chute—two Yale men— one of them had been a judge—and I. We've been begging for a week. We were going out on the road in a few days—to rob. Then—I saw you—in that old women's dance hall—the Venusberg, they call it."

"You've come down here for me, Rod. You'll take me back?
You'll save me from the Venusberg?"

"I couldn't save anybody. Susie, at bottom I'm N. G. I always was—and I knew it. Weak—vain. But you! If you hadn't been a woman—and such a sweet, considerate one you'd have never got down here."

"Such a fool," corrected Susan. "But, once I get up, I'll not be so again. I'll fight under the rules, instead of acting in the silly way they teach us as children."

"Don't say those hard things, Susie!"

"Aren't they true?"

"Yes, but I can't bear to hear them from a woman. . . . I told you that you hadn't changed. But after I'd looked at you a while I saw that you have. You've got a terrible look in your eyes—wonderful and terrible. You had something of that look as a child—the first time I saw you."

"The day after my marriage," said the girl, tearing her face away.

"It was there then," he went on. "But now—it's—it's heartbreaking, Susie when your face is in repose."

"I've gone through a fire that has burned up every bit of me that can burn," said she. "I've been wondering if what's left isn't strong enough to do something with. I believe so—if you'll help me."

"Help you? I—help anybody? Don't mock me, Susie."

"I don't know about anybody else," said she sweetly and gently, "but I do know about me."

"No use—too late. I've lost my nerve." He began to sob.
"It's because I'm unstrung," explained he.

"Don't think I'm a poor contemptible fool of a whiner. . . . Yes, I *am* a whiner! Susie, I ought to have been the woman and you the man. Weak—weak—weak!"

She turned the gas low, bent over him, kissed his brow, caressed him. "Let's do the best we can," she murmured.

He put his arm round her. "I wonder if there *is* any hope," he said. "No—there couldn't be."

"Let's not hope," pleaded she. "Let's just do the best we can."

"What—for instance?"

"You know the theater people. You might write a little play—a sketch—and you and I could act it in one of the ten-cent houses."

"That's not a bad idea!" exclaimed he. "A little comedy—about fifteen or twenty minutes." And he cast about for a plot, found the beginnings of one the ancient but ever acceptable commonplace of a jealous quarrel between two lovers—"I'll lay the scene in Fifth Avenue—there's nothing low life likes so much as high life." He sketched, she suggested. They planned until broad day, then fell asleep, she half sitting up, his head pillowed upon her lap.

She was awakened by a sense of a parching and suffocating heat. She started up with the idea of fire in her drowsy mind. But a glance at him revealed the real cause. His face was fiery red, and from his lips came rambling sentences, muttered, whispered, that indicated the delirium of a high fever. She had first seen it when she and the night porter broke into Burlingham's room in the Walnut Street House, in Cincinnati. She had seen it many a time since; for, while she herself had never been ill, she had been surrounded by illness all the time, and the commonest form of it was one of these fevers, outraged nature's frenzied rise against the ever denser swarms of enemies from without which the slums sent to attack her. Susan ran across the hall and roused Clara, who would watch while she went for a doctor. "You'd better get Einstein in Grand Street," Clara advised.

"Why not Sacci?" asked Susan.

"Our doctor doesn't know anything but the one thing—and he doesn't like to take other kinds of cases. No, get Einstein. . . . You know, he's like all of them—he won't come unless you pay in advance."

"How much?" asked Susan.

"Three dollars. I'll lend you if——"

"No—I've got it." She had eleven dollars and sixty cents in the world.

Einstein pronounced it a case of typhoid. "You must get him to the hospital at once."

Susan and Clara looked at each other in terror. To them, as to the masses everywhere, the hospital meant almost certain death; for they assumed—and they had heard again and again accusations which warranted it—that the public hospital doctors and nurses treated their patients with neglect always, with downright inhumanity often. Not a day passed without their hearing some story of hospital outrage upon poverty, without their seeing someone—usually some child—who was paying a heavy penalty for having been in the charity wards.

Einstein understood their expression. "Nonsense!" said he gruffly. "You girls look too sensible to believe those silly lies."

Susan looked at him steadily. His eyes shifted. "Of course, the pay service *is* better," said he in a strikingly different tone.

"How much would it be at a pay hospital?" asked Susan.

"Twenty-five a week including my services," said Doctor Einstein. "But you can't afford that."

"Will he get the best treatment for that?"

"The very best. As good as if he were Rockefeller or the big chap uptown."

"In advance, I suppose?"

"Would we ever get our money out of people if we didn't get it in advance? We've got to live just the same as any other class."

"I understand," said the girl. "I don't blame you. I don't blame anybody for anything." She said to Clara, "Can you lend me twenty?"

"Sure. Come in and get it." When she and Susan were in the hall beyond Einstein's hearing, she went on: "I've got the twenty and you're welcome to it. But—Lorna hadn't you better— —"

"In the same sort of a case, what'd *you* do?" interrupted Susan.

Clara laughed. "Oh—of course." And she gave Susan a roll of much soiled bills—a five, the rest ones and twos.

"I can get the ambulance to take him free," said Einstein. "That'll save you five for a carriage."

She accepted this offer. And when the ambulance went, with Spenser burning and raving in the tightly wrapped blankets, Susan followed in a street car to see with her own eyes that he was properly installed. It was arranged that she could visit him at any hour and stay as long as she liked.

She returned to the tenement, to find the sentiment of the entire neighborhood changed toward her. Not loss of money, not loss of work, not dispossession nor fire nor death is the supreme calamity among the poor, but sickness. It is their most frequent visitor—sickness in all its many frightful forms—rheumatism and consumption, cancer and typhoid and the rest of the monsters. Yet never do the poor grow accustomed or hardened. And at the sight of the ambulance the neighborhood had been instantly stirred. When the reason for its coming got about, Susan became the object of universal sympathy and respect. She was not sending her friend to be neglected and killed at a charity hospital; she was paying twenty-five a week that he might have a chance for life—twenty-five dollars a week! The neighbors felt that her high purpose justified any means she might be compelled to employ in getting the money. Women who had scowled and spat as she walked by, spoke friendlily to her and wiped their eyes with their filthy skirts, and prayed in church and synagogue that she might prosper until her man was well and the old debt paid. Clara went from group to group, relating the whole story, and the tears flowed at each recital. Money they had none to give; but what they had they gave with that generosity which suddenly transfigures rags and filth and makes foul and distorted bodies lift in the full dignity of membership in the human family. Everywhere in those streets were seen the ravages of disease—rheumatism and rickets and goiter, wen and tumors and cancer, children with only one arm or one leg, twisted spines, sunken chests, distorted hips, scrofulous eyes and necks, all the sad markings of poverty's supreme misery, the ferocious penalties of ignorance, stupidity and want. But Susan's burden of sorrow was not on this account overlooked.

Rafferty, who kept the saloon at the corner and was chief lieutenant to O'Frayne, the District Leader, sent for her and handed her a twenty. "That may help some," said he.

Susan hesitated—gave it back. "Thank you," said she, "and perhaps later I'll have to get it from you. But I don't want to get into debt. I already owe twenty."

"This ain't debt," explained Rafferty. "Take it and forget it."

"I couldn't do that," said the girl. "But maybe you'll lend it to me, if I need it in a week or so?"

"Sure," said the puzzled saloon man—liquor store man, he preferred to be called, or politician. "Any amount you want."

As she went away he looked after her, saying to his barkeeper: "What do you think of that, Terry? I offered her a twenty and she sidestepped."

Terry's brother had got drunk a few days before, had killed a woman and was on his way to the chair. Terry scowled at the boss and said:

"She's got a right to, ain't she? Don't she earn her money honest, without harmin' anybody but herself? There ain't many that can say that—not any that runs factories and stores and holds their noses up as if they smelt their own sins, damn 'em!"

"She's a nice girl," said Rafferty, sauntering away. He was a broad, tolerant and good-humored man; he made allowances for an employee whose brother was in for murder.

Susan had little time to spend at the hospital. She must now earn fifty dollars a week—nearly double the amount she had been averaging. She must pay the twenty-five dollars for Spenser, the ten dollars for her lodgings. Then there was the seven dollars which must be handed to the police captain's "wardman" in the darkness of some entry every Thursday night. She had been paying the patrolman three dollars a week to keep him in a good humor, and two dollars to the janitor's wife; she might risk cutting out these items for the time, as both janitor's wife and policeman were sympathetic. But on the closest figuring, fifty a week would barely meet her absolute necessities—would give her but seven a week for food and other expenses and nothing toward repaying Clara.

Fifty dollars a week! She might have a better chance to make it could she go back to the Broadway-Fifth Avenue district. But however vague other impressions from the life about her might have been, there had been branded into her a deep and terrible fear of the police an omnipotence as cruel as destiny itself—indeed, the visible form of that sinister god at present. Once in the pariah class, once with a "police record," and a man or woman would have to scale the steeps of respectability up to a far loftier height than Susan ever dreamed of again reaching, before that malign and relentless power would abandon its tyranny. She did not dare risk adventuring a part of town where she had no "pull" and where, even should she by chance escape arrest, Freddie Palmer would hear of her; would certainly revenge himself by having her arrested and made an example of. In the Grand Street district she must stay, and she must "stop the nonsense" and "play the game"— must be business-like.

She went to see the "wardman," O'Ryan, who under the guise of being a plain clothes man or detective, collected and turned in to the captain, who took his "bit" and passed up the rest, all the money levied upon saloons, dives, procuresses, dealers in unlawful goods of any kind from opium and cocaine to girls for "hock shops."

O'Ryan was a huge brute of a man, his great hard face bearing the scars of battles against pistol, knife, bludgeon and fist. He was a sour and savage brute, hated and feared by everyone for his tyrannies over the helpless poor and the helpless outcast class. He had primitive masculine notions as to feminine virtue, intact despite the latter day general disposition to concede toleration and even a certain respectability to prostitutes. But by some chance which she and the other girls did not understand he treated Susan with the utmost consideration, made the gangs appreciate that if they annoyed her or tried to drag her into the net of tribute in which they had enmeshed most of the girls worth while, he would regard it as a personal defiance to himself.

Susan waited in the back room of the saloon nearest O'Ryan's lodgings and sent a boy to ask him to come. The boy came back with the astonishing message that she was to come to O'Ryan's flat. Susan was so doubtful that she paused to ask the janitress about it.

"It's all right," said the janitress. "Since his wife died three years ago him and his baby lives alone. There's his old mother but she's gone out. He's always at home when he ain't on duty. He takes care of the baby himself, though it howls all the time something awful."

Susan ascended, found the big policeman in his shirt sleeves, trying to soothe the most hideous monstrosity she had ever seen—a misshapen, hairy animal looking like a monkey, like a rat, like half a dozen repulsive animals, and not at all like a human being. The thing was clawing and growling and grinding its teeth. At sight of Susan it fixed malevolent eyes on her and began to snap its teeth at her.

"Don't mind him," said O'Ryan. "He's only acting up queer."

Susan sat not daring to look at the thing lest she should show her aversion, and not knowing how to state her business when the thing was so clamorous, so fiendishly uproarious. After a time O'Ryan succeeded in quieting it. He seemed to think some explanation was necessary. He began abruptly, his gaze tenderly on the awful creature, his child, lying quiet now in his arms:

"My wife—she died some time ago—died when the baby here was born."

"You spend a good deal of time with it," said Susan.

"All I can spare from my job. I'm afraid to trust him to anybody, he being kind of different. Then, too, I *like* to take care of him. You see, it's all I've got to remember *her* by. I'm kind o' tryin' to do what *she'd* want did." His lips quivered. He looked at his monstrous child. "Yes, I *like* settin' here, thinkin'—and takin' care of him."

This brute of a slave driver, this cruel tyrant over the poor and the helpless—yet, thus tender and gentle—thus capable of the enormous sacrifice of a great, pure love!

"*You've* got a way of lookin' out of the eyes that's like her," he went on—and Susan had the secret of his strange forbearance toward her. "I suppose you've come about being let off on the assessment?"

Already he knew the whole story of Rod and the hospital.

"Yes—that's why I'm bothering you," said she.

"You needn't pay but five-fifty. I can only let you off a dollar and a half—my bit and the captain's. We pass the rest on up—and we don't dare let you off."

"Oh, I can make the money," Susan said hastily. "Thank you,

Mr. O'Ryan, but I don't want to get anyone into trouble."

"We've got the right to knock off one dollar and a half," said O'Ryan. "But if we let you off the other, the word would get up to—to wherever the graft goes—and they'd send down along the line, to have merry hell raised with us. The whole thing's done systematic, and they won't take no excuses, won't allow no breaks in the system nowhere. You can see for yourself—it'd go to smash if they did."

"Somebody must get a lot of money," said Susan.

"Oh, it's dribbled out—and as you go higher up, I don't suppose them that gets it knows where it comes from. The whole world's nothing but graft, anyhow. Sorry I can't let you off."

The thing in his lap had recovered strength for a fresh fit of malevolence. It was tearing at its hairy, hideous face with its claws and was howling and shrieking, the big father gently trying to soothe it—for *her* sake. Susan got away quickly. She halted in the deserted hall and gave way to a spasm of dry sobbing—an overflow of all the emotions that had been accumulating within her. In this world of noxious and repulsive weeds, what sudden startling upshooting of what beautiful flowers! Flowers where you would expect to find the most noisome weeds of all, and vilest weeds where you would expect to find flowers. What a world!

However—the fifty a week must be got—and she must be business-like.

Most of the girls who took to the streets came direct from the tenements of New York, of the foreign cities or of the factory towns of New England. And the world over, tenement house life is an excellent school for the life of the streets. It prevents modesty from developing; it familiarizes the eye, the ear, the nerves, to all that is brutal; it takes away from a girl every feeling that might act as a restraining influence except fear—fear of maternity, of disease, of prison. Thus, practically all the other girls had the advantage over Susan. Soon after they definitely abandoned respectability and appeared in the streets frankly members of the profession, they became bold and rapacious. They had an instinctive feeling that their business was as reputable as any other, more reputable than many held in high repute, that it would be most reputable if it paid better and were less uncertain. They respected themselves for all things, talk to the contrary in the search for the sympathy and pity most human beings crave. They despised the men as utterly as the men despised them. They bargained as shamelessly as the men. Even those who did not steal still felt that stealing was justifiable; for, in the streets the sex impulse shows stripped of all disguise, shows as a brutal male appetite, and the female feels that her yielding to it entitles her to all she can compel and cozen and crib. Susan had been unfitted for her profession—as for all active, unsheltered life—by her early training. The point of view given us in our childhood remains our point of view as to all the essentials of life to the end. Reason, experience, the influence of contact with many phases of the world, may change us seemingly, but the under-instinct remains unchanged. Thus, Susan had never lost, and never would lose her original repugnance; not even drink had ever given her the courage to approach men or to bargain with them. Her shame was a false shame, like most of the shame in the world—a lack of courage, not a lack of desire—and, however we may pretend, there can be no virtue in abstinence merely through cowardice. Still, if there be merit in shrinking, even when the cruelest necessities were goading, that merit was hers in full measure. As a matter of reason and sense, she admitted that the girls who respected themselves and practiced their profession like merchants of other kinds were right, were doing what she ought to do. Anyhow, it was absurd to practice a profession half-heartedly. To play your game, whatever it might be, for all there was in it—that was the obvious first principle of success. Yet—she remained laggard and squeamish.

What she had been unable to do for herself, to save herself from squalor, from hunger, from cold, she was now able to do for the sake of another— to help the man who had enabled her to escape from that marriage, more hideous than anything she had endured since, or ever could be called upon to endure—to save him from certain neglect and probable death in the "charity" hospital. Not by merely tolerating the not too impossible men who joined her without sign from her, and not by merely accepting what they gave, could fifty dollars a week be made. She must dress herself in franker avowal of her profession, must look as expensive as her limited stock of clothing, supplemented by her own taste, would permit. She must flirt, must bargain, must ask for presents, must make herself agreeable, must resort to the crude female arts—which, however, are subtle enough to convince the self-enchanted male even in face of the discouraging fact of the mercenary arrangement. She must crush down her repugnance, must be active, not simply passive—must get the extra dollars by stimulating male appetites, instead of simply permitting them to satisfy themselves. She must seem rather the eager mistress than the reluctant and impatient wife.

And she did abruptly change her manner. There was in her, as her life had shown, a power of endurance, an ability to sacrifice herself in order to do the thing that seemed necessary, and to do it without shuffling or whining. Whatever else her career had done for her, it undoubtedly had strengthened this part of her nature. And now the result of her training showed. With her superior intelligence for the first time free to make the best of her opportunities, she abruptly became equal to the most consummate of her sisters in that long line of her sister-panders to male appetites which extends from the bought wife or mistress or fiancee of the rich grandee down all the social ranks to the wife or street girl cozening for a tipsy day-laborer's earnings on a Saturday night and the work girl teasing her "steady company" toward matrimony on the park bench or in the dark entry of the tenement.

She was able to pay Clara back in less than ten days. In Spenser's second week at the hospital she had him moved to better quarters and better attendance at thirty dollars a week.

Although she had never got rid of her most unprofessional habit of choosing and rejecting, there had been times when need forced her into straits where her lot seemed to her almost as low as that of the slave-like wives of the tenements, made her almost think she would be nearly as well off were she the wife, companion, butt, servant and general vent to some one dull and distasteful provider of a poor living. But now she no longer felt either degraded or heart sick and heart weary. And when he passed the worst crisis her spirits began to return.

And when Roderick should be well, and the sketch written—and an engagement got—Ah, then! Life indeed—life, at last! Was it this hope that gave her the strength to fight down and conquer the craving for opium? Or was it the necessity of keeping her wits and of saving every cent? Or was it because the opium habit, like the drink habit, like every other habit, is a matter of a temperament far more than it is a matter of an appetite—and that she had the appetite but not the temperament? No doubt this had its part in the quick and complete victory. At any rate, fight and conquer she did. The strongest interest always wins. She had an interest stronger than love of opium—an interest that substituted itself for opium and for drink and supplanted them. Life indeed—life, at last!

In his third week Rod began to round toward health. Einstein observed from the nurse's charts that Susan's visits were having an unfavorably exciting effect. He showed her the readings of temperature and pulse, and forbade her to stay longer than five minutes at each of her two daily visits. Also, she must not bring up any topic beyond the sickroom itself. One day Spenser greeted her with, "I'll feel better, now that I've got this off my mind." He held out to her a letter. "Take that to George Fitzalan. He's an old friend of mine—one I've done a lot for and never asked any favors of. He may be able to give you something fairly good, right away."

Susan glanced penetratingly at him, saw he had been brooding over the source of the money that was being spent upon him. "Very well," said she, "I'll go as soon as I can."

"Go this afternoon," said he with an invalid's fretfulness.

"And when you come this evening you can tell me how you got on."

"Very well. This afternoon. But you know, Rod, there's not a ghost of a chance."

"I tell you Fitzalan's my friend. He's got some gratitude. He'll *do* something."

"I don't want you to get into a mood where you'll be awfully depressed if I should fail."

"But you'll not fail."

It was evident that Spenser, untaught by experience and flattered into exaggerating his importance by the solicitude and deference of doctors and nurses to a paying invalid, had restored to favor his ancient enemy— optimism, the certain destroyer of any man who does not shake it off. She went away, depressed and worried. When she should come back with the only possible news, what would be the effect upon him—and he still in a critical stage? As the afternoon must be given to business, she decided to go straight uptown, hoping to catch Fitzalan before he went out to lunch. And twenty minutes after making this decision she was sitting in the anteroom of a suite of theatrical offices in the Empire Theater building. The girl in attendance had, as usual, all the airs little people assume when they are in close, if menial, relations with a person who, being important to them, therefore fills their whole small horizon. She deigned to take in Susan's name and the letter. Susan seated herself at the long table and with the seeming of calmness that always veiled her in her hours of greatest agitation, turned over the pages of the theatrical journals and magazines spread about in quantity.

After perhaps ten silent and uninterrupted minutes a man hurried in from the outside hall, strode toward the frosted glass door marked "Private." With his hand reaching for the knob he halted, made an impatient gesture, plumped himself down at the long table—at its distant opposite end. With a sweep of the arm he cleared a space wherein he proceeded to spread papers from his pocket and to scribble upon them furiously. When Susan happened to glance at him, his head was bent so low and his straw hat was tilted so far forward that she could not see his face. She observed that he was dressed attractively in an extremely light summer suit of homespun; his hands were large and strong and ruddy—the hands of an artist, in good health. Her glance returned to the magazine. After a few minutes she looked up. She was startled to find that the man was giving her a curious, searching inspection—and that he was Brent, the playwright—the same fascinating face, keen, cynical, amused—the same seeing eyes, that, in the Cafe Martin long ago, had made her feel as if she were being read to her most secret thought. She dropped her glance.

His voice made her start. "It's been a long time since I've seen you," he was saying.

She looked up, not believing it possible he was addressing her. But his gaze was upon her. Thus, she had not been mistaken in thinking she had seen recognition in his eyes. "Yes," she said, with a faint smile.

"A longer time for you than for me," said he.

"A good deal has happened to me," she admitted.

"Are you on the stage?"

"No. Not yet."

The girl entered by way of the private door. "Miss Lenox—this way, please." She saw Brent, became instantly all smiles and bows. "Oh—Mr. Fitzalan doesn't know you're here, Mr. Brent," she cried. Then, to Susan, "Wait a minute."

She was about to reënter the private office when Brent stopped her with, "Let Miss Lenox go in first. I don't wish to see Mr. Fitzalan yet." And he stood up, took off his hat, bowed gravely to Susan, said, "I'm glad to have seen you again."

Susan, with some color forced into her old-ivory skin by nervousness and amazement, went into the presence of Fitzalan. As the now obsequious girl closed the door behind her, she found herself facing a youngish man with a remnant of hair that was little more than fuzz on the top of his head. His features were sharp, aggressive, rather hard. He might have sat for the typical successful American young man of forty—so much younger in New York than is forty elsewhere in the United States—and so much older. He looked at Susan with a pleasant sympathetic smile.

"So," said he, "you're taking care of poor Spenser, are you? Tell him I'll try to run down to see him. I wish I could do something for him—something worth while, I mean. But—his request——

"Really, I've nothing of the kind. I couldn't possibly place you—at least, not at present—perhaps, later on——"

"I understand," interrupted Susan. "He's very ill. It would help him greatly if you would write him a few lines, saying you'll give me a place at the first vacancy, but that it may not be soon. I'll not trouble you again. I want the letter simply to carry him over the crisis."

Fitzalan hesitated, rubbed his fuzzy crown with his jeweled hand. "Tell him that," he said, finally. "I'm rather careful about writing letters. . . . Yes, say to him what you suggested, as if it was from me."

"The letter will make all the difference between his believing and not believing," urged Susan. "He has great admiration and liking for you—thinks you would do anything for him."

Fitzalan frowned; she saw that her insistence had roused—or, rather, had strengthened—suspicion. "Really—you must excuse me. What I've heard about him the past year has not——

"But, no matter, I can't do it. You'll let me know how he's getting on? Good day." And he gave her that polite yet positive nod of dismissal which is a necessary part of the equipment of men of affairs, constantly beset as they are and ever engaged in the battle to save their chief asset, time, from being wasted.

Susan looked at him—a straight glance from gray eyes, a slight smile hovering about her scarlet lips. He reddened, fussed with the papers before him on the desk from which he had not risen. She opened the door, closed it behind her. Brent was seated with his back full to her and was busy with his scribbling. She passed him, went on to the outer door. She was waiting for his voice; she knew it would come.

"Miss Lenox!"

As she turned he was advancing. His figure, tall and slim and straight, had the ease of movement which proclaims the man who has been everywhere and so is at home anywhere. He held out a card. "I wish to see you on business. You can come at three this afternoon?"

"Yes," said Susan.

"Thanks," said he, bowing and returning to the table. She went on into the hall, the card between her fingers. At the elevator, she stood staring at the name—Robert Brent—as if it were an inscription in a forgotten language. She was so absorbed, so dazed that she did not ring the bell. The car happened to stop at that floor; she entered as if it were dark. And, in the street, she wandered many blocks down Broadway before she realized where she was.

She left the elevated and walked eastward through Grand Street. She was filled with a new and profound dissatisfaction. She felt like one awakening from a hypnotic trance. The surroundings, inanimate and animate, that had become endurable through custom abruptly resumed their original aspect of squalor and ugliness of repulsion and tragedy. A stranger—the ordinary, unobservant, feebly imaginative person, going along those streets would have seen nothing but tawdriness and poverty. Susan, experienced, imaginative, saw *all*—saw what another would have seen only after it was pointed out, and even then but dimly. And that day her vision was no longer staled and deadened by familiarity, but with vision fresh and with nerves acute. The men—the women—and, saddest, most tragic of all, the children! When she entered her room her reawakened sensitiveness, the keener for its long repose, for the enormous unconscious absorption of impressions of the life about her—this morbid sensitiveness of the soul a-clash with its environment reached its climax. As she threw open the door, she shrank back before the odor—the powerful, sensual, sweet odor of chypre so effective in covering the bad smells that came up from other flats and from the noisome back yards. The room itself was neat and clean and plain, with not a few evidences of her personal taste—in the blending of colors, in the selection of framed photographs on the walls. The one she especially liked was the largest—a nude woman lying at full length, her head supported by her arm, her face gazing straight out of the picture, upon it a baffling expression—of sadness, of cynicism, of amusement perhaps, of experience, yet of innocence. It hung upon the wall opposite the door. When she saw this picture in the department store, she felt at once a sympathy between that woman and herself, felt she was for the first time seeing another soul like her own, one that would have understood her strange sense of innocence in the midst of her own defiled and depraved self—a core of unsullied nature. Everyone else in the world would have mocked at this notion of a something within—a true self to which all that seemed to be her own self was as external as her clothing; this woman of the photograph would understand. So, there she hung—Susan's one prized possession.

The question of dressing for this interview with Brent was most important. Susan gave it much thought before she began to dress, changed her mind again and again in the course of dressing. Through all her vicissitudes she had never lost her interest in the art of dress or her skill at it—and despite the unfavorable surroundings she had steadily improved; any woman anywhere would instantly have recognized her as one of those few favored and envied women who know how to get together a toilet. She finally chose the simplest of the half dozen summer dresses she had made for herself—a plain white lawn, with a short skirt. It gave her an appearance of extreme youth, despite her height and the slight stoop in her shoulders—a mere drooping that harmonized touchingly with the young yet weary expression of her face. To go with the dress she had a large hat of black rough straw with a very little white trimming on it. With this large black hat bewitchingly set upon her gracefully-done dark wavy hair, her sad, dreamy eyes, her pallid skin, her sweet-bitter mouth with its rouged lips seemed to her to show at their best. She felt that nothing was quite so effective for her skin as a white dress. In other colors—though she did not realize—the woman of bought kisses showed more distinctly—never brazenly as in most of the girls, but still unmistakably. In white she took on a glamour of melancholy—and the human countenance is capable of no expression so universally appealing as the look of melancholy that suggests the sadness underlying all life, the pain that pays for pleasure, the pain that pays and gets no pleasure, the sorrow of the passing of all things, the faint foreshadow of the doom awaiting us all. She washed the rouge from her lips, studied the effect in the glass. "No," she said aloud, "without it I feel like a hypocrite—and I don't look half so well." And she put the rouge on again—the scarlet dash drawn startlingly across her strange, pallid face.

CHAPTER XII

AT three that afternoon she stood in the vestibule of Brent's small house in Park Avenue overlooking the oblong of green between East Thirty-seventh Street and East Thirty-eighth. A most reputable looking Englishman in evening dress opened the door; from her reading and her theater-going she knew that this was a butler. He bowed her in. The entire lower floor was given to an entrance hall, done in plain black walnut, almost lofty of ceiling, and with a grand stairway leading to the upper part of the house. There was a huge fireplace to the right; a mirror filled the entire back wall; a broad low seat ran all round the room. In one corner, an enormous urn of dark pottery; in another corner, a suit of armor, the helmet, the breastplate and the gauntlets set with gold of ancient lackluster.

The butler left her there and ascended the polished but dead-finished stairway noiselessly. Susan had never before been in so grand a room. The best private house she had ever seen was Wright's in Sutherland; and while everybody else in Sutherland thought it magnificent, she had felt that there was something wrong, what she had not known. The grandiose New York hotels and restaurants were more showy and more pretentious far than this interior of Brent's. But her unerring instinct of those born with good taste knew at first view of them that they were simply costly; there were beautiful things in them, fine carvings and paintings and tapestries, but personality was lacking. And without personality there can be no unity; without unity there can be no harmony — and without harmony, no beauty.

Looking round her now, she had her first deep draught of esthetic delight in interior decoration. She loved this quiet dignity, this large simplicity — nothing that obtruded, nothing that jarred, everything on the same scale of dark coloring and large size. She admired the way the mirror, without pretense of being anything but a mirror, enhanced the spaciousness of the room and doubled the pleasure it gave by offering another and different view of it.

Last of all Susan caught sight of herself — a slim, slightly stooped figure, its white dress and its big black hat with white trimmings making it stand out strongly against the rather somber background. In a curiously impersonal way her own sad, wistful face interested her. A human being's face is a summary of his career. No man can realize at a thought what he is, can epitomize in just proportion what has been made of him by experience of the multitude of moments of which life is composed. But in some moods and in some lights we do get such an all-comprehending view of ourselves in looking at our own faces. As she had instinctively felt, there was a world of meaning in the contrast between her pensive brow above melancholy eyes and the blood-red line of her rouged lips.

The butler descended. "Mr. Brent is in his library, on the fourth floor," said he. "Will you kindly step this way, ma'am?"

Instead of indicating the stairway, he went to the panel next the chimney piece. She saw that it was a hidden door admitting to an elevator. She entered; the door closed; the elevator ascended rapidly. When it came to a stop the door opened and she was facing Brent.

"Thank you for coming," said he, with almost formal courtesy.

For all her sudden shyness, she cast a quick but seeing look round. It was an overcast day; the soft floods of liquid light—the beautiful light of her beloved City of the Sun—poured into the big room through an enormous window of clear glass which formed the entire north wall. Round the other walls from floor almost to lofty ceiling were books in solid rows; not books with ornamental bindings, but books for use, books that had been and were being used. By way of furniture there were an immense lounge, wide and long and deep, facing the left chimney piece, an immense table desk facing the north light, three great chairs with tall backs, one behind the table, one near the end of the table, the third in the corner farthest from the window; a grand piano, open, with music upon its rack, and a long carved seat at its keyboard. The huge window had a broad sill upon which was built a generous window garden fresh and lively with bright flowers. The woodwork, the ceiling, the furniture were of mahogany. The master of this splendid simplicity was dressed in a blue house suit of some summer material like linen. He was smoking a cigarette, and offered her one from the great carved wood box filled with them on the table desk.

"Thanks," said she. And when she had lighted it and was seated facing him as he sat at his desk, she felt almost at her ease. After all, while his gaze was penetrating, it was also understanding; we do not mind being unmasked if the unmasker at once hails us as brother. Brent's eyes seemed to say to her, "Human!—like me." She smoked and let her gaze wander from her books to window garden, from window garden to piano.

"You play?" said he.

"A very little. Enough for accompaniments to simple songs."

"You sing?"

"Simple songs. I've had but a few lessons from a small-town teacher."

"Let me hear."

She went to the piano, laid her cigarette in a tray ready beside the music rack. She gave him the "Gipsy Queen," which she liked because it expressed her own passion of revolt against restraints of every conventional kind and her love for the open air and open sky. He somehow took away all feeling of embarrassment; she felt so strongly that he understood and was big enough not to have it anywhere in him to laugh at anything sincere. When she finished she resumed her cigarette and returned to the chair near his.

"It's as I thought," said he. "Your voice can be trained—to speak, I mean. I don't know as to its singing value. . . . Have you good health?"

"I never have even colds. Yes, I'm strong."

"You'll need it."

"I have needed it," said she. Into her face came the sad, bitter expression with its curious relief of a faint cynical smile.

He leaned back in his chair and looked at her through a cloud of smoke. She saw that his eyes were not gray, as she had thought, but brown, a hazel brown with points of light sparkling in the irises and taking away all the suggestion of weakness and sentimentality that makes pure brown eyes unsatisfactory in a man. He said slowly:

"When I saw you—in the Martin—you were on the way down. You went, I see."

She nodded. "I'm still there."

"You like it? You wish to stay?"

She shook her head smilingly. "No, but I can stay if it's necessary. I've discovered that I've got the health and the nerves for anything."

"That's a great discovery. . . . Well, you'll soon be on your way up. . . . Do you wish to know why I spoke to you this morning?—Why I remembered you?"

"Why?"

"Because of the expression of your eyes—when your face is in repose."

She felt no shyness—and no sense of necessity of responding to a compliment, for his tone forbade any thought of flattery. She lowered her gaze to conceal the thoughts his words brought—the memories of the things that had caused her eyes to look as Rod and now Brent said.

"Such an expression," the playwright went on, "must mean character. I am sick and tired of the vanity of these actresses who can act just enough never to be able to learn to act well. I'm going to try an experiment with you. I've tried it several times but—No matter. I'm not discouraged. I never give up. . . . Can you stand being alone?"

"I spend most of my time alone. I prefer it."

"I thought so. Yes—you'll do. Only the few who can stand being alone ever get anywhere. Everything worth while is done alone. The big battle—it isn't fought in the field, but by the man sitting alone in his tent, working it all out. The bridge—the tunnel through the great mountains—the railway— the huge business enterprise—all done by the man alone, thinking, plotting to the last detail. It's the same way with the novel, the picture, the statue, the play—writing it, acting it—all done by someone alone, shut in with his imagination and his tools. I saw that you were one of the lonely ones. All you need is a chance. You'd surely get it, sooner or later. Perhaps I can bring it a little sooner. . . . How much do you need to live on?"

"I must have fifty dollars a week—if I go on at—as I am now.

If you wish to take all my time—then, forty."

He smiled in a puzzled way.

"The police," she explained. "I need ten——"

"Certainly—certainly," cried he. "I understand—perfectly. How stupid of me! I'll want all your time. So it's to be forty dollars a week. When can you begin?"

Susan reflected. "I can't go into anything that'll mean a long time," she said. "I'm waiting for a man—a friend of mine to get well. Then we're going to do something together."

Brent made an impatient gesture. "An actor? Well, I suppose I can get him something to do. But I don't want you to be under the influence of any of these absurd creatures who think they know what acting is—when they merely know how to dress themselves in different suits of clothes, and strut themselves about the stage. They'd rather die than give up their own feeble, foolish little identities. I'll see that your actor friend is taken care of, but you must keep away from him—for the time at least."

"He's all I've got. He's an old friend."

"You—care for him?"

"I used to. And lately I found him again—after we had been separated a long time. We're going to help each other up."

"Oh—he's down and out oh? Why?"

"Drink—and hard luck."

"Not hard luck. That helps a man. It has helped you. It has made you what you are."

"What am I?" asked Susan.

Brent smiled mysteriously. "That's what we're going to find out," said he. "There's no human being who has ever had a future unless he or she had a past—and the severer the past the more splendid the future."

Susan was attending with all her senses. This man was putting into words her own inarticulate instincts.

"A past," he went on in his sharp, dogmatic way, "either breaks or makes. You go into the crucible a mere ore, a possibility. You come out slag or steel." He was standing now, looking down at her with quizzical eyes. "You're about due to leave the pot," said he.

"And I've hopes that you're steel. If not——" He shrugged his shoulders—"You'll have had forty a week for your time, and I'll have gained useful experience."

Susan gazed at him as if she doubted her eyes and ears.

"What do you want me to do?" she presently inquired.

"Learn the art of acting—which consists of two parts. First, you must learn to act—thousands of the profession do that. Second, you must learn not to act—and so far I know there aren't a dozen in the whole world who've got that far along. I've written a play I think well of. I want to have it done properly—it, and several other plays I intend to write. I'm going to give you a chance to become famous—better still, great."

Susan looked at him incredulously. "Do you know who I am?" she asked at last.

"Certainly."

Her eyes lowered, the faintest tinge of red changed the amber-white pallor of her cheeks, her bosom rose and fell quickly.

"I don't mean," he went on, "that I know any of the details of your experience. I only know the results as they are written in your face. The details are unimportant. When I say I know who you are, I mean I know that you are a woman who has suffered, whose heart has been broken by suffering, but not her spirit. Of where you came from or how you've lived, I know nothing. And it's none of my business—no more than it's the public's business where *I* came from and how I've learned to write plays."

Well, whether he was guessing any part of the truth or all of it, certainly what she had said about the police and now this sweeping statement of his attitude toward her freed her of the necessity of disclosing herself. She eagerly tried to dismiss the thoughts that had been making her most uneasy. She said:

"You think I can learn to act?"

"That, of course," replied he. "Any intelligent person can learn to act— and also most persons who have no more intelligence in their heads than they have in their feet. I'll guarantee you some sort of career. What I'm interested to find out is whether you can learn *not* to act. I believe you can. But——" He laughed in self-mockery. "I've made several absurd mistakes in that direction. . . . You have led a life in which most women become the cheapest sort of liars—worse liars even than is the usual respectable person, because they haven't the restraint of fearing loss of reputation. Why is it you have not become a liar?"

Susan laughed. "I'm sure I don't know. Perhaps because lying is such a tax on the memory. May I have another cigarette?"

He held the match for her. "You don't paint—except your lips," he went on, "though you have no color. And you don't wear cheap finery. And while you use a strong scent, it's not one of the cheap and nasty kind—it's sensual without being slimy. And you don't use the kind of words one always hears in your circle."

Susan looked immensely relieved. "Then you *do* know who I am!" she cried.

"You didn't suppose I thought you fresh from a fashionable boarding school, did you? I'd hardly look there for an actress who could act. You've got experience—experience—experience—written all over your face— sadly, satirically, scornfully, gayly, bitterly. And what I want is experience— not merely having been through things, but having been through them understandingly. You'll help me in my experiment?"

He looked astonished, then irritated, when the girl, instead of accepting eagerly, drew back in her chair and seemed to be debating. His irritation showed still more plainly when she finally said:

"That depends on him. And he—he thinks you don't like him."

"What's his name?" said Brent in his abrupt, intense fashion.

"What's his name?"

"Spenser—Roderick Spenser."

Brent looked vague.

"He used to be on the *Herald*. He writes plays."

"Oh—yes. I remember. He's a weak fool."

Susan abruptly straightened, an ominous look in eyes and brow.

Brent made an impatient gesture. "Beg pardon. Why be sensitive about him? Obviously because you know I'm right. I said fool, not ass. He's clever, but ridiculously vain. I don't dislike him. I don't care anything about him— or about anybody else in the world. No man does who amounts to anything. With a career it's as Jesus said—leave father and mother, husband and wife—land, ox everything—and follow it."

"What for?" said Susan.

"To save your soul! To be a somebody; to be strong. To be able to give to anybody and everybody—whatever they need. To be happy."

"Are you happy?"

"No," he admitted. "But I'm growing in that direction. . . . Don't waste yourself on Stevens—I beg pardon, Spenser. You're bigger than that. He's a small man with large dreams—a hopeless misfit. Small dreams for small men; large dreams for—" he laughed—"you and me—our sort."

Susan echoed his laugh, but faint-heartedly. "I've watched your name in the papers," she said, sincerely unconscious of flattery. "I've seen you grow more and more famous. But—if there had been anything in me, would I have gone down and down?"

"How old are you?"

"About twenty-one."

"Only twenty-one and that look in your face! Magnificent! I don't believe I'm to be disappointed this time. You ask why you've gone down! You haven't. You've gone *through*."

"Down," she insisted, sadly.

"Nonsense! The soot'll rub off the steel."

She lifted her head eagerly. Her own secret thought put into words.

"You can't make steel without soot and dirt. You can't make anything without dirt. That's why the nice, prim, silly world's full of cabinets exhibiting little chips of raw material polished up neatly in one or two spots. That's why there are so few men and women—and those few have had to make themselves, or are made by accident. You're an accident, I suppose. The women who amount to anything usually are. The last actress I tried to do anything with might have become a somebody if it hadn't been for one thing: She had a hankering for respectability—a yearning to be a society person—to be thought well of by society people. It did for her."

"I'll not sink on that rock," said Susan cheerfully.

"No secret longing for social position?"

"None. Even if I would, I couldn't."

"That's one heavy handicap out of the way. But I'll not let myself begin to hope until I find out whether you've got incurable and unteachable vanity. If you have—then, no hope. If you haven't—there's a fighting chance."

"You forget my compact," Susan reminded him.

"Oh—the lover—Spenser."

Brent reflected, strolled to the big window, his hands deep in his pockets. Susan took advantage of his back to give way to her own feelings of utter amazement and incredulity. She certainly was not dreaming. And the man gazing out at the window was certainly flesh and blood—a great man, if voluble and eccentric. Perhaps to act and speak as one pleased was one of the signs of greatness, one of its perquisites. Was he amusing himself with her? Was he perchance taken with her physically and employing these extraordinary methods as ways of approach? She had seen many peculiarities of sex-approach in men—some grotesque, many terrible, all beyond comprehension. Was this another such?

He wheeled suddenly, surprised her eyes upon him. He burst out laughing, and she felt that he had read her thoughts. However, he merely said:

"Have you anything to suggest—about Spenser?"

"I can't even tell him of your offer now. He's very ill—and sensitive about you."

"About me? How ridiculous! I'm always coming across men I don't know who are full of venom toward me. I suppose he thinks I crowded him. No matter. You're sure you're not fancying yourself in love with him?"

"No, I am not in love with him. He has changed—and so have I."

He smiled at her. "Especially in the last hour?" he suggested.

"I had changed before that. I had been changing right along. But I didn't realize it fully until you talked with me—no, until after you gave me your card this morning."

"You saw a chance—a hope—eh?"

She nodded.

"And at once became all nerves and courage. . . . As to Spenser—I'll have some play carpenter sent to collaborate with him and set him up in the play business. You know it's a business as well as an art. And the chromos sell better than the oil paintings—except the finest ones. It's my chromos that have earned me the means and the leisure to try oils."

"He'd never consent. He's very proud."

"Vain, you mean. Pride will consent to anything as a means to an end. It's vanity that's squeamish and haughty. He needn't know."

"But I couldn't discuss any change with him until he's much better."

"I'll send the play carpenter to him—get Fitzalan to send one of his carpenters." Brent smiled. "You don't think *he*'ll hang back because of the compact, do you?"

Susan flushed painfully. "No," she admitted in a low voice.

Brent was still smiling at her, and the smile was cynical. But his tone soothed where his words would have wounded, as he went on: "A man of his sort—an average, 'there-are-two-kinds-of-women, good-and-bad' sort of man—has but one use for a woman of your sort."

"I know that," said Susan.

"Do you mind it?"

"Not much. I'd not mind it at all if I felt that I was somebody."

Brent put his hand on her shoulder. "You'll do, Miss Lenox," he said with quiet heartiness. "You may not be so big a somebody as you and I would like. But you'll count as one, all right."

She looked at him with intense appeal in her eyes. "Why?" she said earnestly. "*Why* do you do this?"

He smiled gravely down at her—as gravely as Brent could smile—with the quizzical suggestion never absent from his handsome face, so full of life and intelligence. "I've been observing your uneasiness," said he. "Now listen. It would be impossible for you to judge me, to understand me. You are young and as yet small. I am forty, and have lived twenty-five of my forty years intensely. So, don't fall into the error of shallow people and size me up by your own foolish little standards. Do you see what I mean?"

Susan's candid face revealed her guilt. "Yes," said she, rather humbly.

"I see you do understand," said he. "And that's a good sign. Most people, hearing what I said, would have disregarded it as merely my vanity, would have gone on with their silly judging, would have set me down as a conceited ass who by some accident had got a reputation. But to proceed—I have not chosen you on impulse. Long and patient study has made me able to judge character by the face, as a horse dealer can judge horses by looking at them. I don't need to read every line of a book to know whether it's wise or foolish, worth while or not. I don't need to know a human being for years or for hours or for minutes even, before I can measure certain things. I measured you. It's like astronomy. An astronomer wants to get the orbit of a star. He takes its position twice—and from the two observations he can calculate the orbit to the inch. I've got three observations of your orbit. Enough—and to spare."

"I shan't misunderstand again," said Susan.

"One thing more," insisted Brent. "In our relations, we are to be not man and woman, but master and pupil. I shan't waste your time with any— other matters."

It was Susan's turn to laugh. "That's your polite way of warning me not to waste any of your time with—other matters."

"Precisely," conceded he. "A man in my position—a man in any sort of position, for that matter—is much annoyed by women trying to use their sex with him. I wished to make it clear at the outset that— —"

"That I could gain nothing by neglecting the trade of actress for the trade of woman," interrupted Susan. "I understand perfectly."

He put out his hand. "I see that at least we'll get on together. I'll have Fitzalan send the carpenter to your friend at once."

"Today!" exclaimed Susan, in surprise and delight.

"Why not?" He arranged paper and pen. "Sit here and write Spenser's address, and your own. Your salary begins with today. I'll have my secretary mail you a check. And as soon as I can see you again, I'll send you a telegram. Meanwhile—" He rummaged among a lot of paper bound plays on the table "Here's 'Cavalleria Rusticana.' Read it with a view to yourself as either *Santuzzao* or *Lola*. Study her first entrance—what you would do with it. Don't be frightened. I expect nothing from you—nothing whatever. I'm glad you know nothing about acting. You'll have the less to unlearn."

They had been moving towards the elevator. He shook hands again and, after adjusting the mechanism for the descent, closed the door. As it was closing she saw in his expression that his mind had already dismissed her for some one of the many other matters that crowded his life.

CHAPTER XIII

THE Susan Lenox who left Delancey Street at half past two that afternoon to call upon Robert Brent was not the Susan Lenox who returned to Delancey Street at half-past five. A man is wandering, lost in a cave, is groping this way and that in absolute darkness, with flagging hope and fainting strength—has reached the point where he wonders at his own folly in keeping on moving—is persuading himself that the sensible thing would be to lie down and give up. He sees a gleam of light. Is it a reality? Is it an illusion—one more of the illusions that have lured him on and on? He does not know; but instantly a fire sweeps through him, warming his dying strength into vigor.

So it was with Susan.

The pariah class—the real pariah class—does not consist of merely the women formally put beyond the pale for violations of conventional morality and the men with the brand of thief or gambler upon them. Our social, our industrial system has made it far vaster. It includes almost the whole population—all those who sell body or brain or soul in an uncertain market for uncertain hire, to gain the day's food and clothing, the night's shelter. This vast mass floats hither and yon on the tides and currents of destiny. Now it halts, resting sluggishly in a dead calm; again it moves, sometimes slowly, sometimes under the lash of tempest. But it is ever the same vast inertia, with no particle of it possessing an aim beyond keeping afloat and alive. Susan had been an atom, a spray of weed, in this Sargasso Sea.

If you observe a huge, unwieldy crowd so closely packed that nothing can be done with it and it can do nothing with itself, you will note three different types. There are the entirely inert—and they make up most of the crowd. They do not resist; they helplessly move this way and that as the chance waves of motion prompt. Of this type is the overwhelming majority of the human race. Here and there in the mass you will see examples of a second type. These are individuals who are restive and resentful under the sense of helplessness and impotence. They struggle now gently, now furiously. They thrust backward or forward or to one side. They thresh about. But nothing comes of their efforts beyond a brief agitation, soon dying away in ripples. The inertia of the mass and their own lack of purpose conquer them. Occasionally one of these grows so angry and so violent that the surrounding inertia quickens into purpose—the purpose of making an end of this agitation which is serving only to increase the general discomfort. And the agitator is trampled down, disappears, perhaps silently, perhaps with groan or shriek. Continue to look at this crowd, so pitiful, so terrible, such a melancholy waste of incalculable power—continue to observe and you may chance upon an example of the third type. You are likely at first to confuse the third type with the second, for they seem to be much alike. Here and there, of the resentful strugglers, will be one whose resentment is intelligent. He struggles, but it is not aimless struggle. He has seen or suspected in a definite direction a point where he would be more or less free, perhaps entirely free. He realizes how he is hemmed in, realizes how difficult, how dangerous, will be his endeavor to get to that point. And he proceeds to try to minimize or overcome the difficulties, the dangers. He struggles now gently, now earnestly, now violently—but always toward his fixed objective. He is driven back, to one side, is almost overwhelmed. He causes commotions that threaten to engulf him, and must pause or retreat until they have calmed. You may have to watch him long before you discover that, where other strugglers have been aimless, he aims and resolves. And little by little he gains, makes progress toward his goal—and once in a long while one such reaches that goal. It is triumph, success.

Susan, young, inexperienced, dazed; now too despondent, now too hopeful; now too gentle and again too infuriated—Susan had been alternating between inertia and purposeless struggle. Brent had given her the thing she lacked—had given her a definite, concrete, tangible purpose. He had shown her the place where, if she should arrive, she might be free of that hideous slavery of the miserable mass; and he had inspired her with the hope that she could reach it.

And that was the Susan Lenox who came back to the little room in Delancey Street at half-past five.

Curiously, while she was thinking much about Brent, she was thinking even more about Burlingham—about their long talks on the show boat and in their wanderings in Louisville and Cincinnati. His philosophy, his teachings—the wisdom he had, but was unable to apply—began to come back to her. It was not strange that she should remember it, for she had admired him intensely and had listened to his every word, and she was then at the time when the memory takes its clearest and strongest impressions. The strangeness lay in the suddenness with which Burlingham, so long dead, suddenly came to life, changed from a sad and tender memory to a vivid possibility, advising her, helping her, urging her on.

Clara, dressed to go to dinner with her lover, was waiting to arrange about their meeting to make together the usual rounds in the evening. "I've got an hour before I'm due at the hospital," said Susan. "Let's go down to Kelly's for a drink."

While they were going and as they sat in the clean little back room of Kelly's well ordered and select corner saloon, Clara gave her all the news she had gathered in an afternoon of visits among their acquaintances—how, because of a neighborhood complaint, there was to be a fake raid on Gussie's opium joint at midnight; that Mazie had caught a frightful fever; and that Nettie was dying in Governeur of the stab in the stomach her lover had given her at a ball three nights before; that the police had raised the tariff for sporting houses, and would collect seventy-five and a hundred a month protection money where the charge had been twenty-five and fifty—the plea was that the reformers, just elected and hoping for one term only, were compelling a larger fund from vice than the old steady year-in-and-year-out ruling crowd. "And they may raise *us* to fifteen a week," said Clara, "though I doubt it. They'll not cut off their nose to spite their face. If they raised the rate for the streets they'd drive two-thirds of the girls back to the factories and sweat shops. You're not listening, Lorna. What's up?"

"Nothing."

"Your fellow's not had a relapse?"

"No—nothing."

"Need some money? I can lend you ten. I did have twenty, but I gave Sallie and that little Jew girl who's her side partner ten for the bail bondsman. They got pinched last night for not paying up to the police. They've gone crazy about that prize fighter—at least, he thinks he is—that Joe O'Mara, and they're giving him every cent they make. It's funny about Sallie. She's a Catholic and goes to mass regular. And she keeps straight on Sunday—no money'll tempt her—I've seen it tried. Do you want the ten?"

"No. I've got plenty."

"We must look in at that Jolly Rovers' ball tonight. There'll be a lot of fellows with money there.

"We can sure pull off something pretty good. Anyhow, we'll have fun. But you don't care for the dances. Well, they are a waste of time. And because the men pay for a few bum drinks and dance with a girl, they don't want to give up anything more. How's she to live, I want to know?"

"Would you like to get out of this, Clara?" interrupted Susan, coming out of her absent-mindedness.

"Would I! But what's the use of talking?"

"But I mean, would you *really?*"

"Oh—if there was something better. But is there? I don't see how I'd be as well off, respectable. As I said to the rescue woman, what is there in it for a 'reclaimed' girl, as they call it? When they ask a man to reform they can offer him something—and he can go on up and up. But not for girls. Nothing doing but charity and pity and the second table and the back door. I can make more money at this and have a better time, as long as my looks last. And I've turned down already a couple of chances to marry—men that wouldn't have looked at me if I'd been in a store or a factory or living out. I may marry."

"Don't do that," said Susan. "Marriage makes brutes of men, and slaves of women."

"You speak as if you knew."

"I do," said Susan, in a tone that forbade question.

"I ain't exactly stuck on the idea myself," pursued Clara. "And if I don't, why when my looks are gone, where am I worse off than I'd be at the same age as a working girl? If I have to get a job then, I can get it—and I'll not be broken down like the respectable women at thirty—those that work or those that slop round boozing and neglecting their children while their husbands work. Of course, there's chances against you in this business. But so there is in every business. Suppose I worked in a factory and lost a leg in the machinery, like that girl of Mantell, the bricklayer's? Suppose I get an awful disease—to hear some people talk you'd think there wasn't any chances of death or horrible diseases at respectable work. Why, how could anybody be worse off than if they got lung trouble and boils as big as your fist like those girls over in the tobacco factory?"

"You needn't tell me about work," said Susan. "The streets are full of wrecks from work—and the hospitals—and the graveyard over on the Island. You can always go to that slavery. But I mean a respectable life, with everything better."

"Has one of those swell women from uptown been after you?"

"No. This isn't a pious pipe dream."

"You sound like it. One of them swell silk smarties got at me when I was in the hospital with the fever. She was a bird—she was. She handed me a line of grand talk, and I, being sort of weak with sickness, took it in. Well, when she got right down to business, what did she want me to do? Be a dressmaker or a lady's maid. Me work twelve, fourteen, God knows how many hours—be too tired to have any fun—travel round with dead ones—be a doormat for a lot of cheap people that are tryin' to make out they ain't human like the rest of us. *Me!* And when I said, No, thank you,' what do you think?"

"Did she offer to get you a good home in the country?" said Susan.

"That was it. The *country!* The nerve of her! But I called her bluff, all right, all right. I says to her, Are you going to the country to live?' And she reared at *me* daring to question *her*, and said she wasn't. 'You'd find it dead slow, wouldn't you?' says I. And she kind o' laughed and looked almost human. 'Then,' says I, 'no more am I going to the country. I'll take my chances in little old New York,' I says."

"I should think so!" exclaimed Susan.

"I'd like to be respectable, if I could afford it. But there's nothing in that game for poor girls unless they haven't got no looks to sell and have to sell the rest of themselves for some factory boss to get rich off of while they get poorer and weaker every day. And when they say 'God' to me, I say, 'Who's he? He must be somebody that lives up on Fifth Avenue. We ain't seen him down our way.'"

"I mean, go on the stage," resumed Susan.

"I wouldn't mind, if I could get in right. Everything in this world depends on getting in right. I was born four flights up in a tenement, and I've been in wrong ever since."

"I was in wrong from the beginning, too," said Susan, thoughtfully. "In wrong—that's it exactly." Clara's eyes again became eager with the hope of a peep into the mystery of Susan's origin. But Susan went on, "Yes, I've always been in wrong. Always."

"Oh, no," declared Clara. "You've got education—and manners—and ladylike instincts. I'm at home here. I was never so well off in my life. I'm, you might say, on my way up in the world. Most of us girls are—like the fellow that ain't got nothing to eat or no place to sleep and gets into jail— he's better off, ain't he? But you—you don't belong here at all."

"I belong anywhere—and everywhere—and nowhere," said Susan. "Yes, I belong here. I've got a chance uptown. If it pans out, I'll let you in."

Clara looked at her wistfully. Clara had a wicked temper when she was in liquor, and had the ordinary human proneness to lying, to mischievous gossip, and to utter laziness. The life she led, compelling cleanliness and neatness and a certain amount of thrift under penalty of instant ruin, had done her much good in saving her from going to pieces and becoming the ordinary sloven and drag on the energies of some man. "Lorna," she now said, "I do believe you like me a little." "More than that," Susan assured her. "You've saved me from being hard-hearted. I must go to the hospital. So long!"

"How about this evening?" asked Clara.

"I'm staying in. I've got something to do."

"Well—I may be home early—unless I go to the ball."

Susan was refused admittance at the hospital. Spenser, they said, had received a caller, had taxed his strength enough for the day. Nor would it be worth while to return in the morning. The same caller was coming again. Spenser had said she was to come in the afternoon. She received this cheerfully, yet not without a certain sense of hurt—which, however, did not last long.

When she was admitted to Spenser the following afternoon, she faced him guiltily—for the thoughts Brent had set to bubbling and boiling in her. And her guilt showed in the tone of her greeting, in the reluctance and forced intensity of her kiss and embrace. She had compressed into the five most receptive years of a human being's life an experience that was, for one of her intelligence and education, equal to many times five years of ordinary life. And this experience had developed her instinct for concealing her deep feelings into a fixed habit. But it had not made her a liar—had not robbed her of her fundamental courage and self-respect which made her shrink in disdain from deceiving anyone who seemed to her to have the right to frankness. Spenser, she felt as always, had that right—this, though he had not been frank with her; still, that was a matter for his own conscience and did not affect her conscience as to what was courageous and honorable toward him. So, had he been observing, he must have seen that something was wrong. But he was far too excited about his own affairs to note her.

"My luck's turned!" cried he, after kissing her with enthusiasm. "Fitzalan has sent Jack Sperry to me, and we're to collaborate on a play. I told you Fitz was the real thing."

Susan turned hastily away to hide her telltale face.

"Who's Sperry?" asked she, to gain time for self-control.

"Oh, He's a play-smith—and a bear at it. He has knocked together half a dozen successes. He'll supply the trade experience that I lack, and Fitzalan will be sure to put on our piece."

"You're a lot better—aren't you?"

"Better? I'm almost well."

He certainly had made a sudden stride toward health. By way of doing something progressive he had had a shave, and that had restored the look of youth to his face—or, rather, had uncovered it. A strong, handsome face it was—much handsomer than Brent's—and with the subtle, moral weakness of optimistic vanity well concealed. Yes, much handsomer than Brent's, which wasn't really handsome at all—yet was superbly handsomer, also— the handsomeness that comes from being through and through a somebody. She saw again why she had cared for Rod so deeply; but she also saw why she could not care again, at least not in that same absorbed, self-effacing way. Physical attraction—yes. And a certain remnant of the feeling of comradeship, too. But never again utter belief, worshipful admiration—or any other degree of belief or admiration beyond the mild and critical. She herself had grown. Also, Brent's penetrating and just analysis of Spenser had put clearly before her precisely what he was—precisely what she herself had been vaguely thinking of him.

As he talked on and on of Sperry's visit and the new projects, she listened, looking at his character in the light Brent had turned upon it— Brent who had in a few brief moments turned such floods of light upon so many things she had been seeing dimly or not at all. Moderate prosperity and moderate adversity bring out the best there is in a man; the extreme of either brings out his worst. The actual man is the best there is in him, and not the worst, but it is one of the tragedies of life that those who have once seen his worst ever afterward have sense of it chiefly, and cannot return to the feeling they had for him when his worst was undreamed of. "I'm not in love with Brent," thought Susan. "But having known him, I can't ever any more care for Rod. He seems small beside Brent—and he *is* small."

Spenser in his optimistic dreaming aloud had reached a point where it was necessary to assign Susan a role in his dazzling career. "You'll not have to go on the stage," said he. "I'll look out for you. By next week Sperry and I will have got together a scenario for the play and when Sperry reads it to Fitzalan we'll get an advance of at least five hundred. So you and I will take a nice room and bath uptown—as a starter—and we'll be happy again— happier than before."

"No, I'm going to support myself," said Susan promptly.

"Trash!" cried Spenser, smiling tenderly at her. "Do you suppose I'd allow you to mix up in stage life? You've forgotten how jealous I am of you. You don't know what I've suffered since I've been here sick, brooding over what you're doing, to——"

She laid her fingers on his lips. "What's the use of fretting about anything that has to be?" said she, smilingly. "I'm going to support myself. You may as well make up your mind to it."

"Plenty of time to argue that out," said he, and his tone forecast his verdict on the arguing. And he changed the subject by saying, "I see you still cling to your fad of looking fascinating about the feet. That was one of the reasons I never could trust you. A girl with as charming feet and ankles as you have, and so much pride in getting them up well, simply cannot be trustworthy." He laughed. "No, you were made to be taken care of, my dear."

She did not press the matter. She had taken her stand; that was enough for the present. After an hour with him, she went home to get herself something to eat on her gas stove. Spenser's confidence in the future did not move her even to the extent of laying out half a dollar on a restaurant dinner. Women have the habit of believing in the optimistic outpourings of egotistical men, and often hasten men along the road to ruin by proclaiming this belief and acting upon it. But not intelligent women of experience; that sort of woman, by checking optimistic husbands, fathers, sons, lovers, has even put off ruin—sometimes until death has had the chance to save the optimist from the inevitable consequence of his folly. When she finished her chop and vegetable, instead of lighting a cigarette and lingering over a cup of black coffee she quickly straightened up and began upon the play Brent had given her. She had read it several times the night before, and again and again during the day. But not until now did she feel sufficiently calmed down from her agitations of thought and emotion to attack the play understandingly.

Thanks to defective education the most enlightened of us go through life much like a dim-sighted man who has no spectacles. Almost the whole of the wonderful panorama of the universe is unseen by us, or, if seen, is but partially understood or absurdly misunderstood. When it comes to the subtler things, the things of science and art, rarely indeed is there anyone who has the necessary training to get more than the crudest, most imperfect pleasure from them. What little training we have is so limping that it spoils the charm of mystery with which savage ignorance invests the universe from blade of grass to star, and does not put in place of that broken charm the profounder and loftier joy of understanding. To take for illustration the most widely diffused of all the higher arts and sciences, reading: How many so-called "educated" people can read understandingly even a novel, the form of literature designed to make the least demand upon the mind? People say they have read, but, when questioned, they show that they have got merely a glimmering of the real action, the faintest hint of style and characterization, have perhaps noted some stray epigram which they quote with evidently faulty grasp of its meaning.

When the thing read is a play, almost no one can get from it a coherent notion of what it is about. Most of us have nothing that can justly be called imagination; our early training at home and at school killed in the shoot that finest plant of the mind's garden. So there is no ability to fill in the picture which the dramatic author draws in outline. Susan had not seen "Cavalleria Rusticana" either as play or as opera. But when she and Spenser were together in Forty-fourth Street, she had read plays and had dreamed over them; the talk had been almost altogether of plays—of writing plays, of constructing scenes, of productions, of acting, of all the many aspects of the theater. Spenser read scenes to her, got her to help him with criticism, and she was present when he went over his work with Drumley, Riggs, Townsend and the others. Thus, reading a play was no untried art to her.

She read "Cavalleria" through slowly, taking about an hour to it. She saw now why Brent had given it to her as the primer lesson—the simple, elemental story of a peasant girl's ruin under promise of marriage; of her lover's wearying of one who had only crude physical charm; of his being attracted by a young married woman, gay as well as pretty, offering the security in intrigue that an unmarried woman could not offer. Such a play is at once the easiest and the hardest to act—the easiest because every audience understands it perfectly and supplies unconsciously almost any defect in the acting; the hardest because any actor with the education necessary to acting well finds it next to impossible to divest himself or herself of the sophistications of education and get back to the elemental animal.

Santuzza or *Lola*? Susan debated. *Santuzza* was the big and easy part; *Lola*, the smaller part, was of the kind that is usually neglected. But Susan saw possibilities in the character of the woman who won *Turiddu* away—the triumphant woman. The two women represented the two kinds of love— the love that is serious, the love that is light. And experience had taught her why it is that human nature soon tires of intensity, turns to frivolity. She felt that, if she could act, she would try to show that not *Turiddu's* fickleness nor his contempt of the woman who had yielded, but *Santuzza's* sad intensity and *Lola's* butterfly gayety had cost *Santuzza* her lover and her lover his life. So, it was not *Santuzza's* but *Lola's* first entrance that she studied.

In the next morning's mail, under cover addressed "Miss Susan Lenox, care of Miss Lorna Sackville," as she had written it for Brent, came the promised check for forty dollars. It was signed John P. Garvey, Secretary, and was inclosed with a note bearing the same signature:

DEAR MADAM:

Herewith I send you a check for forty dollars for the first week's salary under your arrangement with Mr. Brent. No receipt is necessary. Until further notice a check for the same amount will be mailed you each Thursday. Unless you receive notice to the contrary, please call as before, at three o'clock next Wednesday.

It made her nervous to think of those five days before she should see Brent. He had assured her he would expect nothing from her; but she felt she must be able to show him that she had not been wasting her time—his time, the time for which he was paying nearly six dollars a day. She must work every waking hour, except the two hours each day at the hospital. She recalled what Brent had said about the advantage of being contented alone—and how everything worth doing must be done in solitude. She had never thought about her own feelings as to company and solitude, as it was not her habit to think about herself. But now she realized how solitary she had been, and how it had bred in her habits of thinking and reading—and how valuable these habits would be to her in her work. There was Rod, for example. He hated being alone, must have someone around even when he was writing; and he had no taste for order or system. She understood why it was so hard for him to stick at anything, to put anything through to the finish. With her fondness for being alone, with her passion for reading and thinking about what she read, surely she ought soon to begin to accomplish something—if there was any ability in her.

She found Rod in higher spirits. Several ideas for his play had come to him; he already saw it acted, successful, drawing crowded houses, bringing him in anywhere from five hundred to a thousand a week. She was not troubled hunting for things to talk about with him—she, who could think of but one thing and that a secret from him. He talked his play, a steady stream with not a seeing glance at her or a question about her. She watched the little clock at the side of the bed. At the end of an hour to the minute, she interrupted him in the middle of a sentence. "I must go now," said she, rising.

"Sit down," he cried. "You can stay all day. The doctor says it will do me good to have you to talk with. And Sperry isn't coming until tomorrow."

"I can't do it," said she. "I must go."

He misunderstood her avoiding glance. "Now, Susie—sit down there," commanded he. "We've got plenty of money. You—you needn't bother about it any more."

"We're not settled yet," said she. "Until we are, I'd not dare take the risk." She was subtly adroit by chance, not by design.

"Risk!" exclaimed he angrily. "There's no risk. I've as good as got the advance money. Sit down."

She hesitated. "Don't be angry," pleaded she in a voice that faltered. "But I must go."

Into his eyes came the gleam of distrust and jealousy. "Look at me," he ordered.

With some difficulty she forced her eyes to meet his.

"Have you got a lover?"

"No."

"Then where do you get the money we're living on?" He counted on her being too humiliated to answer in words. Instead of the hanging head and burning cheeks he saw clear, steady eyes, heard a calm, gentle and dignified voice say:

"In the streets."

His eyes dropped and a look of abject shame made his face pitiable. "Good Heavens," he muttered.

"How low we are!"

"We've been doing the best we could," said she simply.

"Isn't there any decency anywhere in you?" he flashed out, eagerly seizing the chance to forget his own shame in contemplating her greater degradation.

She looked out of the window. There was something terrible in the calmness of her profile. She finally said in an even, pensive voice:

"You have been intimate with a great many women, Rod. But you have never got acquainted with a single one."

He laughed good-humoredly. "Oh, yes, I have. I've learned that 'every woman is at heart a rake,' as Mr. Jingle Pope says."

She looked at him again, her face now curiously lighted by her slow faint smile. "Perhaps they showed you only what they thought you'd be able to appreciate," she suggested.

He took this as evidence of her being jealous of him. "Tell me, Susan, did you leave me—in Forty-fourth Street—because you thought or heard I wasn't true to you?"

"What did Drumley tell you?"

"I asked him, as you said in your note. He told me he knew no reason."

So Drumley had decided it was best Rod should not know why she left. Well, perhaps—probably—Drumley was right. But there was no reason why he shouldn't know the truth now. "I left," said she, "because I saw we were bad for each other."

This amused him. She saw that he did not believe. It wounded her, but she smiled carelessly. Her smile encouraged him to say: "I couldn't quite make up my mind whether the reason was jealousy or because you had the soul of a shameless woman. You see, I know human nature, and I know that a woman who once crosses the line never crosses back. I'll always have to watch you, my dear. But somehow I like it. I guess you have—you and I have—a rotten streak in us. We were brought up too strictly. That always makes one either too firm or too loose. I used to think I liked good women. But I don't. They bore me. That shows I'm rotten."

"Or that your idea of what's good is—is mistaken."

"You don't pretend that *you* haven't done wrong?" cried Rod.

"I might have done worse," replied she. "I might have wronged others. No, Rod, I can't honestly say I've ever felt wicked."

"Why, what brought you here?"

She reflected a moment, then smiled. "Two things brought me down," said she. "In the first place, I wasn't raised right. I was raised as a lady instead of as a human being. So I didn't know how to meet the conditions of life. In the second place—" her smile returned, broadened—"I was too—too what's called 'good.'"

"Pity about you!" mocked he.

"Being what's called good is all very well if you're independent or if you've got a husband or a father to do life's dirty work for you—or, perhaps, if you happen to be in some profession like preaching or teaching—though I don't believe the so-called 'goodness' would let you get very far even as a preacher. In most lines, to practice what we're taught as children would be to go to the bottom like a stone. You know this is a hard world, Rod. It's full of men and women fighting desperately for food and clothes and a roof to cover them—fighting each other. And to get on you've got to have the courage and the indifference to your fellow beings that'll enable you to do it."

"There's a lot of truth in that," admitted Spenser. "If I'd not been such a 'good fellow,' as they call it—a fellow everybody liked—if I'd been like

Brent, for instance—Brent, who never would have any friends, who never would do anything for anybody but himself, who hadn't a thought except for his career—why, I'd be where he is."

It was at the tip of Susan's tongue to say, "Yes—strong—able to help others—able to do things worth while." But she did not speak.

Rod went on: "I'm not going to be a fool any longer. I'm going to be too busy to have friends or to help people or to do anything but push my own interests."

Susan, indifferent to being thus wholly misunderstood, was again moving toward the door. "I'll be back this evening, as usual," said she.

Spenser's face became hard and lowering: "You're going to stay here now, or you're not coming back," said he. "You can take your choice. Do you want me to know you've got the soul of a streetwalker?"

She stood at the foot of the bed, gazing at the wall above his head. "I must earn our expenses until we're safe," said she, once more telling a literal truth that was yet a complete deception.

"Why do you fret me?" exclaimed he. "Do you want me to be sick again?"

"Suppose you didn't get the advance right away," urged she.

"I tell you I shall get it! And I won't have you—do as you are doing. If you go, you go for keeps."

She seated herself. "Do you want me to read or take dictation?"

His face expressed the satisfaction small people find in small successes at asserting authority. "Don't be angry," said he. "I'm acting for your good. I'm saving you from yourself."

"I'm not angry," replied she, her strange eyes resting upon him.

He shifted uncomfortably. "Now what does that look mean?" he demanded with an uneasy laugh.

She smiled, shrugged her shoulders.

Sperry—small and thin, a weather-beaten, wooden face suggesting Mr. Punch, sly keen eyes, theater in every tone and gesture Sperry pushed the scenario hastily to completion and was so successful with Fitzalan that on Sunday afternoon he brought two hundred and fifty dollars, Spenser's half of the advance money.

"Didn't I tell you!" said Spenser to Susan, in triumph. "We'll move at once. Go pack your traps and put them in a carriage, and by the time you're back here Sperry and the nurses will have me ready."

It was about three when Susan got to her room. Clara heard her come in and soon appeared, bare feet in mules, hair hanging every which way. Despite the softening effect of the white nightdress and of the framing of abundant hair, her face was hard and coarse. She had been drunk on liquor and on opium the night before, and the effects were wearing off. As she was only twenty years old, the hard coarse look would withdraw before youth in a few hours; it was there only temporarily as a foreshadowing of what Clara would look like in five years or so.

"Hello, Lorna," said she. "Gee, what a bun my fellow and I had on last night! Did you hear us scrapping when we came in about five o'clock?"

"No," replied Susan. "I was up late and had a lot to do, and was kept at the hospital all day. I guess I must have fallen asleep."

"He gave me an awful beating," pursued Clara. "But I got one good crack at him with a bottle." She laughed. "I don't think he'll be doing much flirting till his cheek heals up. He looks a sight!" She opened her nightdress and showed Susan a deep blue-black mark on her left breast. "I wonder if I'll get cancer from that?" said she. "It'd be just my rotten luck. I've heard of several cases of it lately, and my father kicked my mother there, and she got cancer. Lord, how she did suffer!"

Susan shivered, turned her eyes away. Her blood surged with joy that she had once more climbed up out of this deep, dark wallow where the masses of her fellow beings weltered in darkness and drunkenness and disease—was up among the favored ones who, while they could not entirely escape the great ills of life, at least had the intelligence and the means to mitigate them. How fortunate that few of these unhappy ones had the imagination to realize their own wretchedness! "I don't care what becomes of me," Clara was saying. "What is there in it for me? I can have a good time only as long as my looks last—and that's true of every woman, ain't it? What's a woman but a body? Ain't I right?"

"That's why I'm going to stop being a woman as soon as ever I can," said Susan.

"Why, you're packing up!" cried Clara.

"Yes. My friend's well enough to be moved. We're going to live uptown."

"Right away?"

"This afternoon."

Clara dropped into a chair and began to weep. "I'll miss you something fierce!" sobbed she. "You're the only friend in the world I give a damn for, or that gives a damn for me. I wish to God I was like you. You don't need anybody."

"Oh, yes, I do, dear," cried Susan.

"But, I mean, you don't lean on anybody. I don't mean you're hard-hearted—for you ain't. You've pulled me and a dozen other girls out of the hole lots of times. But you're independent. Can't you take me along? I can drop that bum across the hall. I don't give a hoot for him. But a girl's got to make believe she cares for somebody or she'd blow her brains out."

"I can't take you along, but I'm going to come for you as soon as I'm on my feet," said Susan. "I've got to get up myself first. I've learned at least that much."

"Oh, you'll forget all about *me.*"

"No," said Susan.

And Clara knew that she would not. Moaned Clara, "I'm not fit to go. I'm only a common streetwalker. You belong up there. You're going back to your own. But I belong here. I wish to God I was like most of the people down here, and didn't have any sense. No wonder you used to drink so! I'm getting that way, too. The only people that don't hit the booze hard down here are the muttonheads who don't know nothing and can't learn nothing. . . . I used to be contented. But somehow, being with you so much has made me dissatisfied."

"That means you're on your way up," said Susan, busy with her packing.

"It would, if I had sense enough. Oh, it's torment to have sense enough to see, and not sense enough to do!"

"I'll come for you soon," said Susan. "You're going up with me."

Clara watched her for some time in silence. "You're sure you're going to win?" said she, at last.

"Sure," replied Susan.

"Oh, you can't be as sure as that."

"Yes, but I can," laughed she. "I'm done with foolishness. I've made up my mind to get up in the world—*with* my self-respect if possible; if not, then without it. I'm going to have everything—money, comfort, luxury, pleasure. Everything!" And she dropped a folded skirt emphatically upon the pile she had been making, and gave a short, sharp nod. "I was taught a lot of things when I was little—things about being sweet and unselfish and all that. They'd be fine, if the world was Heaven. But it isn't."

"Not exactly," said Clara.

"Maybe they're fine, if you want to get to Heaven," continued Susan. "But I'm not trying to get to Heaven. I'm trying to live on earth. I don't like the game, and I don't like its rules. But—it's the only game, and I can't change the rules. So I'm going to follow them—at least, until I get what I want."

"Do you mean to say you've got any respect for yourself?" said Clara. "*I* haven't. And I don't see how any girl in our line can have."

"I thought I hadn't," was Susan's reply, "until I talked with—with someone I met the other day. If you slipped and fell in the mud—or were thrown into it—you wouldn't say, 'I'm dirty through and through. I can never get clean again'—would you?"

"But that's different," objected Clara.

"Not a bit," declared Susan. "If you look around this world, you'll see that everybody who ever moved about at all has slipped and fallen in the mud—or has been pushed in."

"Mostly pushed in."

"Mostly pushed in," assented Susan. "And those that have good sense get up as soon as they can, and wash as much of the mud off as'll come off—maybe all—and go on. The fools—they worry about the mud. But not I—not any more!... And not you, my dear—when I get you uptown."

Clara was now looking on Susan's departure as a dawn of good luck for herself. She took a headache powder, telephoned for a carriage, and helped carry down the two big packages that contained all Susan's possessions worth moving. And they kissed each other good-by with smiling faces. Susan did not give Clara, the loose-tongued, her new address; nor did Clara, conscious of her own weakness, ask for it.

"Don't put yourself out about me," cried Clara in farewell. "Get a good tight grip yourself, first."

"That's advice I need," answered Susan. "Good-by. Soon—*soon!*"

The carriage had to move slowly through those narrow tenement streets, so thronged were they with the people swarmed from hot little rooms into the open to try to get a little air that did not threaten to burn and choke as it entered the lungs. Susan's nostrils were filled with the stenches of animal and vegetable decay—stenches descending in heavy clouds from the open windows of the flats and from the fire escapes crowded with all manner of rubbish; stenches from the rotting, brimful garbage cans; stenches from the groceries and butcher shops and bakeries where the poorest qualities of food were exposed to the contamination of swarms of disgusting fat flies, of mangy, vermin-harassed children and cats and dogs; stenches from the never washed human bodies, clad in filthy garments and drawn out of shape by disease and toil. Sore eyes, scrofula, withered arm or leg, sagged shoulder, hip out of joint—There, crawling along the sidewalk, was the boy whose legs had been cut off by the street car; and the stumps were horribly ulcered. And there at the basement window drooled and cackled the fat idiot girl whose mother sacrificed everything always to dress her freshly in pink. What a world!—where a few people such a very few!—lived in health and comfort and cleanliness—and the millions lived in disease and squalor, ignorant, untouched of civilization save to wear its cast-off clothes and to eat its castaway food and to live in its dark noisome cellars!—And to toil unceasingly to make for others the good things of which they had none themselves! It made her heartsick—the sadder because nothing could be done about it. Stay and help? As well stay to put out a conflagration barehanded and alone.

As the carriage reached wider Second Avenue, the horses broke into a trot. Susan drew a long breath of the purer air—then shuddered as she saw the corner where the dive into which the cadet had lured her flaunted its telltale awnings. Lower still her spirits sank when she was passing, a few blocks further on, the music hall. There, too, she had had a chance, had let hope blaze high. And she was going forward—into—the region where she had been a slave to Freddie Palmer—no, to the system of which he was a slave no less than she— —

"I *must* be strong! I *must!*" Susan said to herself, and there was desperation in the gleam of her eyes, in the set of her chin. "This time I will fight! And I feel at last that I can."

But her spirits soared no more that day.

CHAPTER XIV

SPERRY had chosen for "Mr. and Mrs. Spenser" the second floor rear of a house on the south side of West Forty-fifth Street a few doors off Sixth Avenue. It was furnished as a sitting-room—elegant in red plush, with oil paintings on the walls, a fringed red silk-plush dado fastened to the mantelpiece with bright brass-headed tacks, elaborate imitation lace throws on the sofa and chairs, and an imposing piece that might have been a cabinet organ or a pianola or a roll-top desk but was in fact a comfortable folding bed. There was a marble stationary washstand behind the hand-embroidered screen in the corner, near one of the two windows. Through a deep clothes closet was a small but satisfactory bathroom.

"And it's warm in winter," said Mrs. Norris, the landlady,
to
Susan. "Don't you hate a cold bathroom?"

Susan declared that she did.

"There's only one thing I hate worse," said Mrs. Norris, "and that's cold coffee."

She had one of those large faces which look bald because the frame of hair does not begin until unusually far back. At fifty, when her hair would be thin, Mrs. Norris would be homely; but at thirty she was handsome in a bold, strong way. Her hair was always carefully done, her good figure beautifully corseted. It was said she was not married to Mr. Norris—because New York likes to believe that people are living together without being married, because Mr. Norris came and went irregularly, and because Mrs. Norris was so particular about her toilet—and everyone knows that when a woman has the man with whom she's satisfied securely fastened, she shows her content or her virtuous indifference to other men—or her laziness—by neglecting her hair and her hips and dressing in any old thing any which way. Whatever the truth as to Mrs. Norris's domestic life, she carried herself strictly and insisted upon keeping her house as respectable as can reasonably be expected in a large city. That is, everyone in it was quiet, was of steady and sedate habit, was backed by references. Not until Sperry had thoroughly qualified as a responsible person did Mrs. Norris accept his assurances as to the Spensers and consent to receive them. Downtown the apartment houses that admit persons of loose character are usually more expensive because that class of tenants have more and expect more than ordinary working people. Uptown the custom is the reverse; to get into a respectable house you must pay more. The Spensers had to pay fourteen a week for their quarters—and they were getting a real bargain, Mrs. Norris having a weakness for literature and art where they were respectable and paid regularly.

"What's left of the two hundred and fifty will not last long," said Spenser to Susan, when they were established and alone. "But we'll have another five hundred as soon as the play's done, and that'll be in less than a month. We're to begin tomorrow. In less than two months the play'll be on and the royalties will be coming in. I wonder how much I owe the doctor and the hospital."

"That's settled," said Susan.

He glanced at her with a frown. "How much was it? You had no right to pay!"

"You couldn't have got either doctor or room without payment in advance." She spoke tranquilly, with a quiet assurance of manner that was new in her, the nervous and sensitive about causing displeasure in others. She added, "Don't be cross, Rod. You know it's only pretense."

"Don't you believe anybody has any decency?" demanded he.

"It depends on what you mean by decency," replied she. "But why talk of the past? Let's forget it."

"I would that I could!" exclaimed he.

She laughed at his heroics. "Put that in your play," said she. "But this isn't the melodrama of the stage. It's the farce comedy of life."

"How you have changed! Has all the sweetness, all the womanliness, gone out of your character?"

She showed how little she was impressed. "I've learned to take terrible things—really terrible things—without making a fuss—or feeling like making a fuss. You can't expect me to get excited over mere staginess. They're fond of fake emotions up in this part of town. But down where I've been so long the real horrors come too thick and fast for there to be any time to fake."

He continued to frown, presently came out of a deep study to say, "Susie, I see I've got to have a serious talk with you."

"Wait till you're well, my dear," said she. "I'm afraid I'll not be very sympathetic with your seriousness."

"No—today. I'm not an invalid. And our relations worry me, whenever I think of them."

He observed her as she sat with hands loosely clasped in her lap; there was an inscrutable look upon her delicate face, upon the clear-cut features so attractively framed by her thick dark hair, brown in some lights, black in others.

"Well?" said she.

"To begin, I want you to stop rouging your lips. It's the only sign of— of what you were. I'd a little rather you didn't smoke. But as respectable women smoke nowadays, why I don't seriously object. And when you get more clothes, get quieter ones. Not that you dress loudly or in bad taste — —"

"Thank you," murmured Susan.

"What did you say?"

"I didn't mean to interrupt. Go on."

"I admire the way you dress, but it makes me jealous. I want you to have nice clothes for the house. I like things that show your neck and suggest your form. But I don't want you attracting men's eyes and their loose thoughts, in the street. . . . And I don't want you to look so damnably alluring about the feet. That's your best trick—and your worst. Why are you smiling—in that fashion?"

"You talk to me as if I were your wife."

He gazed at her with an expression that was as affectionate as it was generous—and it was most generous. "Well, you may be some day—if you keep straight. And I think you will."

The artificial red of her lips greatly helped to make her sweetly smiling face the perfection of gentle irony. "And you?" said she.

"You know perfectly well it's different about a man."

"I know nothing of the sort," replied she. "Among certain kinds of people that is the rule. But I'm not of those kinds. I'm trying to make my way in the world, exactly like a man. So I've got to be free from the rules that may be all very well for ladies. A woman can't fight with her hands tied, any more than a man can—and you know what happens to the men who allow themselves to be tied; they're poor downtrodden creatures working hard at small pay for the men who fight with their hands free."

"I've taken you out of the unprotected woman class, my dear," he reminded her. "You're mine, now, and you're going back where you belong."

"Back to the cage it's taken me so long to learn to do without?" She shook her head. "No, Rod—I couldn't possibly do it—not if I wanted to. . . . You've got several false ideas about me. You'll have to get rid of them, if we're to get along."

"For instance?"

"In the first place, don't delude yourself with the notion that I'd marry you. I don't know whether the man I was forced to marry is dead or whether he's got a divorce. I don't care. No matter how free I was I shouldn't marry you."

He smiled complacently. She noted it without irritation. Truly, small indeed is the heat of any kind that can be got from the warmed-up ashes of a burnt-out passion. She went easily on:

"You have nothing to offer me—neither love nor money. And a woman—unless she's a poor excuse—insists on one or the other. You and I fancied we loved each other for a while. We don't fool ourselves in that way now. At least I don't, though I believe you do imagine I'm in love with you."

"You wouldn't be here if you weren't."

"Put that out of your head, Rod. It'll only breed trouble. I don't like to say these things to you, but you compel me to. I learned long ago how foolish it is to put off unpleasant things that will have to be faced in the end. The longer they're put off the worse the final reckoning is. Most of my troubles have come through my being too weak or good-natured—or whatever it was—to act as my good sense told me. I'm not going to make that mistake any more. And I'm going to start the new deal with absolute frankness with you. I am not in love with you."

"I know you better than you know yourself," said he.

"For a little while after I found you again I did have a return of the old feeling—or something like it. But it soon passed. I couldn't love you. I know you too well."

He struggled hard with his temper, as his vanity lashed at it. She saw, struggled with her old sensitiveness about inflicting even necessary pain upon others, went on:

"I simply like you, Rod—and that's all. We're well acquainted. You're physically attractive to me—not wildly so, but enough—more than any other man—probably more than most husbands are to their wives—or most wives to their husbands. So as long as you treat me well and don't wander off to other women, I'm more than willing to stay on here."

"Really!" said he, in an intensely sarcastic tone. "Really!"

"Now—keep your temper," she warned. "Didn't I keep mine when you were handing me that impertinent talk about how I should dress and the rest of it? No—let me finish. In the second place and in conclusion, my dear Rod, I'm not going to live off you. I'll pay my half of the room. I'll pay for my own clothes—and rouge for my lips. I'll buy and cook what we eat in the room; you'll pay when we go to a restaurant. I believe that's all."

"Are you quite sure?" inquired he with much satire.

"Yes, I think so. Except—if you don't like my terms, I'm ready to leave at once."

"And go back to the streets, I suppose?" jeered he.

"If it were necessary—yes. So long as I've got my youth and my health, I'll do precisely as I please. I've no craving for respectability—not the slightest. I—I——" She tried to speak of her birth, that secret shame of which she was ashamed. She had been thinking that Brent's big fine way of looking at things had cured her of this bitterness. She found that it had not—as yet. So she went on, "I'd prefer your friendship to your ill will—much prefer it, as you're the only person I can look to for what a man can do for a woman, and as I like you. But if I have to take tyranny along with the friendship—" she looked at him quietly and her tones were almost tender, almost appealing—"then, it's good-by, Rod."

She had silenced him, for he saw in her eyes, much more gray than violet though the suggestion of violet was there, that she meant precisely what she said. He was astonished, almost dazed by the change in her. This woman grown was not the Susie who had left him. No—and yet——

She had left him, hadn't she? That showed a character completely hidden from him, perhaps the character he was now seeing. He asked—and there was no sarcasm and a great deal of uneasiness in his tone:

"How do you expect to make a living?"

"I've got a place at forty dollars a week."

"Forty dollars a week! You!" He scowled savagely at her. "There's only one thing anyone would pay you forty a week for."

"That's what I'd have said," rejoined she. "But it seems not to be true. My luck may not last, but while it lasts, I'll have forty a week."

"I don't believe you," said he, with the angry bluntness of jealousy.

"Then you want me to go?" inquired she, with a certain melancholy but without any weakness.

He ignored her question. He demanded:

"Who's giving it to you?"

"Brent."

Spenser leaned from the bed toward her in his excitement. "*Robert Brent?*" he cried.

"Yes. I'm to have a part in one of his plays."

Spenser laughed harshly. "What rot! You're his mistress."

"It wouldn't be strange for you to think I'd accept that position for so little, but you must know a man of his sort wouldn't have so cheap a mistress."

"It's simply absurd."

"He is to train me himself."

"You never told me you knew him."

"I don't."

"Who got you the job?"

"He saw me in Fitzalan's office the day you sent me there. He asked me to call, and when I went he made me the offer."

"Absolute rot. What reason did he give?"

"He said I looked as if I had the temperament he was in search of."

"You must take me for a fool."

"Why should I lie to you?"

"God knows. Why do women lie to men all the time? For the pleasure of fooling them."

"Oh, no. To get money, Rod—the best reason in the world, it being rather hard for a woman to make money by working for it."

"The man's in love with you!"

"I wish he were," said Susan, laughing. "I'd not be here, my dear—you may be sure of that. And I'd not content myself with forty a week. Oh, you don't know what tastes I've got! Wait till I turn myself loose."

"Well—you can—in a few months," said Spenser.

Even as he had been protesting his disbelief in her story, his manner toward her had been growing more respectful—a change that at once hurt and amused her with its cynical suggestions, and also pleased her, giving her a confidence-breeding sense of a new value in herself. Rod went on, with a kind of shamefaced mingling of jest and earnest:

"You stick by me, Susie, old girl, and the time'll come when
I'll be able to give you more than Brent."

"I hope so," said Susan.

He eyed her sharply. "I feel like a fool believing such a fairy story as you've been telling me. Yet I do."

"That's good," laughed she. "Now I can stay. If you hadn't believed me, I'd have had to go. And I don't want to do that—not yet."

His eyes flinched. "Not yet? What does that mean?"

"It means I'm content to stay, at present. Who can answer for tomorrow?" Her eyes lit up mockingly. "For instance—you. Today you think you're going to be true to me don't you? Yet tomorrow—or as soon as you get strength and street clothes, I may catch you in some restaurant telling some girl she's the one you've been getting ready for."

He laughed, but not heartily. Sperry came, and Susan went to buy at a department store a complete outfit for Rod, who still had only nightshirts. As she had often bought for him in the old days, she felt she would have no difficulty in fitting him nearly enough, with her accurate eye supplementing the measurements she had taken. When she got back home two hours and a half later, bringing her purchases in a cab, Sperry had gone and Rod was asleep. She sat in the bathroom, with the gas lighted, and worked at "Cavalleria" until she heard him calling. He had awakened in high good-humor.

"That was an awful raking you gave me before Sperry came," began he. "But it did me good. A man gets so in the habit of ordering women about that it becomes second nature to him. You've made it clear to me that I've even less control over you than you have over me. So, dear, I'm going to be humble and try to give satisfaction, as servants say."

"You'd better," laughed Susan. "At least, until you get on your feet again."

"You say we don't love each other," Rod went on, a becoming brightness in his strong face. "Well—maybe so. But—we suit each other—don't we?"

"That's why I want to stay," said Susan, sitting on the bed and laying her hand caressingly upon his. "I could stand it to go, for I've been trained to stand anything—everything. But I'd hate it."

He put his arm round her, drew her against his breast. "Aren't you happy here?" he murmured.

"Happier than any place else in the world," replied she softly.

After a while she got a small dinner for their two selves on the gas stove she had brought with her and had set up in the bathroom. As they ate, she cross-legged on the bed opposite him, they beamed contentedly at each other. "Do you remember the dinner we had at the St. Nicholas in Cincinnati?" asked she.

"It wasn't as good as this," declared he. "Not nearly so well cooked. You could make a fortune as a cook. But then you do everything well."

"Even to rouging my lips?"

"Oh, forget it!" laughed he. "I'm an ass. There's a wonderful fascination in the contrast between the dash of scarlet and the pallor of that clear, lovely skin of yours."

Her eyes danced. "You are getting well!" she exclaimed. "I'm sorry I bought you clothes. I'll be uneasy every time you're out."

"You can trust me. I see I've got to hustle to keep my job with you. Well, thank God, your friend Brent's old enough to be your father."

"Is he?" cried Susan. "Do you know, I never thought of his age."

"Yes, he's forty at least—more. Are you sure he isn't after *you*, Susie?"

"He warned me that if I annoyed him in that way he'd discharge me."

"Do you like him?"

"I—don't—know" was Susan's slow, reflective answer. "I'm—afraid of him—a little."

Both became silent. Finally Rod said, with an impatient shake of the head, "Let's not think of him."

"Let's try on your new clothes," cried Susan.

And when the dishes were cleared away they had a grand time trying on the things she had bought. It was amazing how near she had come to fitting him. "You ought to feel flattered," said she. "Only a labor of love could have turned out so well."

He turned abruptly from admiring his new suit in the glass and caught her in his arms. "You do love me—you do!" he cried. "No woman would have done all you've done for me, if she didn't."

For answer, Susan kissed him passionately; and as her body trembled with the sudden upheaval of emotions long dormant or indulged only in debased, hateful ways, she burst into tears. She knew, even in that moment of passion, that she did not love him; but not love itself can move the heart more deeply than gratitude and her bruised heart was so grateful for his words and tones and gestures of affection!

Wednesday afternoon, on the way to Brent's house, she glanced up at the clock in the corner tower of the Grand Central Station. It lacked five minutes of three. She walked slowly, timed herself so accurately that, as the butler opened the door, a cathedral chime hidden somewhere in the upper interior boomed the hour musically. The man took her direct to the elevator, and when it stopped at the top floor, Brent himself opened the door, as before. He was dismissing a short fat man whom Susan placed as a manager, and a tall, slim, and most fashionably dressed woman with a beautiful insincere face—anyone would have at once declared her an actress, probably a star. The woman gave Susan a searching, feminine look which changed swiftly to superciliousness. Both the man and the woman were loath to go, evidently had not finished what they had come to say. But Brent, in his abrupt but courteous way, said:

"Tomorrow at four, then. As you see, my next appointment has begun." And he had them in the elevator with the door closed. He turned upon Susan the gaze that seemed to take in everything. "You are in better spirits, I see," said he.

"I'm sorry to have interrupted," said she. "I could have waited."

"But I couldn't," replied he. "Some day you'll discover that your time is valuable, and that to waste it is far sillier than if you were to walk along throwing your money into the gutter. Time ought to be used like money—spent generously but intelligently." He talked rapidly on, with his manner as full of unexpressed and inexpressible intensity as the voice of the violin, with his frank egotism that had no suggestion of vanity or conceit. "Because I systematize my time, I'm never in a hurry, never at a loss for time to give to whatever I wish. I didn't refuse to keep you waiting for your sake but for my own. Now the next hour belongs to you and me—and we'll forget about time—as, if we were dining in a restaurant, we'd not think of the bill till it was presented. What did you do with the play?"

Susan could only look at him helplessly.

He laughed, handed her a cigarette, rose to light a match for her. "Settle yourself comfortably," said he, "and say what's in your head."

With hands deep in the trousers of his house suit, he paced up and down the long room, the cigarette loose between his lips. Whenever she saw his front face she was reassured; but whenever she saw his profile, her nerves trembled—for in the profile there was an expression of almost ferocious resolution, of tragic sadness, of the sternness that spares not. The full face was kind, if keen; was sympathetic—was the man as nature had made him. The profile was the great man—the man his career had made. And Susan knew that the profile was master.

"Which part did you like *Santuzza* or *Lola*?"

"*Lola*," replied she.

He paused, looked at her quickly. Why?"

"Oh, I don't sympathize with the woman—or the man—who's deserted. I pity, but I can't help seeing it's her or his own fault. *Lola* explains why. Wouldn't you rather laugh than cry? *Santuzza* may have been attractive in the moments of passion, but how she must have bored *Turiddu* the rest of the time! She was so intense, so serious—so vain and selfish."

"Vain and selfish? That's interesting." He walked up and down several times, then turned on her abruptly. "Well—go on," he said. "I'm waiting to hear why she was vain and selfish."

"Isn't it vain for a woman to think a man ought to be crazy about her all the time because he once has been? Isn't it selfish for her to want him to be true to her because it gives *her* pleasure, even though she knows it doesn't give *him* pleasure?"

"Men and women are all vain and selfish in love," said he.

"But the women are meaner than the men," replied she, "because they're more ignorant and narrow-minded."

He was regarding her with an expression that made her uneasy.

"But that isn't in the play—none of it," said he.

"Well, it ought to be," replied she. "*Santuzza* is the old-fashioned conventional heroine. I used to like them—until I had lived a little, myself. She isn't true to life. But in *Lola*——"

"Yes—what about *Lola*?" he demanded.

"Oh, she wasn't a heroine, either. She was just human—taking happiness when it offered. And her gayety—and her capriciousness. A man will always break away from a solemn, intense woman to get that sort of sunshine."

"Yes—yes—go on," said Brent.

"And her sour, serious, solemn husband explains why wives are untrue to their husbands. At least, it seems so to me."

He was walking up and down again. Every trace of indolence,
of relaxation, was gone from his gait and from his features.
His mind was evidently working like an engine at full speed.
Suddenly he halted. "You've given me a big idea," said he.
"I'll throw away the play I was working on. I'll do your play."

Susan laughed—pleased, yet a little afraid he was kinder than she deserved. "What I said was only common sense—what my experience has taught me."

"That's all that genius is, my dear," replied he. "As soon as we're born, our eyes are operated on so that we shall never see anything as it is. The geniuses are those who either escape the operation or are reëndowed with true sight by experience." He nodded approvingly at her. "You're going to be a person—or, rather, you're going to show you're a person. But that comes later. You thought of *Lola* as your part?"

"I tried to. But I don't know anything about acting except what I've seen and the talk I've heard."

"As I said the other day, that means you've little to learn.
Now—as to *Lola's* entrance."

"Oh, I thought of a lot of things to do—to show that she, too, loved *Turiddu* and that she had as much right to love—and to be loved—as *Santuzza* had. *Santuzza* had had her chance, and had failed."

Brent was highly amused. "You seem to forget that *Lola* was a married woman—and that if *Santuzza* didn't get a husband she'd be the mother of a fatherless child."

Never had he seen in her face such a charm of sweet melancholy as at that moment. "I suppose the way I was born and the life I've led make me think less of those things than most people do," replied she. "I was talking about natural hearts—what people think inside—the way they act when they have courage."

"When they have courage," Brent repeated reflectively. "But who has courage?"

"A great many people are compelled to have it," said she.

"I never had it until I got enough money to be independent."

"I never had it," said Susan, "until I had no money."

He leaned against the big table, folded his arms on his chest, looked at her with eyes that made her feel absolutely at ease with him. Said he:

"You have known what it was to have no money—none?"

Susan nodded. "And no friends—no place to sleep—worse off than *Robinson Crusoe* when the waves threw him on the island. I had to—to suck my own blood to keep alive."

"You smile as you say that," said he.

"If I hadn't learned to smile over such things," she answered,
"I'd have been dead long ago."

He seated himself opposite her. He asked:

"Why didn't you kill yourself?"

"I was afraid."

"Of the hereafter?"

"Oh no. Of missing the coming true of my dreams about life."

"Love?"

"That—and more. Just love wouldn't satisfy me. I want to see the world—to know the world—and to be somebody. I want to try *everything*."

She laughed gayly—a sudden fascinating vanishing of the melancholy of eyes and mouth, a sudden flashing out of young beauty. "I've been down about as deep as one can go. I want to explore in the other direction."

"Yes—yes," said Brent, absently. "You must see it all."

He remained for some time in a profound reverie, she as unconscious of the passing of time as he for if he had his thoughts, she had his face to study. Try as she would, she could not associate the idea of age with him—any age. He seemed simply a grown man. And the more closely she studied him the greater her awe became. He knew so much; he understood so well. She could not imagine him swept away by any of the petty emotions—the vanities, the jealousies, the small rages, the small passions and loves that made up the petty days of the small creatures who inhabit the world and call it theirs. Could he fall in love? Had he been in love? Yes—he must have been in love many times—for many women must have taken trouble to please a man so well worth while, and he must have passed from one woman to another as his whims or his tastes changed. Could he ever care about her—as a woman? Did he think her worn out as a physical woman? Or would he realize that body is nothing by itself; that unless the soul enters it, it is cold and meaningless and worthless—like the electric bulb when the filament is dark and the beautiful, hot, brilliant and intensely living current is not in it? Could she love him? Could she ever feel equal and at ease, through and through, with a man so superior?

"You'd better study the part of *Lola*—learn the lines," said he, when he had finished his reflecting. "Then—this day week at the same hour—we will begin. We will work all afternoon—we will dine together—go to some theater where I can illustrate what I mean. Beginning with next Wednesday that will be the program every day until further notice."

"Until you see whether you can do anything with me or not?"

"Just so. You are living with Spenser?"

"Yes." Susan could have wished his tone less matter-of-fact.

"How is he getting on?"

"He and Sperry are doing a play for Fitzalan."

"Really? That's good. He has talent. If he'll learn of Sperry and talk less and work more, and steadily, he'll make a lot of money. You are not tied to him in any way?"

"No—not now that he's prospering. Except, of course, that I'm fond of him."

He shrugged his shoulders. "Oh, everybody must have somebody. You've not seen this house. I'll show it to you, as we've still fifteen minutes."

A luxurious house it was—filled with things curious and, some of them, beautiful—things gathered in excursions through Europe, Susan assumed. The only absolutely simple room was his bedroom, big and bare and so arranged that he could sleep practically out of doors. She saw servants—two men besides the butler, several women. But the house was a bachelor's house, with not a trace of feminine influence. And evidently he cared nothing about it but lived entirely in that wonderful world which so awed Susan—the world he had created within himself, the world of which she had alluring glimpses through his eyes, through his tones and gestures even. Small people strive to make, and do make, impression of themselves by laboring to show what they know and think. But the person of the larger kind makes no such effort. In everything Brent said and did and wore, in all his movements, gestures, expressions, there was the unmistakable hallmark of the man worth while. The social life has banished simplicity from even the most savage tribe. Indeed, savages, filled with superstitions, their every movement the result of some notion of proper ceremonial, are the most complex of all the human kind. The effort toward simplicity is not a movement back to nature, for there savage and lower animal are completely enslaved by custom and instinct; it is a movement upward toward the freedom of thought and action of which our best intelligence has given us a conception and for which it has given us a longing. Never had Susan met so simple a man; and never had she seen one so far from all the silly ostentations of rudeness, of unattractive dress, of eccentric or coarse speech wherewith the cheap sort of man strives to proclaim himself individual and free.

With her instinct for recognizing the best at first sight, Susan at once understood. And she was like one who has been stumbling about searching for the right road, and has it suddenly shown to him. She fairly darted along this right road. She was immediately busy, noting the mistakes in her own ideas of manners and dress, of good and bad taste. She realized how much she had to learn. But this did not discourage her. For she realized at the same time that she could learn—and his obvious belief in her as a possibility was most encouraging.

When he bade her good-by at the front door and it closed behind her, she was all at once so tired that it seemed to her she would then and there sink down through sheer fatigue and fall asleep. For no physical exercise so quickly and utterly exhausts as real brain exercise—thinking, studying, learning with all the concentrated intensity of a thoroughbred in the last quarter of the mile race.

CHAPTER XV

SPENSER had time and thought for his play only. He no longer tormented himself with jealousy of the abilities and income and fame of Brent and the other successful writers for the stage; was not he about to equal them, probably to surpass them? As a rule, none of the mean emotions is able to thrive—unless it has the noxious vapors from disappointment and failure to feed upon. Spenser, in spirits and in hope again, was content with himself. Jealousy of Brent about Susan had been born of dissatisfaction with himself as a failure and envy of Brent as a success; it died with that dissatisfaction and that envy. His vanity assured him that while there might be possibly—ways in which he was not without rivals, certainly where women were concerned he simply could not be equaled; the woman he wanted he could have—and he could hold her as long as he wished. The idea that Susan would give a sentimental thought to a man "old enough to be her father"—Brent was forty-one—was too preposterous to present itself to his mind. She loved the handsome, fascinating, youthful Roderick Spenser; she would soon be crazy about him.

Rarely does it occur to a man to wonder what a woman is thinking. During courtship very young men attribute intellect and qualities of mystery and awe to the woman they love. But after men get an insight into the mind of woman and discover how trivial are the matters that of necessity usually engage it, they become skeptical about feminine mentality; they would as soon think of speculating on what profundities fill the brain of the kitten playing with a ball as of seeking a solution of the mystery behind a woman's fits of abstraction. However, there was in Susan's face, especially in her eyes, an expression so unusual, so arresting that Spenser, self-centered and convinced of woman's intellectual deficiency though he was, did sometimes inquire what she was thinking about. He asked this question at breakfast the morning after that second visit to Brent.

"Was I thinking?" she countered.

"You certainly were not listening. You haven't a notion what
I was talking about."

"About your play."

"Of course. You know I talk nothing else," laughed he. "I must bore you horribly."

"No, indeed," protested she.

"No, I suppose not. You're not bored because you don't listen."

He was cheerful about it. He talked merely to arrange his thoughts, not because he expected Susan to understand matters far above one whom nature had fashioned and experience had trained to minister satisfyingly to the physical and sentimental needs of man. He assumed that she was as worshipful before his intellect as in the old days. He would have been even more amazed than enraged had he known that she regarded his play as mediocre claptrap, false to life, fit only for the unthinking, sloppily sentimental crowd that could not see the truth about even their own lives, their own thoughts and actions.

"There you go again!" cried he, a few minutes later. "What *are* you thinking about? I forgot to ask how you got on with Brent. Poor chap—he's had several failures in the past year. He must be horribly cut up. They say he's written out. What does he think he's trying to get at with you?"

"Acting, as I told you," replied Susan. She felt ashamed for him, making this pitiable exhibition of patronizing a great man.

"Sperry tells me he has had that twist in his brain for a long time—that he has tried out a dozen girls or more—drops them after a few weeks or months. He has a regular system about it—runs away abroad, stops the pay after a month or so."

"Well, the forty a week's clear gain while it lasts," said Susan. She tried to speak lightly. But she felt hurt and uncomfortable. There had crept into her mind one of those disagreeable ideas that skurry into some dusky corner to hide, and reappear from time to time making every fit of the blues so much the sadder and aggravating despondency toward despair.

"Oh, I didn't mean to suggest that *you* wouldn't succeed," Spenser hastened to apologize with more or less real kindliness. "Sperry says Brent has some good ideas about acting. So, you'll learn something—maybe enough to enable me to put you in a good position—if Brent gets tired and if you still want to be independent, as you call it."

"I hope so," said Susan absently.

Spenser was no more absorbed in his career than she in hers; only, she realized how useless it would be to try to talk it to him—that he would not give her so much as ears in an attitude of polite attention. If he could have looked into her head that morning and seen what thoughts were distracting her from hearing about the great play, he would have been more amused and disgusted than ever with feminine frivolity of mind and incapacity in serious matters. For, it so happened that at the moment Susan was concentrating on a new dress. He would have laughed in the face of anyone saying to him that this new dress was for Susan in the pursuit of her scheme of life quite as weighty a matter, quite as worthy of the most careful attention, as was his play for him. Yet that would have been the literal truth. Primarily man's appeal is to the ear, woman's to the eye—the reason, by the way, why the theater—preeminently the place to *see*—tends to be dominated by woman.

Susan had made up her mind not only that she would rapidly improve herself in every way, but also how she would go about the improving. She saw that, for a woman at least, dress is as much the prime essential as an arresting show window for a dealer in articles that display well. She knew she was far from the goal of which she dreamed—the position where she would no longer be a woman primarily but a personage. Dress would not merely increase her physical attractiveness; it would achieve the far more important end of gaining her a large measure of consideration. She felt that Brent, even Brent, dealer in actualities and not to be fooled by pretenses, would in spite of himself change his opinion of her if she went to him dressed less like a middle class working girl, more like the woman of the upper classes. At best, using all the advantages she had, she felt there was small enough chance of her holding his interest; for she could not make herself believe that he was not deceiving himself about her. However, to strengthen herself in every way with him was obviously the wisest effort she could make. So, she must have a new dress for the next meeting, one which would make him better pleased to take her out to dinner. True, if she came in rags, he would not be disturbed—for he had nothing of the snob in him. But at the same time, if she came dressed like a woman of his own class, he would be impressed. "He's a man, if he is a genius," reasoned she.

Vital though the matter was, she calculated that she did not dare spend more than twenty-five dollars on this toilet. She must put by some of her forty a week; Brent might give her up at any time, and she must not be in the position of having to choose immediately between submitting to the slavery of the kept woman as Spenser's dependent and submitting to the costly and dangerous and repulsive freedom of the woman of the streets. Thus, to lay out twenty-five dollars on a single costume was a wild extravagance. She thought it over from every point of view; she decided that she must take the risk.

Late in the afternoon she walked for an hour in Fifth Avenue. After some hesitation she ventured into the waiting- and dressing-rooms of several fashionable hotels. She was in search of ideas for the dress, which must be in the prevailing fashion. She had far too good sense and good taste to attempt to be wholly original in dress; she knew that the woman who understands her business does not try to create a fashion but uses the changing and capricious fashion as the means to express a constant and consistent style of her own. She appreciated her limitations in such matters—how far she as yet was from the knowledge necessary to forming a permanent and self-expressive style. She was prepared to be most cautious in giving play to an individual taste so imperfectly educated as hers had necessarily been.

She felt that she had the natural instinct for the best and could recognize it on sight—an instinct without which no one can go a step forward in any of the arts. She had long since learned to discriminate among the vast masses of offering, most of them tasteless or commonplace, to select the rare and few things that have merit. Thus, she had always stood out in the tawdrily or drearily or fussily dressed throngs, had been a pleasure to the eyes even of those who did not know why they were pleased. On that momentous day, she finally saw a woman dressed in admirable taste who was wearing a costume simple enough for her to venture to think of copying the main points. She walked several blocks a few yards behind this woman, then hurried ahead of her, turned and walked toward her to inspect the front of the dress. She repeated this several times between the St. Regis and Sherry's. The woman soon realized, as women always do, what the girl in the shirtwaist and short skirt was about. But she happened to be a good-natured person, and smiled pleasantly at Susan, and got in return a smile she probably did not soon forget.

The next morning Susan went shopping. She had it in mind to get the materials for a costume of a certain delicate shade of violet. A dress of that shade, and a big hat trimmed in tulle to match or to harmonize, with a bunch of silk violets fastened in the tulle in a certain way.

Susan knew she had good looks, knew what was becoming to her darkly and softly fringed violet eyes, pallid skin, to her rather tall figure, slender, not voluptuous yet suggesting voluptuousness. She could see herself in that violet costume. But when she began to look at materials she hesitated. The violet would be beautiful; but it was not a wise investment for a girl with few clothes, with but one best dress. She did not give it up definitely, however, until she came upon a sixteen-yard remnant of soft gray China crêpe. Gray was a really serviceable color for the best dress of a girl of small means. And this remnant, certainly enough for a dress, could be had for ten dollars, where violet China crêpe of the shade she wanted would cost her a dollar a yard. She took the remnant.

She went to the millinery department and bought a large hat frame. It was of a good shape and she saw how it could be bent to suit her face. She paid fifty cents for this, and two dollars and seventy cents for four yards of gray tulle. She found that silk flowers were beyond her means; so she took a bunch of presentable looking violets of the cheaper kind at two dollars and a half. She happened to pass a counter whereon were displayed bargains in big buckles and similar odds and ends of steel and enamel. She fairly pounced upon a handsome gray buckle with violet enamel, which cost but eighty-nine cents. For a pair of gray suede ties she paid two dollars; for a pair of gray silk stockings, ninety cents. These matters, with some gray silk net for the collar, gray silk for a belt, linings and the like, made her total bill twenty-three dollars and sixty-seven cents. She returned home content and studied "Cavalleria" until her purchases arrived.

Spenser was out now, was working all day and in the evenings at Sperry's office high up in the Times Building. So, Susan had freedom for her dressmaking operations. To get them off her mind that she might work uninterruptedly at learning *Lola's* part in "Cavalleria," she toiled all Saturday, far into Sunday morning, was astir before Spenser waked, finished the dress soon after breakfast and the hat by the middle of the afternoon. When Spenser returned from Sperry's office to take her to dinner, she was arrayed. For the first time he saw her in fashionable attire and it was really fashionable, for despite all her disadvantages she, who had real and rare capacity for learning, had educated herself well in the chief business of woman the man-catcher in her years in New York.

He stood rooted to the threshold. It would have justified a vanity less vigorous than Susan or any other normal human being possessed, to excite such a look as was in his eyes. He drew a long breath by way of breaking the spell over speech.

"You are *beautiful!*" he exclaimed.

And his eyes traveled from the bewitching hat, set upon her head coquettishly yet without audacity, to the soft crêpe dress, its round collar showing her perfect throat, its graceful lines subtly revealing her alluring figure, to the feet that men always admired, whatever else of beauty or charm they might fail to realize.

"How you have grown!" he ejaculated. Then, "How did you do it?"

"By all but breaking myself."

"It's worth whatever it cost. If I had a dress suit, we'd go to Sherry's or the Waldorf. I'm willing to go, without the dress suit."

"No. I've got everything ready for dinner at home."

"Then, why on earth did you dress? To give me a treat?"

"Oh, I hate to go out in a dress I've never worn. And a woman has to wear a hat a good many times before she knows how."

"What a lot of fuss you women do make about clothes."

"You seem to like it, all the same."

"Of course. But it's a trifle."

"It has got many women a good provider for life. And not paying attention to dress or not knowing how has made most of the old maids. Are those things trifles?"

Spenser laughed and shifted his ground without any sense of having been pressed to do so. "Men are fools where women are concerned."

"Or women are wise where men are concerned."

"I guess they do know their business—some of them," he confessed. "Still, it's a silly business, you must admit."

"Nothing is silly that's successful," said Susan.

"Depends on what you mean by success," argued he.

"Success is getting what you want."

"Provided one wants what's worth while," said he.

"And what's worth while?" rejoined she. "Why, whatever one happens to want."

To avoid any possible mischance to the *grande toilette* he served the dinner and did the dangerous part of the clearing up. They went to the theater, Rod enjoying even more than she the very considerable admiration she got. When she was putting the dress away carefully that night, Rod inquired when he was to be treated again.

"Oh—I don't know," replied she. "Not soon."

She was too wise to tell him that the dress would not be worn again until Brent was to see it. The hat she took out of the closet from time to time and experimented with it, reshaping the brim, studying the different effects of different angles. It delighted Spenser to catch her at this "foolishness"; he felt so superior, and with his incurable delusion of the shallow that dress is an end, not merely a means, he felt more confident than ever of being able to hold her when he should have the money to buy her what her frivolous and feminine nature evidently craved beyond all else in the world. But— —

When he bought a ready-to-wear evening suit, he made more stir about it than had Susan about her costume—this, when dress to him was altogether an end in itself and not a shrewd and useful means. He spent more time in admiring himself in it before the mirror, and looked at it, and at himself in it, with far more admiration and no criticism at all. Susan noted this—and after the manner of women who are wise or indifferent—or both—she made no comment.

At the studio floor of Brent's house the door of the elevator was opened for Susan by a small young man with a notably large head, bald and bulging. His big smooth face had the expression of extreme amiability that usually goes with weakness and timidity. "I am Mr. Brent's secretary, Mr. Garvey," he explained. And Susan—made as accurate as quick in her judgments of character by the opportunities and the necessities of her experience—saw that she had before her one of those nice feeble folk who either get the shelter of some strong personality as a bird hides from the storm in the thick branches of a great tree or are tossed and torn and ruined by life and exist miserably until rescued by death. She knew the type well; it had been the dominant type in her surroundings ever since she left Sutherland. Indeed, is it not the dominant type in the whole ill-equipped, sore-tried human race? And does it not usually fail of recognition because so many of us who are in fact weak, look—and feel—strong because we are sheltered by inherited money or by powerful friends or relatives or by chance lodgment in a nook unvisited of the high winds of life in the open? Susan liked Garvey at once; they exchanged smiles and were friends.

She glanced round the room. At the huge open window Brent, his back to her, was talking earnestly to a big hatchet-faced man with a black beard. Even as Susan glanced Brent closed the interview; with an emphatic gesture of fist into palm he exclaimed, "And that's final. Good-by." The two men came toward her, both bowed, the hatchet-faced man entered the elevator and was gone. Brent extended his hand with a smile.

"You evidently didn't come to work today," said he with a careless, fleeting glance at the *grande toilette*. "But we are prepared against such tricks. Garvey, take her down to the rear dressing-room and have the maid lay her out a simple costume." To Susan, "Be as quick as you can." And he seated himself at his desk and was reading and signing letters.

Susan, crestfallen, followed Garvey down the stairway. She had confidently expected that he would show some appreciation of her toilette. She knew she had never in her life looked so well. In the long glass in the dressing-room, while Garvey was gone to send the maid, she inspected herself again. Yes—never anything like so well. And Brent had noted her appearance only to condemn it. She was always telling herself that she wished him to regard her as a working woman, a pupil in stagecraft.

But now that she had proof that he did so regard her, she was depressed, resentful. However, this did not last long. While she was changing to linen skirt and shirtwaist, she began to laugh at herself. How absurd she had been, thinking to impress this man who had known so many beautiful women, who must have been satiated long ago with beauty—she thinking to create a sensation in such a man, with a simple little costume of her own crude devising. She reappeared in the studio, laughter in her eyes and upon her lips. Brent apparently did not glance at her; yet he said, "What's amusing you?"

She confessed all, on one of her frequent impulses to candor—those impulses characteristic both of weak natures unable to exercise self-restraint and of strong natures, indifferent to petty criticism and misunderstanding, and absent from vain mediocrity, which always has itself—that is, appearances—on its mind. She described in amusing detail how she had planned and got together the costume how foolish his reception of it had made her feel. "I've no doubt you guessed what was in my head," concluded she. "You see everything."

"I did notice that you were looking unusually well, and that you felt considerably set up over it," said he. "But why not? Vanity's an excellent thing. Like everything else it's got to be used, not misused. It can help us to learn instead of preventing."

"I had an excuse for dressing up," she reminded him. "You said we were to dine together. I thought you wouldn't want there to be too much contrast between us. Next time I'll be more sensible."

"Dress as you like for the present," said he. "You can always change here. Later on dress will be one of the main things, of course. But not now. Have you learned the part?"

And they began. She saw at the far end of the room a platform about the height of a stage. He explained that Garvey, with the book of the play, would take the other parts in *Lola's* scenes, and sent them both to the stage. "Don't be nervous," Garvey said to her in an undertone. "He doesn't expect anything of you. This is simply to get started." But she could not suppress the trembling in her legs and arms, the hysterical contractions of her throat. However, she did contrive to go through the part—Garvey prompting. She knew she was ridiculous; she could not carry out a single one of the ideas of "business" which had come to her as she studied; she was awkward, inarticulate, panic-stricken.

"Rotten!" exclaimed Brent, when she had finished. "Couldn't be worse therefore, couldn't be better."

She dropped to a chair and sobbed hysterically.

"That's right—cry it out," said Brent. "Leave us alone, Garvey."

Brent walked up and down smoking until she lifted her head and glanced at him with a pathetic smile. "Take a cigarette," he suggested. "We'll talk it over. Now, we've got something to talk about."

She found relief from her embarrassment in the cigarette. "You can laugh at me now," she said. "I shan't mind. In fact, I didn't mind, though I thought I did. If I had, I'd not have let you see me cry."

"Don't think I'm discouraged," said Brent. "The reverse. You showed that you have nerve a very different matter from impudence. Impudence fails when it's most needed. Nerve makes one hang on, regardless. In such a panic as yours was, the average girl would have funked absolutely. You stuck it out. Now, you and I will try *Lola's* first entrance. No, don't throw away your cigarette. *Lola* might well come in smoking a cigarette." She did better. What Burlingham had once thoroughly drilled into her now stood her in good stead, and Brent's sympathy and enthusiasm gave her the stimulating sense that he and she were working together. They spent the afternoon on the one thing—*Lola* coming on, singing her gay song, her halt at sight of *Santuzza* and *Turiddu*, her look at *Santuzza*, at *Turiddu*, her greeting for each. They tried it twenty different ways. They discussed what would have been in the minds of all three. They built up "business" for *Lola*, and for the two others to increase the significance of *Lola's* actions.

"As I've already told you," said he, "anyone with a voice and a movable body can learn to act. There's no question about your becoming a good actress. But it'll be some time before I can tell whether you can be what I hope—an actress who shows no sign that she's acting."

Susan showed the alarm she felt. "I'm afraid you'll find at the end that you've been wasting your time," said she.

"Put it straight out of your head," replied he. "I never waste time. To live is to learn. Already you've given me a new play—don't forget that. In a month I'll have it ready for us to use. Besides, in teaching you I teach myself. Hungry?"

"No—that is, yes. I hadn't thought of it, but I'm starved."

"This sort of thing gives one an appetite like a field hand." He accompanied her to the door of the rear dressing-room on the floor below. "Go down to the reception room when you're ready," said he, as he left her to go on to his own suite to change his clothes. "I'll be there."

The maid came immediately, drew a bath for her, afterward helped her to dress. It was Susan's first experience with a maid, her first realization how much time and trouble one saves oneself if free from the routine, menial things. And then and there a maid was set down upon her secret list of the luxurious comforts to which she would treat herself—*when?* The craving for luxury is always a part, usually a powerful part, of an ambitious temperament. Ambition is simply a variously manifested and variously directed impulse toward improvement—a discomfort so keen that it compels effort to change to a position less uncomfortable. There had never been a time when luxury had not attracted her. At the slightest opportunity she had always pushed out for luxuries—for better food, better clothing, more agreeable surroundings. Even in her worst hours of discouragement she had not really relaxed in the struggle against rags and dirt. And when moral horror had been blunted by custom and drink, physical horror had remained acute. For, human nature being a development upward through the physical to the spiritual, when a process of degeneration sets in, the topmost layers, the spiritual, wear away first—then those in which the spiritual is a larger ingredient than the material—then those in which the material is the larger—and last of all those that are purely material. As life educated her, as her intelligence and her knowledge grew, her appreciation of luxury had grown apace and her desire for it. With most human beings, the imagination is a heavy bird of feeble wing; it flies low, seeing only the things of the earth. When they describe heaven, it has houses of marble and streets of gold. Their pretense to sight of higher things is either sheer pretense or sight at second hand. Susan was of the few whose fancy can soar. She saw the earthy things; she saw the things of the upper regions also. And she saw the lower region from the altitudes of the higher—and in their perspective.

As she and Brent stood together on the sidewalk before his house, about to enter his big limousine, his smile told her that he had read her thought—her desire for such an automobile as her very own. "I can't help it," said she. "It's my nature to want these things."

"And to want them intelligently," said he. "Everybody wants, but only the few want intelligently—and they get. The three worst things in the world are sickness, poverty and obscurity. Your splendid health safeguards you against sickness. Your looks and your brains can carry you far away from the other two. Your one danger is of yielding to the temptation to become the wife or the mistress of some rich man. The prospect of several years of heart-breaking hard work isn't wildly attractive at twenty-two."

"You don't know me," said Susan—but the boast was uttered under her breath.

The auto rushed up to Delmonico's entrance, came to a halt abruptly yet gently. The attentiveness of the personnel, the staring and whispering of the people in the palm room showed how well known Brent was. There were several women—handsome women of what is called the New York type, though it certainly does not represent the average New York woman, who is poorly dressed in flimsy ready-made clothes and has the mottled skin that indicates bad food and too little sleep. These handsome women were dressed beautifully as well as expensively, in models got in—not from—Paris. One of them smiled sweetly at Brent, who responded, so Susan thought, rather formally. She felt dowdy in her home-made dress. All her pride in it vanished; she saw only its defects. And the gracefully careless manner of these women—the manners of those who feel sure of themselves—made her feel "green" and out of place. She was disgusted with the folly that had caused her to thrill with pleasure when his order to his chauffeur at his door told her she was actually to be taken to one of the restaurants in which she had wished to exhibit herself with him. She heartily wished she had insisted on going where she would have been as well dressed and as much at home as anyone there.

She lifted her eyes, to distract her mind from these depressing sensations. Brent was looking at her with that amused, mocking yet sympathetic expression which was most characteristic of him. She blushed furiously.

He laughed. "No, I'm not ashamed of your homemade dress," said he. "I don't care what is thought of me by people who don't give me any money. And, anyhow, you are easily the most unusual looking and the most tastefully dressed woman here. The rest of these women are doomed for life to commonplace obscurity. You——

"We'll see your name in letters of fire on the Broadway temples of fame."

"I know you're half laughing at me," said Susan. "But I feel a little better."

"Then I'm accomplishing my object. Let's not think about ourselves. That makes life narrow. Let's keep the thoughts on our work—on the big splendid dreams that come to us and invite us to labor and to dare."

And as they lingered over the satisfactory dinner he had ordered, they talked of acting—of the different roles of "Cavalleria" as types of fundamental instincts and actions—of how best to express those meanings—how to fill out the skeletons of the dramatist into personalities actual and vivid. Susan forgot where she was, forgot to be reserved with him. In her and Rod's happiest days she had never been free from the constraint of his and her own sense of his great superiority. With Brent, such trifles of the petty personal disappeared. And she talked more naturally than she had since a girl at her uncle's at Sutherland. She was amazed by the fountain that had suddenly gushed forth in her mind at the conjuring of Brent's sympathy. She did not recognize herself in this person so open to ideas, so eager to learn, so clear in the expression of her thoughts. Not since the Burlingham days had she spent so long a time with a man in absolute unconsciousness of sex.

They were interrupted by the intrusion of a fashionable young man with the expression of assurance which comes from the possession of wealth and the knowledge that money will buy practically everything and everybody. Brent received him so coldly that, after a smooth sentence or two, he took himself off stammering and in confusion. "I suppose," said Brent when he was gone, "that young ass hoped I would introduce him to you and invite him to sit. But you'll be tempted often enough in the next few years by rich men without my helping to put temptation in your way,"

"I've never been troubled thus far," laughed Susan.

"But you will, now. You have developed to the point where everyone will soon be seeing what it took expert eyes to see heretofore."

"If I am tempted," said Susan, "do you think I'll be able to resist?"

"I don't know," confessed Brent. "You have a strong sense of honesty, and that'll keep you at work with me for a while. Then— —

"If you have it in you to be great, you'll go on. If you're merely the ordinary woman, a little more intelligent, you'll probably—sell out. All the advice I have to offer is, don't sell cheap. As you're not hampered by respectability or by inexperience, you needn't." He reflected a moment, then added, "And if you ever do decide that you don't care to go on with a career, tell me frankly. I may be able to help you in the other direction."

"Thank you," said Susan, her strange eyes fixed upon him.

"Why do you put so much gratitude in your tone and in your eyes?" asked he.

"I didn't put it there," she answered. "It—just came. And I was grateful because—well, I'm human, you know, and it was good to feel—that— that— —"

"Go on," said he, as she hesitated.

"I'm afraid you'll misunderstand."

"What does it matter, if I do?"

"Well—you've acted toward me as if I were a mere machine that you were experimenting with."

"And so you are."

"I understand that. But when you offered to help me, if I happened to want to do something different from what you want me to do, it made me feel that you thought of me as a human being, too."

The expression of his unseeing eyes puzzled her. She became much embarrassed when he said, "Are you dissatisfied with Spenser? Do you want to change lovers? Are you revolving me as a possibility?"

"I haven't forgotten what you said," she protested.

"But a few words from me wouldn't change you from a woman into a sexless ambition."

An expression of wistful sadness crept into the violet-gray eyes, in contrast to the bravely smiling lips. She was thinking of her birth that had condemned her to that farmer Ferguson, full as much as of the life of the streets, when she said:

"I know that a man like you wouldn't care for a woman of my sort."

"If I were you," said he gently, "I'd not say those things about myself. Saying them encourages you to think them. And thinking them gives you a false point of view. You must learn to appreciate that you're not a sheltered woman, with reputation for virtue as your one asset, the thing that'll enable you to get some man to undertake your support. You are dealing with the world as a man deals with it. You must demand and insist that the world deal with you on that basis." There came a wonderful look of courage and hope into the eyes of Lorella's daughter.

"And the world will," he went on. "At least, the only part of it that's important to you—or really important in any way. The matter of your virtue or lack of it is of no more importance than is my virtue or lack of it."

"Do you *really* believe that way?" asked Susan, earnestly.

"It doesn't in the least matter whether I do or not," laughed he. "Don't bother about what I think—what anyone thinks—of you. The point here, as always, is that you believe it, yourself. There's no reason why a woman who is making a career should not be virtuous. She will probably not get far if she isn't more or less so. Dissipation doesn't help man or woman, especially the ruinous dissipation of license in passion. On the other hand, no woman can ever hope to make a career who persists in narrowing and cheapening herself with the notion that her virtue is her all. She'll not amount to much as a worker in the fields of action."

Susan reflected, sighed. "It's very, very hard to get rid of one's sex."

"It's impossible," declared he. "Don't try. But don't let it worry you, either."

"Everyone can't be as strong as you are—so absorbed in a career that they care for nothing else."

This amused him. With forearms on the edge of the table he turned his cigarette slowly round between his fingers, watching the smoke curl up from it. She observed that there was more than a light sprinkle of gray in his thick, carefully brushed hair. She was filled with curiosity as to the thoughts just then in that marvelous brain of his; nor did it lessen her curiosity to know that never would those thoughts be revealed to her. What women had he loved? What women had loved him? What follies had he committed? From how many sources he must have gathered his knowledge of human nature of—woman nature! And no doubt he was still gathering. What woman was it now?

When he lifted his glance from the cigarette, it was to call the waiter and get the bill. "I've a supper engagement," he said, "and it's nearly eleven o'clock."

"Eleven o'clock!" she exclaimed.

"Times does fly—doesn't it?—when a man and a woman, each an unexplored mystery to the other, are dining alone and talking about themselves."

"It was my fault," said Susan.

His quizzical eyes looked into hers—uncomfortably far.

She flushed. "You make me feel guiltier than I am," she protested, under cover of laughing glance and tone of raillery.

"Guilty? Of what?"

"You think I've been trying to—to 'encourage' you," replied she frankly.

"And why shouldn't you, if you feel so inclined?" laughed he.

"That doesn't compel me to be—encouraged."

"Honestly I haven't," said she, the contents of seriousness still in the gay wrapper of raillery. "At least not any more than— —"

"You know, a woman feels bound to 'encourage' a man who piques her by seeming—difficult."

"Naturally, you'd not have objected to baptizing the new hat and dress with my heart's blood." She could not have helped laughing with him. "Unfortunately for you—or rather for the new toilette—my poor heart was bled dry long, long ago. I'm a busy man, too—busy and a little tired."

"I deserve it all," said she. "I've brought it on myself. And I'm not a bit sorry I started the subject. I've found out you're quite human—and that'll help me to work better."

They separated with the smiling faces of those who have added an evening altogether pleasant to memory's store of the past's happy hours— that roomy storehouse which is all too empty even where the life has been what is counted happy. He insisted on sending her home in his auto, himself taking a taxi to the Players' where the supper was given. The moment she was alone for the short ride home, her gayety evaporated like a delicious but unstable perfume.

Why? Perhaps it was the sight of the girls on the stroll. Had she really been one of them?—and only a few days ago? Impossible! Not she not the real self . . . and perhaps she would be back there with them before long. No—never, never, in any circumstances!. . . She had said, "Never!" the first time she escaped from the tenements, yet she had gone back. . . were any of those girls strolling along—were, again, any of them Freddie Palmer's? At the thought she shivered and quailed. She had not thought of him, except casually, in many months. What if he should see her, should still feel vengeful—he who never forgot or forgave—who would dare anything! And she would be defenseless against him. . . . She remembered what she had last read about him in the newspaper. He had risen in the world, was no longer in the criminal class apparently, had moved to the class of semi-criminal wholly respectable contractor-politician. No, he had long since forgotten her, vindictive Italian though he was.

The auto set her down at home. Her tremors about Freddie departed; but the depression remained. She felt physically as if she had been sitting all evening in a stuffy room with a dull company after a heavy, badly selected dinner. She fell easy prey to one of those fits of the blues to which all imaginative young people are at least occasional victims, and by which those cursed and hampered with the optimistic temperament are haunted and harassed and all but or quite undone. She had a sense of failure, of having made a bad impression. She feared he, recalling and reinspecting what she had said, would get the idea that she was not in earnest, was merely looking for a lover—for a chance to lead a life of luxurious irresponsibility. Would it not be natural for him, who knew women well, to assume from her mistakenly candid remarks, that she was like the rest of the women, both the respectable and the free? Why should he believe in her, when she did not altogether believe in herself but suspected herself of a secret hankering after something more immediate, more easy and more secure than the stage career? The longer she thought of it the clearer it seemed to her to be that she had once more fallen victim to too much hope, too much optimism, too much and too ready belief in her fellow-beings—she who had suffered so much from these follies, and had tried so hard to school herself against them.

She fought this mood of depression—fought alone, for Spenser did not notice and she would not annoy him. She slept little that night; she felt that she could not hope for peace until she had seen Brent again.

CHAPTER XVI

TOWARD half-past ten the next day, a few minutes after Rod left for the theater, she was in the bathroom cleaning the coffee machine. There came a knock at the door of the sitting-room bedroom. Into such disorder had her mood of depression worried her nerves that she dropped the coffee machine into the washbowl and jumped as if she were seeing a ghost. Several dire calamities took vague shape in her mind, then the image of Freddie Palmer, smiling sweetly, cruelly. She wavered only a moment, went to the door, and after a brief hesitation that still further depressed her about herself she opened it. The maid—a good-natured sloven who had become devoted to Susan because she gave her liberal fees and made her no extra work—was standing there, in an attitude of suppressed excitement. Susan laughed, for this maid was a born agitator, a person who is always trying to find a thrill or to put a thrill into the most trivial event.

"What is it now, Annie?" Susan asked.

"Mr. Spenser—he's gone, hasn't he?"

"Yes—a quarter of an hour ago."

Annie drew a breath of deep relief. "I was sure he had went," said she, producing from under her apron a note. "I saw it was in a gentleman's writing, so I didn't come up with it till he was out of the way, though the boy brought it a little after nine."

"Oh, bother!" exclaimed Susan, taking the note.

"Well, Mrs. Spenser, I've had my lesson," replied Annie, apologetic but firm. "When I first came to New York, green as the grass that grows along the edge of the spring, what does I do but go to work and take up a note to a lady when her husband was there! Next thing I knew he went to work and hauled her round the floor by the hair and skinned out—yes, beat it for good. And my madam says to me, 'Annie, you're fired. Never give a note to a lady when her gent is by or to a gent when his lady's by. That's the first rule of life in gay New York.' And you can bet I never have since—nor never will."

Susan had glanced at the address on the note, had recognized the handwriting of Brent's secretary. Her heart had straightway sunk as if the foreboding of calamity had been realized. As she stood there uncertainly, Annie seized the opportunity to run on and on. Susan now said absently, "Thank you. Very well," and closed the door. It was a minute or so before she tore open the envelope with an impatient gesture and read:

DEAR MRS. SPENSER:

Mr. Brent requests me to ask you not to come until further notice. It may be sometime before he will be free to resume.

Yours truly,
JOHN C. GARVEY.

It was a fair specimen of Garvey's official style, with which she had become acquainted—the style of the secretary who has learned by experience not to use frills or flourishes but to convey his message in the fewest and clearest words. Had it been a skillfully worded insult Susan, in this mood of depression and distorted mental vision, could not have received it differently. She dropped to a chair at the table and stared at the five lines of neat handwriting until her eyes became circled and her face almost haggard. Precisely as Rod had described! After a long, long time she crumpled the paper and let it fall into the waste-basket. Then she walked up and down the room—presently drifted into the bathroom and resumed cleaning the coffee machine. Every few moments she would pause in the task—and in her dressing afterwards—would be seized by the fear, the horror of again being thrust into that hideous underworld. What was between her and it, to save her from being flung back into its degradation? Two men on neither of whom she could rely. Brent might drop her at any time—perhaps had already dropped her. As for Rod—vain, capricious, faithless, certain to become an unendurable tyrant if he got her in his power—Rod was even less of a necessity than Brent. What a dangerous situation was hers! How slender her chances of escape from another catastrophe. She leaned against wall or table and was shaken by violent fits of shuddering. She felt herself slipping—slipping. It was all she could do to refrain from crying out. In those moments, no trace of the self-possessed Susan the world always saw. Her fancy went mad and ran wild. She quivered under the actuality of coarse contacts—Mrs. Tucker in bed with her—the men who had bought her body for an hour—the vermin of the tenements—the brutal hands of policemen.

Then with an exclamation of impatience or of anger she would shake herself together and go resolutely on—only again to relapse. "Because I so suddenly cut off the liquor and the opium," she said. It was the obvious and the complete explanation. But her heart was like lead, and her sky like ink.

This note, the day after having tried her out as a possibility for the stage and as a woman. She stared down at the crumpled note in the wast-basket. That note—it was herself. He had crumpled her up and thrown her into the waste-basket, where she no doubt belonged.

It was nearly noon before she, dressed with unconscious care, stood in the street doorway looking about uncertainly as if she did not know which way to turn. She finally moved in the direction of the theater where Rod's play was rehearsing. She had gone to none of the rehearsals because Rod had requested it. "I want you to see it as a total surprise the first night," explained he. "That'll give you more pleasure, and also it will make your criticism more valuable to us." And she had acquiesced, not displeased to have all her time for her own affairs. But now she, dazed, stunned almost, convinced that it was all over for her with Brent, instinctively turned to Rod to get human help—not to ask for it, but in the hope that somehow he would divine and would say or do something that would make the way ahead a little less forbidding—something that would hearten her for the few first steps, anyhow. She turned back several times—now, because she feared Rod wouldn't like her coming; again because her experience—enlightened good sense—told her that Rod would—could—not help her, that her sole reliance was herself. But in the end, driven by one of those spasms of terror lest the underworld should be about to engulf her again, she stood at the stage door.

As she was about to negotiate the surly looking man on guard within, Sperry came rushing down the long dark passageway. He was brushing past her when he saw who it was. "Too late!" he cried. "Rehearsal's over."

"I didn't come to the rehearsal," explained Susan. "I thought perhaps Rod would be going to lunch."

"So he is. Go straight back. You'll find him on the stage. I'll join you if you'll wait a minute or so." And Sperry hurried on into the street.

Susan advanced along the passageway cautiously as it was but one remove from pitch dark. Perhaps fifty feet, and she came to a cross passage. As she hesitated, a door at the far end of it opened and she caught a glimpse of a dressing-room and, in the space made by the partly opened door, a woman half-dressed—an attractive glimpse. The woman—who seemed young—was not looking down the passage, but into the room. She was laughing in the way a woman laughs only when it is for a man, for *the* man— and was saying, "Now, Rod, you must go, and give me a chance to finish dressing." A man's arm—Rod's arm—reached across the opening in the doorway. A hand—Susan recognized Rod's well-shaped hand—was laid strongly yet tenderly upon the pretty bare arm of the struggling, laughing young woman—and the door closed—and the passage was soot-dark again. All this a matter of less than five seconds. Susan, ashamed at having caught him, frightened lest she should be found where she had no business to be, fled back along the main passage and jerked open the street door. She ran squarely into Sperry.

"I—I beg your pardon," stammered he. "I was in such a rush—I ought to have been thinking where I was going. Did I hurt you?" This last most anxiously. "I'm so sorry——"

"It's nothing—nothing," laughed Susan. "You are the one that's hurt."

And in fact she had knocked Sperry breathless. "You don't look anything like so strong," gasped he.

"Oh, my appearance is deceptive—in a lot of ways."

For instance, he could have got from her face just then no hint of the agony of fear torturing her—fear of the drop into the underworld.

"Find Rod?" asked he.

"He wasn't on the stage. So—I came out again."

"Wait here," said Sperry. "I'll hunt him up."

"Oh, no—please don't. I stopped on impulse. I'll not bother him." She smiled mischievously. "I might be interrupting."

Sperry promptly reddened. She had no difficulty in reading what was in his mind—that her remark had reminded him of Rod's "affair," and he was cursing himself for having been so stupid as to forget it for the moment and put his partner in danger of detection.

"I—I guess he's gone," stammered Sperry. "Lord, but that was a knock you gave me! Better come to lunch with me."

Susan hesitated, a wistful, forlorn look in her eyes. "Do you really want me?" asked she.

"Come right along," said Sperry in a tone that left no doubt of his sincerity. "We'll go to the Knickerbocker and have something good to eat."

"Oh, no—a quieter place," urged Susan.

Sperry laughed. "You mean less expensive. There's one of the great big differences between you and the make-believe ladies one bumps into in this part of town. *You* don't like to be troublesome or expensive. But we'll go to the Knickerbocker. I feel 'way down today, and I intended to treat myself. You don't look any too gay-hearted yourself."

"I'll admit I don't like the way the cards are running," said Susan. "But—they'll run better—sooner or later."

"Sure!" cried Sperry. "You needn't worry about the play. That's all right. How I envy women!"

"Why?"

"Oh—you have Rod between you and the fight. While I—I've got to look out for myself."

"So have I," said Susan. "So has everyone, for that matter."

"Believe me, Mrs. Spenser," cried Sperry, earnestly, "you can count on Rod. No matter what——"

"Please!" protested Susan. "I count on nobody. I learned long ago not to lean."

"Well, leaning isn't exactly a safe position," Sperry admitted. "There never was a perfectly reliable crutch. Tell me your troubles."

Susan smilingly shook her head. "That'd be leaning. . . . No, thank you. I've got to think it out for myself. I believed I had arranged for a career for myself. It seems to have gone to pieces That's all. Something else will turn up—after lunch."

"Not a doubt in the world," replied he confidently. "Meanwhile—there's Rod."

Susan's laugh of raillery made him blush guiltily. "Yes," said she, "there's Rod." She laughed again, merrily. "There's Rod—but where is there?"

"You're the only woman in the world he has any real liking for," said Sperry, earnest and sincere. "Don't you ever doubt that, Mrs. Spenser."

When they were seated in the café and he had ordered, he excused himself and Susan saw him make his way to a table where sat Fitzalan and another man who looked as if he too had to do with the stage. It was apparent that Fitzalan was excited about something; his lips, his arms, his head were in incessant motion. Susan noted that he had picked up many of Brent's mannerisms; she had got the habit of noting this imitativeness in men—and in women, too—from having seen in the old days how Rod took on the tricks of speech, manner, expression, thought even, of whatever man he happened at the time to be admiring. May it not have been this trait of Rod's that gave her the clue to his character, when she was thinking him over, after the separation?

Sperry was gone nearly ten minutes. He came, full of apologies. "Fitz held on to me while he roasted Brent. You've heard of Brent, of course?"

"Yes," said Susan.

"Fitz has been seeing him off. And he says it's— —"

Susan glanced quickly at him. "Off?" she said.

"To Europe."

Susan had paused in removing her left glove. Rod's description of Brent's way of sidestepping—Rod's description to the last detail. Her hands fluttered uncertainly—fluttering fingers like a flock of birds flushed and confused by the bang of the gun.

"And Fitz says— —"

"For Europe," said Susan. She was drawing her fingers slowly one by one from the fingers of her glove.

"Yes. He sailed, it seems, on impulse barely time to climb aboard. Fitz always lays everything to a woman. He says Brent has been mixed up for a year or so with— — Oh, it doesn't matter. I oughtn't to repeat those things. I don't believe 'em—on principle. Every man—or woman—who amounts to anything has scandal talked about him or her all the time. Good Lord! If Robert Brent bothered with half the affairs that are credited to him, he'd have no time or strength—not to speak of brains—to do plays."

"I guess even the busiest man manages to fit a woman in somehow," observed Susan. "A woman or so."

Sperry laughed. "I guess yes," said he. "But as to Brent, most of the scandal about him is due to a fad of his—hunting for an undeveloped female genius who— —"

"I've heard of that," interrupted Susan. "The service is dreadfully slow here. How long is it since you ordered?"

"Twenty minutes—and here comes our waiter." And then, being one of those who must finish whatever they have begun, he went on. "Well, it's true Brent does pick up and drop a good many ladies of one kind and another. And naturally, every one of them is good-looking and clever or he'd not start in. But—you may laugh at me if you like—I think he's strictly business with all of them. He'd have got into trouble if he hadn't been. And Fitz admits this one woman—she's a society woman—is the only one there's any real basis for talk about in connection with Brent."

Susan had several times lifted a spoonful of soup to her lips and had every time lowered it untasted.

"And Brent's mighty decent to those he tries and has to give up. I know of one woman he carried on his pay roll for nearly two years— —"

"Let's drop Mr. Brent," cried Susan. "Tell me about—about the play."

"Rod must be giving you an overdose of that."

"I've not seen much of him lately. How was the rehearsal?"

"Fair—fair." And Sperry forgot Brent and talked on and on about the play, not checking himself until the coffee was served. He had not observed that Susan was eating nothing. Neither had he observed that she was not listening; but there was excuse for this oversight, as she had set her expression at absorbed attention before withdrawing within herself to think—and to suffer. She came to the surface again when Sperry, complaining of the way the leading lady was doing her part, said: "No wonder Brent drops one after another. Women aren't worth much as workers. Their real mind's always occupied with the search for a man to support 'em."

"Not always," cried Susan, quivering with sudden pain. "Oh, no, Mr. Sperry—not always."

"Yes—there are exceptions," said Sperry, not noting how he had wounded her. "But—well, I never happened to run across one."

"Can you blame them?" mocked Susan. She was ashamed that she had been stung into crying out.

"To be honest—no," said Sperry. "I suspect I'd throw up the sponge and sell out if I had anything a lady with cash wanted to buy. I only *suspect* myself. But I *know* most men would. No, I don't blame the ladies. Why not have a nice easy time? Only one short life—and then—the worms."

She was struggling with the re-aroused insane terror of a fall back to the depths whence she had once more just come—and she felt that, if she fell again, it would mean the very end of hope. It must have been instinct or accident, for it certainly was not any prompting from her calm expression, that moved him to say:

"Now, tell me *your* troubles. I've told you mine. . . . You surely must have some?"

Susan forced a successful smile of raillery. "None to speak of," evaded she.

When she reached home there was a telegram—from Brent:

> Compelled to sail suddenly. Shall be back in a few weeks.
> Don't mind this annoying interruption. R. B.

A very few minutes after she read these words, she was at work on the play. But—a very few minutes thereafter she was sitting with the play in her lap, eyes gazing into the black and menacing future. The misgivings of the night before had been fed and fattened into despairing certainties by the events of the day. The sun was shining, never more brightly; but it was not the light of her City of the Sun. She stayed in all afternoon and all evening. During those hours before she put out the light and shut herself away in the dark a score of Susans, every one different from every other, had been seen upon the little theater of that lodging house parlor-bedroom. There had been a hopeful Susan, a sad but resolved Susan, a strong Susan, a weak Susan; there had been Susans who could not have shed a tear; there had been Susans who shed many tears—some of them Susans all bitterness, others Susans all humility and self-reproach. Any spectator would have been puzzled by this shifting of personality. Susan herself was completely confused. She sought for her real self among this multitude so contradictory. Each successive one seemed the reality; yet none persisted. When we look in at our own souls, it is like looking into a many-sided room lined with mirrors. We see reflections—re-reflections—views at all angles—but we cannot distinguish the soul itself among all these counterfeits, all real yet all false because partial.

"What shall I do? What can I do? What will I do?"—that was her last cry as the day ended. And it was her first cry as her weary brain awakened for the new day.

At the end of the week came the regular check with a note from Garvey—less machine-like, more human. He apologized for not having called, said one thing and another had prevented, and now illness of a near relative compelled him to leave town for a few days, but as soon as he came back he would immediately call. It seemed to Susan that there could be but one reason why he should call—the reason that would make a timid, soft-hearted man such as he put off a personal interview as long as he could find excuses. She flushed hot with rage and shame as she reflected on her position. Garvey pitying her! She straightway sat down and wrote:

DEAR MR. GARVEY: Do not send me any more checks until Mr.
Brent comes back and I have seen him. I am in doubt whether
I shall be able to go on with the work he and I had arranged.

She signed this "Susan Lenox" and dispatched it. At once she felt better in spite of the fact that she had, with characteristic and fatal folly, her good sense warned her, cut herself off from all the income in sight or in prospect. She had debated sending back the check, but had decided that if she did she might give the impression of pique or anger. No, she would give him every chance to withdraw from a bargain with which he was not content; and he would get the idea that it was she who was ending the arrangement, would therefore feel no sense of responsibility for her. She would save her pride; she would spare his feelings. She was taking counsel of Burlingham these days—was recalling the lesson he had taught her, was getting his aid in deciding her course. Burlingham protested vehemently against this sending back of the check; but she let her pride, her aversion to being an object of pity, overrule him.

A few days more, and she was so desperate, so harassed that she altogether lost confidence in her own judgment. While outwardly she seemed to be the same as always with Rod, she had a feeling of utter alienation. Still, there was no one else to whom she could turn. Should she put the facts before him and ask his opinion? Her intelligence said no; her heart said perhaps. While she was hesitating, he decided for her. One morning at breakfast he stopped talking about himself long enough to ask carelessly:

"About you and Brent—he's gone away. What are you doing?"

"Nothing," said she.

"Going to take that business up again, when he comes back?"

"I don't know."

"I wouldn't count on it, if I were you. . . . You're so sensitive that I've hesitated to say anything. But I think that chap was looking for trouble, and when he found you were already engaged, why, he made up his mind to drop it."

"Do you think so?" said Susan indifferently. "More coffee?"

"Yes—a little. If my play's as good as your coffee——
That's enough, thanks. . . . Do you still draw your—your—
—"

His tone as he cast about for a fit word made her flush scarlet. "No—I stopped it until we begin work again."

He did not conceal his thorough satisfaction. "That's right!" he cried. "The only cloud on our happiness is gone. You know, a man doesn't like that sort of thing."

"I know," said Susan drily.

And she understood why that very night he for the first time asked her to supper after the rehearsal with Sperry and Constance Francklyn, the leading lady, with whom he was having one of those affairs which as he declared to Sperry were "absolutely necessary to a man of genius to keep him freshened up—to keep the fire burning brightly." He had carefully coached Miss Francklyn to play the part of unsuspected "understudy"—Susan saw that before they had been seated in Jack's ten minutes. And she also saw that he was himself resolved to conduct himself "like a gentleman." But after he had taken two or three highballs, Susan was forced to engage deeply in conversation with the exasperated and alarmed Sperry to avoid seeing how madly Rod and Constance were flirting. She, however, did contrive to see nothing—at least, the other three were convinced that she had not seen. When they were back in their rooms, Rod—whether through pretense or through sidetracked amorousness or from simple intoxication—became more demonstrative than he had been for a long time.

"No, there's nobody like you," he declared. "Even if I wandered I'd always come back to you."

"Really?" said Susan with careless irony. "That's good.
No,
I can unhook my blouse."

"I do believe you're growing cold."

"I don't feel like being messed with tonight."

"Oh, very well," said he sulkily. Then, forgetting his ill humor after a few minutes of watching her graceful movements and gestures as she took off her dress and made her beautiful hair ready for the night, he burst out in a very different tone: "You don't know how glad I am that you're dependent on me again. You'll not be difficult any more."

A moment's silence, then Susan, with a queer little laugh,
"Men don't in the least mind—do they?"

"Mind what?"

"Being loved for money." There was a world of sarcasm in her accent on that word loved.

"Oh, nonsense. You don't understand yourself," declared he with large confidence. "Women never grow up. They're like babies—and babies, you know, love the person that feeds them."

"And dogs—and cats—and birds—and all the lower orders."
She took a book and sat in a wrapper under the light.

"Come to bed—please, dear," pleaded he.

"No, I'll read a while."

And she held the book before her until he was asleep. Then she sat a long time, her elbows on her knees, her chin supported by her hands, her gaze fixed upon his face—the face of the man who was her master now. She must please him, must accept what treatment he saw fit to give, must rein in her ambitions to suit the uncertain gait and staying power of his ability to achieve. She could not leave him; he could leave her when he might feel so inclined. Her master—capricious, tyrannical, a drunkard. Her sole reliance—and the first condition of his protection was that she should not try to do for herself. A dependent, condemned to become even more dependent.

CHAPTER XVII

SHE now spent a large part of every day in wandering, like a derelict, drifting aimlessly this way or that, up into the Park or along Fifth Avenue. She gazed intently into shop windows, apparently inspecting carefully all the articles on display; but she passed on, unconscious of having seen anything. If she sat at home with a book she rarely turned a page, though her gaze was fastened upon the print as if she were absorbingly interested.

What was she feeling? The coarse contacts of street life and tenement life—the choice between monstrous defilements from human beings and monstrous defilements from filth and vermin. What was she seeing? The old women of the slums—the forlorn, aloof figures of shattered health and looks—creeping along the gutters, dancing in the barrel houses, sleeping on the floor in some vile hole in the wall—sleeping the sleep from which one awakes bitten by mice and bugs, and swarming with lice.

She had entire confidence in Brent's judgment. Brent must have discovered that she was without talent for the stage—for if he had thought she had the least talent, would he not in his kindness have arranged or offered some sort of place in some theater or other? Since she had no stage talent—then—what should she do? What *could* she do? And so her mind wandered as aimlessly as her wandering steps. And never before had the sweet melancholy of her eyes been so moving.

But, though she did not realize it, there was a highly significant difference between this mood of profound discouragement and all the other similar moods that had accompanied and accelerated her downward plunges. Every time theretofore, she had been cowed by the crushing mandate of destiny—had made no struggle against it beyond the futile threshings about of aimless youth. This time she lost neither strength nor courage. She was no longer a child; she was no longer mere human flotsam and jetsam. She did not know which way to turn; but she did know, with all the certainty of a dauntless will, that she would turn some way—and that it would not be a way leading back to the marshes and caves of the underworld. She wandered—she wandered aimlessly; but not for an instant did she cease to keep watch for the right direction—the direction that would be the best available in the circumstances. She did not know or greatly care which way it led, so long as it did not lead back whence she had come.

In all her excursions she had—not consciously but by instinct—kept away from her old beat. Indeed, except in the company of Spenser or Sperry she had never ventured into the neighborhood of Long Acre. But one day she was deflected by chance at the Forty-second Street corner of Fifth Avenue and drifted westward, pausing at each book stall to stare at the titles of the bargain offerings in literature. As she stood at one of these stalls near Sixth Avenue, she became conscious that two men were pressing against her, one on either side. She moved back and started on her way. One of the men was standing before her. She lifted her eyes, was looking into the cruel smiling eyes of a man with a big black mustache and the jaws of a prizefighter. His smile broadened.

"I thought it was you, Queenie," said he. "Delighted to see you."

She recognized him as a fly cop who had been one of Freddie Palmer's handy men. She fell back a step and the other man—she knew him instantly as also a policeman—lined up beside him of the black mustache. Both men were laughing.

"We've been on the lookout for you a long time, Queenie," said the other. "There's a friend of yours that wants to see you mighty bad."

Susan glanced from one to the other, her face pale but calm, in contrast to her heart where was all the fear and horror of the police which long and savage experience had bred. She turned away without speaking and started toward Sixth Avenue.

"Now, what d'ye think of that?" said Black Mustache to his "side kick." "I thought she was too much of a lady to cut an old friend. Guess we'd better run her in, Pete."

"That's right," assented Pete. "Then we can keep her safe till F. P. can get the hooks on her."

Black Mustache laughed, laid his hand on her arm. "You'll come along quietly," said he. "You don't want to make a scene. You always was a perfect lady."

She drew her arm away. "I am a married woman—living with my husband."

Black Mustache laughed. "Think of that, Pete! And she soliciting us. That'll be good news for your loving husband. Come along, Queenie. Your record's against you. Everybody'll know you've dropped back to your old ways."

"I am going to my husband," said she quietly. "You had better not annoy me."

Pete looked uneasy, but Black Mustache's sinister face became more resolute. "If you wanted to live respectable, why did you solicit us two? Come along—or do you want me and Pete to take you by the arms?"

"Very well," said she. "I'll go." She knew the police, knew that Palmer's lieutenant would act as he said—and she also knew what her "record" would do toward carrying through the plot.

She walked in the direction of the station house, the two plain clothes men dropping a few feet behind and rejoining her only when they reached the steps between the two green lamps. In this way they avoided collecting a crowd at their heels. As she advanced to the desk, the sergeant yawning over the blotter glanced up.

"Bless my soul!" cried he, all interest at once. "If it ain't F. P.'s Queenie!"

"And up to her old tricks, sergeant," said Black Mustache. "She solicited me and Pete." Susan was looking the sergeant straight in the eyes. "I am a married woman," said she. "I live with my husband. I was looking at some books in Forty-second Street when these two came up and arrested me."

The sergeant quailed, glanced at Pete who was guiltily hanging his head—glanced at Black Mustache. There he got the support he was seeking. "What's your husband's name?" demanded Black Mustache roughly. "What's your address?"

And Rod's play coming on the next night but one! She shrank, collected herself. "I am not going to drag him into this, if I can help it," said she. "I give you a chance to keep yourselves out of trouble." She was gazing calmly at the sergeant again. "You know these men are not telling the truth. You know they've brought me here because of Freddie Palmer. My husband knows all about my past. He will stand by me. But I wish to spare him."

The sergeant's uncertain manner alarmed Black Mustache. "She's putting up a good, bluff" scoffed he. "The truth is she ain't got no husband. She'd not have solicited us if she was living decent."

"You hear what the officer says," said the sergeant, taking the tone of great kindness. "You'll have to give your name and address—and I'll leave it to the judge to decide between you and the officers." He took up his pen. "What's your name?"

Susan, weak and trembling, was clutching the iron rail before the desk—the rail worn smooth by the nervous hands of ten thousand of the social system's sick or crippled victims.

"Come—what's your name?" jeered Black Mustache.

Susan did not answer.

"Put her down Queenie Brown," cried he, triumphantly.

The sergeant wrote. Then he said: "Age?"

No answer from Susan. Black Mustache answered for her: "About twenty-two now."

"She don't look it," said the sergeant, almost at ease once more. "But brunettes stands the racket better'n blondes. Native parents?"

No answer.

"Native. You don't look Irish or Dutch or Dago—though you might have a dash of the Spinnitch or the Frog-eaters. Ever arrested before?"

No answer from the girl, standing rigid at the bar. Black Mustache said:

"At least oncet, to my knowledge. I run her in myself."

"Oh, she's got a record?" exclaimed the sergeant, now wholly at ease. "Why the hell didn't you say so?"

"I thought you remembered. You took her pedigree."

"I do recollect now," said the sergeant. "Take my advice, Queenie, and drop that bluff about the officers lying. Swallow your medicine—plead guilty—and you'll get off with a fine. If you lie about the police, the judge'll soak it to you. It happens to be a good judge—a friend of Freddie's." Then to the policemen: "Take her along to court, boys, and get back here as soon as you can."

"I want her locked up," objected Black Mustache. "I want F. P. to see her. I've got to hunt for him."

"Can't do it," said the sergeant. "If she makes a yell about police oppression, our holding on to her would look bad. No, put her through."

Susan now straightened herself and spoke. "I shan't make any complaint," said she. "Anything rather than court. I can't stand that. Keep me here."

"Not on your life!" cried the sergeant. "That's a trick. She'd have a good case against us."

"F. P.'ll raise the devil if——" began Black Mustache.

"Then hunt him up right away. To court she's got to go. I don't want to get broke."

The two men fell afoul each other with curse and abuse. They were in no way embarrassed by the presence of Susan. Her "record" made her of no account either as a woman or as a witness. Soon each was so well pleased with the verbal wounds he had dealt the other that their anger evaporated. The upshot of the hideous controversy was that Black Mustache said:

"You take her to court, Pete. I'll hunt up F. P. Keep her till the last."

In after days she could recall starting for the street car with the officer, Pete; then memory was a blank until she was sitting in a stuffy room with a prison odor—the anteroom to the court. She and Pete were alone. He was walking nervously up and down pulling his little fair mustache. It must have been that she had retained throughout the impassive features which, however stormy it was within, gave her an air of strength and calm. Otherwise Pete would not presently have halted before her to say in a low, agitated voice:

"If you can make trouble for us, don't do it. I've got a wife, and three babies—one come only last week—and my old mother paralyzed. You know how it is with us fellows—that we've got to do what them higher up says or be broke."

Susan made no reply.

"And F. P.—he's right up next the big fellows nowadays. What he says goes. You can see for yourself how much chance against him there'd be for a common low-down cop."

She was still silent, not through anger as he imagined but because she had no sense of the reality of what was happening. The officer, who had lost his nerve, looked at her a moment, in his animal eyes a humble pleading look; then he gave a groan and turned away. "Oh, hell!" he muttered.

Again her memory ceased to record until—the door swung open; she shivered, thinking it was the summons to court. Instead, there stood Freddie Palmer. The instant she looked into his face she became as calm and strong as her impassive expression had been falsely making her seem. Behind him was Black Mustache, his face ghastly, sullen, cowed. Palmer made a jerky motion of head and arm. Pete went; and the door closed and she was alone with him.

"I've seen the Judge and you're free," said Freddie.

She stood and began to adjust her hat and veil.

"I'll have those filthy curs kicked off the force."

She was looking tranquilly at him.

"You don't believe me? You think I ordered it done?"

She shrugged her shoulders. "No matter," she said. "It's undone now. I'm much obliged. It's more than I expected."

"You don't believe me—and I don't blame you. You think I'm making some sort of grandstand play."

"You haven't changed—at least not much."

"I'll admit, when you left I was wild and did tell 'em to take you in as soon as they found you. But that was a long time ago. And I never meant them to disturb a woman who was living respectably with her husband. There may have been—yes, there was a time when I'd have done that—and worse. But not any more. You say I haven't changed. Well, you're wrong. In some ways I have. I'm climbing up, as I always told you I would—and as a man gets up he sees things differently. At least, he acts differently. I don't do *that* kind of dirty work, any more."

"I'm glad to hear it," murmured Susan for lack of anything else to say.

He was as handsome as ever, she saw—had the same charm of manner—a charm owing not a little of its potency to the impression he made of the man who would dare as far as any man, and then go on to dare a step farther—the step from which all but the rare, utterly unafraid man shrinks. His look at her could not but appeal to her vanity as woman, and to her woman's craving for being loved; at the same time it agitated her with specters of the days of her slavery to him. He said:

"*You*'ve changed—a lot. And all to the good. The only sign is rouge on your lips and that isn't really a sign nowadays. But then you never did look the professional—and you weren't."

His eyes were appealingly tender as he gazed at her sweet, pensive face, with its violet-gray eyes full of mystery and sorrow and longing. And the clear pallor of her skin, and the slender yet voluptuous lines of her form suggested a pale, beautiful rose, most delicate of flowers yet about the hardiest.

"So—you've married and settled down?"

"No," replied Susan. "Neither the one nor the other."

"Why, you told——"

"I'm supposed to be a married woman."

"Why didn't you give your name and address at the police station?" said he. "They'd have let you go at once."

"Yes, I know," replied she. "But the newspapers would probably have published it. So—I couldn't. As it is I've been worrying for fear I'd be recognized, and the man would get a write-up."

"That was square," said he. "Yes, it'd have been a dirty trick to drag him in."

It was the matter-of-course to both of them that she should have protected her "friend." She had simply obeyed about the most stringent and least often violated article in the moral code of the world of outcasts. If Freddie's worst enemy in that world had murdered him, Freddie would have used his last breath in shielding him from the common foe, the law.

"If you're not married to him, you're free," said Freddie with a sudden new kind of interest in her.

"I told you I should always be free."

They remained facing each other a moment. When she moved to go, he said:

"I see you've still got your taste in dress—only more so."

She smiled faintly, glanced at his clothing. He was dressed with real fashion. He looked Fifth Avenue at its best, and his expression bore out the appearance of the well-bred man of fortune. "I can return the compliment," said she. "And you too have improved."

At a glance all the old fear of him had gone beyond the possibility of return. For she instantly realized that, like all those who give up war upon society and come in and surrender, he was enormously agitated about his new status, was impressed by the conventionalities to a degree that made him almost weak and mildly absurd. He was saying:

"I don't think of anything else but improving—in every way. And the higher I get the higher I want to go. . . . That was a dreadful thing I did to you. I wasn't to blame. It was part of the system. A man's got to do at every stage whatever's necessary. But I don't expect you to appreciate that. I know you'll never forgive me."

"I'm used to men doing dreadful things."

"*You* don't do them."

"Oh, I was brought up badly—badly for the game, I mean.
But
I'm doing better, and I shall do still better. I can't

abolish the system. I can't stand out against it—and live. So, I'm yielding—in my own foolish fashion."

"You don't lay up against me the—the—you know what I mean?"

The question surprised her, so far as it aroused any emotion.

She answered indifferently:

"I don't lay anything up against anybody. What's the use? I guess we all do the best we can—the best the system'll let us."

And she was speaking the exact truth. She did not reason out the causes of a state of mind so alien to the experiences of the comfortable classes that they could not understand it, would therefore see in it hardness of heart. In fact, the heart has nothing to do with this attitude in those who are exposed to the full force of the cruel buffetings of the storms that incessantly sweep the wild and wintry sea of active life. They lose the sense of the personal. Where they yield to anger and revenge upon the instrument the blow fate has used it to inflict, the resentment is momentary. The mood of personal vengeance is characteristic of stupid people leading uneventful lives—of comfortable classes, of remote rural districts. She again moved to go, this time putting out her hand with a smile. He said, with an awkwardness most significant in one so supple of mind and manner:

"I want to talk to you. I've got something to propose—something that'll interest you. Will you give me—say, about an hour?"

She debated, then smiled. "You will have me arrested if I refuse?"

He flushed scarlet. "You're giving me what's coming to me," said he. "The reason—one reason—I've got on so well is that I've never been a liar."

"No—you never were that."

"You, too. It's always a sign of bravery, and bravery's the one thing I respect. Yes, what I said I'd do always I did. That's the only way to get on in politics—and the crookeder the politics the more careful a man has to be about acting on the level. I can borrow a hundred thousand dollars without signing a paper—and that's more than the crooks in Wall Street can do—the biggest and best of them. So, when I told you how things were with me about you, I was on the level."

"I know it," said Susan. "Where shall we go? I can't ask you to come home with me."

"We might go to tea somewhere——"

Susan laughed outright. Tea! Freddie Palmer proposing tea! What a changed hooligan—how ridiculously changed! The other Freddie Palmer—

the real one—the fascinating repelling mixture of all the barbaric virtues and vices must still be there. But how carefully hidden—and what strong provocation would be needed to bring that savage to the surface again. The Italian in him, that was carrying him so far so cleverly, enabled him instantly to understand her amusement. He echoed her laugh. Said he:

"You've no idea the kind of people I'm traveling with—not political swells, but the real thing. What do you say to the Brevoort?"

She hesitated.

"You needn't be worried about being seen with me, no matter how high you're flying," he hastened to say. "I always did keep myself in good condition for the rise. Nothing's known about me or ever will be."

The girl was smiling at him again. "I wasn't thinking of those things," said she. "I've never been to the Brevoort."

"It's quiet and respectable."

Susan's eyes twinkled. "I'm glad it's respectable," said she. "Are you quite sure *you* can afford to be seen with *me?* It's true they don't make the fuss about right and wrong side of the line that they did a few years ago. They've gotten a metropolitan morality. Still—I'm not respectable and never shall be."

"Don't be too hasty about that," protested he, gravely. "But wait till you hear my proposition."

As they walked through West Ninth Street she noted that there was more of a physical change in him than she had seen at first glance. He was less athletic, heavier of form and his face was fuller. "You don't keep in as good training as you used," said she.

"It's those infernal automobiles," cried he. "They're death to figure—to health, for that matter. But I've got the habit, and I don't suppose I'll ever break myself of it. I've taken on twenty pounds in the past year, and I've got myself so upset that the doctor has ordered me abroad to take a cure. Then there's champagne. I can't let that alone, either, though I know it's plain poison."

And when they were in the restaurant of the Brevoort he insisted on ordering champagne—and left her for a moment to telephone for his automobile. It amused her to see a man so masterful thus pettily enslaved. She laughed at him, and he again denounced himself as a weak fool. "Money and luxury are too much for me. They are for everybody. I'm not as strong willed as I used to be," he said. "And it makes me uneasy. That's another reason for my proposition."

"Well—let's hear it," said she. "I happen to be in a position where I'm fond of hearing propositions—even if I have no intention of accepting."

She was watching him narrowly. The Freddie Palmer he was showing to her was a surprising but perfectly logical development of a side of his character with which she had been familiar in the old days; she was watching for that other side—the sinister and cruel side. "But first," he went on, "I must tell you a little about myself. I think I told you once about my mother and father?"

"I remember," said Susan.

"Well, honestly, do you wonder that I was what I used to be?"

"No," she answered. "I wonder that you are what you *seem* to be."

"What I come pretty near being," cried he. "The part that's more or less put on today is going to be the real thing tomorrow. That's the way it is with life—you put on a thing, and gradually learn to wear it. And—I want you to help me."

There fell silence between them, he gazing at his glass of champagne, turning it round and round between his long white fingers and watching the bubbles throng riotously up from the bottom. "Yes," he said thoughtfully, "I want you to help me. I've been waiting for you. I knew you'd turn up again." He laughed. "I've been true to you in a way—a man's way. I've hunted the town for women who suggested you—a poor sort of makeshift—but—I had to do something."

"What were you going to tell me?"

Her tone was business-like. He did not resent it, but straightway acquiesced. "I'll plunge right in. I've been, as you know, a bad one—bad all my life. I was born bad. You know about my mother and father. One of my sisters died in a disreputable resort. The other—well, the last I heard of her, she was doing time in an English pen. I've got a brother—he's a degenerate. Well!—not to linger over rotten smells, I was the only one of the family that had brains. I soon saw that everybody who gets on in the world is bad— which simply means doing disturbing things of one kind and another. And I saw that the ordinary crooks let their badness run their brains, while the get-on kind of people let their brains run their badness. You can be rotten— and sink lower and lower every day. Or you can gratify your natural taste for rottenness and at the same time get up in the world. I made up my mind to do the rotten things that get a man money and power."

"Respectability," said Susan.

"Respectability exactly. So I set out to improve my brains. I went to night school and read and studied. And I didn't stay a private in the gang of toughs. I had the brains to be leader, but the leader's got to be a fighter too. I took up boxing and made good in the ring. I got to be leader. Then I pushed my way up where I thought out the dirty work for the others to do, and I stayed under cover and made 'em bring the big share of the profits to me. And they did it because I had the brains to think out jobs that paid well and that could be pulled off without getting pinched—at least, not always getting pinched."

Palmer sipped his champagne, looked at her to see if she was appreciative. "I thought you'd understand," said he. "I needn't go into details. You remember about the women?"

"Yes, I remember," said Susan. "That was one step in the ladder up?"

"It got me the money to make my first play for respectability. I couldn't have got it any other way. I had extravagant tastes—and the leader has to be always giving up to help this fellow and that out of the hole. And I never did have luck with the cards and the horses."

"Why did you want to be respectable?" she asked.

"Because that's the best graft," explained he. "It means the most money, and the most influence. The coyotes that raid the sheep fold don't get the big share—though they may get a good deal. No, it's the shepherds and the owners that pull off the most. I've been leader of coyotes. I'm graduating into shepherd and proprietor."

"I see," said Susan. "You make it beautifully clear."

He bowed and smiled. "Thank you, kindly. Then, I'll go on. I'm deep in the contracting business now. I've got a pot of money put away. I've cut out the cards—except a little gentlemen's game now and then, to help me on with the right kind of people. Horses, the same way. I've got my political pull copper-riveted. It's as good with the Republicans as with Democrats, and as good with the reform crowd as with either. My next move is to cut loose from the gang. I've put a lot of lieutenants between me and them, instead of dealing with them direct. I'm putting in several more fellows I'm not ashamed to be seen with in Delmonico's."

"What's become of Jim?" asked Susan.

"Dead—a kike shot him all to pieces in a joint in Seventh Avenue about a month ago. As I was saying, how do these big multi-millionaires do the trick? They don't tell somebody to go steal what they happen to want. They tell somebody they want it, and that somebody else tells somebody else to get it, and that somebody else passes the word along until it reaches the poor devils who must steal it or lose their jobs. I studied it all out, and I've framed up my game the same way. Nowadays, every dollar that comes to me has been thoroughly cleaned long before it drops into my pocket. But you're wondering where *you* come in."

"Women are only interested in what's coming to them," said Susan.

"Sensible men are the same way. The men who aren't—they work for wages and salaries. If you're going to live off of other people, as women and the rich do, you've got to stand steady, day and night, for Number One. And now, here's where *you* come in. You've no objection to being respectable?"

"I've no objection to not being disreputable."

"That's the right way to put it," he promptly agreed. "Respectable, you know, doesn't mean anything but appearances. People who are really respectable, who let it strike in, instead of keeping it on the outside where it belongs—they soon get poor and drop down and out."

Palmer's revelation of himself and of a philosophy which life as it had revealed itself to her was incessantly urging her to adopt so grappled her attention that she altogether forgot herself. A man on his way to the scaffold who suddenly sees and feels a cataclysm rocking the world about him forgets his own plight. Unconsciously he was epitomizing, unconsciously she was learning, the whole story of the progress of the race upward from beast toward intellect—the brutal and bloody building of the highway from the caves of darkness toward the peaks of light. The source from which springs, and ever has sprung, the cruelty of man toward man is the struggle of the ambition of the few who see and insist upon better conditions, with the inertia and incompetence of the many who have little sight and less imagination. Ambition must use the inert mass—must persuade it, if possible, must compel it by trick or force if persuasion fails. But Palmer and Susan Lenox were, naturally, not seeing the thing in the broad but only as it applied to themselves.

"I've read a whole lot of history and biography," Freddie went on, "and I've thought about what I read and about what's going on around me. I tell you the world's full of cant. The people who get there don't act on what is always preached. The preaching isn't all lies—at least, I think not. But it doesn't fit the facts a man or a woman has got to meet."

"I realized that long ago," said Susan.

"There's a saying that you can't touch pitch without being defiled. Well—you can't build without touching pitch—at least not in a world where money's king and where those with brains have to live off of those without brains by making 'em work and showing 'em what to work at. It's a hell of a world, but *I* didn't get it up."

"And we've got to live in it," said she, "and get out of it the things we want and need."

"That's the talk!" cried Palmer. "I see you're 'on.' Now—to make a long story short—you and I can get what we want. We can help each other. You were better born than I am—you've had a better training in manners and dress and all the classy sort of things. I've got the money—and brains enough to learn with—and I can help you in various ways. So—I propose that we go up together."

"We've got—pasts," said Susan.

"Who hasn't that amounts to anything? Mighty few. No one that's made his own pile, I'll bet you. I'm in a position to do favors for people—the people we'd need. And I'll get in a position to do more and more. As long as they can make something out of us—or hope to—do you suppose they'll nose into our pasts and root things up that'd injure them as much as us?"

"It would be an interesting game, wouldn't it?" said Susan.

She was reflectively observing the handsome, earnest face before her— an incarnation of intelligent ambition, a Freddie Palmer who was somehow divesting himself of himself—was growing up—away from the rotten soil that had nourished him—up into the air—was growing strongly—yes, splendidly!

"And we've got everything to gain and nothing to lose," pursued he. "We'd not be adventurers, you see. Adventurers are people who haven't any money and are looking round to try to steal it. We'd have money. So, we'd be building solid, right on the rock." The handsome young man—the strongest, the most intelligent, the most purposeful she had ever met, except possibly Brent—looked at her with an admiring tenderness that moved her, the forlorn derelict adrift on the vast, lonely, treacherous sea. "The reason I've waited for you to invite you in on this scheme is that I tried you out and I found that you belong to the mighty few people who do what they say they'll do, good bargain or bad. It'd never occur to you to shuffle out of trying to keep your word."

"It hasn't—so far," said Susan.

"Well—that's the only sort of thing worth talking about as morality. Believe me, for I've been through the whole game from chimney pots to cellar floor."

"There's another thing, too," said the girl.

"What's that?"

"Not to injure anyone else."

Palmer shook his head positively. "It's believing that and acting on it that has kept you down in spite of your brains and looks."

"That I shall never do," said the girl. "It may be weakness—I guess it is weakness. But—I draw the line there."

"But I'm not proposing that you injure anyone—or proposing to do it myself. As I said, I've got up where I can afford to be good and kind and all that. And I'm willing to jump you up over the stretch of the climb that can't be crossed without being—well, anything but good and kind."

She was reflecting.

"You'll never get over that stretch by yourself. It'll always turn you back."

"Just what do you propose?" she asked.

It gave her pleasure to see the keen delight her question, with its implication of hope, aroused in him. Said he:

"That we go to Europe together and stay over there several years—as long as you like as long as it's necessary. Stay till our pasts have disappeared—work ourselves in with the right sort of people. You say you're not married?"

"Not to the man I'm with."

"To somebody else?"

"I don't know. I was."

"Well—that'll be looked into and straightened out. And then we'll quietly marry."

Susan laughed. "You're too fast," said she. "I'll admit I'm interested. I've been looking for a road—one that doesn't lead toward where we've come from. And this is the first road that has offered. But I haven't agreed to go in with you yet—haven't even begun to think it over. And if I did agree—which I probably won't—why, still I'd not be willing to marry. That's a serious matter. I'd want to be very, very sure I was satisfied."

Palmer nodded, with a return of the look of admiration. "I understand. You don't promise until you intend to stick, and once you've promised all hell couldn't change you."

"Another thing—very unfortunate, too. It looks to me as if I'd be dependent on you for money."

Freddie's eyes wavered. "Oh, we'd never quarrel about that," said he with an attempt at careless confidence.

"No," replied she quietly. "For the best of reasons. I'd not consider going into any arrangement where I'd be dependent on a man for money. I've had my experience. I've learned my lesson. If I lived with you several years in the sort of style you've suggested—no, not several years but a few months—you'd have me absolutely at your mercy. You'd thought of that, hadn't you?"

His smile was confession.

"I'd develop tastes for luxuries and they'd become necessities." Susan shook her head. "No—that would be foolish—very foolish."

He was watching her so keenly that his expression was covert suspicion. "What do you suggest?" he asked.

"Not what you suspect," replied she, amused. "I'm not making a play for a gift of a fortune. I haven't anything to suggest."

There was a long silence, he turning his glass slowly and from time to time taking a little of the champagne thoughtfully. She observed him with a quizzical expression. It was apparent to her that he was debating whether he would be making a fool of himself if he offered her an independence outright. Finally she said:

"Don't worry, Freddie. I'd not take it, even if you screwed yourself up to the point of offering it."

He glanced up quickly and guiltily. "Why not?" he said. "You'd be practically my wife. I can trust you. You've had experience, so you can't blame me for hesitating. Money puts the devil in anybody who gets it—man or woman. But I'll trust you——" he laughed—"since I've got to."

"No. The most I'd take would be a salary. I'd be a sort of companion."

"Anything you like," cried he. This last suspicion born of a life of intimate dealings with his fellow-beings took flight. "It'd have to be a big salary because you'd have to dress and act the part. What do you say? Is it a go?"

"Oh, I can't decide now."

"When?"

She reflected. "I can tell you in a week."

He hesitated, said, "All right—a week."

She rose to go. "I've warned you the chances are against my accepting."

"That's because you haven't looked the ground over," replied he, rising. Then, after a nervous moment, "Is the—is the——" He stopped short.

"Go on," said she. "We must be frank with each other."

"If the idea of living with me is—is disagreeable——" And again he stopped, greatly embarrassed—an amazing indication of the state of mind of such a man as he—of the depth of his infatuation, of his respect, of his new-sprung awe of conventionality.

"I hadn't given it a thought," replied she. "Women are not especially sensitive about that sort of thing."

"They're supposed to be. And I rather thought you were."

She laughed mockingly. "No more than other women," said she. "Look how they marry for a home—or money—or social position—and such men! And look how they live with men year after year, hating them. Men never could do that."

"Don't you believe it," replied he. "They can, and they do. The kept man—in and out of marriage—is quite a feature of life in our chaste little village."

Susan looked amused. "Well—why not?" said she. "Everybody's simply got to have money nowadays."

"And working for it is slow and mighty uncertain."

Her face clouded. She was seeing the sad wretched past from filthy tenement to foul workshop. She said:

"Where shall I send you word?"

"I've an apartment at Sherry's now."

"Then—a week from today."

She put out her hand. He took it, and she marveled as she felt a tremor in that steady hand of his. But his voice was resolutely careless as he said, "So long. Don't forget how much I want or need you. And if you do forget that, think of the advantages—seeing the world with plenty of money—and all the rest of it. Where'll you get such another chance? You'll not be fool enough to refuse."

She smiled, said as she went, "You may remember I used to be something of a fool."

"But that was some time ago. You've learned a lot since then—surely."

"We'll see. I've become—I think—a good deal of a—of a New Yorker."

"That means frank about doing what the rest of the world does under a stack of lies. It's a lovely world, isn't it?"

"If I had made it," laughed Susan, "I'd not own up to the fact."

She laughed; but she was seeing the old women of the slums—was seeing them as one sees in the magic mirror the vision of one's future self. And on the way home she said to herself, "It was a good thing that I was arrested today. It reminded me. It warned me. But for it, I might have gone on to make a fool of myself." And she recalled how it had been one of Burlingham's favorite maxims that everything is for the best, for those who know how to use it.

CHAPTER XVIII

SHE wrote Garvey asking an appointment. The reply should have come the next day or the next day but one at the farthest; for Garvey had been trained by Brent to the supreme courtesy of promptness. It did not come until the fourth day; before she opened it Susan knew about what she would read—the stupidly obvious attempt to put off facing her—the cowardice of a kind-hearted, weak fellow. She really had her answer—was left without a doubt for hope to perch upon. But she wrote again, insisting so sharply that he came the following day. His large, tell-tale face was a restatement of what she had read in his delay and between the lines of his note. He was effusively friendly with a sort of mortuary suggestion, like one bearing condolences, that tickled her sense of humor, far though her heart was from mirth.

"Something has happened," began she, "that makes it necessary for me to know when Mr. Brent is coming back."

"Really, Mrs. Spencer——"

"Miss Lenox," she corrected.

"Yes—Miss Lenox, I beg your pardon. But really—in my position—I know nothing of Mr. Brent's plans—and if I did, I'd not be at liberty to speak of them. I have written him what you wrote me about the check—and—and—that is all."

"Mr. Garvey, is he ever—has he——" Susan, desperate, burst out with more than she intended to say: "I care nothing about it, one way or the other. If Mr. Brent is politely hinting that I won't do, I've a right to know it. I have a chance at something else. Can't you tell me?"

"I don't know anything about it—honestly I don't, Miss Lenox," cried he, swearing profusely.

"You put an accent on the 'know,'" said Susan. "You suspect that I'm right, don't you?"

"I've no ground for suspecting—that is—no, I haven't. He said nothing to me—nothing. But he never does. He's very peculiar and uncertain . . . and I don't understand him at all."

"Isn't this his usual way with the failures—his way of letting them down easily?"

Susan's manner was certainly light and cheerful, an assurance that he need have no fear of hysterics or despair or any sort of scene trying to a soft heart. But Garvey could take but the one view of the favor or disfavor of the god of his universe. He looked at her like a dog that is getting a whipping from a friend. "Now, Miss Lenox, you've no right to put me in this painful——"

"That's true," said Susan, done since she had got what she sought. "I shan't say another word. When Mr. Brent comes back, will you tell him I sent for you to ask you to thank him for me—and say to him that I found something else for which I hope I'm better suited?"

"I'm so glad," said Garvey, hysterically. "I'm delighted.
And I'm sure he will be, too. For I'm sure he liked you,
personally—and I must say I was surprised when he went.
But
I must not say that sort of thing. Indeed, I know nothing,
Miss Lenox—I assure you——"

"And please tell him," interrupted Susan, "that I'd have written him myself, only I don't want to bother him."

"Oh, no—no, indeed. Not that, Miss Lenox. I'm so sorry.
But I'm only the secretary. I can't say anything."

It was some time before Susan could get rid of him, though he was eager to be gone. He hung in the doorway, ejaculating disconnectedly, dropping and picking up his hat, perspiring profusely, shaking hands again and again, and so exciting her pity for his misery of the good-hearted weak that she was for the moment forgetful of her own plight. Long before he went, he had greatly increased her already strong belief in Brent's generosity of character—for, thought she, he'd have got another secretary if he hadn't been too kind to turn adrift so helpless and foolish a creature. Well—he should have no trouble in getting rid of her.

She was seeing little of Spenser and they were saying almost nothing to each other. When he came at night, always very late, she was in bed and pretended sleep. When he awoke, she got breakfast in silence; they read the newspapers as they ate. And he could not spare the time to come to dinner. As the decisive moment drew near, his fears dried up his confident volubility. He changed his mind and insisted on her coming to the theater for the final rehearsals. But "Shattered Lives" was not the sort of play she cared for, and she was wearied by the profane and tedious wranglings of the stage director and the authors, by the stupidity of the actors who had to be told every little intonation and gesture again and again. The agitation, the labor seemed grotesquely out of proportion to the triviality of the matter at issue. At the first night she sat in a box from which Spenser, in a high fever and twitching with nervousness, watched the play, gliding out just before the lights were turned up for the intermission. The play went better than she had expected, and the enthusiasm of the audience convinced her that it was a success before the fall of the curtain on the second act. With the applause that greeted the chief climax—the end of the third act—Spenser, Sperry and Fitzalan were convinced. All three responded to curtain calls. Susan had never seen Spenser so handsome, and she admired the calmness and the cleverness of his brief speech of thanks. That line of footlights between them gave her a new point of view on him, made her realize how being so close to his weaknesses had obscured for her his strong qualities—for, unfortunately, while a man's public life is determined wholly by his strong qualities, his intimate life depends wholly on his weaknesses. She was as fond of him as she had ever been; but it was impossible for her to feel any thrill approaching love. Why? She looked at his fine face and manly figure; she recalled how many good qualities he had. Why had she ceased to love him? She thought perhaps some mystery of physical lack of sympathy was in part responsible; then there was the fact that she could not trust him. With many women, trust is not necessary to love; on the contrary, distrust inflames love. It happened not to be so with Susan Lenox. "I do not love him. I can never love him again. And when he uses his power over me, I shall begin to dislike him." The lost illusion! The dead love! If she could call it back to life! But no—there it lay, coffined, the gray of death upon its features. Her heart ached.

After the play Fitzalan took the authors and the leading lady, Constance Francklyn, and Miss Lenox to supper in a private room at Rector's. This was Miss Francklyn's first trial in a leading part. She had small ability as an actress, having never risen beyond the primer stage of mere posing and declamation in which so many players are halted by their vanity—the universal human vanity that is content with small triumphs, or with purely imaginary triumphs. But she had a notable figure of the lank, serpentine kind and a bad, sensual face that harmonized with it. Especially in artificial light she had an uncanny allure of the elemental, the wild animal in the jungle. With every disposition and effort to use her physical charms to further herself she would not have been still struggling at twenty-eight, had she had so much as a thimbleful of intelligence.

"Several times," said Sperry to Susan as they crossed Long Acre together on the way to Rector's, "yes, at least half a dozen times to my knowledge,

Constance had had success right in her hands. And every time she has gone crazy about some cheap actor or sport and has thrown it away."

"But she'll get on now," said Susan.

"Perhaps," was Sperry's doubting reply. "Of course, she's got no brains. But it doesn't take brains to act—that is, to act well enough for cheap machine-made plays like this. And nowadays playwrights have learned that it's useless to try to get actors who can act. They try to write parts that are actor-proof."

"You don't like your play?" said Susan.

"Like it? I love it. Isn't it going to bring me in a pot of money? But as a play"—Sperry laughed. "I know Spenser thinks it's great, but—there's only one of us who can write plays, and that's Brent. It takes a clever man to write a clever play. But it takes a genius to write a clever play that'll draw the damn fools who buy theater seats. And Robert Brent now and then does the trick. How are you getting on with your ambition for a career?"

Susan glanced nervously at him. The question, coming upon the heels of talk about Brent, filled her with alarm lest Rod had broken his promise and had betrayed her confidence. But Sperry's expression showed that she was probably mistaken.

"My ambition?" said she. "Oh—I've given it up."

"The thought of work was too much for you—eh?"

Susan shrugged her shoulders.

A sardonic grin flitted over Sperry's Punch-like face. "The more I see of women, the less I think of 'em," said he. "But I suppose the men'd be lazy and worthless too, if nature had given 'em anything that'd sell or rent. . . . Somehow I'm disappointed in *you*, though."

That ended the conversation until they were sitting down at the table. Then Sperry said:

"Are you offended by my frankness a while ago?"

"No," replied Susan. "The contrary. Some day your saying that may help me."

"It's quite true, there's something about you—a look—a manner—it makes one feel you could do things if you tried."

"I'm afraid that 'something' is a fraud," said she. No doubt it was that something that had misled Brent—that had always deceived her about herself. No, she must not think herself a self-deceived dreamer. Even if it was so, still she must not think it. She must say to herself over and over again "Brent or no Brent, I shall get on—I shall get on" until she had silenced the last disheartening doubt.

Miss Francklyn, with Fitzalan on her left and Spenser on her right, was seated opposite Susan. About the time the third bottle was being emptied the attempts of Spenser and Constance to conceal from her their doings became absurd. Long before the supper was over there had been thrust at her all manner of proofs that Spenser was again untrue, that he was whirling madly in one of those cyclonic infatuations which soon wore him out and left him to return contritely to her. Sperry admired Susan's manners as displayed in her unruffled serenity—an admiration which she did not in the least deserve. She was in fact as deeply interested as she seemed in his discussion of plays and acting, illustrated by Brent's latest production. By the time the party broke up, Susan had in spite of herself collected a formidable array of incriminating evidence, including the stealing of one of Constance's jeweled show garters by Spenser under cover of the tablecloth and a swift kiss in the hall when Constance went out for a moment and Spenser presently suspended his drunken praises of himself as a dramatist, and appointed himself a committee to see what had become of her.

At the door of the restaurant, Spenser said:

"Susan, you and Miss Francklyn take a taxicab. She'll drop you at our place on her way home. Fitz and Sperry and I want one more drink."

"Not for me," said Sperry savagely, with a scowl at Constance.

But Fitzalan, whose arm Susan had seen Rod press, remained silent.

"Come on, my dear," cried Miss Francklyn, smiling sweet insolent treachery into Susan's face.

Susan smiled sweetly back at her. As she was leaving the taxicab in Forty-fifth Street, she said:

"Send Rod home by noon, won't you? And don't tell him I know."

Miss Francklyn, who had been drinking greedily, began to cry. Susan laughed. "Don't be a silly," she urged. "If I'm not upset, why should you be? And how could I blame you two for getting crazy about each other? I wouldn't spoil it for worlds. I want to help it on."

"Don't you love him—really?" cried Constance, face and voice full of the most thrilling theatricalism.

"I'm very fond of him," replied Susan. "We're old, old friends. But as to love—I'm where you'll be a few months from now."

Miss Francklyn dried her eyes. "Isn't it the devil!" she exclaimed. "Why *can't* it last?"

"Why, indeed," said Susan. "Good night—and don't forget to send him by twelve o'clock." And she hurried up the steps without waiting for a reply.

She felt that the time for action had again come—that critical moment which she had so often in the past seen come and had let pass unheeded. He was in love with another woman; he was prosperous, assured of a good income for a long time, though he wrote no more successes. No need to consider him. For herself, then—what? Clearly, there could be no future for her with Rod. Clearly, she must go.

Must go—must take the only road that offered. Up before her—as in every mood of deep depression—rose the vision of the old women of the slums—the solitary, bent, broken forms, clad in rags, feet wrapped in rags— shuffling along in the gutters, peering and poking among filth, among garbage, to get together stuff to sell for the price of a drink. The old women of the tenements, the old women of the gutters, the old women drunk and dancing as the lecherous-eyed hunchback played the piano.

She must not this time wait and hesitate and hope; this time she must take the road that offered—and since it must be taken she must advance along it as if of all possible roads it was the only one she would have freely chosen.

Yet after she had written and sent off the note to Palmer, a deep sadness enveloped her—a grief, not for Rod, but for the association, the intimacy, their life together, its sorrows and storms perhaps more than the pleasures and the joys. When she left him before, she had gone sustained by the feeling that she was doing it for him, was doing a duty. Now, she was going merely to save herself, to further herself. Life, life in that great and hard school of practical living, New York, had given her the necessary hardiness to go, aided by Rod's unfaithfulness and growing uncongeniality. But not while she lived could she ever learn to be hard. She would do what she must—she was no longer a fool. But she could not help sighing and crying a little as she did it.

It was not many minutes after noon when Spenser came. He looked so sheepish and uncomfortable that Susan thought Constance had told him. But his opening sentence of apology was:

"I took too many nightcaps and Fitz had to lug me home with him."

"Really?" said Susan. "How disappointed Constance must have been!"

Spenser was not a good liar. His face twisted and twitched so that Susan laughed outright. "Why, you look like a caught married man," cried she. "You forget we're both free."

"Whatever put that crazy notion in your head—about Miss
Francklyn?" demanded he.

"When you take me or anyone for that big a fool, Rod, you only show how foolish you yourself are," said she with the utmost good humor. "The best way to find out how much sense a person has is to see what kind of lies he thinks'll deceive another person."

"Now—don't get jealous, Susie," soothed he. "You know how a man is."

The tone was correctly contrite, but Susan felt underneath the confidence that he would be forgiven—the confidence of the egotist giddied by a triumph. Said she:

"Don't you think mine's a strange way of acting jealous?"

"But you're a strange woman."

Susan looked at him thoughtfully. "Yes, I suppose I am," said she. "And you'll think me stranger when I tell you what I'm going to do."

He started up in a panic. And the fear in his eyes pleased her, at the same time that it made her wince.

She nodded slowly. "Yes, Rod—I'm leaving."

"I'll drop Constance," cried he. "I'll have her put out of the company."

"No—go on with her till you've got enough—or she has."

"I've got enough, this minute," declared he with convincing energy and passion. "You must know, dearest, that to me Constance—all the women I've ever seen—aren't worth your little finger. You're all that they are, and a whole lot more besides." He seized her in his arms. "You wouldn't leave me—you couldn't! You understand how men are—how they get these fits of craziness about a pair of eyes or a figure or some trick of voice or manner. But that doesn't affect the man's heart. I love you, Susan. I adore you."

She did not let him see how sincerely he had touched her. Her eyes were of their deepest violet, but he had never learned that sign. She smiled mockingly; the fingers that caressed his hair were trembling. "We've tided each other over, Rod. The play's a success. You're all right again—and so am I. Now's the time to part."

"Is it Brent, Susie?"

"I quit him last week."

"There's no one else. You're going because of Constance!"

She did not deny. "You're free and so am I," said she practically. "I'm going. So—let's part sensibly. Don't make a silly scene."

She knew how to deal with him—how to control him through his vanity. He drew away from her, chilled and sullen. "If you can live through it, I guess I can," said he. "You're making a damn fool of yourself—leaving a man that's fond of you—and leaving when he's successful."

"I always was a fool, you know," said she. She had decided against explaining to him and so opening up endless and vain argument. It was enough that she saw it was impossible to build upon or with him, saw the necessity of trying elsewhere—unless she would risk—no, invite—finding herself after a few months, or years, back among the drift, back in the underworld.

He gazed at her as she stood smiling gently at him—smiling to help her hide the ache at her heart, the terror before the vision of the old women of the tenement gutters, earning the wages, not of sin, not of vice, not of stupidity, but of indecision, of over-hopefulness—of weakness. Here was the kind of smile that hurts worse than tears, that takes the place of tears and sobs and moans. But he who had never understood her did not understand her now. Her smile infuriated his vanity. "You can *laugh!*" he sneered. "Well—go to the filth where you belong! You were born for it." And he flung out of the room, went noisily down the stairs. She heard the front door's distant slam; it seemed to drop her into a chair. She sat there all crouched together until the clock on the mantel struck two. This roused her hastily to gather into her trunk such of her belongings as she had not already packed. She sent for a cab. The man of all work carried down the trunk and put it on the box. Dressed in a simple blue costume as if for traveling, she entered the cab and gave the order to drive to the Grand Central Station.

At the corner she changed the order and was presently entering the Beaux Arts restaurant where she had asked Freddie to meet her. He was there, smoking calmly and waiting. At sight of her he rose. "You'll have lunch?" said he.

"No, thanks."

"A small bottle of champagne?"

"Yes—I'm rather tired."

He ordered the champagne. "And," said he, "it'll be the real thing—which mighty few New Yorkers get even at the best places." When it came he sent the waiter away and filled the glasses himself. He touched the brim of his glass to the bottom of hers. "To the new deal," said he.

She smiled and nodded, and emptied the glass. Suddenly it came to her why she felt so differently toward him. She saw the subtle, yet radical change that always transforms a man of force of character when his position in the world notably changes. This man before her, so slightly different in physical characteristics from the man she had fled, was wholly different in expression.

"When shall we sail?" asked he. "Tomorrow?"

"First—there's the question of money," said she.

He was much amused. "Still worrying about your independence."

"No," replied she. "I've been thinking it out, and I don't feel any anxiety about that. I've changed my scheme of life. I'm going to be sensible and practice what life has taught me. It seems there's only one way for a woman to get up. Through some man."

Freddie nodded. "By marriage or otherwise, but always through a man."

"So I've discovered," continued she. "So, I'm going to play the game. And I think I can win now. With the aid of what I'll learn and with the chances I'll have, I can keep my feeling of independence. You see, if you and I don't get on well together, I'll be able to look out for myself. Something'll turn up."

"Or—*somebody*—eh?"

"Or somebody."

"That's candid."

"Don't you want me to be candid? But even if you don't, I've got to be."

"Yes—truth—especially disagreeable truth—is your long suit," said he. "Not that I'm kicking. I'm glad you went straight at the money question. We can settle it and never think of it again. And neither of us will be plotting to take advantage of the other, or fretting for fear the other is plotting. Sometimes I think nearly all the trouble in this world comes through failure to have a clear understanding about money matters."

Susan nodded. Said she thoughtfully, "I guess that's why I came—one of the main reasons. You are wonderfully sensible and decent about money."

"And the other chap isn't?"

"Oh, yes—and no. He likes to make a woman feel dependent.
He thinks—but that doesn't matter. He's all right."

"Now—for our understanding with each other," said Palmer. "You can have whatever you want. The other day you said you wanted some sort of a salary. But if you've changed——"

"No—that's what I want."

"So much a year?"

"So much a week," replied she. "I want to feel, and I want you to feel, that we can call it off at any time on seven days' notice."

"But that isn't what I want," said he—and she, watching him closely if furtively, saw the strong lines deepen round his mouth.

She hesitated. She was seeing the old woman's dance hall, was hearing the piano as the hunchback played and the old horrors reeled about, making their palsy rhythmic. She was seeing this, yet she dared. "Then you don't want me," said she, so quietly that he could not have suspected her agitation. Never had her habit of concealing her emotion been so useful to her.

He sat frowning at his glass—debating. Finally he said:

"I explained the other day what I was aiming for. Such an arrangement as you suggest wouldn't help. You see that?"

"It's all I can do—at present," replied she firmly. And she was now ready to stand or fall by that decision. She had always accepted the other previous terms—or whatever terms fate offered. Result—each time, disaster. She must make no more fatal blunders. This time, her own terms or not at all.

He was silent a long time. She knew she had convinced him that her terms were final. So, his delay could only mean that he was debating whether to accept or to go his way and leave her to go hers. At last he laughed and said:

"You've become a true New Yorker. You know how to drive a hard bargain." He looked at her admiringly. "You certainly have got courage. I happen to know a lot about your affairs. I've ways of finding out things. And I know you'd not be here if you hadn't broken with the other fellow first. So, if I turned your proposition down you'd be up against it—wouldn't you?"

"Yes," said she. "But—I won't in any circumstances tie myself. I must be free."

"You're right," said he. "And I'll risk your sticking. I'm a good gambler."

"If I were bound, but didn't want to stay, would I be of much use?"

"Of no use. You can quit on seven minutes' notice, instead of seven days."

"And you, also," said she.

Laughingly they shook hands. She began to like him in a new and more promising way. Here was a man, who at least was cast in a big mold. Nothing small and cheap about him—and Brent had made small cheap men forever intolerable to her. Yes, here was a man of the big sort; and a big man couldn't possibly be a bad man. No matter how many bad things he might do, he would still be himself, at least, a scorner of the pettiness and sneakiness and cowardice inseparable from villainy.

"And now," said he, "let's settle the last detail. How much a week? How would five hundred strike you?"

"That's more than twelve times the largest salary I ever
got.
It's many times as much as I made in the——"

"No matter," he hastily interposed. "It's the least you can hold down the job on. You've got to spend money—for clothes and so on."

"Two hundred is the most I can take," said she. "It's the outside limit."

He insisted, but she remained firm. "I will not accustom myself to much more than I see any prospect of getting elsewhere," explained she. "Perhaps later on I'll ask for an increase—later on, when I see how things are going and what my prospects elsewhere would be. But I must begin modestly."

"Well, let it go at two hundred for the present. I'll deposit a year's salary in a bank, and you can draw against it. Is that satisfactory? You don't want me to hand you two hundred dollars every Saturday, do you?"

"No. That would get on my nerves," said she.

"Now—it's all settled. When shall we sail?"

"There's a girl I've got to look up before I go."

"Maud? You needn't bother about her. She's married to a piker from up the state—a shoe manufacturer. She's got a baby, and is fat enough to make two or three like what she used to be."

"No, not Maud. One you don't know."

"I hoped we could sail tomorrow. Why not take a taxi and go after her now?"

"It may be a long search."

"She's a——?" He did not need to finish his sentence in order to make himself understood.

Susan nodded.

"Oh, let her— —"

"I promised," interrupted she.

"Then—of course." Freddie drew from his trousers pocket a huge roll of bills. Susan smiled at this proof that he still retained the universal habit of gamblers, politicians and similar loose characters of large income, precariously derived. He counted off three hundreds and four fifties and held them out to her. "Let me in on it," said he.

Susan took the money without hesitation. She was used to these careless generosities of the men of that class—generosities passing with them and with the unthinking for evidences of goodness of heart, when in fact no generosity has any significance whatever beyond selfish vanity unless it is a sacrifice of necessities—real necessities.

"I don't think I'll need money," said she. "But I may."

"You've got a trunk and a bag on the cab outside," he went on.

"I've told them at Sherry's that I'm to be married."

Susan flushed. She hastily lowered her eyes. But she need not have feared lest he should suspect the cause of the blush . . . a strange, absurd resentment of the idea that she could be married to Freddie Palmer. Live with him—yes. But marry—now that it was thus squarely presented to her, she found it unthinkable. She did not pause to analyze this feeling, indeed could not have analyzed it, had she tried. It was, however, a most interesting illustration of how she had been educated at last to look upon questions of sex as a man looks on them. She was like the man who openly takes a mistress whom he in no circumstances would elevate to the position of wife.

"So," he proceeded, "you might as well move in at Sherry's."

"No," objected she. "Let's not begin the new deal until we sail."

The wisdom of this was obvious. "Then we'll take your things over to the Manhattan Hotel," said he. "And we'll start the search from there."

But after registering at the Manhattan as Susan Lenox, she started out alone. She would not let him look in upon any part of her life which she could keep veiled.

CHAPTER XIX

SHE left the taxicab at the corner of Grand Street and the Bowery, and plunged into her former haunts afoot. Once again she had it forced upon her how meaningless in the life history are the words "time" and "space." She was now hardly any distance, as measurements go, from her present world, and she had lived here only a yesterday or so ago. Yet what an infinity yawned between! At the Delancey Street apartment house there was already a new janitress, and the kinds of shops on the ground floor had changed. Only after two hours of going up and down stairs, of knocking at doors, of questioning and cross-questioning, did she discover that Clara had moved to Allen Street, to the tenement in which Susan herself had for a few weeks lived—those vague, besotted weeks of despair.

When we go out into the streets with bereavement in mind, we see nothing but people dressed in mourning. And a similar thing occurs, whatever the emotion that oppresses us. It would not have been strange if Susan, on the way to Allen Street afoot, had seen only women of the streets, for they swarm in every great thoroughfare of our industrial cities. They used to come out only at night. But with the passing of the feeling against them that existed when they were a rare, unfamiliar, mysteriously terrible minor feature of life, they issue forth boldly by day, like all the other classes, making a living as best they can. But on that day Susan felt as if she were seeing only the broken down and cast-out creatures of the class—the old women, old in body rather than in years, picking in the gutters, fumbling in the garbage barrels, poking and peering everywhere for odds and ends that might pile up into the price of a glass of the poison sold in the barrel houses. The old women—the hideous, lonely old women—and the diseased, crippled children, worse off than the cats and the dogs, for cat and dog were not compelled to wear filth-soaked rags. Prosperous, civilized New York!

A group of these children were playing some rough game, in imitation of their elders, that was causing several to howl with pain. She heard a woman, being shown about by a settlement worker or some such person, say:

"Really, not at all badly dressed—for street games. I must confess I don't see signs of the misery they talk so much about."

A wave of fury passed through Susan. She felt like striking the woman full in her vain, supercilious, patronizing face—striking her and saying: "You smug liar! What if you had to wear such clothes on that fat, overfed body of yours! You'd realize then how filthy they are!"

She gazed in horror at the Allen Street house. Was it possible that *she* had lived there? In the filthy doorway sat a child eating a dill pickle—a scrawny, ragged little girl with much of her hair eaten out by the mange. She recalled this little girl as the formerly pretty and lively youngster, the daughter of the janitress. She went past the child without disturbing her, knocked at the janitress' door. It presently opened, disclosing in a small and foul room four prematurely old women, all in the family way, two with babies in arms. One of these was the janitress. Though she was not a Jewess, she was wearing one of the wigs assumed by orthodox Jewish women when they marry. She stared at Susan with not a sign of recognition.

"I am looking for Miss Clara," said Susan.

The janitress debated, shifted her baby from one arm to the other, glanced inquiringly at the other women. They shook their heads; she looked at Susan and shook her head. "There ain't a Clara," said she. "Perhaps she's took another name?"

"Perhaps," conceded Susan. And she described Clara and the various dresses she had had. At the account of one with flounces on the skirts and lace puffs in the sleeves, the youngest of the women showed a gleam of intelligence. "You mean the girl with the cancer of the breast," said she.

Susan remembered. She could not articulate; she nodded.

"Oh, yes," said the janitress. "She had the third floor back, and was always kicking because Mrs. Pfister kept a guinea pig for her rheumatism and the smell came through."

"Has she gone?" asked Susan.

"Couple of weeks."

"Where?"

The janitress shrugged her shoulders. The other women shrugged their shoulders. Said the janitress:

"Her feller stopped coming. The cancer got awful bad. I've saw a good many—they're quite plentiful down this way. I never see a worse'n hers. She didn't have no money. Up to the hospital they tried a new cure on her that made her gallopin' worse. The day before I was going to have to go to work and put her out—she left."

"Can't you give me any idea?" urged Susan.

"She didn't take her things," said the janitress meaningly. "Not a stitch."

"The—the river?"

The janitress shrugged her shoulders. "She always said she would, and I guess——"

Again the fat, stooped shoulders lifted and lowered. "She was most crazy with pain."

There was a moment's silence, then Susan murmured, "Thank you," and went back to the hall. The house was exhaling a frightful stench—the odor of cheap kerosene, of things that passed there for food, of animals human and lower, of death and decay. On her way out she dropped a dollar into the lap of the little girl with the mange. A parrot was shrieking from an upper window. On the topmost fire escape was a row of geraniums blooming sturdily. Her taxicab had moved up the street, pushed out of place by a hearse—a white hearse, with polished mountings, the horses caparisoned in white netting, and tossing white plumes. A baby's funeral—this mockery of a ride in state after a brief life of squalor. It was summer, and the babies were dying like lambs in the shambles. In winter the grown people were slaughtered; in summer the children. Across the street, a few doors up, the city dead wagon was taking away another body—in a plain pine box—to the Potter's Field where find their way for the final rest one in every ten of the people of the rich and splendid city of New York.

Susan hurried into her cab. "Drive fast," she said.

When she came back to sense of her surroundings she was flying up wide and airy Fifth Avenue with gorgeous sunshine bathing its palaces, with wealth and fashion and ease all about her. Her dear City of the Sun! But it hurt her now, was hateful to look upon. She closed her eyes; her life in the slums, her life when she was sharing the lot that is really the lot of the human race as a race, passed before her—its sights and sounds and odors, its hideous heat, its still more hideous cold, its contacts and associations, its dirt and disease and degradation. And through the roar of the city there came to her a sound, faint yet intense—like the still, small voice the prophet heard—but not the voice of God, rather the voice of the multitude of aching hearts, aching in hopeless poverty—hearts of men, of women, of children——

The children! The multitudes of children with hearts that no sooner begin to beat than they begin to ache. She opened her eyes to shut out these sights and that sound of heartache.

She gazed round, drew a long breath of relief. She had almost been afraid to look round lest she should find that her escape had been only a dream. And now the road she had chosen—or, rather, the only road she could take—the road with Freddie Palmer—seemed attractive, even dazzling. What she could not like, she would ignore—and how easily she, after her experience, could do that! What she could not ignore she would tolerate would compel herself to like.

Poor Clara!—Happy Clara!—better off in the dregs of the river than she had ever been in the dregs of New York. She shuddered. Then, as so often, the sense of the grotesque thrust in, as out of place as jester in cap and bells at a bier—and she smiled sardonically. "Why," thought she, "in being squeamish about Freddie I'm showing that I'm more respectable than the respectable women. There's hardly one of them that doesn't swallow worse doses with less excuse or no excuse at all—and without so much as a wry face."

CHAPTER XX

IN the ten days on the Atlantic and the Mediterranean Mr. and Mrs. Palmer, as the passenger list declared them, planned the early stages of their campaign. They must keep to themselves, must make no acquaintances, no social entanglements of any kind, until they had effected the exterior transformation which was to be the first stride—and a very long one, they felt—toward the conquest of the world that commands all the other worlds. Several men aboard knew Palmer slightly—knew him vaguely as a big politician and contractor. They had a hazy notion that he was reputed to have been a thug and a grafter. But New Yorkers have few prejudices except against guilelessness and failure. They are well aware that the wisest of the wise Hebrew race was never more sagacious than when he observed that "he who hasteth to be rich shall not be innocent." They are too well used to unsavory pasts to bother much about that kind of odor; and where in the civilized world—or in that which is not civilized—is there an odor from reputation—or character—whose edge is not taken off by the strong, sweet, hypnotic perfume of money? Also, Palmer's appearance gave the lie direct to any scandal about him. It could not be—it simply could not be— that a man of such splendid physical build, a man with a countenance so handsome, had ever been a low, wicked fellow! Does not the devil always at once exhibit his hoofs, horns, tail and malevolent smile, that all men may know who and what he is? A frank, manly young leader of men—that was the writing on his countenance. And his Italian blood put into his good looks an ancient and aristocratic delicacy that made it incredible that he was of low origin. He spoke good English, he dressed quietly; he did not eat with his knife; he did not retire behind a napkin to pick his teeth, but attended to them openly, if necessity compelled—and splendid teeth they were, set in a wide, clean mouth, notably attractive for a man's. No, Freddie Palmer's past would not give him any trouble whatever; in a few years it would be forgotten, would be romanced about as the heroic struggles of a typical American rising from poverty.

"Thank God," said Freddie, "I had sense enough not to get a jail smell on me!"

Susan colored painfully—and Palmer, the sensitive, colored also. But he had the tact that does not try to repair a blunder by making a worse one; he pretended not to see Susan's crimson flush.

Her past would not be an easy matter—if it should ever rise to face her publicly. Therefore it must not rise till Freddie and she were within the walls of the world they purposed to enter by stealth, and had got themselves well intrenched. Then she would be Susan Lenox of Sutherland, Indiana, who had come to New York to study for the stage and, after many trials from all of which she had emerged with unspotted virtue, whatever vicious calumny might in envy say, had captured the heart and the name of the handsome, rich young contractor. There would be nasty rumors, dreadful stories, perhaps. But in these loose and cynical days, with the women more and more audacious and independent, with the universal craving for luxury beyond the reach of laboriously earned incomes, with marriage decaying in city life among the better classes—in these easy-going days, who was not suspected, hinted about, attacked? And the very atrociousness of the stories would prevent their being believed. One glance at Susan would be enough to make doubters laugh at their doubts.

The familiar types of fast women of all degrees come from the poorest kinds of farms and from the tenements. In America, practically not until the panics and collapses of recent years which have tumbled another and better section of the middle class into the abyss of the underworld—not until then did there appear in the city streets and houses of ill repute any considerable number of girls from good early surroundings. Before that time, the clamor for luxury—the luxury that civilization makes as much a necessity as food—had been satisfied more or less by the incomes of the middle class; and any girl of that class, with physical charm and shrewdness enough to gain a living as outcast woman, was either supported at home or got a husband able to give her at least enough of what her tastes craved to keep her in the ranks of the reputable. Thus Susan's beauty of refinement, her speech and manner of the lady, made absurd any suggestion that she could ever have been a fallen woman. The crimson splash of her rouged lips did not suggest the *cocotte*, but the lady with a dash of gayety in her temperament. This, because of the sweet, sensitive seriousness of her small, pallid face with its earnest violet-gray eyes and its frame of abundant dark hair, simply and gracefully arranged. She was of the advance guard of a type which the swift downfall of the middle class, the increasing intelligence and restlessness and love of luxury among women, and the decay of formal religion with its exactions of chastity as woman's one diamond-fine jewel, are now making familiar in every city. The demand for the luxurious comfort which the educated regard as merely decent existence is far outstripping the demand for, and the education of, women in lucrative occupations other than prostitution.

Luckily Susan had not been arrested under her own name; there existed no court record which could be brought forward as proof by some nosing newspaper.

Susan herself marveled that there was not more trace of her underworld experience in her face and in her mind. She could not account for it. Yet the matter was simple enough to one viewing it from the outside. It is what we think, what we feel about ourselves, that makes up our expression of body and soul. And never in her lowest hour had her soul struck its flag and surrendered to the idea that she was a fallen creature. She had a temperament that estimated her acts not as right and wrong but as necessity. Men, all the rest of the world, might regard her as nothing but sex symbol; she regarded herself as an intelligence. And the filth slipped from her and could not soak in to change the texture of her being. She had no more the feeling or air of the *cocotte* than has the married woman who lives with her husband for a living. Her expression, her way of looking at her fellow beings and of meeting their looks, was that of the woman of the world who is for whatever reason above that slavery to opinion, that fear of being thought bold or forward which causes women of the usual run to be sensitive about staring or being stared at. Sometimes—in *cocottes*, in stage women, in fashionable women—this expression is self-conscious, or supercilious. It was not so with Susan, for she had little self-consciousness and no snobbishness at all. It merely gave the charm of worldly experience and expertness to a beauty which, without it, might have been too melancholy.

Susan, become by sheer compulsion philosopher about the vagaries of fat, did not fret over possible future dangers. She dismissed them and put all her intelligence and energy to the business in hand—to learning and to helping Palmer learn the ways of that world which includes all worlds.

Toward the end of the voyage she said to him:

"About my salary—or allowance—or whatever it is—— I've been thinking things over. I've made up my mind to save some money. My only chance is that salary. Have you any objection to my saving it—as much of it as I can?"

He laughed. "Tuck away anything and everything you can lay your hands on," said he. "I'm not one of those fools who try to hold women by being close and small with them. I'd not want you about if you were of the sort that could be held that way."

"No—I'll put by only from my salary," said she. "I admit I've no right to do that. But I've become sensible enough to realize that I mustn't ever risk being out again with no money. It has got on my mind so that I'd not be able to think of much else for worrying—unless I had at least a little."

"Do you want me to make you independent?"

"No," replied she. "Whatever you gave me I'd have to give back if we separated."

"*That* isn't the way to get on, my dear," said he.

"It's the best I can do—as yet," replied she. "And it's quite an advance on what I was. Yes, I *am* learning—slowly."

"Save all your salary, then," said Freddie. "When you buy anything charge it, and I'll attend to the bill."

Her expression told him that he had never made a shrewder move in his life. He knew he had made himself secure against losing her; for he knew what a force gratitude was in her character.

Her mind was now free—free for the educational business in hand. She appreciated that he had less to learn than she. Civilization, the science and art of living, of extracting all possible good from the few swift years of life, has been—since the downfall of woman from hardship, ten or fifteen thousand years ago—the creation of the man almost entirely. Until recently among the higher races such small development of the intelligence of woman as her seclusion and servitude permitted was sporadic and exotic. Nothing intelligent was expected of her—and it is only under the compulsion of peremptory demand that any human being ever is roused from the natural sluggishness. But civilization, created *by* man, was created *for* woman. Woman has to learn how to be the civilized being which man has ordained that she shall be—how to use for man's comfort and pleasure the ingenuities and the graces he has invented.

It is easy for a man to pick up the habits, tastes, manners and dress of male citizens of the world, if he has as keen eyes and as discriminating taste as had Palmer, clever descendant of the supple Italian. But to become a female citizen of the world is not so easy. For Susan to learn to be an example of the highest civilization, from her inmost thoughts to the outermost penumbra of her surroundings—that would be for her a labor of love, but still a labor. As her vanity was of the kind that centers on the advantages she actually had, instead of being the more familiar kind that centers upon non-existent charms of mind and person, her task was possible of accomplishment—for those who are sincerely willing to learn, who sincerely know wherein they lack, can learn, can be taught. As she had given these matters of civilization intelligent thought she knew where to begin—at the humble, material foundation, despised and neglected by those who talk most loudly about civilization, art, culture, and so on. They aspire to the clouds and the stars at once—and arrive nowhere except in talk and pretense and flaunting of ill-fitting borrowed plumage. They flap their gaudy artificial wings; there is motion, but no ascent. Susan wished to build—and build solidly. She began with the so-called trifles.

When they had been at Naples a week Palmer said:

"Don't you think we'd better push on to Paris?"

"I can't go before Saturday," replied she. "I've got several fittings yet."

"It's pretty dull here for me—with you spending so much time in the shops. I suppose the women's shops are good"—hesitatingly—"but I've heard those in Paris are better."

"The shops here are rotten. Italian women have no taste in dress. And the Paris shops are the best in the world."

"Then let's clear out," cried he. "I'm bored to death. But I didn't like to say anything, you seemed so busy."

"I am busy. And—can you stand it three days more?"

"But you'll only have to throw away the stuff you buy here. Why buy so much?"

"I'm not buying much. Two ready-to-wear Paris dresses—models they call them—and two hats."

Palmer looked alarmed. "Why, at that rate," protested he, "it'll take you all winter to get together your winter clothes, and no time left to wear 'em."

"You don't understand," said she. "If you want to be treated right in a shop—be shown the best things—have your orders attended to, you've got to come looking as if you knew what the best is. I'm getting ready to make a good first impression on the dressmakers and milliners in Paris."

"Oh, you'll have the money, and that'll make 'em step round."

"Don't you believe it," replied she. "All the money in the world won't get you *fashionable* clothes at the most fashionable place. It'll only get you *costly* clothes."

"Maybe that's so for women's things. It isn't for men's."

"I'm not sure of that. When we get to Paris, we'll see. But certainly it's true for women. If I went to the places in the rue de la Paix dressed as I am now, it'd take several years to convince them that I knew what I wanted and wouldn't be satisfied with anything but the latest and best. So I'm having these miserable dressmakers fit those dresses on me until they're absolutely perfect. It's wearing me out, but I'll be glad I did it."

Palmer had profound respect for her as a woman who knew what she was about. So he settled himself patiently and passed the time investigating the famous Neapolitan political machine with the aid of an interpreter guide whom he hired by the day. He was enthusiastic over the dresses and the hats when Susan at last had them at the hotel and showed herself to him in them. They certainly did work an amazing change in her. They were the first real Paris models she had ever worn.

"Maybe it's because I never thought much about women's clothes before," said Freddie, "but those things seem to be the best ever. How they do show up your complexion and your figure! And I hadn't any idea your hair was as grand as all that. I'm a little afraid of you. We've got to get acquainted all over again. These clothes of mine look pretty poor, don't they? Yet I paid all kinds of money for 'em at the best place in Fifth Avenue."

He examined her from all points of view, going round and round her, getting her to walk up and down to give him the full effect of her slender yet voluptuous figure in that beautifully fitted coat and skirt. He felt that his dreams were beginning to come true.

"We'll do the trick!" cried he. "Don't you think about money when you're buying clothes. It's a joy to give up for clothes for you. You make 'em look like something."

"Wait till I've shopped a few weeks in Paris," said Susan.

"Let's start tonight," cried he. "I'll telegraph to the Ritz for rooms."

When she began to dress in her old clothes for the journey, he protested. "Throw all these things away," he urged. "Wear one of the new dresses and hats."

"But they're not exactly suitable for traveling."

"People'll think you lost your baggage. I don't want ever to see you again looking any way except as you ought to look."

"No, I must take care of those clothes," said she firmly. "It'll be weeks before I can get anything in Paris, and I must keep up a good front."

He continued to argue with her until it occurred to him that as his own clothes were not what they should be, he and she would look much better matched if she dressed as she wished. He had not been so much in jest as he thought when he said to her that they would have to get acquainted all over again. Those new clothes of hers brought out startlingly—so clearly that even his vanity was made uneasy—the subtle yet profound difference of class between them. He had always felt this difference, and in the old days it had given him many a savage impulse to degrade her, to put her beneath him as a punishment for his feeling that she was above him. Now he had his ambition too close at heart to wish to rob her of her chief distinction; he was disturbed about it, though, and looked forward to Paris with uneasiness.

"You must help me get my things," said he.

"I'd be glad to," said she. "And you must be frank with me, and tell me where I fall short of the best of the women we see."

He laughed. The idea that he could help her seemed fantastic. He could not understand it—how this girl who had been brought up in a jay town away out West, who had never had what might be called a real chance to get in the know in New York, could so quickly pass him who had been born and bred in New York, had spent the last ten years in cultivating style and all the other luxurious tastes. He did not like to linger on this puzzle; the more he worked at it, the farther away from him Susan seemed to get. Yet the puzzle would not let him drop it.

They came in at the Gare de Lyon in the middle of a beautiful October afternoon. Usually, from late September or earlier until May or later, Paris has about the vilest climate that curses a civilized city. It is one of the bitterest ironies of fate that a people so passionately fond of the sun, of the outdoors, should be doomed for two-thirds of the year to live under leaden, icily leaking skies with rarely a ray of real sunshine. And nothing so well illustrates the exuberant vitality, the dauntless spirit of the French people, as the way they have built in preparation for the enjoyment of every bit of the light and warmth of any chance ray of sunshine. That year it so fell that the winter rains did not close in until late, and Paris reveled in a long autumn of almost New York perfection. Susan and Palmer drove to the Ritz through Paris, the lovely, the gay.

"This is the real thing—isn't it?" said he, thrilled into speech by that spectacle so inspiring to all who have the joy of life in their veins—the Place de l'Opéra late on a bright afternoon.

"It's the first thing I've ever seen that was equal to what I had dreamed about it," replied she.

They had chosen the Ritz as their campaign headquarters because they had learned that it was the most fashionable hotel in Paris—which meant in the world. There were hotels more grand, the interpreter-guide at Naples had said; there were hotels more exclusive. There were even hotels more comfortable. "But for fashion," said he, "it is the summit. There you see the most beautiful ladies, most beautifully dressed. There you see the elegant world at tea and at dinner."

At first glance they were somewhat disappointed in the quiet, unostentatious general rooms. The suite assigned them—at a hundred and twenty francs a day—was comfortable, was the most comfortable assemblage of rooms either had ever seen. But there was nothing imposing. This impression did not last long, however. They had been misled by their American passion for looks. They soon discovered that the guide at Naples had told the literal truth. They went down for tea in the garden, which was filled as the day was summer warm. Neither spoke as they sat under a striped awning umbrella, she with tea untasted before her, he with a glass of whiskey and soda he did not lift from the little table. Their eyes and their thoughts were too busy for speech; one cannot talk when one is thinking. About them were people of the world of which neither had before had any but a distant glimpse. They heard English, American, French, Italian. They saw men and women with that air which no one can define yet everyone knows on sight—the assurance without impertinence, the politeness without formality, the simplicity that is more complex than the most elaborate ornamentation of dress or speech or manner. Susan and Freddie lingered until the departure of the last couple—a plainly dressed man whose clothes on inspection revealed marvels of fineness and harmonious color; a quietly dressed woman whose costume from tip of plume to tip of suede slipper was a revelation of how fine a fine art the toilet can be made.

"Well—we're right in it, for sure," said Freddie, dropping to a sofa in their suite and lighting a cigarette.

"Yes," said Susan, with a sigh. "In it—but not of it."

"I almost lost my nerve as I sat there. And for the life of me I can't tell why."

"Those people know how," replied Susan. "Well—what they've learned we can learn."

"Sure," said he energetically. "It's going to take a lot of practice—a lot of time. But I'm game." His expression, its suggestion of helplessness and appeal, was a clear confession of a feeling that she was his superior.

"We're both of us ignorant," she hastened to say. "But when we get our bearings—in a day or two—we'll be all right."

"Let's have dinner up here in the sitting-room. I haven't got the nerve to face that gang again today"

"Nonsense!" laughed she. "We mustn't give way to our feelings—not for a minute. There'll be a lot of people as badly off as we are. I saw some this afternoon—and from the way the waiters treated them, I know they had money or something. Put on your evening suit, and you'll be all right. I'm the one that hasn't anything to wear. But I've got to go and study the styles. I must begin to learn what to wear and now to wear it. We've come to the right place, Freddie. Cheer up!"

He felt better when he was in evening clothes which made him handsome indeed, bringing out all his refinement of feature and coloring. He was almost cheerful when Susan came into the sitting-room in the pale gray of her two new toilettes. It might be, as she insisted, that she was not dressed properly for fashionable dining; but there would be no more delicate, no more lady-like loveliness. He quite recovered his nerve when they faced the company that had terrified him in prospect. He saw many commonplace looking people, not a few who were downright dowdy. And presently he had the satisfaction of realizing that not only Susan but he also was getting admiring attention. He no longer floundered panic-stricken; his feet touched bottom and he felt foolish about his sensations of a few minutes before.

After all, the world over, dining in a restaurant is nothing but dining in a restaurant. The waiter and the head waiter spoke English, were gracefully, tactfully, polite; and as he ordered he found his self-confidence returning with the surging rush of a turned tide on a low shore. The food was wonderful, and the champagne, "English taste," was the best he had ever drunk. Halfway through dinner both he and Susan were in the happiest frame of mind. The other people were drinking too, were emerging from caste into humanness. Women gazed languorously and longingly at the handsome young American; men sent stealthy or open smiles of adoration at Susan whenever Freddie's eyes were safely averted. But Susan was more careful than a woman of the world to which she aspired would have been; she ignored the glances and without difficulty assumed the air of wife.

"I don't believe we'll have any trouble getting acquainted with these people," said Freddie.

"We don't want to, yet," replied she.

"Oh, I feel we'll soon be ready for them," said he.

"Yes—that," said she. "But that amounts to nothing. This isn't to be merely a matter of clothes and acquaintances—at least, not with me."

"What then?" inquired he.

"Oh—we'll see as we get our bearings." She could not have put into words the plans she was forming—plans for educating and in every way developing him and herself. She was not sure at what she was aiming, but only of the direction. She had no idea how far she could go herself—or how far he would consent to go. The wise course was just to work along from day to day—keeping the direction.

"All right. I'll do as you say. You've got this game sized up better than I."

Is there any other people that works as hard as do the Parisians? Other peoples work with their bodies; but the Parisians, all classes and masses too, press both mind and body into service. Other peoples, if they think at all, think how to avoid work; the Parisians think incessantly, always, how to provide themselves with more to do. Other peoples drink to stupefy themselves lest peradventure in a leisure moment they might be seized of a thought; Parisians drink to stimulate themselves, to try to think more rapidly, to attract ideas that might not enter and engage a sober and therefore somewhat sluggish brain. Other peoples meet a new idea as if it were a mortal foe; the Parisians as if it were a long-lost friend. Other peoples are agitated chiefly, each man or woman, about themselves; the Parisians are full of their work, their surroundings, bother little about themselves except as means to what they regard as the end and aim of life—to make the world each moment as different as possible from what it was the moment before, to transform the crass and sordid universe of things with the magic of ideas. Being intelligent, they prefer good to evil; but they have God's own horror of that which is neither good nor evil, and spew it out of their mouths.

At the moment of the arrival of Susan and Palmer the world that labors at amusing itself was pausing in Paris on its way from the pleasures of sea and mountains to the pleasures of the Riviera and Egypt. And as the weather held fine, day after day the streets, the cafés, the restaurants, offered the young adventurers an incessant dazzling panorama of all they had come abroad to seek. A week passed before Susan permitted herself to enter any of the shops where she intended to buy dresses, hats and the other and lesser paraphernalia of the woman of fashion.

"I mustn't go until I've seen," said she. "I'd yield to the temptation to buy and would regret it."

And Freddie, seeing her point, restrained his impatience for making radical changes in himself and in her. The fourth day of their stay at Paris he realized that he would buy, and would wish to buy, none of the things that had tempted him the first and second days. Secure in the obscurity of the crowd of strangers, he was losing his extreme nervousness about himself. That sort of emotion is most characteristic of Americans and gets them the reputation for profound snobbishness. In fact, it is not snobbishness at all. In no country on earth is ignorance in such universal disrepute as in America. The American, eager to learn, eager to be abreast of the foremost, is terrified into embarrassment and awe when he finds himself in surroundings where are things that he feels he ought to know about—while a stupid fellow, in such circumstances, is calmly content with himself, wholly unaware of his own deficiencies.

Susan let full two weeks pass before she, with much hesitation, gave her first order toward the outfit on which Palmer insisted upon her spending not less than five thousand dollars. Palmer had been going to the shops with her. She warned him it would make prices higher if she appeared with a prosperous looking man; but he wanted occupation and everything concerning her fascinated him now. His ignorance of the details of feminine dress was giving place rapidly to a knowledge which he thought profound— and it was profound, for a man. She would not permit him to go with her to order, however, or to fittings. All she would tell him in advance about this first dress was that it was for evening wear and that its color was green. "But not a greeny green," said she.

"I understand. A green something like the tint in your skin at the nape of your neck."

"Perhaps," admitted she. "Yes."

"We'll go to the opera the evening it comes home. I'll have my new evening outfit from Charvet's by that time."

It was about ten days after this conversation that she told him she had had a final fitting, had ordered the dress sent home. He was instantly all excitement and rushed away to engage a good box for the opera. With her assistance he had got evening clothes that sent through his whole being a glow of self-confidence—for he knew that in those clothes, he looked what he was striving to be. They were to dine at seven. He dressed early and went into their sitting-room. He was afraid he would spoil his pleasure of complete surprise by catching a glimpse of the *grande toilette* before it was finished. At a quarter past seven Susan put her head into the sitting-room—only her head. At sight of his anxious face, his tense manner, she burst out laughing. It seemed, and was, grotesque that one so imperturbable of surface should be so upset.

"Can you stand the strain another quarter of an hour?" said she.

"Don't hurry," he urged. "Take all the time you want. Do the thing up right." He rose and came toward her with one hand behind him. "You said the dress was green, didn't you?"

"Yes."

"Well—here's something you may be able to fit in somewhere." And he brought the concealed hand into view and held a jewel box toward her.

She reached a bare arm through the crack in the door and took it. The box, the arm, the head disappeared. Presently there was a low cry of delight that thrilled him. The face reappeared. "Oh—Freddie!" she exclaimed, radiant. "You must have spent a fortune on them."

"No. Twelve thousand—that's all. It was a bargain. Go on dressing. We'll talk about it afterward." And he gently pushed her head back—getting a kiss in the palm of his hand—and drew the door to.

Ten minutes later the door opened part way again. "Brace yourself," she called laughingly. "I'm coming."

A breathless pause and the door swung wide. He stared with eyes amazed and bewitched. There is no more describing the effects of a harmonious combination of exquisite dress and exquisite woman than there is reproducing in words the magic and the thrill of sunrise or sunset, of moonlight's fanciful amorous play, or of starry sky. As the girl stood there, her eyes starlike with excitement, her lips crimson and sensuous against the clear old-ivory pallor of her small face in its frame of glorious dark hair, it seemed to him that her soul, more beautiful counterpart of herself, had come from its dwelling place within and was hovering about her body like an aureole. Round her lovely throat was the string of emeralds. Her shoulders were bare and also her bosom, over nearly half its soft, girlish swell. And draped in light and clinging grace about her slender, sensuous form was the most wonderful garment he had ever seen. The great French designers of dresses and hats and materials have a genius for taking an idea—a pure poetical abstraction—and materializing it, making it visible and tangible without destroying its spirituality. This dress of Susan's did not suggest matter any more than the bar of music suggests the rosined string that has given birth to it. She was carrying the train and a pair of long gloves in one hand. The skirt, thus drawn back, revealed her slim, narrow foot, a slender slipper of pale green satin, a charming instep with a rosiness shimmering through the gossamer web of pale green silk, the outline of a long, slender leg whose perfection was guaranteed by the beauty of her bare arm.

His expression changed slowly from bedazzlement to the nearest approach to the old slumbrous, smiling wickedness she had seen since they started. And her sensitive instinct understood; it was the menace of an insane jealousy, sprung from fear—fear of losing her. The look vanished, and once again he was Freddie Palmer the delighted, the generous and almost romantically considerate, because everything was going as he wished.

"No wonder I went crazy about you," he said.

"Then you're not disappointed?"

He came to her, unclasped the emeralds, stood off and viewed her again. "No—you mustn't wear them," said he.

"Oh!" she cried, protesting. "They're the best of all."

"Not tonight," said he. "They look cheap. They spoil the effect of your neck and shoulders. Another time, when you're not quite so wonderful, but not tonight."

As she could not see herself as he saw her, she pleaded for the jewels. She loved jewels and these were the first she had ever had, except two modest little birthday rings she had left in Sutherland. But he led her to the long mirror and convinced her that he was right. When they descended to the dining-room, they caused a stir. It does not take much to make fashionable people stare; but it does take something to make a whole room full of them quiet so far toward silence that the discreet and refined handling of dishes in a restaurant like the Ritz sounds like a vulgar clatter. Susan and Palmer congratulated themselves that they had been at the hotel long enough to become acclimated and so could act as if they were unconscious of the sensation they were creating. When they finished dinner, they found all the little tables in the long corridor between the restaurant and the entrance taken by people lingering over coffee to get another and closer view. And the men who looked at her sweet dreaming violet-gray eyes said she was innocent; those who looked at her crimson lips said she was gay; those who saw both eyes and lips said she was innocent—as yet. A few very dim-sighted, and very wise, retained their reason sufficiently to say that nothing could be told about a woman from her looks—especially an American woman. She put on the magnificent cloak, white silk, ermine lined, which he had seen at Paquin's and had insisted on buying. And they were off for the opera in the aristocratic looking auto he was taking by the week.

She had a second triumph at the opera—was the center that drew all glasses the instant the lights went up for the intermission. There were a few minutes when her head was quite turned, when it seemed to her that she had arrived very near to the highest goal of human ambition—said goal being the one achieved and so self-complacently occupied by these luxurious, fashionable people who were paying her the tribute of interest and admiration. Were not these people at the top of the heap? Was she not among them, of them, by right of excellence in the things that made them, distinguished them?

Ambition, drunk and heavy with luxury, flies sluggishly and low.
And her ambition was—for the moment—in danger of that fate.

During the last intermission the door of their box opened. At once Palmer sprang up and advanced with beaming face and extended hand to welcome the caller.

"Hello, Brent, I *am* glad to see you! I want to introduce you to Mrs. Palmer"—that name pronounced with the unconscious pride of the possessor of *the* jewel.

Brent bowed. Susan forced a smile.

"We," Palmer hastened on, "are on a sort of postponed honeymoon. I didn't announce the marriage—didn't want to have my friends out of pocket for presents. Besides, they'd have sent us stuff fit only to furnish out a saloon or a hotel—and we'd have had to use it or hurt their feelings. My wife's a Western girl—from Indiana. She came on to study for the stage. But"—he laughed delightedly—"I persuaded her to change her mind."

"You are from the West?" said Brent in the formal tone one uses in addressing a new acquaintance. "So am I. But that's more years ago than you could count. I live in New York—when I don't live here or in the Riviera."

The moment had passed when Susan could, without creating an impossible scene, admit and compel Brent to admit that they knew each other. What did it matter? Was it not best to ignore the past? Probably Brent had done this deliberately, assuming that she was beginning a new life with a clean slate.

"Been here long?" said Brent to Palmer.

As he and Palmer talked, she contrasted the two men. Palmer was much the younger, much the handsomer. Yet in the comparison Brent had the advantage. He looked as if he amounted to a great deal, as if he had lived and had understood life as the other man could not. The physical difference between them was somewhat the difference between look of lion and look of tiger. Brent looked strong; Palmer, dangerous. She could not imagine either man failing of a purpose he had set his heart upon. She could not imagine Brent reaching for it in any but an open, direct, daring way. She knew that the descendant of the supple Italians, the graduate of the street schools of stealth and fraud, would not care to have anything unless he got it by skill at subtlety. She noted their dress. Brent was wearing his clothes in that elegantly careless way which it was one of Freddie's dreams—one of the vain ones—to attain. Brent's voice was much more virile, was almost harsh, and in pronouncing some words made the nerves tingle with a sensation of mingled irritation and pleasure. Freddie's voice was manly enough, but soft and dangerous, suggestive of hidden danger. She compared the two men, as she knew them. She wondered how they would seem to a complete stranger. Palmer, she thought, would be able to attract almost any woman he might want; it seemed to her that a woman Brent wanted would feel rather helpless before the onset he would make.

It irritated her, this untimely intrusion of Brent who had the curious quality of making all other men seem less in the comparison. Not that he assumed anything, or forced comparisons; on the contrary, no man could have insisted less upon himself. Not that he compelled or caused the transfer of all interest to himself. Simply that, with him there, she felt less hopeful of Palmer, less confident of his ability to become what he seemed—and go beyond it. There are occasional men who have this same quality that Susan was just then feeling in Brent—men whom women never love yet who make it impossible for them to begin to love or to continue to love the other men within their range.

She was not glad to see him. She did not conceal it. Yet she knew that he would linger—and that she would not oppose. She would have liked to say to him: "You lost belief in me and dropped me. I have begun to make a life for myself. Let me alone. Do not upset me—do not force me to see what I must not see if I am to be happy. Go away, and give me a chance." But we do not say these frank, childlike things except in moments of closest intimacy— and certainly there was no suggestion of intimacy, no invitation to it, but the reverse, in the man facing her at the front of the box.

"Then you are to be in Paris some time?" said Brent, addressing her.

"I think so," said Susan.

"Sure," cried Palmer. "This is the town the world revolves round. I felt like singing 'Home, Sweet Home' as we drove from the station."

"I like it better than any place on earth," said Brent. "Better even than New York. I've never been quite able to forgive New York for some of the things it made me suffer before it gave me what I wanted."

"I, too," said Freddie. "My wife can't understand that. She doesn't know the side of life we know. I'm going to smoke a cigarette. I'll leave you here, old man, to entertain her."

When he disappeared, Susan looked out over the house with an expression of apparent abstraction. Brent—she was conscious—studied her with those seeing eyes—hazel eyes with not a bit of the sentimentality and weakness of brown in them. "You and Palmer know no one here?"

"Not a soul."

"I'll be glad to introduce some of my acquaintances to you—French people of the artistic set. They speak English. And you'll soon be learning French."

"I intend to learn as soon as I've finished my fall shopping."

"You are not coming back to America?"

"Not for a long time."

"Then you will find my friends useful."

She turned her eyes upon his. "You are very kind," said she.

"But I'd rather—we'd rather—not meet anyone just yet."

His eyes met hers calmly. It was impossible to tell whether he understood or not. After a few seconds he glanced out over the house. "That is a beautiful dress," said he. "You have real taste, if you'll permit me to say so. I was one of those who were struck dumb with admiration at the Ritz tonight."

"It's the first grand dress I ever possessed," said she.

"You love dresses—and jewels—and luxury?"

"As a starving man loves food."

"Then you are happy?"

"Perfectly so—for the first time in my life."

"It is a kind of ecstasy—isn't it? I remember how it was with me. I had always been poor—I worked my way through prep school and college. And I wanted *all* the luxuries. The more I had to endure—the worse food and clothing and lodgings—the madder I became about them, until I couldn't think of anything but getting the money to buy them. When I got it, I gorged myself. . . . It's a pity the starving man can't keep on loving food—keep on being always starving and always having his hunger satisfied."

"Ah, but he can."

He smiled mysteriously. "You think so, now. Wait till you are gorged."

She laughed. "You don't know! I could never get enough—never!"

His smile became even more mysterious. As he looked away, his profile presented itself to her view—an outline of sheer strength, of tragic sadness—the profile of those who have dreamed and dared and suffered. But the smile, saying no to her confident assertion, still lingered.

"Never!" she repeated. She must compel that smile to take away its disquieting negation, its relentless prophecy of the end of her happiness. She must convince him that he had come back in vain, that he could not disturb her.

"You don't suggest to me the woman who can be content with just people and just things. You will always insist on luxury. But you will demand more." He looked at her again. "And you will get it," he added, in a tone that sent a wave through her nerves.

Her glance fell. Palmer came in, bringing an odor of cologne and of fresh cigarette fumes. Brent rose. Palmer laid a detaining hand on his shoulder. "Do stay on, Brent, and go to supper with us."

"I was about to ask you to supper with me. Have you been to the Abbaye?"

"No. We haven't got round to that yet. Is it lively?"

"And the food's the best in Paris. You'll come?"

Brent was looking at Susan. Palmer, not yet educated in the smaller— and important—refinements of politeness, did not wait for her reply or think that she should be consulted. "Certainly," said he. "On condition that you dine with us tomorrow night."

"Very well," agreed Brent. And he excused himself to take leave of his friends. "Just tell your chauffeur to go to the Abbaye—he'll know," he said as he bowed over Susan's hand. "I'll be waiting. I wish to be there ahead and make sure of a table."

As the door of the box closed upon him Freddie burst out with that enthusiasm we feel for one who is in a position to render us good service and is showing a disposition to do so. "I've known him for years," said he, "and he's the real thing. He used to spend a lot of time in a saloon I used to keep in Allen Street."

"Allen Street?" ejaculated Susan, shivering.

"I was twenty-two then. He used to want to study types, as he called it. And I gathered in types for him—though really my place was for the swell crooks and their ladies. How long ago that seems—and how far away!"

"Another life," said Susan.

"That's a fact. This is my second time on earth. *Our* second time.
I tell you it's fighting for a foothold that makes men and women
the wretches they are. Nowadays, I couldn't hurt a fly— could you?
But then you never were cruel. That's why you stayed down so long."

Susan smiled into the darkness of the auditorium—the curtain was up, and they were talking in undertones. She said, as she smiled:

"I'll never go down and stay down for that reason again."

Her tone arrested his attention; but he could make nothing of it or of her expression, though her face was clear enough in the reflection from the footlights.

"Anyhow, Brent and I are old pals," continued he, "though we haven't seen so much of each other since he made a hit with the plays. He always used to predict I'd get to the top and be respectable. Now that it's come true, he'll help me. He'll introduce us, if we work it right."

"But we don't want that yet," protested Susan.

"You're ready and so am I," declared Palmer in the tone she knew had the full strength of his will back of it.

Faint angry hissing from the stalls silenced them, but as soon as they were in the auto Susan resumed. "I have told Mr. Brent we don't want to meet his friends yet."

"Now what the hell did you do that for?" demanded Freddie. It was the first time she had crossed him; it was the first time he had been reminiscent of the Freddie she used to know.

"Because," said she evenly, "I will not meet people under false pretenses."

"What rot!"

"I will not do it," replied she in the same quiet way.

He assumed that she meant only one of the false pretenses—the one that seemed the least to her. He said:

"Then we'll draw up and sign a marriage contract and date it a couple of years ago, before the new marriage law was passed to save rich men's drunken sons from common law wives."

"I am already married," said Susan. "To a farmer out in Indiana."

Freddie laughed. "Well, I'll be damned! You! You!" He looked at her ermine-lined cloak and laughed again. "An Indiana farmer!" Then he suddenly sobered. "Come to think of it," said he, "that's the first thing you ever told me about your past."

"Or anybody else," said Susan. Her body was quivering, for we remember the past events with the sensations they made upon us at the time. She could smell that little room in the farmhouse. Allen Street and all the rest of her life in the underworld had for her something of the vagueness of dreams—not only now but also while she was living that life. But not Ferguson, not the night when her innocent soul was ravished as a wolf rips up and munches a bleating lamb. No vagueness of dreams about that, but a reality to make her shudder and reel whenever she thought of it—a reality vivider now that she was a woman grown in experiences and understanding.

"He's probably dead—or divorced you long ago."

"I do not know."

"I can find out—without stirring things up. What was his name?"

"Ferguson."

"What was his first name?"

She tried to recall. "I think—it was Jim. Yes, it was Jim." She fancied she could hear the voice of that ferocious sister snapping out that name in the miserable little coop of a general room in that hot, foul, farm cottage.

"Where did he live?"

"His farm was at the edge of Zeke Warham's place—not far from
Beecamp, in Jefferson County."

She lapsed into silence, seemed to be watching the gay night streets of the Montmartre district—the cafés, the music halls, the sidewalk shows, the throngs of people every man and woman of them with his or her own individual variation upon the fascinating, covertly terrible face of the Paris mob. "What are you thinking about?" he asked, when a remark brought no answer.

"The past," said she. "And the future."

"Well—we'll find out in a few days that your farmer's got no claim on you—and we'll attend to that marriage contract and everything'll be all right."

"Do you want to marry me?" she asked, turning on him suddenly.

"We're as good as married already," replied he. "Your tone sounds as if *you* didn't want to marry *me*." And he laughed at the absurdity of such an idea.

"I don't know whether I do or not," said she slowly.

He laid a gentle strong hand on her knee. Gentle though it was, she felt its strength through the thickness of her cloak. "When the time comes," said he in the soft voice with the menace hidden in it, "you'll know whether you do or don't. You'll know you *do*—Queenie."

The auto was at the curb before the Abbaye. And on the steps, in furs and a top hat, stood the tall, experienced looking, cynical looking playwright. Susan's eyes met his, he lifted his hat, formal, polite.

"I'll bet he's got the best table in the place," said Palmer, before opening the door, "and I'll bet it cost him a bunch."

CHAPTER XXI

BRENT had an apartment in the rue de Rivoli, near the Hotel Meurice and high enough to command the whole Tuileries garden. From his balcony he could see to the east the ancient courts of the Louvre, to the south the varied, harmonious façades of the Quay d'Orsay with the domes and spires of the Left Bank behind, to the west the Obélisque, the long broad reaches of the Champs Elysées with the Arc de Triomphe at the boundary of the horizon. On that balcony, with the tides of traffic far below, one had a sense of being at the heart of the world, past, present, and to come. Brent liked to feel at home wherever he was; it enabled him to go tranquilly to work within a few minutes after his arrival, no matter how far he had journeyed or how long he had been away. So he regarded it as an economy, an essential to good work, to keep up the house in New York, a villa in Petite Afrique, with the Mediterranean washing its garden wall, this apartment at Paris; and a telegram a week in advance would reserve him the same quarters in the quietest part of hotels at Luzerne, at St. Moritz and at Biarritz.

Susan admired, as he explained his scheme of life to her and Palmer when they visited his apartment. Always profound tranquillity in the midst of intense activity. He could shut his door and he as in a desert; he could open it, and the most interesting of the sensations created by the actions and reactions of the whole human race were straightway beating upon his senses. As she listened, she looked about, her eyes taking in impressions to be studied at leisure. These quarters of his in Paris were fundamentally different from those in New York, were the expression of a different side of his personality. It was plain that he loved them, that they came nearer to expressing his real—that is, his inmost—self.

"Though I work harder in Paris than in New York," he explained, "I have more leisure because it is all one kind of work—writing—at which I'm never interrupted. So I have time to make surroundings for myself. No one has time for surroundings in New York."

She observed that of the scores of pictures on the walls, tables, shelves of the three rooms they were shown, every one was a face—faces of all nationalities, all ages, all conditions—faces happy and faces tragic, faces homely, faces beautiful, faces irradiating the fascination of those abnormal developments of character, good and bad, which give the composite countenance of the human race its distinction, as the characteristics themselves give it intensities of light and shade. She saw angels, beautiful and ugly, devils beautiful and ugly.

When she began to notice this peculiarity of those rooms, she was simply interested. What an amazing collection! How much time and thought it must have taken! How he must have searched—and what an instinct he had for finding the unusual, the significant! As she sat there and then strolled about and then sat again, her interest rose into a feverish excitement. It was as if the ghosts of all these personalities, not one of them commonplace, were moving through the rooms, were pressing upon her. She understood why Brent had them there—that they were as necessary to him as cadavers and skeletons and physiological charts to an anatomist. But they oppressed, suffocated her; she went out on the balcony and watched the effects of the light from the setting sun upon and around the enormously magnified Arc.

"You don't like my rooms," said Brent.

"They fascinate me," replied she. "But I'd have to get used to these friends of yours. You made their acquaintance one or a few at a time. It's very upsetting, being introduced to all at once."

She felt Brent's gaze upon her—that unfathomable look which made her uneasy, yet was somehow satisfying, too. He said, after a while, "Palmer is to give me his photograph. Will you give me yours?" He was smiling. "Both of you belong in my gallery."

"Of course she will," said Palmer, coming out on the balcony and standing beside her. "I want her to have some taken right away—in the evening dress she wore to the Opera last week. And she must have her portrait painted."

"When we are settled," said Susan. "I've no time for anything now but shopping."

They had come to inspect the apartment above Brent's, and had decided to take it; Susan saw possibilities of making it over into the sort of environment of which she had dreamed. In novels the descriptions of interiors, which weary most readers, interested her more than story or characters. In her days of abject poverty she used these word paintings to construct for herself a room, suites of rooms, a whole house, to replace, when her physical eyes closed and her eyes of fancy opened wide, the squalid and nauseous cell to which poverty condemned her. In the streets she would sometimes pause before a shop window display of interior furnishings; a beautiful table or chair, a design in wall or floor covering had caught her eyes, had set her to dreaming—dreaming on and on—she in dingy skirt and leaky shoes. Now—the chance to realize her dreams had come. Palmer had got acquainted with some high-class sports, American, French and English, at an American bar in the rue Volney. He was spending his afternoons and some of his evenings with them—in the evenings winning large sums from them at cards at which he was now as lucky as at everything else. Palmer, pleased by Brent's manner toward Susan—formal politeness, indifference to sex—was glad to have him go about with her. Also Palmer was one of those men who not merely imagine they read human nature but actually can read it. He *knew* he could trust Susan. And it had been his habit—as it is the habit of all successful men—to trust human beings, each one up to his capacity for resisting temptation to treachery.

"Brent doesn't care for women—as women," said he. "He never did. Don't you think he's queer?"

"He's different," replied Susan. "He doesn't care much for people—to have them as intimates. I understand why. Love and friendship bore one—or fail one—and are unsatisfactory—and disturbing. But if one centers one's life about things—books, pictures, art, a career—why, one is never bored or betrayed. He has solved the secret of happiness, I think."

"Do you think a woman could fall in love with him?" he asked, with an air of the accidental and casual.

"If you mean, could I fall in love with him," said she, "I should say no. I think it would either amuse or annoy him to find that a woman cared about him."

"Amuse him most of all," said Palmer. "He knows the ladies—that they love us men for what we can give them."

"Did you ever hear of anyone, man or woman, who cared about a person who couldn't give them anything?"

Freddie's laugh was admission that he thought her right. "The way to get on in politics," observed he, "is to show men that it's to their best interest to support you. And that's the way to get on in everything else—including love."

Susan knew that this was the truth about life, as it appeared to her also. But she could not divest herself of the human aversion to hearing the cold, practical truth. She wanted sugar coating on the pill, even though she knew the sugar made the medicine much less effective, often neutralized it altogether. Thus Palmer's brutally frank cynicism got upon her nerves, whereas Brent's equally frank cynicism attracted her because it was not brutal. Both men saw that life was a coarse practical joke. Palmer put the stress on the coarseness, Brent upon the humor.

Brent recommended and introduced to her a friend of his, a young French Jew named Gourdain, an architect on the way up to celebrity. "You will like his ideas and he will like yours," said Brent.

She had acquiesced in his insistent friendship for Palmer and her, but she had not lowered by an inch the barrier of her reserve toward him. His speech and actions at all times, whether Palmer was there or not; suggested that he respected the barrier, regarded it as even higher and thicker than it was. Nevertheless she felt that he really regarded the barrier as non-existent. She said:

"But I've never told you my ideas."

"I can guess what they are. Your surroundings will simply be an extension of your dress."

She would not have let him see—she would not have admitted to herself—how profoundly the subtle compliment pleased her.

Because a man's or a woman's intimate personal taste is good it by no means follows that he or she will build or decorate or furnish a house well. In matters of taste, the greater does not necessarily include the less, nor does the less imply the greater. Perhaps Susan would have shown she did not deserve Brent's compliment, would have failed ignominiously in that first essay of hers, had she not found a Gourdain, sympathetic, able to put into the concrete the rather vague ideas she had evolved in her dreaming. An architect is like a milliner or a dressmaker. He supplies the model, product of his own individual taste. The person who employs him must remold that form into an expression of his own personality—for people who deliberately live in surroundings that are not part of themselves are on the same low level with those who utter only borrowed ideas. That is the object and the aim of civilization—to encourage and to compel each individual to be frankly himself—herself. That is the profound meaning of freedom. The world owes more to bad morals and to bad taste that are spontaneous than to all the docile conformity to the standards of morals and of taste, however good. Truth—which simply means an increase of harmony, a decrease of discord, between the internal man and his environment—truth is a product, usually a byproduct, of a ferment of action.

Gourdain—chiefly, no doubt, because Susan's beauty of face and figure and dress fascinated him—was more eager to bring out her individuality than to show off his own talents. He took endless pains with her, taught her the technical knowledge and vocabulary that would enable her to express herself, then carried out her ideas religiously. "You are right, *mon ami,*" said he to Brent. "She is an orchid, and of a rare species. She has a glorious imagination, like a bird of paradise balancing itself into an azure sky, with every plume raining color and brilliancy."

"Somewhat exaggerated," was Susan's pleased, laughing comment when Brent told her.

"Somewhat," said Brent. "But my friend Gourdain is stark mad about women's dressing well. That lilac dress you had on yesterday did for him. He *was* your servant; he *is* your slave."

Abruptly—for no apparent cause, as was often the case—Susan had that sickening sense of the unreality of her luxurious present, of being about to awaken in Vine Street with Etta—or in the filthy bed with old Mrs. Tucker. Absently she glanced down at her foot, holding it out as if for inspection. She saw Brent's look of amusement at her seeming vanity.

"I was looking to see if my shoes were leaky," she explained.

A subtle change came over his face. He understood instantly.

"Have you ever been—cold?" she asked, looking at him strangely.

"One cold February—cold and damp—I had no underclothes—and no overcoat."

"And dirty beds—filthy rooms—filthy people?"

"A ten-cent lodging house with a tramp for bedfellow."

They were looking at each other, with the perfect understanding and sympathy that can come only to two people of the same fiber who have braved the same storms. Each glanced hastily away.

Her enthusiasm for doing the apartment was due full as much to the fact that it gave her definitely directed occupation as to its congeniality. That early training of hers from Aunt Fanny Warham had made it forever impossible for her in any circumstances to become the typical luxuriously sheltered woman, whether legally or illegally kept—the lie-abed woman, the woman who dresses only to go out and show off, the woman who wastes her life in petty, piffling trifles—without purpose, without order or system, without morals or personal self-respect. She had never lost the systematic instinct—the instinct to use time instead of wasting it—that Fanny Warham had implanted in her during the years that determine character. Not for a moment, even without distinctly definite aim, was she in danger of the creeping paralysis that is epidemic among the rich, enfeebling and slowing down mental and physical activity. She had a regular life; she read, she walked in the Bois; she made the best of each day. And when this definite thing to accomplish offered, she did not have to learn how to work before she could begin the work itself.

All this was nothing new to Gourdain. He was born and bred in a country where intelligent discipline is the rule and the lack of it the rare exception—among all classes—even among the women of the well-to-do classes.

The finished apartment was a disappointment to Palmer. Its effects were too quiet, too restrained. Within certain small limits, those of the man of unusual intelligence but no marked originality, he had excellent taste— or, perhaps, excellent ability to recognize good taste. But in the large he yearned for the grandiose. He loved the gaudy with which the rich surround themselves because good taste forbids them to talk of their wealth and such surroundings do the talking for them and do it more effectively. He would have preferred even a vulgar glitter to the unobtrusiveness of those rooms. But he knew that Susan was right, and he was a very human arrant coward about admitting that he had bad taste.

"This is beautiful—exquisite," said he, with feigned enthusiasm. "I'm afraid, though, it'll be above their heads."

"What do you mean?" inquired Susan.

Palmer felt her restrained irritation, hastened to explain. "I mean the people who'll come here. They can't appreciate it. You have to look twice to appreciate this—and people, the best of 'em, look only once and a mighty blind look it is."

But Susan was not deceived. "You must tell me what changes you want," said she. Her momentary irritation had vanished. Since Freddie was paying, Freddie must have what suited him.

"Oh, I've got nothing to suggest. Now that I've been studying it out, I couldn't allow you to make any changes. It does grow on one, doesn't it, Brent?"

"It will be the talk of Paris," replied Brent.

The playwright's tone settled the matter for Palmer. He was content. Said he:

"Thank God she hasn't put in any of those dirty old tapestry rags—and the banged up, broken furniture and the patched crockery."

At the same time she had produced an effect of long tenancy. There was nothing that glittered, nothing with the offensive sheen of the brand new. There was in that delicately toned atmosphere one suggestion which gave the same impression as the artificial crimson of her lips in contrast with the pallor of her skin and the sweet thoughtful melancholy of her eyes. This suggestion came from an all-pervading odor of a heavy, languorously sweet, sensuous perfume—the same that Susan herself used. She had it made at a perfumer's in the faubourg St. Honoré by mixing in a certain proportion several of the heaviest and most clinging of the familiar perfumes. "You don't like my perfume?" she said to Brent one day.

He was in the library, was inspecting her *selections* of books. Instead of answering her question, he said:

"How did you find out so much about books? How did you find time to read so many?"

"One always finds time for what one likes."

"Not always," said he. "I had a hard stretch once—just after I struck New York. I was a waiter for two months. Working people don't find time for reading—and such things."

"That was one reason why I gave up work," said she.

"That—and the dirt—and the poor wages—and the hopelessness—and a few other reasons," said he.

"Why don't you like the perfume I use?"

"Why do you say that?"

"You made a queer face as you came into the drawing-room."

"Do *you* like it?"

"What a queer question!" she said. "No other man would have asked it."

"The obvious," said he, shrugging his shoulders.

"I couldn't help knowing you didn't like it."

"Then why should I use it?"

His glance drifted slowly away from hers. He lit a cigarette with much attention to detail.

"Why should I use perfume I don't like?" persisted she.

"What's the use of going into that?" said he.

"But I do like it—in a way," she went on after a pause. "It is—it seems to me the odor of myself."

"Yes—it is," he admitted.

She laughed. "Yet you made a wry face."

"I did."

"At the odor?"

"At the odor."

"Do you think I ought to change to another perfume?"

"You know I do not. It's the odor of your soul. It is different at different times—sometimes inspiringly sweet as the incense of heaven, as my metaphoric friend Gourdain would say—sometimes as deadly sweet as the odors of the drugs men take to drag them to hell—sometimes repulsively sweet, making one heart sick for pure, clean smell-less air yet without the courage to seek it. Your perfume is many things, but always—always strong and tenacious and individual."

A flush had overspread the pallor of her skin; her long dark lashes hid her eyes.

"You have never been in love," he went on.

"So you told me once before." It was the first time either had referred to their New York acquaintance.

"You did not believe me then. But you do now?"

"For me there is no such thing as love," replied she. "I understand affection—I have felt it. I understand passion. It is a strong force in my life—perhaps the strongest."

"No," said he, quiet but positive.

"Perhaps not," replied she carelessly, and went on, with her more than manlike candor, and in her manner of saying the most startling things in the calmest way:

"I understand what is called love—feebleness looking up to strength or strength pitying feebleness. I understand because I've felt both those things. But love—two equal people united perfectly, merged into a third person who is neither yet is both—that I have not felt. I've dreamed it. I've imagined it—in some moments of passion. But"—she laughed and shrugged her shoulders and waved the hand with the cigarette between its fingers—"I have not felt it and I shall not feel it. I remain I." She paused, considered, added, "And I prefer that."

"You are strong," said he, absent and reflective. "Yes, you are strong."

"I don't know," replied she. "Sometimes I think so. Again——" She shook her head doubtfully.

"You would be dead if you were not. As strong in soul as in body."

"Probably," admitted she. "Anyhow, I am sure I shall always be—alone. I shall visit—I shall linger on my threshold and talk. Perhaps I shall wander in perfumed gardens and dream of comradeship. But I shall return *chez moi.*"

He rose—sighed—laughed—at her and at himself. "Don't delay too long," said he.

"Delay?"

"Your career."

"My career? Why, I am in the full swing of it. I'm at work in the only profession I'm fit for."

"The profession of woman?"

"Yes—the profession of female."

He winced—and at this sign, if she did not ask herself what pleased her, she did not ask herself why. He said sharply, "I don't like that."

"But *you* have only to *hear* it. Think of poor me who have to *live* it."

"Have to? No," said he.

"Surely you're not suggesting that I drop back into the laboring classes! No, thank you. If you knew, you'd not say anything so stupid."

"I do know, and I was not suggesting that. Under this capitalistic system the whole working class is degraded. They call what they do 'work,' but that word ought to be reserved for what a man does when he exercises mind and body usefully. What the working class is condemned to by capitalism is not work but toil."

"The toil of a slave," said Susan.

"It's shallow twaddle or sheer want to talk about the dignity and beauty of labor under this system," he went on. "It is ugly and degrading. The fools or hypocrites who talk that way ought to be forced to join the gangs of slaves at their tasks in factory and mine and shop, in the fields and the streets. And even the easier and better paid tasks, even what the capitalists themselves do—those things aren't dignified and beautiful. Capitalism divides all men except those of one class—the class to which I luckily belong—divides all other men into three unlovely classes—slave owners, slave drivers and slaves. But you're not interested in those questions."

"In wage slavery? No. I wish to forget about it. Any alternative to being a wage slave or a slave driver—or a slave owner. Any alternative."

"You don't appreciate your own good fortune," said he. "Most human beings—all but a very few—have to be in the slave classes, in one way or another. They have to submit to the repulsive drudgery, with no advancement except to slave driver. As for women—if they have to work, what can they do but sell themselves into slavery to the machines, to the capitalists? But you—you needn't do that. Nature endowed you with talent—unusual talent, I believe. How lucky you are! How superior to the great mass of your fellow beings who must slave or starve, because they have no talent!"

"Talent?—I?" said Susan. "For what, pray?"

"For the stage."

She looked amused. "You evidently don't think me vain—or you'd not venture that jest."

"For the stage," he repeated.

"Thanks," said she drily, "but I'll not appeal from your verdict."

"My verdict? What do you mean?"

"I prefer to talk of something else," said she coldly, offended by his unaccountable disregard of her feelings.

"This is bewildering," said he. And his manner certainly fitted the words.

"That I should have understood? Perhaps I shouldn't—at least, not so quickly—if I hadn't heard how often you have been disappointed, and how hard it has been for you to get rid of some of those you tried and found wanting."

"Believe me—I was not disappointed in you." He spoke earnestly, apparently with sincerity. "The contrary. Your throwing it all up was one of the shocks of my life."

She laughed mockingly—to hide her sensitiveness.

"One of the shocks of my life," he repeated.

She was looking at him curiously—wondering why he was thus uncandid.

"It puzzled me," he went on. "I've been lingering on here, trying to solve the puzzle. And the more I've seen of you the less I understand. Why did you do it? How could *you* do it?"

He was walking up and down the room in a characteristic pose—hands clasped behind his back as if to keep them quiet, body erect, head powerfully thrust forward. He halted abruptly and wheeled to face her. "Do you mean to tell me you didn't get tired of work and drop it for—" he waved his arm to indicate her luxurious surroundings—"for this?"

No sign of her agitation showed at the surface. But she felt she was not concealing herself from him.

He resumed his march, presently to halt and wheel again upon her. But before he could speak, she stopped him.

"I don't wish to hear any more," said she, the strange look in her eyes. It was all she could do to hide the wild burst of emotion that had followed her discovery. Then she had not been without a chance for a real career! She might have been free, might have belonged to herself— —

"It is not too late," cried he. "That's why I'm here."

"It is too late," she said.

"It is not too late," repeated he, harshly, in his way that swept aside opposition. "I shall get you back." Triumphantly, "The puzzle is solved!"

She faced him with a look of defiant negation. "That ocean I crossed— it's as narrow as the East River into which I thought of throwing myself many a time—it's as narrow as the East River beside the ocean between what I am and what I was. And I'll never go back. Never!"

She repeated the "never" quietly, under her breath. His eyes looked as if they, without missing an essential detail, had swept the whole of that to which she would never go back. He said:

"Go back? No, indeed. Who's asking you to go back? Not I. I'm not *asking* you to go anywhere. I'm simply saying that you will—*must*—go forward. If you were in love, perhaps not. But you aren't in love. I know from experience how men and women care for each other—how they form these relationships. They find each other convenient and comfortable. But they care only for themselves. Especially young people. One must live quite a while to discover that thinking about oneself is living in a stuffy little cage with only a little light, through slats in the top that give no view. . . . It's an unnatural life for you. It can't last. You—centering upon yourself—upon comfort and convenience. Absurd!"

"I have chosen," said she.

"No—you can't do it," he went on, as if she had not spoken. "*You* can't spend your life at dresses and millinery, at chattering about art, at thinking about eating and drinking—at being passively amused—at attending to your hair and skin and figure. You may think so, but in reality you are getting ready for *me* . . . for your career. You are simply educating yourself. I shall have you back."

She held the cigarette to her lips, inhaled the smoke deeply, exhaled it slowly.

"I will tell you why," he went on, as if he were answering a protest. "Every one of us has an individuality of some sort. And in spite of everything and anything, except death or hopeless disease, that individuality will insist upon expressing itself."

"Mine is expressing itself," said she with a light smile—the smile of a light woman.

"You can't rest in this present life of yours. Your individuality is too strong. It will have its way—and for all your mocking smiling, you know I am right. I understand how you were tempted into it——"

She opened her lips—changed her mind and stopped her lips with her cigarette.

"I don't blame you—and it was just as well. This life has taught you—will teach you—will advance you in your career. . . . Tell me, what gave you the idea that I was disappointed?"

She tossed her cigarette into the big ash tray. "As I told you, it is too late." She rose and looked at him with a strange, sweet smile. "I've got any quantity of faults," said she. "But there's one I haven't got. I don't whine."

"You don't whine," assented he, "and you don't lie—and you don't shirk. Men and women have been canonized for less. I understand that for some reason you can't talk about——"

"Then why do you continue to press me?" said she, a little coldly.

He accepted the rebuke with a bow. "Nevertheless," said he, with raillery to carry off his persistence, "I shall get you. If not sooner, then when the specter of an obscure—perhaps poor—old age begins to agitate the rich hangings of youth's banquet hall."

"That'll be a good many years yet," mocked she. And from her lovely young face flashed the radiant defiance of her perfect youth and health.

"Years that pass quickly," retorted he, unmoved.

She was still radiant, still smiling, but once more she was seeing the hideous old women of the tenements. Into her nostrils stole the stench of the foul den in which she had slept with Mrs. Tucker and Mrs. Reardon—and she was hearing the hunchback of the dive playing for the drunken dancing old cronies, with their tin cups of whiskey.

No danger of that now? How little she was saving of her salary from Palmer! She could not "work" men—she simply could not. She would never put by enough to be independent and every day her tastes for luxury had firmer hold upon her. No danger? As much danger as ever—a danger postponed but certain to threaten some day—and then, a fall from a greater height—a certain fall. She was hearing the battered, shattered piano of the dive.

"For pity's sake Mrs. Palmer!" cried Brent, in a low voice.

She started. The beautiful room, the environment of luxury and taste and comfort came back.

Gourdain interrupted and then Palmer.

The four went to the Cafe Anglais for dinner. Brent announced that he was going to the Riviera soon to join a party of friends. "I wish you would visit me later," said he, with a glance that included them all and rested, as courtesy required, upon Susan. "There's room in my villa—barely room."

"We've not really settled here," said Susan. "And we've taken up French seriously."

"The weather's frightful," said Palmer, with a meaning glance at her. "I think we ought to go."

But her expression showed that she had no intention of going, no sympathy with Palmer's desire to use this excellent, easy ladder of Brent's offering to make the ascent into secure respectability.

"Next winter, then," said Brent, who was observing her.

"Or—in the early spring, perhaps."

"Oh, we may change our minds and come," Palmer suggested eagerly. "I'm going to try to persuade my wife."

"Come if you can," said Brent cordially. "I'll have no one stopping with me."

When they were alone, Palmer sent his valet away and fussed about impatiently until Susan's maid had unhooked her dress and had got her ready for bed. As the maid began the long process of giving her hair a thorough brushing, he said, "Please let her go, Susan. I want to tell you something."

"She does not know a word of English."

"But these French are so clever that they understand perfectly with their eyes."

Susan sent the maid to bed and sat in a dressing gown brushing her hair. It was long enough to reach to the middle of her back and to cover her bosom. It was very thick and wavy. Now that the scarlet was washed from her lips for the night, her eyes shone soft and clear with no relief for their almost tragic melancholy. He was looking at her in profile. Her expression was stern as well as sad—the soul of a woman who has suffered and has been made strong, if not hard.

"I got a letter from my lawyers today," he began. "It was about that marriage. I'll read."

At the word "marriage," she halted the regular stroke of the brush. Her eyes gazed into the mirror of the dressing table through her reflection deep into her life, deep into the vistas of memory. As he unfolded the letter, she leaned back in the low chair, let her hands drop to her lap.

"'As the inclosed documents show,'" he read, "'we have learned and have legally verified that Jeb—not James—Ferguson divorced his wife Susan Lenox about a year after their marriage, on the ground of desertion; and two years later he fell through the floor of an old bridge near Brooksburg and was killed.'"

The old bridge—she was feeling its loose flooring sag and shift under the cautious hoofs of the horse. She was seeing Rod Spenser on the horse, behind him a girl, hardly more than a child—under the starry sky exchanging confidences—talking of their futures.

"So, you see, you are free," said Palmer. "I went round to an American lawyer's office this afternoon, and borrowed an old legal form book. And I've copied out this form——"

She was hardly conscious of his laying papers on the table before her.

"It's valid, as I've fixed things. The lawyer gave me some paper. It has a watermark five years old. I've dated back two years—quite enough. So when we've signed, the marriage never could be contested—not even by ourselves."

He took the papers from the table, laid them in her lap. She started. "What were you saying?" she asked. "What's this?"

"What were you thinking about?" said he.

"I wasn't thinking," she answered, with her slow sweet smile of self-concealment. "I was feeling—living—the past. I was watching the procession."

He nodded understandingly. "That's a kind of time-wasting that can easily be overdone."

"Easily," she agreed. "Still, there's the lesson. I have to remind myself of it often—always, when there's anything that has to be decided."

"I've written out two of the forms," said he. "We sign both.

You keep one, I the other. Why not sign now?"

She read the form—the agreement to take each other as lawful husband and wife and to regard the contract as in all respects binding and legal.

"Do you understand it?" laughed he nervously, for her manner was disquieting.

"Perfectly."

"You stared at the paper as if it were a puzzle."

"It is," said she.

"Come into the library and we'll sign and have it over with."

She laid the papers on the dressing table, took up her brush, drew it slowly over her hair several times.

"Wake up," cried he, good humoredly. "Come on into the library." And he went to the threshold.

She continued brushing her hair. "I can't sign," said she. There was the complete absence of emotion that caused her to be misunderstood always by those who did not know her peculiarities. No one could have suspected the vision of the old women of the dive before her eyes, the sound of the hunchback's piano in her ears, the smell of foul liquors and foul bodies and foul breaths in her nostrils. Yet she repeated:

"No—I can't sign."

He returned to his chair, seated himself, a slight cloud on his brow, a wicked smile on his lips. "Now what the devil!" said he gently, a jeer in his quiet voice. "What's all this about?"

"I can't marry you," said she. "I wish to live on as we are."

"But if we do that we can't get up where we want to go."

"I don't wish to know anyone but interesting men of the sort that does things—and women of my own sort. Those people have no interest in conventionalities."

"That's not the crowd we set out to conquer," said he. "You seem to have forgotten."

"It's you who have forgotten," replied she.

"Yes—yes—I know," he hastened to say. "I wasn't accusing you of breaking your agreement. You've lived up to it—and more. But, Susan, the people you care about don't especially interest me. Brent—yes. He's a man of the world as well as one of the artistic chaps. But the others—they're beyond me. I admit it's all fine, and I'm glad you go in for it. But the only crowd that's congenial to me is the crowd that we've got to be married to get in with."

She saw his point—saw it more clearly than did he. To him the world of fashion and luxurious amusement seemed the only world worth while. He accepted the scheme of things as he found it, had the conventional ambitions—to make in succession the familiar goals of the conventional human success—power, wealth, social position. It was impossible for him to get any other idea of a successful life, of ambitions worthy a man's labor. It was evidence of the excellence of his mind that he was able to tolerate the idea of the possibility of there being another mode of success worth while.

"I'm helping you in your ambitions—in doing what you think is worth while," said he. "Don't you think you owe it to me to help me in mine?"

He saw the slight change of expression that told him how deeply he had touched her.

"If I don't go in for the high society game," he went on, "I'll have nothing to do. I'll be adrift—gambling, drinking, yawning about and going to pieces. A man's got to have something to work for—and he can't work unless it seems to him worth doing."

She was staring into the mirror, her elbows on the table, her chin upon her interlaced fingers. It would be difficult to say how much of his gentleness to her was due to her physical charm for him, and how much to his respect for her mind and her character. He himself would have said that his weakness was altogether the result of the spell her physical charm cast over him. But it is probable that the other element was the stronger.

"You'll not be selfish, Susan?" urged he. "You'll give me a square deal."

"Yes—I see that it does look selfish," said she. "A little while ago I'd not have been able to see any deeper than the looks of it. Freddie, there are some things no one has a right to ask of another, and no one has a right to grant."

The ugliness of his character was becoming less easy to control. This girl whom he had picked up, practically out of the gutter, and had heaped generosities upon, was trying his patience too far. But he said, rather amiably:

"Certainly I'm not asking any such thing of you in asking you to become a respectable married woman, the wife of a rich man."

"Yes—you are, Freddie," replied she gently. "If I married you, I'd be signing an agreement to lead your life, to give up my own—an agreement to become a sort of woman I've no desire to be and no interest in being; to give up trying to become the only sort of woman I think is worth while. When we were discussing my coming with you, you made this same proposal in another form. I refused it then. And I refuse it now. It's harder to refuse now, but I'm stronger."

"Stronger, thanks to the money you've got from me—the money and the rest of it," sneered he.

"Haven't I earned all I've got?" said she, so calmly that he did not realize how the charge of ingratitude, unjust though it was, had struck into her.

"You have changed!" said he. "You're getting as hard as the rest of us. So it's all a matter of money, of give and take—is it? None of the generosity and sentiment you used to be full of? You've simply been using me."

"It can be put that way," replied she. "And no doubt you honestly see it that way. But I've got to see my own interest and my own right, Freddie. I've learned at last that I mustn't trust to anyone else to look after them for me."

"Are you riding for a fall—Queenie?"

At "Queenie" she smiled faintly. "I'm riding the way I always have," answered she. "It has carried me down. But—it has brought me up again." She looked at him with eyes that appealed, without yielding. "And I'll ride that way to the end—up or down," said she. "I can't help it."

"Then you want to break with me?" he asked—and he began to look dangerous.

"No," replied she. "I want to go on as we are. . . . I'll not be interfering in your social ambitions, in any way. Over here it'll help you to have a mistress who—" she saw her image in the glass, threw him an arch glance—"who isn't altogether unattractive won't it? And if you found you could go higher by marrying some woman of the grand world—why, you'd be free to do it."

He had a way of looking at her that gave her—and himself—the sense of a delirious embrace. He looked at her so, now. He said:

"You take advantage of my being crazy about you—*damn* you!"

"Heaven knows," laughed she, "I need every advantage I can find."

He touched her—the lightest kind of touch. It carried the sense of embrace in his look still more giddily upward. "Queenie!" he said softly.

She smiled at him through half closed eyes that with a gentle and shy frankness confessed the secret of his attraction for her. There was, however, more of strength than of passion in her face as a whole. Said she:

"We're getting on well—as we are aren't we? I can meet the most amusing and interesting people—my sort of people. You can go with the people and to the places you like and you'll not be bound. If you should take a notion to marry some woman with a big position—you'd not have to regret being tied to—Queenie."

"But—I want you—I want you," said he. "I've got to have you."

"As long as you like," said she. "But on terms I can accept—always on terms I can accept. Never on any others—never! I can't help it. I can yield everything but that."

Where she was concerned he was the primitive man only. The higher his passion rose, the stronger became his desire for absolute possession. When she spoke of terms—of the limitations upon his possession of her— she transformed his passion into fury. He eyed her wickedly, abruptly demanded:

"When did you decide to make this kick-up?"

"I don't know. Simply—when you asked me to sign, I found I couldn't."

"You don't expect *me* to believe that."

"It's the truth." She resumed brushing her hair.

"Look at me!"

She turned her face toward him, met his gaze.

"Have you fallen in love with that young Jew?"

"Gourdain? No."

"Have you a crazy notion that your looks'll get you a better husband? A big fortune or a title?"

"I haven't thought about a husband. Haven't I told you I wish to be free?"

"But that doesn't mean anything."

"It might," said she absently.

"How?"

"I don't know. If one is always free—one is ready for—whatever comes. Anyhow, I must be free—no matter what it costs."

"I see you're bent on dropping back into the dirt I picked you out of."

"Even that," she said. "I must be free."

"Haven't you any desire to be respectable—decent?"

"I guess not," confessed she. "What is there in that direction for me?"

"A woman doesn't stay young and good-looking long."

"No." She smiled faintly. "But does she get old and ugly any slower for being married?"

He rose and stood over her, looked smiling danger down at her. She leaned back in her chair to meet his eyes without constraint. "You're trying to play me a trick," said he. "But you're not going to get away with the goods. I'm astonished that you are so rotten ungrateful."

"Because I'm not for sale?"

"Queenie balking at selling herself," he jeered. "And what's the least you ever did sell for?"

"A half-dollar, I think. No—two drinks of whiskey one cold night. But what I sold was no more myself than—than the coat I'd pawned and drunk up before I did it."

The plain calm way in which she said this made it so terrible that he winced and turned away. "We have seen hell—haven't we?" he muttered. He turned toward her with genuine passion of feeling. "Susan," he cried, "don't be a fool. Let's push our luck, now that things are coming our way. We need each other—we want to stay together—don't we?"

"*I* want to stay. I'm happy."

"Then—let's put the record straight."

"Let's keep it straight," replied she earnestly. "Don't ask me to go where I don't belong. For I can't, Freddie—honestly, I can't."

A pause. Then, "You will!" said he, not in blustering fury, but in that cool and smiling malevolence which had made him the terror of his associates from his boyhood days among the petty thieves and pickpockets of Grand Street. He laid his hand gently on her shoulder. "You hear me. I say you will."

She looked straight at him. "Not if you kill me," she said. She rose to face him at his own height. "I've bought my freedom with my body and with my heart and with my soul. It's all I've got. I shall keep it."

He measured her strength with an expert eye. He knew that he was beaten. He laughed lightly and went into his dressing-room.

CHAPTER XXII

THEY met the next morning with no sign in the manner of either that there had been a drawn battle, that there was an armed truce. She knew that he, like herself, was thinking of nothing else. But until he had devised some way of certainly conquering her he would wait, and watch, and pretend that he was satisfied with matters as they were. The longer she reflected the less uneasy she became—as to immediate danger. In Paris the methods of violence he might have been tempted to try in New York were out of the question. What remained? He must realize that threats to expose her would be futile; also, he must feel vulnerable, himself, to that kind of attack—a feeling that would act as a restraint, even though he might appreciate that she was the sort of person who could not in any circumstances resort to it. He had not upon her a single one of the holds a husband has upon a wife. True, he could break with her. But she must appreciate how easy it would now be for her in this capital of the idle rich to find some other man glad to "protect" a woman so expert at gratifying man's vanity of being known as the proprietor of a beautiful and fashionable woman. She had discovered how, in the aristocracy of European wealth, an admired mistress was as much a necessary part of the grandeur of great nobles, great financiers, great manufacturers, or merchants, as wife, as heir, as palace, as equipage, as chef, as train of secretaries and courtiers. She knew how deeply it would cut, to find himself without his show piece that made him the envied of men and the desired of women. Also, she knew that she had an even stronger hold upon him—that she appealed to him as no other woman ever had, that she had become for him a tenacious habit. She was not afraid that he would break with her. But she could not feel secure; in former days she had seen too far into the mazes of that Italian mind of his, she knew too well how patient, how relentless, how unforgetting he was. She would have taken murder into account as more than a possibility but for his intense and intelligent selfishness; he would not risk his life or his liberty; he would not deprive himself of his keenest pleasure. He was resourceful; but in the circumstances what resources were there for him to draw upon?

When he began to press upon her more money than ever, and to buy her costly jewelry, she felt still further reassured. Evidently he had been unable to think out any practicable scheme; evidently he was, for the time, taking the course of appeal to her generous instincts, of making her more and more dependent upon his liberality.

Well—was he not right? Love might fail; passion might wane; conscience, aiding self-interest with its usual servility, might overcome the instincts of gratitude. But what power could overcome the loyalty resting upon money interest? No power but that of a longer purse than his. As she was not in the mood to make pretenses about herself to herself, she smiled at this cynical self-measuring. "But I shan't despise myself for being so material," said she to herself, "until I find a *genuine* case of a woman, respectable or otherwise, who has known poverty and escaped from it, and has then voluntarily given up wealth to go back to it. I should not stay on with him if he were distasteful to me. And that's more than most women can honestly say. Perhaps even I should not stay on if it were not for a silly, weak feeling of obligation—but I can't be sure of that." She had seen too much of men and women preening upon noble disinterested motives when in fact their real motives were the most calculatingly selfish; she preferred doing herself less than justice rather than more.

She had fifty-five thousand francs on deposit at Munroe's—all her very own. She had almost two hundred thousand francs' worth of jewels, which she would be justified in keeping—at least, she hoped she would think so—should there come a break with Freddie. Yet in spite of this substantial prosperity—or was it because of this prosperity?—she abruptly began again to be haunted by the old visions, by warnings of the dangers that beset any human being who has not that paying trade or profession which makes him or her independent—gives him or her the only unassailable independence.

The end with Freddie might be far away. But end, she saw, there would be the day when he would somehow get her in his power and so would drive her to leave him. For she could not again become a slave. Extreme youth, utter inexperience, no knowledge of real freedom—these had enabled her to endure in former days. But she was wholly different now. She could not sink back. Steadily she was growing less and less able to take orders from anyone. This full-grown passion for freedom, this intolerance of the least restraint—how dangerous, if she should find herself in a position where she would have to put up with the caprices of some man or drop down and down!

What real, secure support had she? None. Her building was without solid foundations. Her struggle with Freddie was a revelation and a warning. There were days when, driving about in her luxurious car, she could do nothing but search among the crowds in the streets for the lonely old women in rags, picking and peering along the refuse of the cafés—weazened, warped figures swathed in rags, creeping along, mumbling to themselves, lips folded in and in over toothless gums.

One day Brent saw again the look she often could not keep from her face when that vision of the dance hall in the slums was horrifying her. He said impulsively:

"What is it? Tell me—what is it, Susan?"

It was the first and the last time he ever called her by her only personal name. He flushed deeply. To cover his confusion—and her own—she said in her most frivolous way:

"I was thinking that if I am ever rich I shall have more pairs of shoes and stockings and take care of more orphans than anyone else in the world."

"A purpose! At last a purpose!" laughed he. "Now you will go to work."

Through Gourdain she got a French teacher—and her first woman friend.

The young widow he recommended, a Madame Clélie Délière, was the most attractive woman she had ever known. She had all the best French characteristics—a good heart, a lively mind, was imaginative yet sensible, had good taste in all things. Like most of the attractive French women, she was not beautiful, but had that which is of far greater importance—charm. She knew not a word of English, and it was perhaps Susan's chief incentive toward working hard at French that she could not really be friends with this fascinating person until she learned to speak her language. Palmer—partly by nature, partly through early experience in the polyglot tenement district of New York—had more aptitude for language than had Susan. But he had been lazy about acquiring French in a city where English is spoken almost universally. With the coming of young Madame Délière to live in the apartment, he became interested.

It was not a month after her coming when you might have seen at one of the fashionable gay restaurants any evening a party of four—Gourdain was the fourth—talking French almost volubly. Palmer's accent was better than Susan's. She could not—and felt she never could—get the accent of the trans-Alleghany region out of her voice—and so long as that remained she would not speak good French. "But don't let that trouble you," said Clélie. "Your voice is your greatest charm. It is so honest and so human. Of the Americans I have met, I have liked only those with that same tone in their voices."

"But I haven't that accent," said Freddie with raillery.

Madame Clélie laughed. "No—and I do not like you," retorted she. "No one ever did. You do not wish to be liked. You wish to be feared." Her lively brown eyes sparkled and the big white teeth in her generous mouth glistened. "You wish to be feared—and you *are* feared, Monsieur Freddie."

"It takes a clever woman to know how to flatter with the truth," said he. "Everybody always has been afraid of me—and is—except, of course, my wife."

He was always talking of "my wife" now. The subject so completely possessed his mind that he aired it unconsciously. When she was not around he boasted of "my wife's" skill in the art of dress, of "my wife's" taste, of "my wife's" shrewdness in getting her money's worth. When she was there, he was using the favorite phrase "my wife" this—"my wife" that—"my wife" the other—until it so got on her nerves that she began to wait for it and to wince whenever it came—never a wait of many minutes. At first she thought he was doing this deliberately either to annoy her or in pursuance of some secret deep design. But she soon saw that he was not aware of his inability to keep off the subject or of his obsession for that phrase representing the thing he was intensely wishing and willing—"chiefly," she thought, "because it is something he cannot have." She was amazed at his display of such a weakness. It gave her the chance to learn an important truth about human nature—that self-indulgence soon destroys the strongest nature—and she was witness to how rapidly an inflexible will disintegrates if incessantly applied to an impossibility. When a strong arrogant man, unbalanced by long and successful self-indulgence, hurls himself at an obstruction, either the obstruction yields or the man is destroyed.

One morning early in February, as she was descending from her auto in front of the apartment house, she saw Brent in the doorway. Never had he looked so young or so well. His color was fine, his face had become almost boyish; upon his skin and in his eyes was that gloss of perfect health which until these latter days of scientific hygiene was rarely seen after twenty-five in a woman or after thirty in a man. She gathered in all, to the smallest detail—such as the color of his shirt—with a single quick glance. She knew that he had seen her before she saw him—that he had been observing her. Her happiest friendliest smile made her small face bewitching as she advanced with outstretched hand.

"When did you come?" she asked.

"About an hour ago."

"From the Riviera?"

"No, indeed. From St. Moritz—and skating and skiing and tobogganing. I rather hoped I looked it. Doing those things in that air—it's being born again."

"I felt well till I saw you," said she. "Now I feel dingy and half sick."

He laughed, his glance sweeping her from hat to boots. Certainly his eyes could not have found a more entrancing sight. She was wearing a beautiful dress of golden brown cloth, sable hat, short coat and muff, brown suede boots laced high upon her long slender calves. And when she had descended from the perfect little limousine made to order for her, he had seen a ravishing flutter of lingerie of pale violet silk. The sharp air had brought no color to her cheeks to interfere with the abrupt and fascinating contrast of their pallor with the long crimson bow of her mouth. But her skin seemed transparent and had the clearness of health itself. Everything about her, every least detail, was of Parisian perfection.

"Probably there are not in the world," said he, "so many as a dozen women so well put together as you are. No, not half a dozen. Few women carry the art of dress to the point of genius."

"I see they had only frumps at St. Moritz this season," laughed she.

But he would not be turned aside. "Most of the well dressed women stop short with being simply frivolous in spending so much time at less than perfection—like the army of poets who write pretty good verse, or the swarm of singers who sing pretty well. I've heard of you many times this winter. You are the talk of Paris."

She laughed with frank delight. It was indeed a pleasure to discover that her pains had not been in vain.

"It is always the outsider who comes to the great city to show it its own resources," he went on. "I knew you were going to do this. Still happy?"

"Oh, yes."

But he had taken her by surprise. A faint shadow flitted across her face. "Not so happy, I see."

"You see too much. Won't you lunch with us? We'll have it in about half an hour."

He accepted promptly and they went up together. His glance traveled round the drawing-room; and she knew he had noted all the changes she had made on better acquaintance with her surroundings and wider knowledge of interior furnishing. She saw that he approved, and it increased her good humor. "Are you hurrying through Paris on your way to somewhere else?" she asked.

"No, I stop here—I think—until I sail for America."

"And that will be soon?"

"Perhaps not until July. I have no plans. I've finished a play a woman suggested to me some time ago. And I'm waiting."

A gleam of understanding came into her eyes. There was controlled interest in her voice as she inquired:

"When is it to be produced?"

"When the woman who suggested it is ready to act in it."

"Do I by any chance know her?"

"You used to know her. You will know her again."

She shook her head slowly, a pensive smile hovering about her eyes and lips. "No—not again. I have changed."

"We do not change," said he. "We move, but we do not change. You are the same character you were when you came into the world. And what you were then, that you will be when the curtain falls on the climax of your last act. Your circumstances will change—and your clothes—and your face, hair, figure—but not *you*."

"Do you believe that?"

"I *know* it."

She nodded slowly, the violet-gray eyes pensive. "Birds in the strong wind—that's what we are. Driven this way or that—or quite beaten down. But the wind doesn't change sparrow to eagle—or eagle to gull—does it?"

She had removed her coat and was seated on an oval lounge gazing into the open fire. He was standing before it, looking taller and stronger than ever, in a gray lounging suit. A cigarette depended loosely from the corner of his mouth. He said abruptly:

"How are you getting on with your acting?"

She glanced in surprise.

"Gourdain," Brent explained. "He had to talk to somebody about how wonderful you are. So he took to writing me—two huge letters a week—all about you."

"I'm fond of him. And he's fond of Clélie. She's my——"

"I know all," he interrupted. "The tie between them is their fondness for you. Tell me about the acting."

"Oh—Clélie and I have been going to the theater every few days—to help me with French. She is mad about acting, and there's nothing I like better."

"Also, *you* simply have to have occupation."

She nodded. "I wasn't brought up to fit me for an idler. When I was a child I was taught to keep busy—not at nothing, but at something. Freddie's a lot better at it than I."

"Naturally," said Brent. "You had a home, with order and a system—an old-fashioned American home. He—well, he hadn't."

"Clélie and I go at our make-believe acting quite seriously. We have to—if we're to fool ourselves that it's an occupation."

"Why this anxiety to prove to me that you're not really serious?"

Susan laughed mockingly for answer, and went on:

"You should see us do the two wives in 'L'Enigme'—or mother and daughter in that diary scene in 'L'Autre Danger'!"

"I must. . . . When are you going to resume your career?"

She rose, strolled toward an open door at one end of the salon, closed it—strolled toward the door into the hall, glanced out, returned without having closed it. She then said:

"Could I study here in Paris?"

Triumph gleamed in his eyes. "Yes. Boudrin—a splendid teacher—speaks English. He—and I—can teach you."

"Tell me what I'd have to do."

"We would coach you for a small part in some play that's to be produced here."

"In French?"

"I'll have an American girl written into a farce. Enough to get you used to the stage—to give you practice in what he'll teach you—the trade side of the art."

"And then?"

"And then we shall spend the summer learning your part in my play. Two or three weeks of company rehearsals in New York in

September. In October—your name out over the Long Acre Theater in letters of fire."

"Could that be done?"

"Even if you had little talent, less intelligence, and no experience. Properly taught, the trade part of every art is easy. Teachers make it hard partly because they're dull, chiefly because there'd be small money for them if they taught quickly, and only the essentials. No, journeyman acting's no harder to learn than bricklaying or carpentering. And in America— everywhere in the world but a few theaters in Paris and Vienna—there is nothing seen but journeyman acting. The art is in its infancy as an art. It even has not yet been emancipated from the swaddling clothes of declamation. Yes, you can do well by the autumn. And if you develop what I think you have in you, you can leap with one bound into fame. In America or England, mind you—because there the acting is all poor to 'pretty good'."

"You are sure it could be done? No—I don't mean that. I mean, is there really a chance—any chance—for me to make my own living? A real living?"

"I guarantee," said Brent.

She changed from seriousness to a mocking kind of gayety—that is, to a seriousness so profound that she would not show it. And she said:

"You see I simply must banish my old women—and that hunchback and his piano. They get on my nerves."

He smiled humorously at her. But behind the smile his gaze—grave, sympathetic—pierced into her soul, seeking the meaning he knew she would never put into words.

At the sound of voices in the hall she said:

"We'll talk of this again."

At lunch that day she, for the first time in many a week, listened without irritation while Freddie poured forth his unending praise of "my wife." As Brent knew them intimately, Freddie felt free to expatiate upon all the details of domestic economy that chanced to be his theme, with the exquisite lunch as a text. He told Brent how Susan had made a study of that branch of the art of living; how she had explored the unrivaled Parisian markets and groceries and shops that dealt in specialties; how she had developed their breakfasts, dinners, and lunches to works of art. It is impossible for anyone, however stupid, to stop long in Paris without beginning to idealize the material side of life—for the French, who build solidly, first idealize food, clothing, and shelter, before going on to take up the higher side of life—as a sane man builds his foundation before his first story, and so on, putting the observation tower on last of all, instead of making an ass of himself trying to hang his tower to the stars. Our idealization goes forward haltingly and hypocritically because we try to build from the stars down, instead of from the ground up. The place to seek the ideal is in the homely, the commonplace, and the necessary. An ideal that does not spring deep-rooted from the soil of practical life may be a topic for a sermon or a novel or for idle conversation among silly and pretentious people. But what use has it in a world that must *live*, and must be taught to live?

Freddie was unaware that he was describing a further development of Susan—a course she was taking in the university of experience—she who had passed through its common school, its high school, its college. To him her clever housekeeping offered simply another instance of her cleverness in general. His discourse was in bad taste. But its bad taste was tolerable because he was interesting—food, like sex, being one of those universal subjects that command and hold the attention of all mankind. He rose to no mean height of eloquence in describing their dinner of the evening before— the game soup that brought to him visions of a hunting excursion he had once made into the wilds of Canada; the way the *barbue* was cooked and served; the incredible duck—and the salad! Clélie interrupted to describe that salad as like a breath of summer air from fields and limpid brooks. He declared that the cheese—which Susan had found in a shop in the Marche St. Honoré—was more wonderful than the most wonderful *petit Suisse*. "And the coffee!" he exclaimed. "But you'll see in a few minutes. We have *coffee* here."

"*Quelle histoire!*" exclaimed Brent, when Freddie had concluded. And he looked at Susan with the ironic, quizzical gleam in his eyes.

She colored. "I am learning to live," said she. "That's what we're on earth for—isn't it?"

"To learn to live—and then, to live," replied he.

She laughed. "Ah, that comes a little later."

"Not much later," rejoined he, "or there's no time left for it."

It was Freddie who, after lunch, urged Susan and Clélie to "show Brent what you can do at acting."

"Yes—by all means," said Brent with enthusiasm.

And they gave—in one end of the salon which was well suited for it— the scene between mother and daughter over the stolen diary, in "L'Autre Danger." Brent said little when they finished, so little that Palmer was visibly annoyed. But Susan, who was acquainted with his modes of expression, felt a deep glow of satisfaction. She had no delusions about her attempts; she understood perfectly that they were simply crude attempts. She knew she had done well—for her—and she knew he appreciated her improvement.

"That would have gone fine—with costumes and scenery—eh?" demanded Freddie of Brent.

"Yes," said Brent absently. "Yes—that is—Yes."

Freddie was dissatisfied with this lack of enthusiasm. He went on insistently:

"I think she ought to go on the stage—she and Madame Clélie, too."

"Yes," said Brent, between inquiry and reflection.

"What do *you* think?"

"I don't think she ought," replied Brent. "I think she *must*." He turned to Susan. "Would you like it?"

Susan hesitated. Freddie said—rather lamely, "Of course she would. For my part, I wish she would."

"Then I will," said Susan quietly.

Palmer looked astounded. He had not dreamed she would assent. He knew her tones—knew that the particular tone meant finality. "You're joking," cried he, with an uneasy laugh. "Why, you wouldn't stand the work for a week. It's hard work—isn't it, Brent?"

"About the hardest," said Brent. "And she's got practically everything still to learn."

"Shall we try, Clélie?" said Susan.

Young Madame Délière was pale with eagerness. "Ah—but that would be worth while!" cried she.

"Then it's settled," said Susan. To Brent: "We'll make the arrangements at once—today."

Freddie was looking at her with a dazed expression. His glance presently drifted from her face to the fire, to rest there thoughtfully as he smoked his cigar. He took no part in the conversation that followed. Presently he left the room without excusing himself. When Clélie seated herself at the piano to wander vaguely from one piece of music to another, Brent joined Susan at the fire and said in English:

"Palmer is furious."

"I saw," said she.

"I am afraid. For—I know him."

She looked calmly at him. "But I am not."

"Then you do not know him."

The strangest smile flitted across her face.

After a pause Brent said: "Are you married to him?"

Again the calm steady look. Then: "That is none of your business."

"I thought you were not," said Brent, as if she had answered his question with a clear negative. He added, "You know I'd not have asked if it had been 'none of my business.'"

"What do you mean?"

"If you had been his wife, I could not have gone on. I've all the reverence for a home of the man who has never had one. I'd not take part in a home-breaking. But—since you are free——"

"I shall never be anything else but free. It's because I wish to make sure of my freedom that I'm going into this."

Palmer appeared in the doorway.

That night the four and Gourdain dined together, went to the theater and afterward to supper at the Cafe de Paris. Gourdain and young Madame Délière formed an interesting, unusually attractive exhibit of the parasitism that is as inevitable to the rich as fleas to a dog. Gourdain was a superior man, Clélie a superior woman. There was nothing of the sycophant, or even of the courtier, about either. Yet they already had in their faces that subtle indication of the dependent that is found in all professional people who habitually work for and associate with the rich only. They had no sense of dependence; they were not dependents, for they gave more than value received. Yet so corrupting is the atmosphere about rich people that Gourdain, who had other rich clients, no less than Clélie who got her whole living from Palmer, was at a glance in the flea class and not in the dog class. Brent looked for signs of the same thing in Susan's face. The signs should have been there; but they were not. "Not yet," thought he. "And never will be now."

Palmer's abstraction and constraint were in sharp contrast to the gayety of the others. Susan drank almost nothing. Her spirits were soaring so high that she did not dare stimulate them with champagne. The Cafe de Paris is one of the places where the respectable go to watch *les autres* and to catch a real gayety by contagion of a gayety that is mechanical and altogether as unreal as play-acting. There is something fantastic about the official temples of Venus; the pleasure-makers are so serious under their masks and the pleasure-getters so quaintly dazzled and deluded. That is, Venus's temples are like those of so many other religions in reverence among men—disbelief and solemn humbuggery at the altar; belief that would rather die than be undeceived, in the pews. Palmer scarcely took his eyes from Susan's face. It amused and pleased her to see how uneasy this made Brent—and how her own laughter and jests aggravated his uneasiness to the point where he was almost showing it. She glanced round that brilliant room filled with men and women, each of them carrying underneath the placidity of stiff evening shirt or the scantiness of audacious evening gown the most fascinating emotions and secrets—love and hate and jealousy, cold and monstrous habits and desires, ruin impending or stealthily advancing, fortune giddying to a gorgeous climax, disease and shame and fear—yet only signs of love and laughter and lightness of heart visible. And she wondered whether at any other table there was gathered so curious an assemblage of pasts and presents and futures as at the one over which Freddie Palmer was presiding somberly. . . . Then her thoughts took another turn. She fell to noting how each man was accompanied by a woman—a gorgeously dressed woman, a woman revealing, proclaiming, in every line, in every movement, that she was thus elaborately and beautifully toiletted to please man, to appeal to his senses, to gain his gracious approval. It was the world in miniature; it was an illustration of the position of woman—of her own position. Favorite; pet. Not the equal of man, but an appetizer, a dessert. She glanced at herself in the glass, mocked her own radiant beauty of face and form and dress. Not really a full human being; merely a decoration. No more; and no worse off than most of the women everywhere, the favorites licensed or unlicensed of law and religion. But just as badly off, and just as insecure. Free! No rest, no full breath until freedom had been won! At any cost, by straight way or devious—free!

"Let's go home," said she abruptly. "I've had enough of this."

She was in a dressing gown, all ready for bed and reading, when Palmer came into her sitting-room. She was smoking, her gaze upon her book. Her thick dark hair was braided close to her small head. There was delicate lace on her nightgown, showing above the wadded satin collar of the dressing gown. He dropped heavily into a chair.

"If anyone had told me a year ago that a skirt could make a damn fool of me," said he bitterly, "I'd have laughed in his face. Yet—here I am! How nicely I did drop into your trap today—about the acting!"

"Trap?"

"Oh, I admit I built and baited and set it, myself—ass that I was! But it was your trap—yours and Brent's, all the same. . . . A skirt—and not a clean one, at that."

She lowered the book to her lap, took the cigarette from between her lips, looked at him. "Why not be reasonable, Freddie?" said she calmly. Language had long since lost its power to impress her. "Why irritate yourself and annoy me simply because I won't let you tyrannize over me? You know you can't treat me as if I were your property. I'm not your wife, and I don't have to be your mistress."

"Getting ready to break with me eh?"

"If I wished to go, I'd tell you—and go."

"You'd give me the shake, would you?—without the slightest regard for all I've done for you!"

She refused to argue that again. "I hope I've outgrown doing weak gentle things through cowardice and pretending it's through goodness of heart."

"You've gotten hard—like stone."

"Like you—somewhat." And after a moment she added, "Anything that's strong is hard—isn't it? Can a man or a woman get anywhere without being able to be what you call 'hard' and what I call 'strong'?"

"Where do *you* want to get?" demanded he.

She disregarded his question, to finish saying what was in her mind— what she was saying rather to give herself a clear look at her own thoughts and purposes than to enlighten him about them. "I'm not a sheltered woman," pursued she. "I've got no one to save me from the consequences of doing nice, sweet, womanly things."

"You've got me," said he angrily.

"But why lean if I'm strong enough to stand alone? Why weaken myself just to gratify your mania for owning and bossing? But let me finish what I was saying. I never got any quarter because I was a woman. No woman does, as a matter of fact; and in the end, the more she uses her sex to help her shirk, the worse her punishment is. But in my case— —

"I was brought up to play the weak female, to use my sex as my shield. And that was taken from me and—I needn't tell *you* how I was taught to give and take like a man—no, not like a man—for no man ever has to endure what a woman goes through if she is thrown on the world. Still, I'm not whining. Now that it's all over I'm the better for what I've been through. I've learned to use all a man's weapons and in addition I've got a woman's."

"As long as your looks last," sneered he.

"That will be longer than yours," said she pleasantly, "if you keep on with the automobiles and the champagne. And when my looks are gone, my woman's weapons. . .

"Why, I'll still have the man's weapons left—shan't I?—knowledge, and the ability to use it."

His expression of impotent fury mingled with compelled admiration and respect made his face about as unpleasant to look at as she had ever seen it. But she liked to look. His confession of her strength made her feel stronger. The sense of strength was a new sensation with her—new and delicious. Nor could the feeling that she was being somewhat cruel restrain her from enjoying it.

"I have never asked quarter," she went on. "I never shall. If fate gets me down, as it has many a time, why I'll he able to take my medicine without weeping or whining. I've never asked pity. I've never asked charity. That's why I'm here, Freddie—in this apartment, instead of in a filthy tenement attic—and in these clothes instead of in rags—and with you respecting me, instead of kicking me toward the gutter. Isn't that so?"

He was silent.

"Isn't it so?" she insisted.

"Yes," he admitted. And his handsome eyes looked the love so near to hate that fills a strong man for a strong woman when they clash and he cannot conquer. "No wonder I'm a fool about you," he muttered.

"I don't purpose that any man or woman shall use me," she went on, "in exchange for merely a few flatteries. I insist that if they use me, they must let me use them. I shan't be mean about it, but I shan't be altogether a fool, either. And what is a woman but a fool when she lets men use her for nothing but being called sweet and loving and womanly? Unless that's the best she can do, poor thing!"

"You needn't sneer at respectable women."

"I don't," replied she. "I've no sneers for anybody. I've discovered a great truth, Freddie the deep-down equality of all human beings—all of them birds in the same wind and battling with it each as best he can. As for myself—with money, with a career that interests me, with position that'll give me any acquaintances and friends that are congenial, I don't care what is said of me."

As her plan unfolded itself fully to his understanding, which needed only a hint to enable it to grasp all, he forgot his rage for a moment in his interest and admiration. Said he:

"You've used me. Now you're going to use Brent—eh? Well—what will you give *him* in exchange?"

"He wants someone to act certain parts in certain plays."

"Is that *all* he wants?"

"He hasn't asked anything else."

"And if he did?"

"Don't be absurd. You know Brent."

"He's not in love with you," assented Palmer. "He doesn't want you that way. There's some woman somewhere, I've heard—and he doesn't care about anybody but her."

He was speaking in a careless, casual way, watching her out of the corner of his eye. And she, taken off guard, betrayed in her features the secret that was a secret even from herself. He sprang up with a bound, sprang at her, caught her up out of her chair, the fingers of one hand clasping her throat.

"I thought so!" he hissed. "You love him—damn you! You love him! You'd better look out, both of you!"

There came a knock at the door between her bedroom and that of Madame Clélie. Palmer released her, stood panting, with furious eyes on the door from which the sound had come. Susan called, "It's all right, Clélie, for the present." Then she said to Palmer, "I told Clélie to knock if she ever heard voices in this room—or any sound she didn't understand." She reseated herself, began to massage her throat where his fingers had clutched it. "It's fortunate my skin doesn't mar easily," she went on. "What were you saying?"

"I know the truth now. You love Brent. That's the milk in the cocoanut."

She reflected on this, apparently with perfect tranquillity, apparently with no memory of his furious threat against her and against Brent. She said:

"Perhaps I was simply piqued because there's another woman."

"You are jealous."

"I guess I was—a little."

"You admit that you love him, you——"

He checked himself on the first hissing breath of the foul epithet. She said tranquilly:

"Jealousy doesn't mean love. We're jealous in all sorts of ways—and of all sorts of things."

"Well—*he* cares nothing about *you*."

"Nothing."

"And never will. He'd despise a woman who had been——"

"Don't hesitate. Say it. I'm used to hearing it, Freddie—and to being it. And not 'had been' but 'is.' I still am, you know."

"You're not!" he cried. "And never were—and never could be—for some unknown reason, God knows why."

She shrugged her shoulders, lit another cigarette. He went on:

"You can't get it out of your head that because he's interested in you he's more or less stuck on you. That's the way with women. The truth is, he wants you merely to act in his plays."

"And I want that, too."

"You think I'm going to stand quietly by and let this thing go on—do you?"

She showed not the faintest sign of nervousness at this repetition, more carefully veiled, of his threat against her—and against Brent. She chose the only hopeful course; she went at him boldly and directly. Said she with amused carelessness:

"Why not? He doesn't want me. Even if I love him, I'm not giving him anything you want."

"How do you know what I want?" cried he, confused by this unexpected way of meeting his attack. "You think I'm simply a brute—with no fine instincts or feelings——"

She interrupted him with a laugh. "Don't be absurd, Freddie," said she. "You know perfectly well you and I don't call out the finer feelings in each other. If either of us wanted that sort of thing, we'd have to look elsewhere."

"You mean Brent—eh?"

She laughed with convincing derision. "What nonsense!" She put her arms round his neck, and her lips close to his. The violet-gray eyes were half closed, the perfume of the smooth amber-white skin, of the thick, wavy, dark hair, was in his nostrils. And in a languorous murmur she soothed his subjection to a deep sleep with, "As long as you give me what I want from you, and I give you what you want from me why should we wrangle?"

And with a smile he acquiesced. She felt that she had ended the frightful danger—to Brent rather than to herself—that suddenly threatened from those wicked eyes of Palmer's. But it might easily come again. She did not dare relax her efforts, for in the succeeding days she saw that he was like one annoyed by a constant pricking from a pin hidden in the clothing and searched for in vain. He was no longer jealous of Brent. But while he didn't know what was troubling him, he did know that he was uncomfortable.

CHAPTER XXIII

IN but one important respect was Brent's original plan modified. Instead of getting her stage experience in France, Susan joined a London company making one of those dreary, weary, cheap and trashy tours of the smaller cities of the provinces with half a dozen plays by Jones, Pinero, and Shaw.

Clélie stayed in London, toiling at the language, determined to be ready to take the small part of French maid in Brent's play in the fall. Brent and Palmer accompanied Susan; and every day for several hours Brent and the stage manager—his real name was Thomas Boil and his professional name was Herbert Streathern—coached the patient but most unhappy Susan line by line, word by word, gesture by gesture, in the little parts she was playing. Palmer traveled with them, making a pretense of interest that ill concealed his boredom and irritation. This for three weeks; then he began to make trips to London to amuse himself with the sports, amateur and professional, with whom he easily made friends—some of them men in a position to be useful to him socially later on. He had not spoken of those social ambitions of his since Susan refused to go that way with him—but she knew he had them in mind as strongly as ever. He was the sort of man who must have an objective, and what other objective could there be for him who cared for and believed in the conventional ambitions and triumphs only—the successes that made the respectable world gape and grovel and envy?

"You'll not stick at this long," he said to Susan.

"I'm frightfully depressed," she admitted. "It's tiresome—and hard—and so hideously uncomfortable! And I've lost all sense of art or profession. Acting seems to be nothing but a trade, and a poor, cheap one at that."

He was not surprised, but was much encouraged by this candid account of her state of mind. Said he:

"It's my private opinion that only your obstinacy keeps you from giving it up straight off. Surely you must see it's nonsense. Drop it and come along—and be comfortable and happy. Why be obstinate? There's nothing in it."

"Perhaps it *is* obstinacy," said she. "I like to think it's something else."

"Drop it. You want to. You know you do."

"I want to, but I can't," replied she.

He recognized the tone, the expression of the eyes, the sudden showing of strength through the soft, young contour. And he desisted.

Never again could there be comfort, much less happiness, until she had tried out her reawakened ambition. She had given up all that had been occupying her since she left America with Freddie; she had abandoned herself to a life of toil. Certainly nothing could have been more tedious, more tormenting to sensitive nerves, than the schooling through which Brent was putting her. Its childishness revolted her and angered her. Experience had long since lowered very considerably the point at which her naturally sweet disposition ceased to be sweet—a process through which every good-tempered person must pass unless he or she is to be crushed and cast aside as a failure. There were days, many of them, when it took all her good sense, all her fundamental faith in Brent, to restrain her from an outbreak. Streathern regarded Brent as a crank, and had to call into service all his humility as a poor Englishman toward a rich man to keep from showing his contempt. And Brent seemed to be—indeed was—testing her forbearance to the uttermost. He offered not the slightest explanation of his method. He simply ordered her blindly to pursue the course he marked out. She was sorely tempted to ask, to demand, explanations. But there stood out a quality in Brent that made her resolve ooze away, as soon as she faced him. Of one thing she was confident. Any lingering suspicions Freddie might have had of Brent's interest in her as a woman, or even of her being interested in him as a man, must have been killed beyond resurrection. Freddie showed that he would have hated Brent, would have burst out against him, for the unhuman, inhuman way he was treating her, had it not been that Brent was so admirably serving his design to have her finally and forever disgusted and done with the stage.

Finally there came a performance in which the audience—the gallery part of it—"booed" her—not the play, not the other players, but her and no other. Brent came along, apparently by accident, as she made her exit. He halted before her and scanned her countenance with those all-seeing eyes of his. Said he:

"You heard them?"

"Of course," replied she.

"That was for you," said he and he said it with an absence of sympathy that made it brutal.

"For only me," said she—frivolously.

"You seem not to mind."

"Certainly I mind. I'm not made of wood or stone."

"Don't you think you'd better give it up?"

She looked at him with a steely light from the violet eyes, a light that had never been there before.

"Give up?" said she. "Not even if you give me up. This thing has got to be put through."

He simply nodded. "All right," he said. "It will be."

"That booing—it almost struck me dead. When it didn't, I for the first time felt sure I was going to win."

He nodded again, gave her one of his quick expressive, fleeting glances that somehow made her forget and forgive everything and feel fresh and eager to start in again. He said:

"When the booing began and you didn't break down and run off the stage, I knew that what I hoped and believed about you was true."

Streathern joined them. His large, soft eyes were full of sympathetic tears. He was so moved that he braved Brent. He said to Susan:

"It wasn't your fault, Miss Lenox. You were doing exactly as
Mr. Brent ordered, when the booing broke out."

"Exactly," said Brent.

Streathern regarded him with a certain nervousness and veiled pity. Streathern had been brought into contact with many great men. He had found them, each and every one, with this same streak of wild folly, this habit of doing things that were to him obviously useless and ridiculous. It was a profound mystery to him why such men succeeded while he himself who never did such things remained in obscurity. The only explanation was the abysmal stupidity, ignorance, and folly of the masses of mankind. What a harbor of refuge that reflection has ever been for mediocrity's shattered and sinking vanity! Yet the one indisputable fact about the great geniuses of long ago is that in their own country and age "the common people heard them gladly." Streathern could not now close his mouth upon one last appeal on behalf of the clever and lovely and so amiable victim of Brent's mania.

"I say, Mr. Brent," pleaded he, "don't you think—Really now, if you'll permit a chap not without experience to say so—Don't you think that by drilling her so much and so—so *beastly* minutely—you're making her wooden—machine-like?"

"I hope so," said Brent, in a tone that sent Streathern scurrying away to a place where he could express himself unseen and unheard.

In her fifth week she began to improve. She felt at home on the stage; she felt at home in her part, whatever it happened to be. She was giving what could really be called a performance. Streathern, when he was sure Brent could not hear, congratulated her. "It's wonderfully plucky of you, my dear," said he, "quite amazingly plucky—to get yourself together and go straight ahead, in spite of what your American friend has been doing to you."

"In spite of it." cried Susan. "Why, don't you see that it's because of what he's been doing? I felt it, all the time. I see it now."

"Oh, really—do you think so?" said Streathern.

His tone made it a polite and extremely discreet way of telling her he thought she had become as mad as Brent. She did not try to explain to him why she was improving. In that week she advanced by long strides, and Brent was radiant.

"Now we'll teach you scales," said he. "We'll teach you the mechanics of expressing every variety of emotion. Then we'll be ready to study a strong part."

She had known in the broad from the outset what Brent was trying to accomplish—that he was giving her the trade side of the art, was giving it to her quickly and systematically. But she did not appreciate how profoundly right he was until she was "learning scales." Then she understood why most so called "professional" performances are amateurish, haphazard, without any precision. She was learning to posture, and to utter every emotion so accurately that any spectator would recognize it at once.

"And in time your voice and your body," said Brent, "will become as much your servants as are Paderewski's ten fingers. He doesn't rely upon any such rot as inspiration. Nor does any master of any art. A mind can be inspired but not a body. It must be taught. You must first have a perfect instrument. Then, if you are a genius, your genius, having a perfect instrument to work with, will produce perfect results. To ignore or to neglect the mechanics of an art is to hamper or to kill inspiration. Geniuses—a few— and they not the greatest—have been too lazy to train their instruments.

But anyone who is merely talented dares not take the risk. And you—we'd better assume—are merely talented."

Streathern, who had a deserved reputation as a coach, was disgusted with Brent's degradation of an art. As openly as he dared, he warned Susan against the danger of becoming a mere machine—a puppet, responding stiffly to the pulling of strings. But Susan had got over her momentary irritation against Brent, her doubt of his judgment in her particular case. She ignored Streathern's advice that she should be natural, that she should let her own temperament dictate variations on his cut and dried formulae for expression. She continued to do as she was bid.

"If you are *not* a natural born actress," said Brent, "at least you will be a good one—so good that most critics will call you great. And if you *are* a natural born genius at acting, you will soon put color in the cheeks of these dolls I'm giving you—and ease into their bodies—and nerves and muscles and blood in place of the strings."

In the seventh week he abruptly took her out of the company and up to London to have each day an hour of singing, an hour of dancing, and an hour of fencing. "You'll ruin her health," protested Freddie. "You're making her work like a ditch digger."

Brent replied, "If she hasn't the health, she's got to abandon the career. If she has health, this training will give it steadiness and solidity. If there's a weakness anywhere, it'll show itself and can be remedied."

And he piled the work on her, dictated her hours of sleep, her hours for rest and for walking, her diet—and little he gave her to eat. When he had her thoroughly broken to his regimen, he announced that business compelled his going immediately to America. "I shall be back in a month," said he.

"I think I'll run over with you," said Palmer. "Do you mind, Susan?"

"Clélie and I shall get on very well," she replied. She would be glad to have both out of the way that she might give her whole mind to the only thing that now interested her. For the first time she was experiencing the highest joy that comes to mortals, the only joy that endures and grows and defies all the calamities of circumstances—the joy of work congenial and developing.

"Yes—come along," said Brent to Palmer. "Here you'll be tempting her to break the rules." He added, "Not that you would succeed. She understands what it all means, now—and nothing could stop her. That's why I feel free to leave her."

"Yes, I understand," said Susan. She was gazing away into space; at sight of her expression Freddie turned hastily away.

On a Saturday morning Susan and Clélie, after waiting on the platform at Euston Station until the long, crowded train for Liverpool and the *Lusitania* disappeared, went back to the lodgings in Half Moon Street with a sudden sense of the vastness of London, of its loneliness and dreariness, of its awkward inhospitality to the stranger under its pall of foggy smoke. Susan was thinking of Brent's last words:

She had said, "I'll try to deserve all the pains you've taken, Mr. Brent."

"Yes, I have done a lot for you," he had replied. "I've put you beyond the reach of any of the calamities of life—beyond the need of any of its consolations. Don't forget that if the steamer goes down with all on board."

And then she had looked at him—and as Freddie's back was half turned, she hoped he had not seen—in fact, she was sure he had not, or she would not have dared. And Brent—had returned her look with his usual quizzical smile; but she had learned how to see through that mask. Then— she had submitted to Freddie's energetic embrace—had given her hand to Brent—"Good-by," she had said; and "Good luck," he.

Beyond the reach of *any* of the calamities? Beyond the need of *any* of the consolations? Yes—it was almost literally true. She felt the big interest—the career—growing up within her, and expanding, and already overstepping all other interests and emotions.

Brent had left her and Clélie more to do than could be done; thus they had no time to bother either about the absent or about themselves. Looking back in after years on the days that Freddie was away, Susan could recall that from time to time she would find her mind wandering, as if groping in the darkness of its own cellars or closets for a lost thought, a missing link in some chain of thought. This even awakened her several times in the night— made her leap from sleep into acute and painful consciousness as if she had recalled and instantly forgotten some startling and terrible thing.

And when Freddie unexpectedly came—having taken passage on the *Lusitania* for the return voyage, after only six nights and five days in New York—she was astonished by her delight at seeing him, and by the kind of delight it was. For it rather seemed a sort of relief, as from a heavy burden of anxiety.

"Why didn't you wait and come with Brent?" asked she.

"Couldn't stand it," replied he. "I've grown clear away from New York—at least from the only New York I know. I don't like the boys any more. They bore me. They—offend me. And I know if I stayed on a few days they'd begin to suspect. No, it isn't Europe. It's—you. You're responsible for the change in me."

He was speaking entirely of the internal change, which indeed was great. For while he was still fond of all kinds of sporting, it was not in his former crude way; he had even become something of a connoisseur of pictures and was cultivating a respect for the purity of the English language that made him wince at Susan's and Brent's slang. But when he spoke thus frankly and feelingly of the change in him, Susan looked at him—and, not having seen him in two weeks and three days, she really saw him for the first time in many a month. She could not think of the internal change he spoke of for noting the external change. He had grown at least fifty pounds heavier than he had been when they came abroad. In one way this was an improvement; it gave him a dignity, an air of consequence in place of the boyish good looks of the days before the automobile and before the effects of high living began to show. But it made of him a different man in Susan's eyes—a man who now seemed almost a stranger to her.

"Yes, you *have* changed," replied she absently. And she went and examined herself in a mirror.

"You, too," said Freddie. "You don't look older—as I do. But—there's a—a—I can't describe it."

Susan could not see it. "I'm just the same," she insisted.

Palmer laughed. "You can't judge about yourself. But all this excitement—and studying—and thinking—and God knows what— — You're not at all the woman I came abroad with."

The subject seemed to be making both uncomfortable; they dropped it.

Women are bred to attach enormous importance to their physical selves—so much so that many women have no other sense of self-respect, and regard themselves as possessing the entirety of virtue if they have chastity or can pretend to have it. The life Susan had led upsets all this and forces a woman either utterly to despise herself, even as she is despised of men, or to discard the sex measure of feminine self-respect as ridiculously inadequate, and to seek some other measure. Susan had sought this other measure, and had found it. She was, therefore, not a little surprised to find— after Freddie had been back three or four days—that he was arousing in her the same sensations which a strange man intimately about would have aroused in her in the long past girlhood of innocence. It was not physical repulsion; it was not a sense of immorality. It was a kind of shyness, a feeling of violated modesty. She felt herself blushing if he came into the room when she was dressing. As soon as she awakened in the morning she sprang from bed beside him and hastened into her dressing-room and closed the door, resisting an impulse to lock it. Apparently the feeling of physical modesty which she had thought dead, killed to the last root, was not dead, was once more stirring toward life.

"What are you blushing about?" asked he, when she, passing through the bedroom, came suddenly upon him, very scantily dressed.

She laughed confusedly and beat a hurried retreat. She began to revolve the idea of separate bedrooms; she resolved that when they moved again she would arrange it on some pretext—and she was looking about for a new place on the plea that their quarters in Half Moon Street were too cramped. All this close upon his return, for it was before the end of the first week that she, taking a shower bath one morning, saw the door of the bathroom opening to admit him, and cried out sharply:

"Close that door!"

"It's I," Freddie called, to make himself heard above the noise of the water. "Shut off that water and listen."

She shut off the water, but instead of listening, she said, nervous but determined:

"Please close the door. I'll be out directly."

"Listen, I tell you," he cried, and she now noticed that his voice was curiously, arrestingly, shrill.

"Brent—has been hurt—badly hurt." She was dripping wet. She thrust her arms into her bathrobe, flung wide the partly open door. He was standing there, a newspaper in his trembling hand. "This is a dispatch from New York—dated yesterday," he began. "Listen," and he read:

"During an attempt to rob the house of Mr. Robert Brent, the distinguished playwright, early this morning, Mr. Brent was set upon and stabbed in a dozen places, his butler, James Fourget, was wounded, perhaps mortally, and his secretary, Mr. J. C. Garvey, was knocked insensible. The thieves made their escape. The police have several clues. Mr. Brent is hovering between life and death, with the chances against him."

Susan, leaning with all her weight against the door jamb, saw Palmer's white face going away from her, heard his agitated voice less and less distinctly—fell to the floor with a crash and knew no more.

When she came to, she was lying in the bed; about it or near it were Palmer, her maid, his valet, Clélie, several strangers. Her glance turned to Freddie's face and she looked into his eyes amid a profound silence. She saw in those eyes only intense anxiety and intense affection. He said:

"What is it, dear? You are all right. Only a fainting spell."

"Was that true?" she asked.

"Yes, but he'll pull through. The surgeons save everybody nowadays. I've cabled his secretary, Garvey, and to my lawyers. We'll have an answer soon. I've sent out for all the papers."

"She must not be agitated," interposed a medical looking man with stupid brown eyes and a thin brown beard sparsely veiling his gaunt and pasty face.

"Nonsense!" said Palmer, curtly. "My wife is not an invalid. Our closest friend has been almost killed. To keep the news from her would be to make her sick."

Susan closed her eyes. "Thank you," she murmured. "Send them all away—except Clélie. . . . Leave me alone with Clélie."

Pushing the others before him, Freddie moved toward the door into the hall. At the threshold he paused to say:

"Shall I bring the papers when they come?"

She hesitated. "No," she answered without opening her eyes.

"Send them in. I want to read them, myself."

She lay quiet, Clélie stroking her brow. From time to time a shudder passed over her. When, in answer to a knock, Clélie took in the bundle of newspapers, she sat up in bed and read the meager dispatches. The long accounts were made long by the addition of facts about Brent's life. The short accounts added nothing to what she already knew. When she had read all, she sank back among the pillows and closed her eyes. A long, long silence in the room. Then a soft knock at the door. Clélie left the bedside to answer it, returned to say:

"Mr. Freddie wishes to come in with a telegram."

Susan started up wildly. Her eyes were wide and staring—a look of horror. "No—no!" she cried. Then she compressed her lips, passed her hand slowly over her brow. "Yes—tell him to come in."

Her gaze was upon the door until it opened, leaped to his face, to his eyes, the instant he appeared. He was smiling—hopefully, but not gayly.

"Garvey says"—and he read from a slip of paper in his hand—" 'None of the wounds necessarily mortal. Doctors refuse to commit themselves, but I believe he has a good chance.'"

He extended the cablegram that she might read for herself, and said, "He'll win, my dear. He has luck, and lucky people always win in big things."

Her gaze did not leave his face. One would have said that she had not heard, that she was still seeking what she had admitted him to learn. He sat down where Clélie had been, and said:

"There's only one thing for us to do, and that is to go over at once."

She closed her eyes. A baffled, puzzled expression was upon her deathly pale face.

"We can sail on the *Mauretania* Saturday," continued he.
"I've telephoned and there are good rooms."

She turned her face away.

"Don't you feel equal to going?"

"As you say, we must."

"The trip can't do you any harm." His forced composure abruptly vanished and he cried out hysterically: "Good God! It's incredible." Then he got himself in hand again, and went on: "No wonder it bowled you out. I had my anxiety about you to break the shock. But you—— How do you feel now?"

"I'm going to dress."

"I'll send you in some brandy." He bent and kissed her. A shudder convulsed her—a shudder visible even through the covers. But he seemed not to note it, and went on: "I didn't realize how fond I was of Brent until I saw that thing in the paper. I almost fainted, myself. I gave Clélie a horrible scare."

"I thought you were having an attack," said Clélie. "My husband looked exactly as you did when he died that way."

Susan's strange eyes were gazing intently at him—the searching, baffled, persistently seeking look. She closed them as he turned from the bed. When she and Clélie were alone and she was dressing, she said:

"Freddie gave you a scare?"

"I was at breakfast," replied Clélie, "was pouring my coffee. He came into the room in his bathrobe—took up the papers from the table opened to the foreign news as he always does. I happened to be looking at him"— Clélie flushed—"he is very handsome in that robe—and all at once he dropped the paper—grew white—staggered and fell into a chair. Exactly like my husband."

Susan, seated at her dressing-table, was staring absently out of the window. She shook her head impatiently, drew a long breath, went on with her toilet.

CHAPTER XXIV

A FEW minutes before the dinner hour she came into the drawing room. Palmer and Madame Délière were already there, near the fire which the unseasonable but by no means unusual coolness of the London summer evening made extremely comfortable—and, for Americans, necessary. Palmer stood with his back to the blaze, moodily smoking a cigarette. That evening his now almost huge form looked more degenerated than usual by the fat of high living and much automobiling. His fleshy face, handsome still and of a refined type, bore the traces of anxious sorrow. Clélie, sitting at the corner of the fireplace and absently turning the leaves of an illustrated French magazine, had in her own way an air as funereal as Freddie's. As Susan entered, they glanced at her.

Palmer uttered and half suppressed an ejaculation of amazement. Susan was dressed as for opera or ball—one of her best evening dresses, the greatest care in arranging her hair and the details of her toilette. Never had she been more beautiful. Her mode of life since she came abroad with Palmer, the thoughts that had been filling her brain and giving direction to her life since she accepted Brent as her guide and Brent's plans as her career, had combined to give her air of distinction the touch of the extraordinary— the touch that characterizes the comparatively few human beings who live the life above and apart from that of the common run—the life illuminated by imagination. At a glance one sees that they are not of the eaters, drinkers, sleepers, and seekers after the shallow easy pleasures money provides ready-made. They shine by their own light; the rest of mankind shines either by light reflected from them or not at all.

Looking at her that evening as she came into the comfortable, old-fashioned English room, with its somewhat heavy but undeniably dignified furniture and draperies, the least observant could not have said that she was in gala attire because she was in gala mood. Beneath the calm of her surface expression lay something widely different. Her face, slim and therefore almost beyond the reach of the attacks of time and worry, was of the type to which a haggard expression is becoming. Her eyes, large and dreamy, seemed to be seeing visions of unutterable sadness, and the scarlet streak of her mouth seemed to emphasize their pathos. She looked young, very young; yet there was also upon her features the stamp of experience, the experience of suffering. She did not notice the two by the fire, but went to the piano at the far end of the room and stood gazing out into the lovely twilight of the garden.

Freddie, who saw only the costume, said in an undertone to Clélie, "What sort of freak is this?"

Said Madame Délière: "An uncle of mine lost his wife. They were young and he loved her to distraction. Between her death and the funeral he scandalized everybody by talking incessantly of the most trivial details— the cards, the mourning, the flowers, his own clothes. But the night of the funeral he killed himself."

Palmer winced as if Clélie had struck him. Then an expression of terror, of fear, came into his eyes. "You don't think she'd do that?" he muttered hoarsely.

"Certainly not," replied the young Frenchwoman. "I was simply trying to explain her. She dressed because she was unconscious of what she was doing. Real sorrow doesn't think about appearances." Then with quick tact she added: "Why should she kill herself? Monsieur Brent is getting well. Also, while she's a devoted friend of his, she doesn't love him, but you."

"I'm all upset," said Palmer, in confused apology.

He gazed fixedly at Susan—a straight, slim figure with the carriage and the poise of head that indicate self-confidence and pride. As he gazed Madame Clélie watched him with fascinated eyes. It was both thrilling and terrifying to see such love as he was revealing—a love more dangerous than hate. Palmer noted that he was observed, abruptly turned to face the fire.

A servant opened the doors into the dining-room, Madame Délière rose. "Come, Susan," said she.

Susan looked at her with unseeing eyes.

"Dinner is served."

"I do not care for dinner," said Susan, seating herself at the piano.

"Oh, but you— —"

"Let her alone," said Freddie, curtly. "You and I will go in."

Susan, alone, dropped listless hands into her lap. How long she sat there motionless and with mind a blank she did not know. She was aroused by a sound in the hall—in the direction of the outer door of their apartment. She started up, instantly all alive and alert, and glided swiftly in the direction of the sound. A servant met her at the threshold. He had a cablegram on a tray.

"For Mr. Palmer," said he.

But she, not hearing, took the envelope and tore it open. At a sweep her eyes took in the unevenly typewritten words:

> Brent died at half past two this afternoon.
> GARVEY.

She gazed wonderingly at the servant, reread the cablegram.

The servant said: "Shall I take it to Mr. Palmer, ma'am?"

"No. That is all, thanks," replied she.

And she walked slowly across the room to the fire. She shivered, adjusted one of the shoulder straps of her low-cut pale green dress. She read the cablegram a third time, laid it gently, thoughtfully, upon the mantel. "Brent died at half past two this afternoon." Died. Yes, there was no mistaking the meaning of those words. She knew that the message was true. But she did not feel it. She was seeing Brent as he had been when they said good-by. And it would take something more than a mere message to make her feel that the Brent so vividly alive, so redolent of life, of activity, of energy, of plans and projects, the Brent of health and strength, had ceased to be. "Brent died at half past two this afternoon." Except in the great crises we all act with a certain theatricalism, do the thing books and plays and the example of others have taught us to do. But in the great crises we do as we feel. Susan knew that Brent was dead. If he had meant less to her, she would have shrieked or fainted or burst into wild sobs. But not when he was her whole future. She *knew* he was dead, but she did not *believe* it. So she stood staring at the flames, and wondering why, when she knew such a frightful thing, she should remain calm. When she had heard that he was injured, she had felt, now she did not feel at all. Her body, her brain, went serenely on in their routine. The part of her that was her very self—had it died, and not Brent?

She turned her back to the fire, gazed toward the opposite wall. In a mirror there she saw the reflection of Palmer, at table in the adjoining room. A servant was holding a dish at his left and he was helping himself. She observed his every motion, observed his fattened body, his round and large face, the forming roll of fat at the back of his neck. All at once she grew cold—cold as she had not been since the night she and Etta Brashear walked the streets of Cincinnati. The ache of this cold, like the cold of death, was an agony. She shook from head to foot. She turned toward the mantel again, looked at the cablegram. But she did not take it in her hands. She could see—in the air, before her eyes—in clear, sharp lettering—"Brent died at half past two this afternoon. Garvey."

The sensation of cold faded into a sensation of approaching numbness. She went into the hall—to her own rooms. In the dressing-room her maid, Clemence, was putting away the afternoon things she had taken off. She stood at the dressing table, unclasping the string of pearls. She said to Clemence tranquilly:

"Please pack in the small trunk with the broad stripes three of my plainest street dresses—some underclothes—the things for a journey—only necessaries. Some very warm things, please, Clemence, I've suffered from cold, and I can't bear the idea of it. And please telephone to the—to the Cecil for a room and bath. When you have finished I shall pay you what I owe and a month's wages extra. I cannot afford to keep you any longer."

"But, madame"—Clemence fluttered in agitation—"Madame promised to take me to America."

"Telephone for the rooms for Miss Susan Lenox," said Susan.

She was rapidly taking off her dress. "If I took you to America I should have to let you go as soon as we landed."

"But, madame—" Clemence advanced to assist her.

"Please pack the trunk," said Susan. "I am leaving here at once."

"I prefer to go to America, even if madame——"

"Very well. I'll take you. But you understand?"

"Perfectly, madame——"

A sound of hurrying footsteps and Palmer was at the threshold. His eyes were wild, his face distorted. His hair, usually carefully arranged over the rapidly growing bald spot above his brow, was disarranged in a manner that would have been ludicrous but for the terrible expression of his face. "Go!" he said harshly to the maid; and he stood fretting the knob until she hastened out and gave him the chance to close the door. Susan, calm and apparently unconscious of his presence, went on with her rapid change of costume. He lit a cigarette with fingers trembling, dropped heavily into a chair near the door. She, seated on the floor, was putting on boots.

When she had finished one and was beginning on the other he said stolidly:

"You think I did it"—not a question but an assertion.

"I know it," replied she. She was so seated that he was seeing her in profile.

"Yes—I did," he went on. He settled himself more deeply in the chair, crossed his leg. "And I am glad that I did."

She kept on at lacing the boot. There was nothing in her expression to indicate emotion, or even that she heard.

"I did it," continued he, "because I had the right. He invited it. He knew me—knew what to expect. I suppose he decided that you were worth taking the risk. It's strange what fools men—all men—we men—are about women. . . . Yes, he knew it. He didn't blame me."

She stopped lacing the boot, turned so that she could look at him.

"Do you remember his talking about me one day?" he went on, meeting her gaze naturally. "He said I was a survival of the Middle Ages—had a medieval Italian mind—said I would do anything to gain my end—and would have a clear conscience about it. Do you remember?"

"Yes."

"But you don't see why I had the right to kill him?"

A shiver passed over her. She turned away again, began again to lace the boot—but now her fingers were uncertain.

"I'll explain," pursued he. "You and I were getting along fine. He had had his chance with you and had lost it. Well, he comes over here—looks us up—puts himself between you and me—proceeds to take you away from me. Not in a square manly way but under the pretense of giving you a career. He made you restless—dissatisfied. He got you away from me. Isn't that so?"

She was sitting motionless now.

Palmer went on in the same harsh, jerky way:

"Now, nobody in the world—not even you—knew me better than Brent did. He knew what to expect—if I caught on to what was doing. And I guess he knew I would be pretty sure to catch on."

"He never said a word to me that you couldn't have heard," said Susan.

"Of course not," retorted Palmer. "That isn't the question. It don't matter whether he wanted you for himself or for his plays. The point is that he took you away from me—he, my friend—and did it by stealth. You can't deny that."

"He offered me a chance for a career—that was all," said she. "He never asked for my love—or showed any interest in it. I gave him that."

He laughed—his old-time, gentle, sweet, wicked laugh. He said:

"Well—it'd have been better for him if you hadn't. All it did for him was to cost him his life."

Up she sprang. "Don't say that!" she cried passionately—so passionately that her whole body shook. "Do you suppose I don't know it? I know that I killed him. But I don't feel that he's dead. If I did, I'd not be able to live. But I can't! I can't! For me he is as much alive as ever."

"Try to think that—if it pleases you," sneered Palmer. "The fact remains that it was *you* who killed him."

Again she shivered. "Yes," she said, "I killed him."

"And that's why I hate you," Palmer went on, calm and deliberate—except his eyes; they were terrible. "A few minutes ago—when I was exulting that he would probably die—just then I found that opened cable on the mantel. Do you know what it did to me? It made me hate you. When I read it——" Freddie puffed at his cigarette in silence. She dropped weakly to the chair at the dressing table.

"Curse it!" he burst out. "I loved him. Yes, I was crazy about him—and am still. I'm glad I killed him. I'd do it again. I had to do it. He owed me his life. But that doesn't make me forgive *you*."

A long silence. Her fingers wandered among the articles spread upon the dressing table. He said:

"You're getting ready to leave?"

"I'm going to a hotel at once."

"Well, you needn't. I'm leaving. You're done with me. But I'm done with you." He rose, bent upon her his wicked glance, sneering and cruel. "You never want to see me again. No more do I ever want to see you again. I wish to God I never had seen you. You cost me the only friend I ever had that I cared about. And what's a woman beside a friend—a *man* friend? You've made a fool of me, as a woman always does of a man—always, by God! If she loves him, she destroys him. If she doesn't love him, he destroys himself."

Susan covered her face with her bare arms and sank down at the dressing table. "For pity's sake," she cried brokenly, "spare me—spare me!"

He seized her roughly by the shoulder. "Just flesh!" he said. "Beautiful flesh—but just female. And look what a fool you've made of me—and the best man in the world dead—over yonder! Spare you? Oh, you'll pull through all right. You'll pull through everything and anything—and come out stronger and better looking and better off. Spare you! Hell! I'd have killed you instead of him if I'd known I was going to hate you after I'd done the other thing. I'd do it yet—you dirty skirt!"

He jerked her unresisting form to its feet, gazed at her like an insane fiend. With a sob he seized her in his arms, crushed her against his breast, sunk his fingers deep into her hair, kissed it, grinding his teeth as he kissed. "I hate you, damn you—and I love you!" He flung her back into the chair— out of his life. "You'll never see me again!" And he fled from the room— from the house.

CHAPTER XXV

THE big ship issued from the Mersey into ugly waters—into the weather that at all seasons haunts and curses the coasts of Northern Europe. From Saturday until Wednesday Susan and Madame Délière had true Atlantic seas and skies; and the ship leaped and shivered and crashed along like a brave cavalryman in the rear of a rout—fighting and flying, flying and fighting. Four days of hours whose every waking second lagged to record itself in a distinct pang of physical wretchedness; four days in which all emotions not physical were suspended, in which even the will to live, most tenacious of primal instincts in a sane human being, yielded somewhat to the general lassitude and disgust. Yet for Susan Lenox four most fortunate days; for in them she underwent a mental change that enabled her to emerge delivered of the strain that threatened at every moment to cause a snap.

On the fifth day her mind, crutched by her resuming body, took up again its normal routine. She began to dress herself, to eat, to exercise—the mechanical things first, as always—then to think. The grief that had numbed her seemed to have been left behind in England where it had suddenly struck her down—England far away and vague across those immense and infuriated waters, like the gulf of death between two incarnations. No doubt that grief was awaiting her at the other shores; no doubt there she would feel that Brent was gone. But she would be better able to bear the discovery. The body can be accustomed to the deadliest poisons, so that they become harmless—even useful—even a necessary aid to life. In the same way the mind can grow accustomed to the cruelest calamities, tolerate them, use them to attain a strength and power the hot-housed soul never gets.

When a human being is abruptly plunged into an unnatural unconsciousness by mental or physical catastrophes, the greatest care is taken that the awakening to normal life again be slow, gradual, without shock. Otherwise the return would mean death or insanity or lifelong affliction with radical weakness. It may be that this sea voyage with its four days of agitations that lowered Susan's physical life to a harmony of wretchedness with her mental plight, and the succeeding days of gradual calming and restoration, acted upon her to save her from disaster. There will be those readers of her story who, judging her, perhaps, by themselves—as revealed in their judgments, rather than in their professions—will think it was quite unnecessary to awaken her gradually; they will declare her a hard-hearted person, caring deeply about no one but herself, or one of those curiosities of human nature that are interested only in things, not at all in persons, even in themselves. There may also be those who will see in her a soft and gentle heart for which her intelligence finally taught her to construct a shield— more or less effective—against buffetings which would have destroyed or, worse still, maimed her. These will feel that the sea voyage, the sea change, suspending the normal human life, the life on land, tided her over a crisis that otherwise must have been disastrous.

However this may be—and who dares claim the definite knowledge of the mazes of human character and motive to be positive about the matter?— however it may be, on Thursday afternoon they steamed along a tranquil and glistening sea into the splendor and majesty of New York Harbor. And Susan was again her calm, sweet self, as the violet-gray eyes gazing pensively from the small, strongly-featured face plainly showed. Herself again, with the wound—deepest if not cruelest of her many wounds— covered and with its poison under control. She was ready again to begin to live—ready to fulfill our only certain mission on this earth, for we are not here to succumb and to die, but to adapt ourselves and live. And those who laud the succumbers and the diers—yea, even the blessed martyrs of sundry and divers fleeting issues usually delusions—may be paying ill-deserved tribute to vanity, obstinacy, lack of useful common sense, passion for futile and untimely agitation—or sheer cowardice. Truth—and what is truth but right living?—truth needs no martyrs; and the world needs not martyrs, not corpses rotting in unmarked or monumented graves, but intelligent men and women, healthy in body and mind, capable of leading the human race as fast as it is able to go in the direction of the best truth to which it is able at that time to aspire.

As the ship cleared Quarantine Susan stood on the main deck well forward, with Madame Clélie beside her. And up within her, defying all rebuke, surged the hope that cannot die in strong souls living in healthy bodies.

She had a momentary sense of shame, born of the feeling that it is basest, most heartless selfishness to live, to respond to the caress of keen air upon healthy skin, of glorious light upon healthy eyes, when there are others shut out and shut away from these joys forever. Then she said to herself, "But no one need apologize for being alive and for hoping. I must try to justify him for all he did for me."

A few miles of beautiful water highway between circling shores of green, and afar off through the mist Madame Clélie's fascinated eyes beheld a city of enchantment. It appeared and disappeared, reappeared only to disappear again, as its veil of azure mist was blown into thick or thin folds by the light breeze. One moment the Frenchwoman would think there was nothing ahead but more and ever more of the bay glittering in the summer sunlight. The next moment she would see again that city—or was it a mirage of a city?—towers, mighty walls, domes rising mass above mass, summit above summit, into the very heavens from the water's edge where there was a fringe of green. Surely the vision must be real; yet how could tiny man out of earth and upon earth rear in such enchantment of line and color those enormous masses, those peak-like piercings of the sky?

"Is that—*it?*" she asked in an awed undertone.

Susan nodded. She, too, was gazing spellbound. Her beloved City of the Sun.

"But it is beautiful—beautiful beyond belief. And I have always heard that New York was ugly."

"It is beautiful—and ugly—both beyond belief!" replied Susan.

"No wonder you love it!"

"Yes—I love it. I have loved it from the first moment I saw it. I've never stopped loving it—not even— —" She did not finish her sentence but gazed dreamily at the city appearing and disappearing in its veils of thin, luminous mist. Her thoughts traveled again the journey of her life in New York. When she spoke again, it was to say:

"Yes—when I first saw it—that spring evening—I called it my City of the Stars, then, for I didn't know that it belonged to the sun— Yes, that spring evening I was happier than I ever had been—or ever shall be again."

"But you will be happy again dear," said Clélie, tenderly pressing her arm.

A faint sad smile—sad but still a smile—made Susan's beautiful face lovely. "Yes, I shall be happy—not in those ways—but happy, for I shall be busy. . . . No, I don't take the tragic view of life—not at all. And as I've known misery, I don't try to hold to it."

"Leave that," said Clélie, "to those who have known only the comfortable make-believe miseries that rustle in crêpe and shed tears—whenever there's anyone by to see."

"Like the beggars who begin to whine and exhibit their aggravated sores as soon as a possible giver comes into view," said Susan. "I've learned to accept what comes, and to try to make the best of it, whatever it is. . . . I say I've learned. But have I? Does one ever change? I guess I was born that sort of philosopher."

She recalled how she put the Warhams out of her life as soon as she discovered what they really meant to her and she to them—how she had put Jeb Ferguson out of her life—how she had conquered the grief and desolation of the loss of Burlingham—how she had survived Etta's going away without her—the inner meaning of her episodes with Rod—with Freddie Palmer——

And now this last supreme test—with her soul rising up and gathering itself together and lifting its head in strength——

"Yes, I was born to make the best of things," she repeated.

"Then you were born lucky," sighed Clélie, who was of those who must lean if they would not fall and lie where they fell.

Susan gave a curious little laugh—with no mirth, with a great deal of mockery. "Do you know, I never thought so before, but I believe you're right," said she. Again she laughed in that queer way. "If you knew my life you'd think I was joking. But I'm not. The fact that I've survived and am what I am proves I was born lucky." Her tone changed, her expression became unreadable. "If it's lucky to be born able to live. And if that isn't luck, what is?"

She thought how Brent said she was born lucky because she had the talent that enables one to rise above the sordidness of that capitalism he so often denounced—the sordidness of the lot of its slaves, the sordidness of the lot of its masters. Brent! If it were he leaning beside her—if he and she were coming up the bay toward the City of the Sun!

A billow of heartsick desolation surged over her.
Alone—always alone. And still alone. And always to be alone.

Garvey came aboard when the gangway was run out. He was in black wherever black could be displayed. But the grief shadowing his large, simple countenance had the stamp of the genuine. And it was genuine, of the most approved enervating kind. He had done nothing but grieve since his master's death—had left unattended all the matters the man he loved and grieved for would have wished put in order. Is it out of charity for the weakness of human nature and that we may think as well as possible of it—is that why we admire and praise most enthusiastically the kind of love and the kind of friendship and the kind of grief that manifest themselves in obstreperous feeling and wordiness, with no strength left for any attempt to *do?* As Garvey greeted them the tears filled Clélie's eyes and she turned away. But Susan gazed at him steadily; in her eyes there were no tears, but a look that made Garvey choke back sobs and bend his head to hide his expression. What he saw—or felt—behind her calmness filled him with awe, with a kind of terror. But he did not recognize what he saw as grief; it did not resemble any grief he had felt or had heard about.

"He made a will just before he died," he said to Susan. "He left everything to you."

Then she had not been mistaken. He had loved her, even as she loved him. She turned and walked quickly from them. She hastened into her cabin, closed the door and flung herself across the bed. And for the first time she gave way. In that storm her soul was like a little land bird in the clutch of a sea hurricane. She did not understand herself. She still had no sense that he was dead; yet had his dead body been lying there in her arms she could not have been more shaken by paroxysms of grief, without tears or sobs—grief that vents itself in shrieks and peals of horrible laughter-like screams—she smothered them in the pillows in which she buried her face. Clélie came, opened the door, glanced in, closed it. An hour passed—an hour and a half. Then Susan appeared on deck—amber-white pallor, calm, beautiful, the fashionable woman in traveling dress.

"I never before saw you with your lips not rouged!" exclaimed Clélie.

"You will never see them rouged again," said Susan.

"But it makes you look older."

"Not so old as I am," replied she.

And she busied herself about the details of the landing and the customs, waving aside Garvey and his eager urgings that she sit quietly and leave everything to him. In the carriage, on the way to the hotel, she roused herself from her apparently tranquil reverie and broke the strained silence by saying:

"How much shall I have?"

The question was merely the protruding end of a train of thought years long and pursued all that time with scarcely an interruption. It seemed abrupt; to Garvey it sounded brutal. Off his guard, he showed in flooding color and staring eye how profoundly it shocked him. Susan saw, but she did not explain; she was not keeping accounts in emotion with the world. She waited patiently. After a long pause he said in a tone that contained as much of rebuke as so mild a dependent dared express:

"He left about thirty thousand a year, Miss Lenox."

The exultant light that leaped to Susan's eye horrified him. It even disturbed Clélie, though she better understood Susan's nature and was not nearly so reverent as Garvey of the hypocrisies of conventionality. But Susan had long since lost the last trace of awe of the opinion of others. She was not seeking to convey an impression of grief. Grief was too real to her. She would as soon have burst out with voluble confession of the secret of her love for Brent. She saw what Garvey was thinking; but she was not concerned. She continued to be herself—natural and simple. And there was no reason why she should conceal as a thing to be ashamed of the fact that Brent had accomplished the purpose he intended, had filled her with honest exultation—not with delight merely, not with triumph, but with that stronger and deeper joy which the unhoped for pardon brings to the condemned man.

She must live on. The thought of suicide, of any form of giving up— the thought that instantly possesses the weak and the diseased—could not find lodgment in that young, healthy body and mind of hers. She must live on; and suddenly she discovered that she could live *free!* Not after years of doubtful struggles, of reverses, of success so hardly won that she was left exhausted. But now—at once—*free!* The heavy shackles had been stricken off at a blow. She was free—forever free! Free, forever free, from the wolves of poverty and shame, of want and rags and filth, the wolves that had been pursuing her with swift, hideous padded stride, the wolves that more than once had dragged her down and torn and trampled her, and lapped her blood. Free to enter of her own right the world worth living in, the world from which all but a few are shut out, the world which only a few of those privileged to enter know how to enjoy. Free to live the life worth while the life of leisure to work, instead of slaving to make leisure and luxury and comfort for others. Free to achieve something beside food, clothing, and shelter. Free to live as *she* pleased, instead of for the pleasure of a master or masters. Free—free—free! The ecstasy of it surged up in her, for the moment possessing her and submerging even thought of how she had been freed.

She who had never acquired the habit of hypocrisy frankly exulted in countenance exultant beyond laughter. She could conceal her feelings, could refrain from expressing. But if she expressed at all, it must be her true self—what she honestly felt. Garvey hung his head in shame. He would not have believed Susan could be so unfeeling. He would not let his eyes see the painful sight. He would try to forget, would deny to himself that he had seen. For to his shallow, conventional nature Susan's expression could only mean delight in wealth, in the opportunity that now offered to idle and to luxuriate in the dead man's money, to realize the crude dreamings of those lesser minds whose initial impulses toward growth have been stifled by the routine our social system imposes upon all but the few with the strength to persist individual.

Free! She tried to summon the haunting vision of the old women with the tin cups of whisky reeling and staggering in time to the hunchback's playing. She could remember every detail, but these memories would not assemble even into a vivid picture and the picture would have been far enough from the horror of actuality in the vision she formerly could not banish. As a menace, as a prophecy, the old women and the hunchback and the strumming piano had gone forever. Free—secure, independent—free!

After a long silence Garvey ventured stammeringly:

"He said to me—he asked me to request—he didn't make it a condition—just a wish—a hope, Miss Lenox—that if you could, and felt it strongly enough— — "

"Wished what?" said Susan, with a sharp impatience that showed how her nerves were unstrung.

"That you'd go on—go on with the plays—with the acting."

The violet eyes expressed wonder. "Go on?" she inquired, "Go on?" Then in a tone that made Clélie sob and Garvey's eyes fill she said:

"What else is there to live for, now?"

"I'm—I'm glad for his sake," stammered Garvey.

He was disconcerted by her smile. She made no other answer—aloud. For *his* sake! For her own sake, rather. What other life had she but the life *he* had given her? "And he knew I would," she said to herself. "He said that merely to let me know he left me entirely free. How like him, to do that!"

At the hotel she shut herself in; she saw no one, not even Clélie, for nearly a week. Then—she went to work—and worked like a reincarnation of Brent.

She inquired for Sperry, found that he and Rod had separated as they no longer needed each other; she went into a sort of partnership with Sperry for the production of Brent's plays—he, an excellent coach as well as stage director, helping her to finish her formal education for the stage. She played with success half a dozen of the already produced Brent plays. At the beginning of her second season she appeared in what has become her most famous part—*Roxy* in Brent's last play, "The Scandal." With the opening night her career of triumph began. Even the critics—therefore, not unnaturally, suspicious of an actress who was so beautiful, so beautifully dressed, so well supported, and so well outfitted with actor-proof plays even the critics conceded her ability. She was worthy of the great character Brent had created—the wayward, many-sided, ever gay *Roxy Grandon*.

When, at the first night of "The Scandal," the audience lingered, cheering Brent's picture thrown upon a drop, cheering Susan, calling her out again and again, refusing to leave the theater until it was announced that she could answer no more calls, as she had gone home—when she was thus finally and firmly established in her own right—she said to Sperry:

"Will you see to it that every sketch of me that appears tomorrow says that I am the natural daughter of Lorella Lenox?"

Sperry's Punch-like face reddened.

"I've been ashamed of that fact," she went on. "It has made me ashamed to be alive in the bottom of my heart."

"Absurd," said Sperry.

"Exactly," replied Susan. "Absurd. Even stronger than my shame about it has been my shame that I could be so small as to feel ashamed of it. Now— tonight" she was still in her dressing-room. As she paused they heard the faint faraway thunders of the applause of the lingering audience—"Listen!" she cried. "I am ashamed no longer. Sperry, *Ich bin ein Ich!*"

"I should say," laughed he. "All you have to say is 'Susan Lenox' and you answer all questions."

"At last I'm proud of it," she went on. "I've justified myself. I've justified my mother. I am proud of her, and she would be proud of me. So see that it's done, Sperry."

"Sure," said he. "You're right."

He took her hand and kissed it. She laughed, patted him on the shoulder, kissed him on both cheeks in friendly, sisterly fashion.

He had just gone when a card was brought to her—"Dr. Robert Stevens"—with "Sutherland, Indiana," penciled underneath. Instantly she remembered, and had him brought to her—the man who had rescued her from death at her birth. He proved to be a quiet, elderly gentleman, subdued and aged beyond his fifty-five years by the monotonous life of the drowsy old town. He approached with a manner of embarrassed respect and deference, stammering old-fashioned compliments. But Susan was the simple, unaffected girl again, so natural that he soon felt as much at ease as with one of his patients in Sutherland.

She took him away in her car to her apartment for supper with her and Clélie, who was in the company, and Sperry. She kept him hour after hour, questioning him about everyone and everything in the old town, drawing him out, insisting upon more and more details. The morning papers were brought and they read the accounts of play and author and players. For once there was not a dissent; all the critics agreed that it was a great performance of a great play. And Susan made Sperry read aloud the finest and the longest of the accounts of Brent himself—his life, his death, his work, his lasting fame now peculiarly assured because in Susan Lenox there had been found a competent interpreter of his genius.

After the reading there fell silence. Susan, her pallid face and her luminous, inquiring violet eyes inscrutable, sat gazing into vacancy. At last Doctor Stevens moved uneasily and rose to go. Susan roused herself, accompanied him to the adjoining room. Said the old doctor.

"I've told you about everybody. But you've told me nothing about the most interesting Sutherlander of all—yourself."

Susan looked at him. And he saw the wound hidden from all the world—the wound she hid from herself as much of the time as she could. He, the doctor, the professional confessor, had seen such wounds often; in all the world there is hardly a heart without one. He said:

"Since sorrow is the common lot, I wonder that men can be so selfish or so unthinking as not to help each other in every way to its consolations. Poor creatures that we are—wandering in the dark, fighting desperately, not knowing friend from foe!"

"But I am glad that you saved me," said she.

"You have the consolations—success—fame—honor."

"There is no consolation," replied she in her grave sweet way. "I had the best. I—lost him. I shall spend my life in flying from myself."

After a pause she went on: "I shall never speak to anyone as I have spoken to you. You will understand all. I had the best—the man who could have given me all a woman seeks from a man—love, companionship, sympathy, the shelter of strong arms. I had that. I have lost it. So— —"

A long pause. Then she added:

"Usually life is almost tasteless to me. Again—for an hour or two it is a little less so—until I remember what I have lost. Then—the taste is very bitter—very bitter."

And she turned away.

She is a famous actress, reputed great. Some day she will be indeed great—when she has the stage experience and the years. Except for Clélie, she is alone. Not that there have been no friendships in her life. There have even been passions. With men and women of her vigor and vitality, passion is inevitable. But those she admits find that she has little to give, and they go away, she making no effort to detain them; or she finds that she has nothing to give, and sends them away as gently as may be. She has the reputation of caring for nothing but her art—and for the great establishment for orphans up the Hudson, into which about all her earnings go. The establishment is named for Brent and is dedicated to her mother. Is she happy? I do not know. I do not think she knows. Probably she is—as long as she can avoid pausing to think whether she is or not. What better happiness can intelligent mortal have, or hope for? Certainly she is triumphant, is lifted high above the storms that tortured her girlhood and early youth, the sordid woes that make life an unrelieved tragedy of calamity threatened and calamity realized for the masses of mankind. The last time I saw her— —

It was a few evenings ago, and she was crossing the sidewalk before her house toward the big limousine that was to take her to the theater. She is still young; she looked even younger than she is. Her dress had the same exquisite quality that made her the talk of Paris in the days of her sojourn there. But it is not her dress that most interests me, nor the luxury and perfection of all her surroundings. It is not even her beauty—that is, the whole of her beauty.

Everything and every being that is individual in appearance has some one quality, trait, characteristic, which stands out above all the rest to make a climax of interest and charm. With the rose it is its perfume; with the bird, perhaps the scarlet or snowy feathers upon its breast. Among human beings who have the rare divine dower of clear individuality the crown and cap of distinction differs. In her—for me, at least—the consummate fascination is not in her eyes, though I am moved by the soft glory of their light, nor in the lovely oval contour of her sweet, healthily pallid face. No, it is in her mouth—sensitive, strong yet gentle, suggestive of all the passion and suffering and striving that have built up her life. Her mouth—the curve of it—I think it is, that sends from time to time the mysterious thrill through her audiences. And I imagine those who know her best look always first at those strangely pale lips, curved in a way that suggests bitterness melting into sympathy, sadness changing into mirth—a way that seems to say: "I have suffered—but, see! I have stood fast!"

Can a life teach any deeper lesson, give any higher inspiration?

As I was saying, the last time I saw her she was about to enter her automobile. I halted and watched the graceful movements with which she took her seat and gathered the robes about her. And then I noted her profile, by the light of the big lamps guarding her door. You know that profile? You have seen its same expression in every profile of successful man or woman who ever lived. Yes, she may be happy—doubtless is more happy than unhappy. But—I do not envy her—or any other of the sons and daughters of men who is blessed—and cursed—with imagination.

And Freddie—and Rod—and Etta—and the people of Sutherland—and all the rest who passed through her life and out? What does it matter? Some went up, some down—not without reason, but, alas! not for reason of desert. For the judgments of fate are, for the most part, not unlike blows from a lunatic striking out in the dark; if they land where they should, it is rarely and by sheer chance. Ruth's parents are dead; she is married to Sam Wright. He lost his father's money in wheat speculation in Chicago—in one of the most successful of the plutocracy's constantly recurring raids upon the hoardings of the middle class. They live in a little house in one of the back streets of Sutherland and he is head clerk in Arthur Sinclair's store—a position he owes to the fact that Sinclair is his rich brother-in-law. Ruth has children and she is happier in them than she realizes or than her discontented face and voice suggest. Etta is fat and contented, the mother of many, and fond of her fat, fussy August, the rich brewer. John Redmond—a congressman, a possession of the Beef Trust, I believe—but not so highly prized a possession as was his abler father.

Freddie? I saw him a year ago at the races at Auteuil. He is huge and loose and coarse, is in the way soon to die of Bright's disease, I suspect. There was a woman with him—very pretty, very *chic*. I saw no other woman similarly placed whose eyes held so assiduously, and without ever a wandering flutter, to the face of the man who was paying. But Freddie never noticed her. He chewed savagely at his cigar, looking about the while for things to grumble at or to curse. Rod? He is still writing indifferent plays with varying success. He long since wearied of Constance Francklyn, but she clings to him and, as she is a steady moneymaker, he tolerates her.

Brent? He is statelily ensconced up at Woodlawn. Susan has never been to his grave—there. His grave in her heart—she avoids that too, when she can. But there are times—there always will be times— —

If you doubt it, look at her profile.

Yes, she has learned to live. But—she has paid the price.